Praise for In Leah's Wake

"Pulled me right along as I constantly compared it to my own life."
Jennifer Donovan, *5 Minutes for Books*, Top 50 Book Blog

"Easily the best read that I have enjoyed in 2011."
Bonnie Erina Wheeler, author of *Fate Fixed: An Erris Coven Novel*

"A very moving and, at times, heartbreaking story which will be loved by many, whether they are parents or not."
A. Rose, Amazon UK, TOP 100 REVIEWER

"Multiple ripples of meaning contribute to the overall intensity of this deeply moving psychological drama."
Cynthia Harrison, author of *Sister Issues*

"Emotional, beautiful and touching."
Niina, *For the Love of Reading!* (Helsinki, Finland)

"I'm adding Terri Giuliano Long to my list of authors I want to be stranded with."
Susie Kline, *Motherhoot*

"The story draws you in with a great hook in the first chapter and keeps you on your toes."
Coral Russell, author of *Amador Lockdown*

"No one reading this can remain untouched or unmoved."
Susan Roebuck, author of *Perfect Score*

"An excellent novel for teenagers and parents alike."
Denise Du Vernay, co-author of *The Simpsons in the Classroom*

"A book to read, share, then read again."
Bri Clark, author of *The Familial Witch*

"There is someone in the story everyone can find a way to relate to."
MB Mulhall, author of *Near Death*

"Ms. Long leaves the reader with the sense that even through the worst storms that can happen within a family, there is a possibility of redemption for them all."

Paula Tohline Calhoun, *Reflections from a Cloudy Mirror*

"Will keep you turning the pages...worth every second spent reading it."

Courtney Conant, author of *The Blood Moon of Winter*

"As a therapist, I found this an accurate description of what can happen when youth are pushed too hard, parents stop communicating, and the family system breaks down."

Susan Salluce, author of *Out of Breath*

"*In Leah's Wake* is an irresistible read. By turns howlingly funny and achingly sad, the book details the vivid, harrowing journey of a fragile family that unravels - and finds redemption - thanks to a teenager's rebellion. Along the way, there are unflinching truths about adolescence and contemporary society, told in prose that leaps off the page like poetry."

Holly Robinson, author of *Sleeping Tigers*

"An incredibly strong debut, this book is fantastic on many fronts."

Naomi Blackburn, Founder *Sisterhood of the Traveling Book*

"Beautifully written and impeccably bold."

Miranda Elizabeth Wheeler, *Ricochet Reviews*

"Exquisitely written and profoundly emotional."

Steve Capell, *True Media Solutions*

"*In Leah's Wake* is a fantastic depiction of the way families interact."

Catherine Coffman, *Cat's Thoughts*

"*In Leah's Wake* is a story about our responsibility toward those we love. With such thoughtful characterization and beautifully woven prose, the reader may find it difficult to believe that this is Terri Giuliano Long's debut novel."

Emlyn Chand, author of *Farsighted*

In Leah's Wake

a novel

By

Terri Giuliano Long

Published February 2012

ISBN10: 0-615-60832-9
ISBN13: 978-0-615-60832-7

Contributing Editors: Kira McFadden
Sara-Jayne Slack

For my husband, Dave, and our beautiful daughters, Jen, Lib, Natty, and KK.

"…little heart of mine, believe me, everyone is really responsible to all men for all men and for everything. I don't know how to explain it to you, but I feel it is so, painfully even. And how is it we went on living, getting angry and not knowing?"

Fyodor Dostoevsky
The Grand Inquisitor

Prologue

 February

Justine strikes a pose before the full-length mirror on her closet door. Chin up, hands at her sides. She draws a breath. "My dear..." she begins, and stops midsentence. Wrinkles her nose. She's got it all wrong.

She's too—*stiff*. Too grown up. Too *some*thing.

With her fingers, she sweeps the hair out of her pale, darkly fringed eyes and tugs at the hem of her pink baby-doll pajamas. When she learned five months ago she'd been selected to give the candidates' address at her Confirmation, Justine was ecstatic. Now, the very idea of standing in front of the whole congregation and telling hundreds, maybe thousands, of people about how her own family has taught her what it means to be part of God's larger family makes her sick to her stomach.

She has no choice. She made a commitment.

Folding her hands primly, she sets them on her imaginary podium. Glancing at her cheat sheet, she pulls her lower face into a smile and begins again. "My fellow Confirmation candidates," she says this time.

Justine balls the paper and tosses it onto her bed. *My fellow Confirmation candidates. What a dork.* She sounds about twenty instead of thirteen.

She unclasps her necklace, places the gold cross in her jewelry box, and logs onto her computer, launching the Word document for her Confirmation speech. She scans the opening paragraph. "I've learned from my own family what it means to be part of God's larger family," she reads. *Learned from my own family what it means to be part of God's larger family?* Please. Could she have been any more naïve?

She hits *delete*.

Typing furiously, she begins a brand new essay, the words tumbling out. In a rush of emotion, Justine describes how miserable she feels. And how very, very alone.

PART ONE

JUST DO IT

One

Just Do It

Zoe and Will Tyler sat at their dining room table playing poker. The table, a nineteenth century, hand-carved mahogany, faced the bay window overlooking their sprawling front yard. Husband and wife sat facing one another, a bowl of Tostitos and a half-empty bottle of Chablis positioned between them. Their favorite Van Morrison disc—*Tupelo Honey*—spun on the player, the music drifting out of speakers built into the dining room walls.

Dog, their old yellow Lab, lay on a blanket under the window.

Zoe fanned her cards. She was holding a straight. If she laid it down she'd win her third hand in a row, and her husband would quit. If she didn't, she would be cheating herself.

"Full moon," she said, glancing out the window. "No wonder I had trouble sleeping last night."

The full moon made her anxious. For one of her graduate school internships, she'd worked on the psych ward at City Hospital in Boston. When the moon was full the floor erupted, the patients noisy and agitated. Zoe's superiors had pooh-poohed the lunar effect, chalked it up to irrationality and superstition. Zoe had witnessed the flaring tempers, seen the commotion with her own two eyes, and she'd found the effect impossible to deny—and the nurses concurred.

Will set his empty glass on the table. With his fingers, he drummed an impatient tattoo. "You planning to take your turn any time soon? Be nice if we ended this game before midnight."

"For Pete's sake, Will." Her husband had the attention span of a titmouse. He reminded her of Mick, a six-year-old ADD patient she counseled—sweet kid, when he wasn't ransacking her office, tossing the sand out of the turtle-shaped box, or tweaking her African violets.

"What's so funny?" he asked, sulking.

She shook her head—*nothing, Mick*—and forced a straight face.

"You're laughing at me."

"Don't be silly. Why would I laugh at you?"

He peered at the window. Smirking, he finger-combed his baby-fine hair, graying at the temples, carving a mini-pyramid at his crown.

"Nice 'do. Could use a little more gel," she said, feeling mean spirited the instant the words slipped out of her mouth. Her husband was exhausted. He'd spent the week in California on business. Though he had yet to fill her in on the details, it was obvious his trip had not gone well. "Sorry," she said. "Just kidding." She took another look at her cards, hesitated, and laid down the straight.

"Congratulations." Scowling, he pushed away from the table. "You win again."

"Way to go, grumpy. Quit."

"I'm getting water," he said, flattening his hair. "Want a glass?"

Dog lifted her head, her gaze following Will to the door. She yawned and settled back down.

Her husband stomped across the kitchen, his footfalls moving toward the family room. The music stopped abruptly and then the opening chords of a Robbie Robertson tune belted out of the speakers. Zoe appreciated the gesture. She loved Robbie Robertson; "Showdown at Big Sky" was one of her favorite songs. That didn't mean the entire state of Massachusetts wanted to hear it.

From the kitchen, heading his way, she caught his eye. "Turn it down," she mouthed, gesturing. "You'll wake Justine."

He pulled a face and lowered the music.

Exasperated, she returned to the dining room. She bundled the cards, put the deck in the sideboard drawer, and gathered the dishes.

The toilet flushed in the half-bath off the back hall. Then she heard her husband rattling around the kitchen, slamming the cabinet doors. In April, Will had won a major contract for his company, North American Construction. For five months, he'd been flying back and forth to the West Coast, spending two weeks a month on the job site in San Francisco. Zoe hadn't minded his traveling at first. A glut of office and manufacturing space had tanked construction starts in the northeast; with sales in a slump, his commissions had steadily dwindled. To compensate, they'd initially relied on their savings. In January, they'd remortgaged the house.

The project spared them bankruptcy. But his schedule was brutal. Will hated traveling, being away from the family, living out of a suitcase. He missed her and the kids. Now, with soccer season in full tilt, it was especially hard. Last year, when she was only a sophomore, their daughter had been named "Player of the Year" on the *Boston Globe* All-Scholastic team. The sports reporter from the *Cortland Gazette* had called Leah the "best soccer player in the state." Head coaches from the top colleges in the northeast—Harvard, Dartmouth, Boston College—had sent congratulatory letters, expressing their interest.

Since her first day on the field, Will had trained and guided their daughter. He wanted to be here now to meet the prospective coaches and help her sort through her options. Zoe knew how tough this was on him. It didn't seem to occur to Will that his traveling disrupted her life, too. Last year she'd developed a motivational seminar, called, "Success Skills for Women on the Move." With the girls practically grown, the workshops were her babies. The extra workload at home added to the demands of her fulltime job at the counseling center, left her no time for marketing or promotion, and the workshops had stagnated. Zoe understood her husband's frustration. It irked her that he failed to recognize hers.

Will appeared in the doorway a few minutes later, empty-handed. Her husband was tall, a hair shy of six-one. He'd played football in college, and at forty-five still had the broad shoulders and narrow waist of an athlete. Amazing, really: after eighteen years of marriage, she still found him achingly sexy. Crow's feet creased the corners of his intelligent blue eyes and fine lines etched his cheekbones, giving his boyish features a look of intensity and purpose. Zoe recognized those qualities from the start, but it was only now, as he was aging, they showed on his face.

After work, he'd changed into jeans and a gray sweatshirt with the words "Harvard Soccer Camp" across the chest. He pushed up his sleeves and peered around the room as though looking for something.

"Zoe?" Normally, he called her "Honey" or "Zo."

"I put the cards away." She thumbed the sideboard. "You quit, remember?"

"Where's Leah?"

"She went to the football game with Cissy. They hardly see each other lately. I thought it was nice."

"She ought to be home by now."

She glanced at the cuckoo clock on the east-facing wall. Their daughter was a junior in high school. They'd agreed before the start of the school year to extend her weekend curfew to eleven. It was ten minutes past.

"You know Leah. She probably lost track of the time."

Will, nodding, went to the window.

Their driveway, half the length of a soccer field, sloped down from the cul-de-sac, ending in a turnaround at the foot of their three-car garage. In summer, the oak and birch trees bordering the property obscured their view of the street. Now, with the trees nearly bare, they could see the flash of headlights as vehicles entered the circle.

Dog hauled herself to her feet and pressed her nose to the glass.

Will stretched his neck, wincing. His back was bothering him again, residual pain from a football injury he'd suffered in college.

Zoe came up behind him, pushing Dog's blanket aside with her foot. "You're tight," she said, squeezing his shoulders.

He dropped his chin. "That feels good. Thanks. I've got to get one of those donut pillows for the plane."

"Try to relax. You know Leah. She has no sense of time."

"I can't see why Hillary won't set a curfew. All the other coaches have one."

"You're blowing this out of proportion, don't you think?"

A flash of headlights caught their attention. An SUV entered the cul-de-sac and rounded the circle, light sweeping across their lawn.

"She has a game in the morning," Will said.

"I know."

Will ruffled Dog's ears. "Reardon's coming specifically to see her. She plays like crap when she's tired."

The Harvard coach. She should have known. "So she doesn't go to Harvard," she said, a tired remark. "She'll go someplace else."

"There *is* no place else."

No place with such fantastic opportunities, great connections... *blah, blah, blah.* They'd been over this a million times. If their daughter expressed any interest at all in Harvard, Zoe would do back flips to support her. As far as she could tell, Harvard wasn't even on Leah's radar screen. It was a moot point, anyway. Leah's grades had been slipping. If she did apply for admission, she'd likely be denied.

"Reardon's got pull. He's been talking to Hillary about her," he said. "She can't afford to blow this opportunity."

What opportunity? "Face it, Will. She doesn't want to go to Harvard."

"If she plays her cards right, she can probably get a boat."

"Please," Zoe said, set to blast him. He'd received a full football scholarship from Penn State. What did he do? Dropped out of college. Was that what he wanted? For their daughter to burn out and quit? Noting the purple rings under his eyes, she held back. "You're exhausted." His plane had barely touched ground at Logan Airport when he was ordered to NAC's corporate office in Waltham for a marketing meeting. He hadn't had time to stop at home to change his clothes, never mind take a short nap. "Why don't you go to bed? I'll wait up."

The look he returned implied that she'd lost it.

"Relax, Will. For all we know, they had a flat."

"She would have called."

"So call her." *Duh.*

"I did. I got voicemail."

Shoot. "You know Leah. Her battery probably died." She was grasping at straws. Leah was sixteen. That phone was her lifeline. Still, it could be true. It was possible. Right?

Leah had totally lost track of time. She and Todd had been hanging out at the water tower for hours, perched on the hood of Todd's jeep drinking vodka and OJ, admiring the beautiful night. This was the most perfect place in the universe, maybe. Big sky, lots of trees. From up here, they could see the whole town. In the valley, lights began to blink out. Leaning on her elbows, Leah gazed at the heavens.

"Look," she said, mesmerized by the inky black sky, the billions and billions of stars. "The Big Dipper." As she stared into space, time fell away, the past merging seamlessly with the future.

Todd set the flask on the hood of his truck and put his arm around her, drawing her close. So close she could smell the spicy deodorant under his armpits. Just being with Todd Corbett made her feel dizzy all over. Todd was, by far, the hottest boy she had ever laid eyes on. His hair was long on top, short on the sides. He had full lips, and the most fabulous blue eyes, like…like crystals or something. A Romanesque nose, the exact nose she'd once told Cissy she'd die for, only now that she'd seen it on Todd, she realized that particular nose was meant for a boy. Best of all, he had this incredible aura, all purple and blue, like James Dean or Kurt Cobain.

She curled her legs under her and laid her head on Todd's chest.

They'd met at a party the Friday before school started. Todd had been on tour for the past two years, working as a roadie for a heavy metal band called Cobra. Leah knew he was back—it was all anybody was talking about—and recognized him instantly from all the descriptions. She couldn't believe her luck. Todd Corbett! And alone! She'd heard he was hot. He was even better looking in person. Thinking back, she couldn't believe she'd been so brazen. She left Cissy in the lurch, sashayed right over to him, and took a seat beside him on the living room floor.

The movie he was watching was stupid. People clopped across a field like zombies with their arms outstretched. They reminded her of herself and Justine when they were little, playing blind. Even the makeup looked phony.

"What are you watching?" she asked.

"*Night of the Living Dead*. Flick's a classic. Hey, haven't I seen you someplace before?"

Maybe, though she couldn't imagine where. Todd couldn't possibly have remembered her from high school. She was only a freshman when he dropped out.

"Leah Tyler, right? You're that soccer chick."

The wind swished through the trees. Leah shivered. Todd shrugged out of his worn leather bomber and draped it over her shoulders. From the pocket of his jeans, he retrieved a plastic bag of weed and rolled a joint. He licked the edge of the paper, lit it, inhaling deeply, and handed it to her, the smell rich and exotic and sweet.

Leah had never smoked marijuana until she met Todd. She used to be scared, which was dumb: weed was totally harmless. She had to admit, she'd been disappointed the first few times. She pulled, her chest searing, struggling to hold the ice-hot smoke in her lungs.

Suddenly, she was coughing, waving her arms.

"You okay, babe?" Todd rescued the joint. With his free hand, he patted her back.

Once she was breathing easily again, he laughed, a gentle chuckle that made her feel dignified rather than cheesy or stupid. He pinched the joint between his index finger and thumb, took a hit to demonstrate, and brought it to her lips. "That's it, babe. Good."

They smoked the joint to its stub and he showed her how to fashion a roach clip from twigs. Afterward, he offered to drive her home. "Don't want you getting in trouble or nothing."

"That's okay," Leah said dreamily. "I don't have to go yet."

Todd hopped off the hood of the jeep, pulled a flannel blanket from the back of the truck, and spread it out on the grass under a giant oak tree.

Leah watched him smooth it out, his hands dancing, the whole world intensely colored, brilliantly alive. She heard the lonely trill of a cricket, calling from deep in the valley, smelled the damp autumn earth, felt the cool blue breeze on her face. Todd glided toward her, floating on air. He scooped her into his arms, lifting her from the hood of his jeep, and laid her on the blanket.

And he kissed her.

———◦◦———

At eleven thirty, Zoe dialed Leah's cell phone again. When Leah didn't pick up, she tried Cissy, both times reaching voicemail.

"I don't believe those two," Zoe said, infuriated. "I'll bet they changed their ringers. The little devils probably know it's us."

"That's your daughter for you," Will huffed.

"She's *my* daughter now?"

By eleven forty-five, Zoe was chewing her cuticles and Will was pacing.

"This is it," Will announced. "I'm calling the cops."

"You can't be serious. What will you tell them?"

He opened his cell phone. "I can't sit here and do nothing." He glared at the screen.

"She's only forty-five minutes late. They'll think we're crazy."

He clicked his cell shut. "Fine," he said, digging his keys out of his pocket. "Then I'll find her myself."

Find her? Where on earth did he plan to look?

"I'll start at the high school."

"The game was over hours ago."

"Then I'll drive by the Hanson's." He headed for the garage, Dog at his heels.

"And do what?" Cissy's mom, a nurse, worked the early shift at St. John's. Judy was probably in bed by now. He'd frighten her if he knocked on the door. "Will? Answer me."

He swiveled to face her. "Look for the car," he snapped, and ushered Dog out the door.

Zoe stood, at a loss, staring at the door her husband had closed. The house, she realized when she came to, was an icebox.

She rooted through the hall closet, found a fleece jacket of Will's, pulled it on, and kicked off her shoes, the ceramic tile cool under her bare feet. She crossed the hall to the laundry, tossed a load of clean clothes into the dryer, and wandered back to the kitchen. To calm herself, she tried to think positive thoughts. *Leah's responsible. She can handle herself. If the girls had been in a car accident, the police would have called.* Naturally, by focusing on avoiding negativity, she conjured it. Twenty, even thirty minutes late Zoe could understand. She often lost track of time herself. She would be in her office transcribing her notes, look up, see the clock, and realize she was supposed to have picked up one of the girls—at school, at the mall, at a friend's—fifteen or twenty minutes earlier. She'd rush around her office, collecting her folders and purse, cursing herself for being neglectful, and drive like a madwoman to her destination. Nearly an hour, though? Something was wrong.

Damn it, Leah. Where are you?

Her stomach knotted. She locked the slider in the breakfast nook of the kitchen and headed to the family room to wait, phone in hand, in case Will or Leah called.

In the arched doorway, she paused, rubbing her neck.

This house held such promise when they bought it, such hope. In the airy rooms, the soaring ceilings, the sweeping light, she'd seen a family home—welcoming, safe, with space to fill, room for the girls to grow, to thrive. Now, this huge house, with its massive stone fireplace and enormous windows that turned into gaping black holes after dark, felt cavernous and lonely.

Zoe stepped down into the family room, her bare feet sinking into the plush carpet. Yawning, she tugged the mohair blanket from the back of the sofa, and curled into the oversized chair by the fireplace, pulling the blanket over her shoulders.

Closing her eyes, Zoe breathed deeply, centering herself, and counted backward from ten. Leah's face gradually materialized and her body slowly came into focus. Concentrating, directing her energy outward, she enclosed her child in a protective circle of light.

Be safe, she whispered. *Please, baby. Be safe.*

The Hansons lived on the opposite side of the center behind a cluster of renovated mill buildings that, in Cortland, passed for an industrial park. Will drove across town, along winding, tree-lined country lanes flanked by stone walls built in the seventeenth century by the farmers who'd settled the town. In the moonlit valley, the roads were weathered and buckling. The forest thinned. He drove past a farm, the rolling meadow indigo in the moonlight. A herd of deer grazed on the alfalfa. Dog lay beside him, curled on the passenger seat. The radio blared head-jarring ZZ Top, *Tres Hombres*—Texas boogie, re-mastered, Gibbons tearing it up on his bluesy guitar. Not the most mature music, true. A former musician, Will's taste was wide and eclectic. *My Favorite Things*, 1961, Coltrane's first recording on soprano sax, lay on the console by his elbow. Nosing out from under it, a Dvořák nocturne for strings, a primo piece, better suited to a quieter mood.

The Hanson house sat on a corner in a modest sub-division built in the late eighties, a neighborhood of center-entry colonials— garrisons, salt boxes, expanded Capes—on cramped one-acre lots.

Will slowed as he approached the Hanson's newly remodeled Cape, he and Dog rubber-necking together. Onion lamps lit the front entry and flanked the garage door with matching pole lights lining the drive. The windows were dark, the driveway empty.

Will turned onto the adjacent street, hoping to find a lit room at the back of the house, an indication someone might be awake.

Nothing—not even a porch lamp.

Frustrated, he rounded the block and passed by the house once more, hoping by now maybe Cissy had returned. "Damn," he muttered and headed for the high school on the off chance that the girls were still there.

The high school looked like a prison, with its concrete walls and spare Brutalist architecture. Will turned onto the sloping driveway behind the school, passing the rubber track where the soccer players practiced their sprints. He passed the service entrance, swung by the gym, doubled back, and circled the deserted lot, scanning the playing fields. Discouraged, he parked by the ticket booth at the football stadium and sat, trying to decide what to do next.

They'd had no idea, he and Zoe, how easy they'd had it when the girls were young. Back then, every little thing had seemed like a crisis. They would glance at the window and catch six-year-old Leah perched on the rail of the deck, clutching the rope swing he'd hung from the oak tree in the yard. In a panic, they'd tear out of the house, always an instant too late.

"Leah," he'd hollered, his stomach churning, "careful!"

Zoe covered her eyes, both parents envisioning their daughter rocketing into a tree.

They'd worried about random accidents, obsessed over tragedies they saw on *News Center 5* or read about in the *Globe*: the girls would fall into the hidden shaft of a well or drown in a neighbor's backyard pool; a stranger would kidnap one of their daughters while she played outdoors. It was tough being a parent, the welfare of their children totally dependent on them, yet as long as they were vigilant, their children would be safe.

Now that she was older, independent, they had no way to keep tabs on their daughter. Once she left the house, her fate was out of their hands. She could be almost anywhere, doing anything, with anyone. They had no way to protect her.

"What do you say, girl?" he said finally. "Shall we take off?"

As a last-ditch effort, he took another run by the Hanson's place.

Will eased the BMW into the garage and cut the engine. He dreaded the next few minutes, the relief in Zoe's eyes shifting to surprise and then anguish as she realized he was alone. His wife was counting on him. He felt like a failure for letting her down. He loved his wife and his daughters. Caring for his family, shouldering their burdens felt right. It never had been and never would be a chore. A shrink might deem his protectiveness a pathology, a superhero complex or something: he *wanted* to be their savior.

While he was gone, an anxious silence had settled over the house. Clothes whirred in the dryer, the rhythmic thud echoing down the hallway. He paused by the dining room, dimmed the lights, and tossed his keys on the kitchen counter.

His wife had fallen asleep in the family room, clutching the portable phone, her head resting on the wing of her chair.

In sleep, her face and shoulders relaxed, and she was the beautiful woman he'd married—long nose set in relief by full lips and wild dark hair. She had luminous eyes, small breasts, a spicy Mediterranean ass. Her eyelids fluttered and he pictured her, yawning, tugging her ear. *Your voice is a cello*, she once told him. *Soulful. Like warm chocolate. Or honey. Listening makes me feel safe.*

They fought constantly now. He was losing her. They were losing each other.

Gently, so he wouldn't wake her, he pried the phone from her hands, and pulled the blanket over her shoulders. He carried the phone to the kitchen, set it on the island where she would see it, poured a tall glass of spring water, and went to the living room.

He eased onto his leather recliner by the window. Dog settled beside him on the floor. In no time, the hound was snoring. He plucked an issue of *Sports Illustrated* from the pleated pocket on the side of his chair, flipped through the magazine, and tossed it aside.

On the windowsill, by an eight-by-ten studio portrait of the girls, taken when Justine was a toddler, sat a framed snapshot of Leah. They'd been in Cortland for about a year when he snapped the shot. Leah was not quite seven, the youngest child on the under-ten team. Her uniform was two sizes too big; her baggie, blue tee-shirt skimmed the hem of her shorts. The team was in the midst of a game, Leah racing to the net, the ball jouncing in front of her, her blonde ponytail flying, her tiny face focused, intense.

His daughter was an exceptional player. Fast, agile, fiercely competitive. The best player from Massachusetts *ever*, some coaches said. Since she was a child, Will groomed her, encouraged her, and fostered her talent. Youth soccer, traveling teams. Scholarship to Harvard—that was their plan. They'd practiced, strategized, prepared. Through the rain, the sleet, the snow, he'd been right there with her. That was her dream, wasn't it? To play pro. But Harvard first. Time and again, they'd discussed the importance of a good education, the one thing in this life that could never be taken away.

Will pushed her, he knew. He wanted the best for his kids. He'd do whatever it took to help them succeed, prevent them from repeating his mistakes. In spring of his junior year, he'd left Penn State, trading his education for a long shot at a music career. In one hour, the time it took to inform his dean he was quitting, walk to the registrar's office, sign the requisite forms, he'd screwed up his life. Look at him: forty-five, stuck in a dead-end job, kissing the ass of guys who ought to be working for him. He refused to sit back and watch Leah throw her life away. Kids needed guidance, a motivational coach to keep them focused, drive them when they didn't feel like practicing, pump them up when they lost confidence, someone to spur them on when they wanted to quit.

God help me. Tell him that he hadn't pushed her away.

Two

Just Do It II

The clock ticked past one. One fifteen. Two. He felt like a rat, gnawing the bars of his cage.

Since the moment the obstetrician handed him his baby girl, her tiny fists clenched, her head bruised by a difficult birth, Will had been dreading this night. She'd been late before. Never this late. He imagined his daughter lost, wandering down the country roads in the dark.

Christ—he imagined her raped.

At two thirty, he headed upstairs to her room, hoping that he might find something—a phone number, a scribbled name, anything that would provide a clue as to his daughter's whereabouts.

Her room was a pigsty, dirty clothes on the floor, her cleats, shin guards, and shoes scattered across her bed. Her bureau drawers were open, off track. He stuffed her panties and bras in the top drawer, pushed it shut, and rifled through the drawer in her nightstand, pawing through candy wrappers, empty CD sleeves, a dog-eared copy of *Hamlet*. Spirits flagging, he rummaged through her closet, opening shoe boxes, fishing through pockets. Kneeling, he reached under her bed. He felt a wire-bound notebook, pulled it out, flipped through pages—notes, poems she'd scribbled, pledges to herself: *Practice harder. Do better in school. Be nicer to Mom.*

He closed the notebook and slid it back in its hiding place under the bed. Rising, he caught sight of the Nike poster taped to her wall, the top right corner furled. "Just Do It," the poster commanded. *Just Do It.* Will shook his head, dejected, and turned away.

He was about to call the cops, report her missing, when a vehicle rumbled down the drive. He raced downstairs, his heart hammering, figuring at this hour the news could only be bad.

At the foot of the staircase, he stopped to collect himself, and reluctantly opened the door.

A black Jeep Wrangler, its top down, was parked by the light post. And there she was, sneaking toward the garage, the arm of a boy he had never seen before draped over her shoulder. *Thank God,* he thought. Then, *Goddamn, all this time I've been waiting.*

"Leah," he called, choking a shout. "Get in here."

Leah froze, eyes narrowed, glaring at Will. She whispered into the kid's ear and the punk drew her closer. The kid appeared to be about Will's height. Jeans, leather jacket. Weighed a buck-fifty, tops. It took every ounce of determination Will could muster not to bolt out of the house and pound the piss out of the kid. He watched with mounting impatience as they slunk through the shadows under the garage, up the brick walkway leading to the house.

"Get in here," he repeated as she wobbled onto the stoop.

Leah looked up at him, a loopy grin plastered in place. "Dad," she said brightly, her bloodshot eyes darting. "This is Todd."

Todd? Please. Blonde hair, pretty boy lashes. A diamond stud in his ear. Had to be twenty, twenty-one. Too damn old for Leah.

Will fixed the punk in his sights. The cocky bastard stared right back.

Leah, shouldering away from the boy, gazed up at her father again, wheedling. "Well, Daddy? Aren't you gonna say hello?"

When she exhaled, he caught a whiff of alcohol on her breath. *Christ.* He grabbed her wrist. "Beat it," he growled at the kid. "Get lost."

"Let me *go*," Leah hissed, jerking free.

He seized his daughter's arm. *Get her inside. Just get her inside.*

"Asshole!" she shrieked, batting him away. "Don't touch me."

In a flash, she was five or six, feet planted, tiny fists clenched, sassing him about something. She wanted to go outside; she didn't want to pick up her toys. His child was in trouble, spinning out of control. He yanked her inside, pivoting, pulling her clear of the door. "*Stay* there," he barked and turned his attention to the boy.

In his peripheral vision, he saw his daughter slip, hit the wall, and—*Good God*—slump to the floor.

The kid glowered at Will, his lanky body strung as tight as a bow. Seething, Will reached, but the boy, too quick, shot down the steps and across the lawn. In a rage, Will took off, screaming at him as he hopped into the jeep. S*omething, something, something*…the words ripping through the hurricane in his head.

"*Will?*"

His wife stood on the stoop. Turning, he peered at her blankly, and spun back toward the truck.

"Will," she said again. "Are you *trying* to wake the neighbors?"

The jeep charged up the hill, squealing, its engine roaring.

"What's wrong with you?" she demanded when they went in.

With his palms, he rubbed his eyes. "I-I don't know. I lost it."

Hearing movement, he looked up. Their younger daughter, tiny dark-haired Justine in pink baby-doll pajamas, stood on the landing, peering down at them, Dog at her side. She met his gaze, her expression inscrutable, and retreated to her bedroom, trailed by the Lab.

Leah was nowhere in sight.

"She's in bed," Zoe said. "I sent her up."

"What did she say?"

Zoe hedged. "Nothing."

"She said something."

"Let's talk about it in the morning. When everyone's calm."

"I want to know what she said."

His wife shrugged. "That you're crazy. Okay? She said you're psycho. Look, I'm going up. We'll talk tomorrow. Are you coming?"

"In a while," he told her. He was too worked up to sleep.

For a long time, he sat in his recliner with his eyes closed, replaying the events of the night: seizing his daughter in rage, then watching her fall. Over and over the vision played, like a horror movie on an endless reel, the nightmare rousing him with a jolt and starting all over each time he fell back to sleep. He longed to wake her, sit on the edge of her bed the way he used to when she was a child, and tell her a story. *Once upon a time, in a land far, far away.*

He loved her. He never intended to hurt her.

It was nearly dawn when he turned off the lights. He paused at the entry to Leah's room and then tiptoed inside and stood over her bed. Leah was a fitful sleeper. Her blankets lay in a tangle at her feet. He pulled the sheets and blankets over her, tucking her in, and kissed her forehead. As he left the room, he caught sight of the poster, lit by a shaft of early morning light. *Just Do It.* How many times over the years had he repeated that slogan? No guts, no glory. Put up or shut up. Do what needs to be done. Do it. Just do it.

Just do it.

Three

A Girl Who Knows What She Wants

When Leah woke the next morning, her head felt as big as a beach ball. She'd stay here all day if she could, in her warm bed, cocooned in the blankets and sheets, but she had to pee. She dragged herself up, shivering as she threw off the covers. She'd never been this sick in her life. She probably had cancer. *Oh God*, she was going to barf. She dropped her head between her knees, staying put until her stomach settled, and dragged herself to the bathroom.

She could hear her father in the kitchen, fixing breakfast. The sugary smell of maple bacon made her gag. In a minute, he'd be up here, ordering her downstairs to eat. Her team had a game this morning at ten, which meant she had to be on the field—she checked her alarm clock—in an hour. She flopped back onto her bed and pulled the covers defiantly over her head. No way was she playing soccer today. Not after last night, after her father freaked out.

She turned onto her side, burying her face in her pillow. Around midnight last night, Todd had retrieved a blanket from his truck and spread it over a pillow of pine needles and leaves. She pictured him on his elbows, staring down at her, the planes of his face accentuated by the shadows. He pushed her hair away from her eyes.

His hand slid from her shoulder to her hips.

"Todd," she whispered. *Todd.*

Her shades snapped up, startling her. In the harsh light, Todd's face vanished. Hearing her name—*Todd?*—she rolled onto her back.

When she looked up, her father was standing over her bed. "Time to get up, Leah. The Harvard coach is coming today."

The *nerve* of that man.

She curled into a ball, pulling the covers over her head. Her father's hand slid under the covers, and he wiggled her big toe, the way he used to when she was little. She yanked her foot back.

"Come on, kiddo," he coaxed. "You have to get up." He'd made blueberry pancakes. As if his stupid pancakes made up for last night.

"Go a*way*," she spat, her words garbled by the mountain of blankets and sheets.

"Leah, your team is—"

Who cares *if you're tired?* she heard in her head. *The competition is practicing, even when you're not...*"depending on you, Leah," *...dedication is what counts...*"talk to you, honey,"*...suck it up...get up, get up...do it...time to get up...time for soccer...time...practice...do it ...just do it...Just do it.*

Leah clapped her hands over her ears. "Go away," she cried. "Get out. Get away from me!"

Why did her father do this to her? Why couldn't he let her be?

"I'd like to talk to you, Leah. Please."

She threw off the covers. "Forget it. You can't make me play."

The toilet flushed in the bathroom between her room and Justine's. The faucet sputtered and water splashed into the sink. Leah's sister was washing her hands. Now she was brushing her teeth. Perfect little angel, never in trouble. Perfect little *dork*. Leah hated her sister. She hated them all—her mother, her father, Justine. Her parents didn't care about her. They cared about controlling her. They expected perfection, wanted perfect robots for kids. Well, guess what? She wasn't a robot. Her name wasn't Justine.

"Fine." Her father sat on her bed. "Stay home if you want to."

She pulled the covers down slightly, exposing only her eyes.

Her father leaned forward, dropping his hands between his knees. "I'm sorry, baby," he said quietly, staring at the floor. "I blew it."

Good. She had him right where she wanted him. Leah covered her head, her elbows up, creating an air tunnel so she could breathe. She'd forgive her father. Eventually. First, she'd make him suffer.

Her father's weight shifted. Then she felt the spring of the mattress. *No*. This wasn't the way it went. He couldn't leave. Her father never gave up. They talked until they'd worked things out.

"Dad?" Leah shot out of bed and darted to the landing. "Dad," she called again, leaning over the railing. "Daddy?"

By the time Zoe reached the office park, she'd worked herself into a funk. She had no idea how she would get through the day. She'd lain awake for hours last night, agonizing about Leah. Zoe's daughters knew very well their grandmother had been an alcoholic. The drinking had destroyed Zoe's family. The broken promises. The endless lies. After his wife died, Zoe's father had moved to a trailer park in Gloucester, a mile from the middle-class neighborhood where Zoe had grown up, cutting himself off from the rest of the world. Zoe and her younger brother, Ethan, had bought his groceries and paid the taxes on his trailer. After their father passed away, Ethan had fled to Hawaii; he lived in a shack on Oahu, taught part-time at the university, and spent the rest of his time on a surfboard.

At five that morning, Will had climbed into bed. He'd reached for her, touched her arm, set a warm hand on her shoulder. Lying on her side, she'd pretended to sleep. Every fifteen minutes, she checked the digital clock, always hoping that it was earlier than it actually was. At six thirty, she'd finally given up, put on sweats and gone downstairs, brewed a pot of Earl Gray tea, and scanned the morning *Globe*.

It was a miserable morning, low clouds scudding across an angry gray sky. She parked her Volvo behind the building in a spot reserved for tenants. Normally, she walked to her second floor office, a penitent's offering to the exercise god she'd forsaken. Today, anxiety fueling her fatigue, she waited for the elevator.

She'd worked for Cortland Child Services for eight years. She used to love this job. Physicians trusted her and they rewarded her with a constant flow of referrals. *Too* popular, she'd been forced to close her practice to new patients. Now she dreaded coming to work.

Early on, patients had treated her with respect; they'd listened eagerly, followed her advice. Today, everybody knew everything. Parents, armed with information gleaned from the Web, came for validation, seeking letters attributing their child's misbehavior to brilliance, drugs to give their child an edge. Zoe's education and experience meant nothing. She was merely a tool, a service provider.

She accidentally pressed *down*, forcing her to ride to the basement and back up.

The stress at home had ratcheted her anxiety, adding to her unease. The small things she used to let slide began to get to her: a missed appointment, a defiant gesture, an insolent remark. Doing a half-assed job made her feel crappy; these days, she felt like crap most of the time.

Zoe's mood lifted as she opened her office door. The office, with its soft coral walls, was her sanctuary. Sunlight filtered through the blinds on the picture window, the flecks of sand in the carpet around the turtle-shaped sandbox glittering. Zoe's grad school books lined the top shelf of a wall-to-wall bookcase. On the lower shelves were toys for the kids: cars and trucks, picture books, puzzles, stuffed animals, dolls.

From her iPod, she selected a soothing Thai instrumental piece, and logged onto her antiquated desktop computer. Her refusal to upgrade to a laptop was a running joke in the office. Zoe still handwrote her notes and transcribed them at the end of each day, the inconvenience a small price to pay for the ability to give her patients her undivided attention.

In no time, she printed and scanned her notes.

With ten minutes to spare before her first appointment, she decided to run a check on the Corbett boy. Last night, in her drunken stupor, Leah had blurted his name. Zoe typed Corbett's name in the Google dialogue box; feeling guilty, she immediately backspaced. A Google search felt invasive, like reading her child's diary or listening to a phone conversation. Yet how else was she to obtain information? She could hardly rely on Leah to fill her in. Besides, Corbett had gotten her daughter drunk and driven her home at three o'clock. That revoked any right he had to privacy.

She tapped her desk, impatient for the page to populate.

On the first page she spotted an entry, dated July 10, 2006, the keywords *Corbett* and *Massachusetts* emboldened. The URL linked to the Website for the *Dallas Star*.

She hit the link, her pulse racing as she scrolled down the page.

MASSACHUSETTS MAN ARRESTED IN TEXAS DRUG BUST

EL PASO, Texas—A Massachusetts man was arrested early this morning outside the Roadhouse restaurant in downtown El Paso on suspicion of drug possession and trafficking. Todd Corbett, 19, from Massachusetts, works as a sound technician for the alternative rock band, Cobra.

"We expect to hand down an indictment later today," said Assistant District Attorney Len Ahearn. Ahearn declined further comment regarding the details of Corbett's arrest, citing a judge's gag order. If prosecuted, Corbett faces a sentence of up to twenty years in prison and a $10,000 fine.

A later article reported the dismissal of the charges.

Zoe had expected to find something—a DUI, a petty theft, a drunk and disorderly—nothing along these lines. Leah pushed boundaries, yes. There was no way she was mixed up with a drug dealer.

Zoe returned to the first article, reread it, and logged on to boston.com, the Website for the *Globe*. In the "Metro" section of the July 11 edition, she found a single paragraph that began:

"Todd Corbett of Cortland, Massachusetts, was arrested..."

Reeling, she logged off. Zoe was a therapist. She worked with teenagers. If her daughter were involved with drugs, she'd know. She'd recognize the signs. Moods? What sixteen-year-old girl wasn't moody? Slipping grades? Zoe and Will had both flunked high school biology; they'd never done drugs. Leah had missed her curfew a few times, until last night never by more than ten minutes. Granted, she'd lied about being with Cissy. That Cissy had been MIA for a month was certainly strange. But girls fight. Junior year, Zoe's best friend had dumped her cold, all because the girl's crush had called Zoe "pretty." Normal teenage behavior—all of it.

Zoe's stomach went hollow.

———⟐———

Leah's father started in on her immediately after the game. Her team won, two to one. Evidently, Leah wasn't her usual self. "What's that supposed to mean? You couldn't breathe?"

She. Couldn't. Breathe. Which word did he not understand?

"Where's your inhaler? Look in the glove compartment."

It wasn't in there. She twisted the knob, letting the door bounce down. One-by-one, she removed the maps—Massachusetts, Ohio, Vermont—and laid them on the seat, along with a wrench, the BMW manual, and a pile of receipts. Triumphant, she stuffed it all back in.

"See," she said, with an I-told-you-so-smirk. "It's not in there." What did he expect from her? She'd scored the winning goal.

"You looked like crap," he said. She'd be lucky if Reardon still wanted her after today. She wasn't hustling, he ranted, and ticked off all the reasons the Harvard coach had probably lost interest.

Leah turned to the window and, chewing her thumbnail, stared at the empty cornfields, the crumbling stone walls, the hills rolling off to nowhere. So she hadn't played her best today. Who cared? Harvard was her father's dream, not hers. She'd been to the college plenty of times. She'd visited for the first time when she was eleven after her father had arranged a tour; she'd attended their soccer camp; she'd been to the stadium to watch their women's team play. She was not impressed. The buildings were old, the dorm rooms rundown. The kids clumped through the Yard, their shoulders stooped from the weight of their backpacks, looking frazzled and harried. Why would she want to go to a school where she would be miserable? College was supposed to be fun.

She'd taken tons of virtual tours on the Web, found plenty of schools she did like—UCLA, for example. But why bring them up? Her father would never send her to UCLA. No matter which college she chose, unless it was Harvard, her father would be disappointed. Nothing she did pleased him, so why bother trying?

Her father was still blathering on.

"Coach Thomas says Wake Forest wants to recruit me," Leah announced, surprising them both. "Maybe I'll go there. Or maybe I won't go to college. You don't have a degree. And you did all right."

"Wake Forest?" her father said incredulously. "You want to go to *Wake Forest?*"

———◈———

After Leah scrambled out, Will sat in his car, decompressing. Most kids would give their eyeteeth for a shot at Harvard. Not his daughter. No, to her it was no big deal. Who needed a scholarship? She could always go to their backyard and pluck one off the scholarship tree. Or maybe she assumed that he had the two hundred grand stashed in a mattress. Or one hundred. Or fifty. Or ten, for that matter.

The last time Leah played this badly—flat, no oomph—she'd had the flu. That day she'd had an excuse. Will had seen the Harvard coach on the sidelines, jotting notes. He'd gone over, said, "Hello," shot the breeze for a few minutes. Reardon had been friendly enough;

as the game progressed, the coach's body language told Will more than he'd wanted to know.

Leah had been a hyperactive little kid. He'd signed her up for soccer to give her an outlet, a release for her pent-up energy. Her talent had stunned everyone, Will included. With soccer—if they could direct her energy, harness her talent—his daughter could go places. He'd talked to coaches, read every rags-to-riches sports story he could lay his hands on, learned about the strategies the parents of the world's elite athletes—Larry Bird, Chris Evert, Tiger Woods— used to motivate their kids, and he'd patterned himself after them.

Their efforts had paid off. She was a star. She had the world by the tail—assuming she stayed on the field. It was all or nothing. Their single-minded devotion to soccer had closed other options. He'd hemmed her in. Now she resented him. If he'd realized this would be the result, he'd have backed off, let her find her own way.

Should've, would've, could've. Wish in one hand, piss in the other. See which fills faster.

When he looked up, Justine was headed down the garage steps. She grinned, side-stepping his golf bag, and crossed the garage.

He scooped her off her feet, planted a smooch on her forehead. "Hey, Princess," he said. "How ya doing?"

"I made sandwiches. Turkey and cheese. Want one?"

"I'd love a sandwich," he told her. "But I need to go to my office to fetch my laptop. Would you like to take a ride? We can stop for ice cream."

"I'm supposed to go to Holly's. I'm just waiting for her to call."

"I'll bring some back then." He winked. "Frozen pudding, right?"

"No!" She pretended to pout. "Chocolate—"

"Marshmallow chip," he said, laughing, wondering how he'd gotten so lucky with her.

Leah was lounging on her futon, her long legs crossed at the ankles, the cordless phone lying facedown on her thighs. In the adjoining room, her sister was pounding on her heavy bag, probably pretending she was Buffy the Vampire Slayer again. Leah banged on the wall. "Cool it, Justine," she hollered. "I can't hear myself think."

The sound died down and she picked up her phone, dialing Todd's number. She got a busy signal again. What was up with that?

Who didn't have call waiting today? It was so annoying. She'd been trying his line every ten minutes since she got home.

Leah went to her desk, booted her computer, and logged into Facebook. No one in the news stream. Checked her e-mail—junk. Bored, she opened the program her parents had ordered from *The Princeton Review* when she was a freshman to help her study for the SATs. While the file loaded, she paged through the workbook.

The math questions were easy. When she looked at a problem, she immediately saw the logic—the same way she recognized the conflation of angles, saw play patterns taking shape on the soccer field, and knew, better than the coach waving from the sidelines, exactly where she needed to be. English had always been tougher.

The first question was easy. *Apple is to fruit as asparagus is to____. Vegetable.*

The next made her think. *Hillary is to mountaineer as Columbus is to ____.*

The answer was supposed to be explorer, but imperialist fit, too. After all, hadn't America belonged to the natives? Her teachers acted as if Columbus were a hero, and the entire country celebrated a day in his honor, when in fact his so-called discovery had led to the death of thousands of indigenous people and the disruption of a way of life that was every bit as significant as the lives of the Fifteenth Century Europeans. Where did people get off insisting one lifestyle was intrinsically better than another? Who had the right to judge?

Leah closed the program and shut down her computer.

Why was she taking this test? She had no idea what she wanted to study, what she wanted to be. What was the point in going to college? The truth was, hardly anyone her age had a clear idea of what they wanted to do when they were older. Oh, the kids all pretended to know, but it was obvious to her they were only repeating dreams their parents laid out.

Just last week in social studies, the discussion had turned to careers. Her teacher, Mr. Mulvany, constantly went on tangents. They'd been talking about the war in Afghanistan and somebody said something about enlisting in the army; next thing she knew, they were talking about the U.S. social and economic outlook, then their careers.

Leah hadn't minded the shift. She was tired of talking about the war. Everybody had an opinion about the invasion and whether the U.S. ought to be there, the talk always distant, impersonal, as if regardless of the outcome, the speaker would not be affected. How could people discuss something so important, yet not really care?

The discussion in social studies had the same dispassionate tone. Mr. Mulvany went around the room, asking each student what profession he or she planned to pursue. Their answers were shockingly vague. Law, one student replied; business, said somebody else. Not a single kid named anything specific. What *branch* of law? Leah wanted to shout. What *sort* of business? Each time one of Leah's classmates named a lofty profession, Mr. Mulvany would nod appreciatively, as if to say, *See? Cortland High is doing its job.*

When her turn came, Leah mumbled her answer. A soccer player, she said, the choice they all expected to hear. Since she was little, she'd dreamed of playing in the Olympics, the first step toward a professional soccer career. Lately, she wondered if playing pro soccer was something she really wanted to do. The adults in her life all pushed her in that direction, told her she'd be a fool not to play.

Had she simply adopted their dream?

Someone tapped on the door. Leah was about to tell her dad to buzz off when Cissy Hanson strutted into the room, glossy black hair cascading over her shoulders. She looked, in a red cashmere sweater and skin-tight jeans, as if she'd just stepped out of *Glamour.*

"What do *you* want?" Leah asked.

Except for soccer, where she had no other choice, Leah hadn't spoken to Cissy in weeks. The girl was a tool, spreading vicious rumors about Todd. According to Cissy, Todd had been arrested in El Paso for dealing coke. Cissy's mom worked with Todd's mom in the emergency room at St. John's. Supposedly, his mom had told her mom the story. After his arrest, the band had fired him, she'd claimed. The liar. When Leah heard the rumors—Cissy didn't have the guts to tell Leah directly—she'd confronted Todd herself, demanding to know what had happened. The arrest wasn't even his fault. The roadies framed him.

Cissy waved a pair of Leah's jeans. "Thought you'd want these."

Leah shot Cissy a narrow look and told her to put the jeans on the bed. Cissy never returned anything without being haunted. She'd borrowed those jeans a month ago. Why return them today?

Cissy folded the jeans. Bending, she laid them at the foot of the bed, the light glinting off a small silver charm at the base of her throat. The other half of Leah's Best Friends necklace. She and Cissy had bought the necklaces when they were in the eighth grade. Leah had been wearing hers for so long the necklace had become a part of her, like a birthmark or a mole. She didn't notice it anymore.

Hard to believe she and Cissy had ever been friends, never mind best friends. They'd met when they were ten, the year Leah's dad coached their team. Cissy's father had walked out on the family the summer before, and her mom had trouble getting Cissy to practice. To help her out, the Tylers volunteered to drive. Cissy looked like a geek with her pixie haircut and plastic-rimmed glasses. She didn't talk much, either. And she wouldn't look at you. Leah had put up with Cissy, but she didn't think all that much of her. She never teased her, as all the other kids did. Cissy was just *there*. In time, Cissy had grown on her, weirdness and all. By the end of the year, they were inseparable. When her mom started her workshops last year, Leah had practically lived at the Hanson's. Cissy's mother had been engaged to a doctor and she'd allowed the girls to help with the wedding arrangements, so there was always plenty to do.

"So what's up?" Leah asked. "What are you really doing here?"

Cissy sat on the floor, raking her fingers over the rug. "You played awesome today."

Leah rolled her eyes. "I played like crap."

"My stepdad knows the Harvard coach, you know. They went to college together."

As if Leah cared.

"Mr. Reardon wants to recruit you. He kept telling my dad what an amazing athlete you are," Cissy said, and launched into a blow-by-blow account of Coach Reardon's reaction to each of Leah's plays.

"Seriously?" Leah asked, her anger softening. "He likes me?"

"Likes you?" Cissy shook her head vehemently. "He thinks you're *great*."

Maybe Leah had been too hard on Cissy, refusing to return her messages, ignoring her calls. Leah missed having a best friend, a girl she could talk to, someone to share her secrets. They had been best friends for far too long to let a boy stand between them—any boy, even Todd Corbett. Once they were better acquainted, Cissy would realize she had misjudged Todd, and they could all be friends. Maybe the three of them could hang out one day soon, go to lunch or a movie. It didn't have to be either-or, Leah suddenly saw. She had plenty of love to share with them both.

Leah was about to suggest a date, when Cissy spoke up. "I talked to your dad."

Weird. "When?"

"After the game."

"What did he say?"

Cissy picked at the rug. "He told me what happened last night."

"My father told you *what*?"

Cissy shrugged, biting her lower lip, her nose twitching.

"Let's go, Cissy. Spit it out."

"The kid's bad news, Lee."

How dare she? "Get out. Now."

"It's for your own good, Lee. The kid's a drug deal—"

"Get out." Leah scooped the jeans off the foot of her bed and hurled them at the wall. "I said, 'get out.' Get *out!*"

Leah slammed the door behind Cissy and threw herself on her bed, sobbing. What had possessed her to trust Cissy Hanson, think they could ever be friends again? Cissy was no friend. She never had been. She'd used Leah to weasel her way into the popular crowd. Leah hated that girl. She wished Cissy would die. Well, maybe not die, but go away. Someplace far, like maybe Alaska.

Someone touched Leah's shoulder.

"Go away." Flinching, she pulled the pillow over her head.

"Lee? You okay? Did you and Cissy get in a fight?"

It was only her sister. With the back of her hand, Leah wiped her eyes. "I'm fine," she said, sitting.

Leah's sister was not much bigger than the life-sized dolls the girls had played with when they were younger, her tiny hands and feet two-thirds the size of Leah's. Her bone structure was exotic, like their mother's, but her features had not yet developed, her cheeks fleshy and round. In a couple of years, once Justine grew a few inches and thinned out, Leah would have to guard her boyfriend. Now, her sister looked like a chubby pixie.

"What is it, Jus?"

Justine's eyes brightened and she handed Leah an envelope.

Too bad their parents had listened to the principal and allowed Justine to skip second grade. If they'd kept her in her own grade, with friends her age, she might have had half a chance to be cool.

Leah glanced at the postmark—Cornell—folded the envelope into an airplane, and sent it sailing toward her nightstand. The plane, missing its target by an inch, drifted lazily to the floor.

Confused, Justine scooped the envelope up.

"Keep it," Leah said. It was just another recruiting letter. Coaches weren't even supposed to contact her yet. According to MIAA rules, college coaches were not allowed to talk to a potential recruit until the summer before senior year. Rules, evidently, didn't apply to adults. She got at least one letter a week. "I don't want it."

Her sister looked shocked. "How come?"

Leah mulled it over. Whatever she said would fly directly from her sister's lips to their parents' ears. Maybe that would be good. Their parents trusted Justine. Maybe if she told them Leah's plans, they'd listen. "I'm not going to college," Leah explained, her fledgling confidence finding its wings. "I might travel for a while."

"But you have to go, Lee. What would you do for a job?"

Good question. She hadn't thought that far ahead. Miraculously, a plan materialized: she would be a famous rock star! She didn't say that, of course. Her sister would laugh. Leah played no instruments, after all. She could sing a little, though, and she could certainly dance.

"I might try out for one of those reality shows," Leah said, inspired, picturing herself on *Dancing with the Stars* or *American Idol*. "Lots of famous people got their start that way."

Justine picked up Leah's Paddington Bear, and stroked its head.

"So how's your project coming?" Leah asked, a nasty hint dusted with sugar.

"Great," Justine said, her eyes lighting up. She had this idea. She'd love an opinion. "Do you mind?"

Leah flipped through the red vinyl CD case on her nightstand. Every other kid in the world had an iPod. Not her. No, she was stuck with father's used CD player. She needed a job so she'd have money to buy her own things.

Most of her CDs were ancient, bought before she met Todd: Michelle Branch, Justin Timberlake. Leah winced. *Britney Spears.*

Leah plucked her new Ani DiFranco CD out of its plastic sleeve, went to her bureau, and slid the CD into the changer.

Justine's idea had something to do with the Milky Way, some new discovery she'd read about in *Science*. Something about planetary movement. Leah heard a few words here and there, nodded now and again, so her sister would think she was listening. She couldn't get Todd out of her head.

Todd was cool and good-looking, but there was much more to him than that. He was mature. He didn't get caught up in appearances. He didn't expect her to measure up to some arbitrary standard. He didn't judge her, didn't expect her to pretend she was someone she wasn't. He couldn't care less whether her picture was in the newspaper or if, until recently, she had been the most popular girl at Cortland High. When Leah complained about practice, when she said she hated soccer and told him she didn't want to play anymore, he advised her to do whatever felt right. Forget what people thought or what anyone said. If she wasn't happy playing soccer, she should quit. With Todd, she felt freer, more like *herself* than she did with anyone else.

"...orbit." Justine stopped talking and looked over at Leah. "So what do you think?"

"Yeah," Leah said. "Awesome."

"No, I mean what do you *think*? Is it a good idea?"

"I don't know, Justine." She'd gotten a *D* on her last science test. Their parents had gone ballistic. Had Justine forgotten already?

"Never mind," Justine said. She'd figure it out. "So what happened last night? I heard you crying."

"Nothing, really," Leah said, and told her sister the story.

"Who's Todd?"

"This guy I'm seeing."

Justine's eyes widened. She wanted to know exactly what Todd looked like, where Leah had met him, how long they'd been dating.

"Not too long," Leah said. "Six weeks and one day." But she expected it to last. "This is it, Jus. He's the one."

"Really? You think so?"

"Yeah," Leah said. "I do."

"That's cool."

Maybe her little sister wasn't such a geek after all. A ceramic cast of Justine's hand sat on her nightstand. Justine had made it in kindergarten. Leah wondered what Justine would say if she knew that Leah used the hand as an ashtray. Maybe Leah should tell her. Make it a test, to see if her sister was trustworthy. Before she had a chance to broach the subject, Justine said, "'Bye," and got up.

"Where are you going? I thought you wanted to hang out."

To Holly's, Justine informed her, to plan their costumes. Halloween was, after all, only a month away. "Hey? Want to come?"

"I don't know, Jus." Sixteen was way too old for trick-or-treating. Leah pictured the three girls, prancing around the neighborhood, making fools of themselves. Come to think of it, it might be a hoot to see the scandalized look on their neighbors' faces when they saw a sixteen-year-old girl at their door.

Justine was still waiting. "Just Do It," said the poster on the wall above Leah's bed. *Just do it.*

Leah shrugged. "Maybe." If she wasn't grounded. She'd think about it, Leah promised. She'd see.

Four

Women on the Move

On Saturday afternoon after work, Zoe had a long talk with Will. They'd discussed his over-reaction the previous night—he needed to get his anxiety under control, they'd agreed—and she'd showed him a printout of the article about Corbett.

"When we talk to her, we need to present a unified front," Zoe had said. It would be hard, considering how disturbed they were by the news. "We need talk this through rationally." Be as nonjudgmental as possible. Ask honest questions; listen to what she has to say. Show Leah they were on her side. If they could help her see how dangerous this Todd person was, she might get rid of the boy on her own.

When they finished strategizing, they called Leah into the living room and closed the French doors. The conversation began on a reasonable note, Zoe asking Leah nicely why she'd been late. Did she have any idea how worried they'd been?

"Dad and I were frantic, Leah. We love you. We thought something terrible happened."

Their daughter answered their questions, less fully than they'd hoped, but at least she didn't shut them out. She and Todd were at the water tower; she'd lost track of time; they hadn't done anything wrong. For ten minutes, Zoe and Will listened patiently. Just as it seemed that they were on the verge of a breakthrough, Will called Todd a loser, and the accusations and counter-accusations had flown.

The battle escalated, their voices rising, Zoe begging them to calm down. Will brought up the underage drinking, mentioned cops, and Leah had fled the room, sobbing, scrambled up to her bedroom, and slammed the door.

After dinner, Zoe popped corn and they'd all watched television together. Will had apologized. Still, there was unresolved tension.

If I can convince her to come to the workshop, Zoe thought on Sunday morning, *she'll see that I care; maybe I'll get through to her.*

Zoe expected a moderate turnout for her workshop today. She checked her list. Fifteen preregistered. Even if a few women brought friends, the gathering would be intimate, a perfect setting to introduce Leah. Justine sometimes accompanied Zoe to the seminars; at twelve, Zoe's younger daughter could still be persuaded to tag along with her mother. Whenever Zoe invited Leah, her elder daughter declined. Normally, Zoe took such rejection in stride. At Leah's age, she'd have refused a walk to their mailbox with her mother. Today, she persisted.

"So what do you say?" Zoe stacked the blueberry pancakes on a plate and turned off the griddle.

"I don't know, Mom," Leah poured a glass of orange juice and set it on the counter. "Why don't you ask Jus? She'll probably go."

"She has that introductory Mass for Confirmation candidates," Zoe reminded her. "Then a reception in the church hall afterward."

"I would," Leah said, staring into her juice. "But I've got a ton of homework."

"Please," Zoe wheedled. "It'll be fun."

"Success Skills, Ma? That's not exactly my speed."

"My back has been bothering me," Zoe said, rubbing the base of her spine. It was true. "I could use some help setting up."

"Well." Leah looked doubtful. "If you *really* need help."

On the way to the seminar, Leah's mom gave her a crash course on Success Skills.

"Understanding *how* to achieve your goal is crucial to success," her mother explained. "First, we work on developing a plan…"

Leah had been angry with her mother for taking part in the so-called "discussion" yesterday. Leah understood why her parents were pissed. She'd worried them. In their shoes, she'd have been worried, too. Still, her father had no right to call Todd a loser. How could he say something so mean? Her father didn't even *know* Todd. Besides, it was her fault they had been late. Todd offered to drive her home earlier. The truth was, the fight was not her mom's fault. Her dad was the jerk. He was wrong to blame Todd for her behavior. It was just as wrong for her to displace blame on her mom.

Leah tuned the radio to her mom's favorite soft rock station, and fastened her seatbelt. Her mother had a soothing voice, rising and falling like waves. Soon, Leah was daydreaming. She said, "Uh-huh," when it seemed appropriate, nodded now and again to show interest.

Her mother, Leah suddenly noticed, had stopped talking. "So," Leah said. "How do you get them started?"

She advised them to find a mentor, her mother replied, someone whose skills they could emulate. "Say you want to be a pianist, for example." Her mom's eyes slid sideways. *A pianist?* Leah detested piano. When she was little, her parents had forced her to take lessons.

She would sit in front of the keyboard for hours, banging the keys, pretending to practice, until her exasperated mother finally let her get up.

"Hypothetically," her mom said. Leah grinned, relieved that her mom hadn't completely forgotten her childhood years. "Anyway, you look for the best pianist, someone who plays music you're interested in, and copy her routine."

"Like Ani?"

"Ani?"

"You know, Ani DiFranco? The CD I played after breakfast."

"Okay, say Ani practices scales for an hour a day."

"I don't think Ani practices, Ma. She's just naturally good."

"Right," said her mother, with a dubious sideways glance.

The light turned red as they approached the intersection. Across the street, a heavyset girl in a navy-blue sweatshirt emerged from Dunkin' Donuts, toting a bag in one hand, a coffee cup in the other. Hope, her name was. Todd had introduced the girls the weekend before last at a bonfire across town. They'd talked for five minutes, then Hope said she had to jet, she had to meet Lupo, her boyfriend— Todd's best friend, it turned out—and took off. Hope opened the front door on the passenger side of a dilapidated black Cadillac, with an "I Heart Jesus" sticker affixed to its trunk. The car's left taillight was missing. Leah reached across her mother's lap, tooted the horn, and then tooted again, waving both arms, so Hope could easily see her.

Hope pulled a sour face and climbed into the car.

"Who was that?" her mom asked. "Do you know that girl?"

"No." Leah slouched, chewing her thumbnail. "Not really."

The light turned green, and the car pitched into the crossroad.

"I've got an idea," her mother exclaimed. They could be a team. Leah would handle administrative duties at first, circulating flyers, placing ads. Once they felt comfortable, she'd teach Leah to present.

Leah rolled her eyes. Her mother conjured up some nutty ideas, but *this* was the looniest yet. "I'm still in school, Ma. Remember?"

"No problem, sweetie." Her mom leaned toward the wheel, smiling broadly. These programs took time to catch on. By the time they developed a following, Leah would be out of high school, and she'd have plenty of free time in college. Her mom painted scenes of herself and Leah crisscrossing the country, conducting their workshops. They'd be far more than business partners, she said. They would be friends. "Who knows? Maybe we'll be on *Oprah* one day."

As wacky as the idea sounded, Leah was tempted. She'd enjoy traveling, seeing new places. Plus, it would be nice to do something for other people for a change. The workshops had clearly been good for her mom. Since last year, her mother's confidence had soared. Though Leah thought little about it, she'd noticed. Her mom seemed happier, less frustrated, less moody. But they were different. Leah lacked her mom's drive. Soccer was all she'd ever done well. She couldn't imagine standing before an audience, dispensing advice. Leah pictured herself and her mom, lying side by side on a lumpy bed in some motel room in Paducah, boning up on material. Never in a million years. Even if the idea intrigued her, she'd never leave Todd.

"There are weeds in every garden." On her flip chart, Leah's mother drew weeds, invading a patch of roughly sketched daisies. "We must learn to deal with disappointment."

The hall, with its speckled linoleum floor and pallid blue walls, resembled the emergency room at St. John's, where Leah had worked last summer, running errands for Cissy's mom. In place of the hospital odors of rubbing alcohol, medication, and disease, the hall smelled of incense and candles. A wooden cross behind the podium gave an impression of a crucifixion, not at all like the life-sized suffering Jesus above the altar in St. Theresa's Catholic Church, where Leah's family worshiped.

A woman in the front row raised her hand. As soon as Leah's mom completed her sentence, she called on her. The woman's polyester slacks crackled as she stood. "Deal with disappointment?" The woman sighed. "Sounds easy. But how do you *do* it?"

"We're here," Leah's mother replied, with a sweep of her hand. "That's the first step."

Beaming, the woman took her seat.

Leah was proud of her mom. She looked so professional standing by the podium with her flip chart. As she talked, she jotted down bullets, her audience scribbling furiously on their notepads.

Weeds in every garden? The advice was cheesy, unoriginal, and yet, maybe because she put so much of herself in her words, her mother sounded totally convincing.

During the break, the participants milled around the room, napkins and cookies in hand, chatting and taking turns stopping by the podium to ask questions. They were seated now, listening carefully again, their chairs rearranged into a semicircle for this part of the program.

"As I was saying—" Leah's mom scanned the audience. "We mustn't be afraid to break self-destructive patterns."

The obese woman sitting beside Leah pulled a bag of barbecue chips from her purse and offered it to Leah. Leah thanked her and set the bag on the floor under her chair.

"We have to stand up for ourselves. Eliminate the negativity in our lives. We've got to be strong." Zoe paused, giving the message a chance to sink in. "Avoid toxic relationships. Or people who bring us down," she added, directing a meaning-filled smile at Leah.

Leah squirmed. Her mom was right. If she were ever to fly, be her own person, she had to stop kowtowing to all the adults in her life. She had to take control, break free. Since she met Todd, she'd grown stronger, more independent. But she had a long way to go.

As the afternoon wore on, people opened up. They talked about their lives, their long-term goals, the changes they intended to make after the workshop.

"Be specific," Leah's mother said, gesturing for them to speak out. "The more specific, the better our chances of accomplishing our goals."

The woman beside Leah leapt out of her seat. "I'm cleaning out the refrigerator," she announced. "The instant I get home." She pumped her fist and everyone cheered.

"I'm ordering flyers for my business," shouted somebody else.

"Finishing my degree."

"Traveling to Italy!"

"Getting my realtor's license."

Quit biting my nails, Leah vowed silently. *Be my own person.*

On the way home, Zoe's daughter said, "I'm impressed, Ma." They were at an intersection, waiting for the light to change. Zoe looked at her and smiled. "Thank you, honey." *This is my real daughter*, she thought. *This is my Leah.*

"I mean it." Leah turned the radio up. "You're great with them." Why on Earth were they always fighting? It was absurd. Look at them now. It was easy to get along. It's all about listening, Zoe thought, congratulating herself on her insight. And mutual respect.

The car behind them honked. The light had turned. Startled, Zoe stepped too heavily on the gas. The car jerked into the intersection.

Leah grabbed the handhold above her door, letting out a yelp.

"Sorry," Zoe said sheepishly. "Think there's a Success Skills workshop for driving?"

"Driver's Ed," Leah said, giggling. When they finally stopped laughing, she asked, "Can I ask you something, Mom?"

"Certainly, sweetheart. Anything."

"What made you do it? The seminars, I mean."

"Tough question." She'd been unhappy. No, unhappy was the wrong word. Frustrated. Discontented, maybe. "Something," Zoe said quietly, "was missing." She signaled their turn onto Main Street. Don't get her wrong: she loved her family. She squeezed Leah's forearm. "How can I explain it? I thought if I could help people make important changes in their lives, I'd be doing something worthwhile."

"Was it hard?" Leah reminded her of the long hours she'd spent developing, organizing, and marketing her workshops. She reminded Zoe of her so-called friends and colleagues, who'd warned her that in a tiny suburb like theirs she'd never attract enough attendees to make the venture worthwhile, who'd insisted she was wasting her time.

"Don't you get tired? Do you ever think about quitting?"

"Sure," Zoe admitted. "Sometimes. Then I think about the women I'm helping and I get excited again." She told Leah about the cards and letters she received after the workshops, thanking her, telling her—she laughed—she was an angel. "The confidence I see in their eyes at the end of the day. That's what makes it all worthwhile."

After that, Leah grew quiet.

They passed a cornfield, the harvested stalks lying in the furrows to be shredded for compost. Soon the fields gave way to forest.

Leah yawned. Within minutes, she was asleep.

Zoe turned off the radio and plugged a CD into the changer. The Liszt piano solos had been a gift from a student. "You'll like the freethinking music," the woman had said, and she had been right. What a perfect ending to a perfect day. For the first time in ages, she and Leah had talked about something real and important. As soon as she and Will straightened out their finances, she'd quit her job at the counseling center and focus on the workshops. If she grew the business, maybe she and Leah really could work together one day.

She stroked Leah's temples, pushing the hair out of her daughter's eyes. Zoe felt sick about their blowout yesterday. The business with this Todd person was her fault as much as Leah's. If she'd paid closer attention to her daughter, Leah would not have looked for affirmation from a person like Corbett.

That's all in the past, Zoe vowed. From now on, she planned to be available for her children. She'd rearrange her patient schedule so that she was there when Justine came home from school. She'd pick up Leah after practice; she'd attend every game. She would set aside at least four hours of individual quality time, per week, for each of the girls. She'd pack healthy, appetizing lunches. Bake cookies. Sew Halloween outfits. She'd be the perfect mother. *Better than perfect*, she thought, then brought herself up short. *Let's not get ahead of ourselves. Let's take this one step at a time.*

On Old Orchard Road, a mile from home, Leah opened her eyes. "I was having this crazy dream," she said, yawning.

"What were you dreaming about?"

Leah rubbed her eyes. "I can't remember. What's this music?"

"Liszt. *Hungarian Rhapsodies*. A student gave it to me. Like it?"

"It's cool," Leah said, fingering her belly ring. "Kind of...wild."

"It's gypsy music." Zoe eyed Leah's belly ring. "Did it hurt? Getting pierced?"

"Not too much. You still mad?"

Zoe squeezed Leah's thigh. "No, sweets. But I wish you'd talked to me first."

"You weren't home," Leah said, a hint of accusation in her tone.

"Sorry. I'd like to have been there for you. That's all I meant."

"Dad was pissed." Leah scraped her thumbnail, chipping the garish blue polish.

Zoe remembered. Will had been angry with her, too. In the Tyler household, by order of both parents, belly rings were forbidden. *If you'd stay on top of things, she might not have done this*, he'd charged, after the girls had gone to bed. *So it's my fault?* Zoe shot back. *Like you're ever around?* The argument ended in a stalemate.

"Dad doesn't mean to be so hard on you, honey. He just worries."

Slouching, Leah slid her hands under her thighs. "He doesn't need to. I'm not a baby."

"I know, sweetie." Zoe signaled their turn onto Lily Farm Road. "It's just, it's scary being a parent. The decisions you make now—"

"Will affect the rest of my life. God, Mom. Can't you say something different for once?"

"We're your parents, sweetie. It's our job to provide guidance."

"You're such a *hypocrite*. All day long you tell those women to make their own decisions. But not me? I'm supposed to listen to you?"

Zoe tightened her grip on the wheel. True, she advised students to take control of their lives. But that was advice for adults. "You'll be an adult soon enough, Leah. Then you can make all your own decisions. For now—"

"I'm an adult already."

"You're sixteen, honey. I know you feel like an adult—"

"Well, guess what, Mom?" Leah shifted aggressively toward her door. "In November I'll be seventeen. And you'll have no say over me."

Zoe felt her jaw clench. She was well aware of the state law governing the legal age of adulthood. Leah's age was immaterial. Leah was her daughter. Zoe loved her. *Because she loved her*, there were some decisions—dating a drug dealer, for example—that she could not allow her to make. Zoe knew all too well from the teenagers she cared for in her practice, that poor decisions often left permanent scars. It was her job as mother to keep Leah off that path.

"I'm sorry, Leah. Until you're a responsible adult—living on your own—your father and I make the rules."

"So I'm irresponsible now?"

Zoe felt closer to Leah today than she'd felt in ages. She refused to end the day with a fight. She reached for Leah's arm. "Honey, listen. All I said is—"

Leah jerked away. "You said I'm a baby."

Patience, Zoe told herself. *Deep breath*. She eased the Volvo alongside the mailbox, pulled out the mail and set it on the console, then turned into their driveway. "Think about it, honey." She forced a smile. "How would you feel if your daughter came in at three—"

"So that's why you were so big on me coming with you today." Leah scooped her team jacket from the floor. "So you could get me alone. Try to get me to dump him. I hate to break it to you, *Mom*. You wasted your time. It's up to me who I go out with."

"Leah, please." Zoe pressed the button for the garage door. Leah's dollhouse sat on the metal shelf at the back of the garage. Until last summer, Leah had kept the dollhouse on a table next to her bed. One day, she'd decided she was too old for a dollhouse and carried it down here. Leah wasn't a baby. Zoe knew that. She wanted to protect her daughter. That was her only goal. "Sweetie," she said, trying again, "I didn't say anything about your boyfriend."

"Right, so lie to me now."

"Honey, think about it for a minute—"

Leah clapped her hands over her ears.

"—honestly, sweetheart. What do you expect?"

"La, la, la, la, la," Leah sang.

"Damn it, Leah." Zoe pried her daughter's hands away from her head. "He had you out *drinking*. How many times have we talked—"

"La, la, la, la, la," Leah trilled, her voice drowning Zoe's.

"—about drinking?" Zoe shouted. "The kid used to be a roadie. This is not a good guy."

"I don't need this." Leah flipped the lock on her door.

Zoe caught Leah's wrist. "The kid sells drugs, for God's sake."

"I'm done with you," Leah shouted, wrenching free. "I'm never going with you again. Anywhere. Ever."

"No problem," Zoe spat back. She was sorry she'd talked the little brat into coming. She should have known this would happen. "Believe me, I have no intention of asking again."

"I hate you," Leah cried. "I hate you. I'm not pretending I don't anymore."

Leah slammed the door, and went hurtling into the house.

The histrionic gypsy music rang in Zoe's ears. She slapped the dash, her fingers fumbling with the dial.

She'd lost her cool, said all the wrong things. Leah was spewing words, trying to hurt Zoe as much as Zoe had hurt her. Leah wanted reassurance. She wanted to be told she was capable and smart. She wanted to know Zoe was proud of her, that she trusted her to make her own decisions. Zoe had let her down. She'd seen the ache in her daughter's eyes, the disappointment. Maybe this was what people meant by the term "growing pains," not the pain children experienced in their joints as their limbs grew, but the ache they felt in their hearts.

Zoe stared at the discarded playthings in their garage, Leah's dollhouse, her tricycle, her wooden blocks dissolving in a watery blur. *If only you knew how hard it is to watch you stumble, to see you in pain.*

Pull yourself together, Zoe told herself. *Don't let your failures defeat you.* Yet here she was, her failures an anchor, sucking her under the sea.

Five

Blue Ribbon Day

Looking back, this is the day Zoe sees: in May, she turned thirty. Will is away, in California. They live in Hudson in a red Cape Cod-style house they bought two years earlier, when Will's commission finally outpaced his draw. At night, terrified to be alone with her children in the secluded house, she has trouble falling asleep. After she tucks the girls in bed, she blocks all the doors, sits in the living room with Dog at her feet, paging through magazines with the TV and radio off, listening for intruders. At dawn, she finally falls asleep.

It's late morning, the end of October—her father's birthday. Today is the seven week anniversary of Zoe's abortion. Exhausted, not yet recovered from the procedure, Zoe is dozing, dreaming about the baby she lost. Her head aches when she comes to.

Rubbing the sleep from her eyes, she sees Leah standing at her elbow, cuddling her filthy pink blanket, a bright yellow tutu stretched over her playsuit. The elastic legs of the tutu pinch her legs; her shorts bunch at the thighs. Leah plugs her thumb in her mouth, bringing the blanket's satin edge to her nose.

The child is four, too old for a blanket.

For the past eight months, since the birth of her sister, Leah's behavior has steadily regressed. Zoe was alarmed at first, when her four-year-old suddenly began wetting her pants, mangling her once clearly articulated words. The pediatrician assured her it is normal.

"A new sibling is stressful," he said. "She feels displaced. You'll be surprised how fast she adjusts."

"Take your thumb out of your mouth, honey. You're not a baby anymore. Here—"Zoe curls her fingers. "Give Mommy the blanket."

"I wanna play wif Hammy," Leah says, thumb garbling her words.

"Take your thumb out of your mouth." Zoe extends her hand. "And give me the blanket."

Leah shakes her head furiously.

Zoe's neck aches. She grimaces, rolling her head left and right. "Fine," she says, too tired to argue. "Have it your way."

The door of the cuckoo clock on the wall in front of the staircase swings open and a bright red rooster springs out. "Cuckoo," the bird sings. "Cuckoo, cuckoo." *Noon.* She's expecting her parents for lunch in an hour.

She's serving tuna salad and chips. She needs to make a dessert.

"How about if you go outside for a while? Play on your swings? Dog's out there."

"Don't wanna go outside," Leah says, unplugging her mouth. Leah turns the blanket over in her hands, twists until the blanket looks like a filthy pink beach ball. "I wanna play wif Hammy. Hammy likes me, Daddy says."

The hamster reminds Zoe of a rat. Will brought it home last month after one of his trips. In a flash, Zoe sees Leah clinging to her father's legs, begging him not to go. Their daughter asked for her father over and over, at least a dozen times a day, the entire time he was gone.

Where my Daddy? Why he leave? In a time zone three hours earlier than theirs, he phoned them at night, after she'd fallen asleep. Zoe sees him standing in the doorway two weeks later, hands behind his back, a guilty grin on his face. Peering over his shoulder, she sees the aquarium, a Habitrail, a month's supply of wood chips. A giant bag of pellets leans against his luggage.

"Where's my girl?" With a flourish, he produces his gift. "Where's Leah?"

"For God's sake, Will. She doesn't need another *pet.*" Zoe had her hands full already with that puppy he brought home six months ago. The Lab wasn't even housebroken yet. Poor thing—they still called her Dog.

Will pretended Zoe was kidding. "This isn't a joke," she told him. "You've been gone three weeks this month. Your daughter is starting to forget what you look like."

He turned away. He had no choice, he told her. Problem on one of the jobs. His responsibility. He'd negotiated the contract. He'd much rather be home. Didn't she know that? She shook her head, listening, but not quite believing.

Leah refuses to budge.

This child is her father's daughter. She's inherited his dazzling blue eyes, his height—at four, she reaches her mother's waist—Will's sturdy build and silky blonde hair. The stubborn streak, too, comes directly from him.

"I wanna play wif Hammy." Leah paws Zoe's arm, climbs onto her. Zoe sets her back down.

"Later, okay? We'll get him out after lunch."

Leah huffs. It is almost comical, the way she stands, feet apart, legs braced as though ready to fight, eyes flashing, tiny fists pressed to her hips. A miniature Will, Zoe thinks, picturing her husband in nearly that same stance the night before he left.

"California?" Zoe said. "And you're not taking us?"

She and Will lived in California before they were married. He was a folk artist then, in his other life, as he calls it. He was playing a gig and she was in the audience. Her friends were noisy, rude. Enraged, he'd ended the show early. She looked for him afterward to apologize. They talked for hours that night, and he'd driven her home. Within three months, they were living together. She misses those days, California, the loving, spontaneous couple she and Will used to be.

He would be on site all day. He laid a starched white shirt in his suitcase. "You and the kids would have nothing to do."

Sure they would. They could go to the beach, for example, and she ticked off a list.

"That's ridiculous. I've got work. Besides, we don't have the money."

"Damn it," she said. "Why don't we have the money? Where does it go?" Look around. Where it always goes. *Where it always goes?* Toward your three-piece suits, she wanted to say, your nights on the town. "Not here," she did say, "into the house, as you promised."

They'd made all sorts of plans when they bought the house. They talked about renovating the kitchen. Will promised to raise the ceiling in their bedroom, finish the basement, build a playroom for the kids, none of which he'd done. Here he was, palms upturned, as if he had no idea what she was talking about.

"Will—please?"

"Jesus Christ, Zoe." He looked at her hard and turned away.

"What? Tell me, damn it. I want to know."

Fine. Look at her. How many more days did she plan on wearing those sweatpants? She'd gained fifteen pounds over the summer. Her jeans were too tight. Turning, she felt his eyes on her back. *And when, by the way, did she plan to wash her hair?* Zoe raked her fingers over her head. She imagined every horrid thing her husband might be thinking and shuddered.

"Listen—" He lowered his voice, took hold of her hand, spun her around. "I know it takes time. But for God's sake, Zoe." *Would she rather she'd died?*

The IUD her doctor had inserted after Justine was born was still intact when she discovered she was pregnant again. Her doctor attempted to remove it without surgery and couldn't. One chance in a thousand, he'd told them. It was possible to continue the pregnancy— the choice was hers—but he did not recommend it. With the IUD in situ, he warned, she was at risk for septicemia. Septic shock could kill her.

"Think of the kids," Will said. "It's time to pull yourself together."

Leah clambers onto her mother's lap, asks to play the kissing game. Her daughter places both hands at the base of Zoe's neck, and yanks.

"Not now, sweetie." Zoe pries Leah's hands from her neck. "Mommy has a headache."

Leah squints. For an instant, Zoe thinks she might hate this child, so like her father.

Yes, it takes time. Of course it takes time.

Her husband, Zoe suddenly realizes, is having an affair. Though she has no tangible proof, she knows. The thought has been winding forward for weeks. She hasn't wanted to see.

Zoe is trembling. Leah says something and Zoe blinks back.

Leah gazes up at her. Zoe sees the confusion in her daughter's eyes and feels bad. "Mommy doesn't feel good," Zoe explains. "Check on Justine, sweetie? Make sure she's okay."

"I wanna play wif Hammy."

"Please, Leah. Mommy has lots to do. You can play with Dog for a while. We'll get Hammy out of his cage as soon as I'm done. Right now—"

Before Zoe finishes the sentence, Leah scoots off.

The pastry shells are cooling on an aluminum cookie tray on top of the stove. Zoe's headache is worse. She took a Percocet tablet fifteen minutes ago and feels woozy. Doctor Marquette prescribed the medication after the surgery, to ease the pain. Two weeks later, Zoe was still having cramps and he refilled the prescription. She's been back a dozen times since, working his guilt.

Dizzy, she grabs the back of a chair. When she regains her balance, she carries the tray to the counter. The kitchen is warm from the heat of the oven. She pushes the sleeves of her sweater to her elbows. When the shells are cool, she spoons whipped cream into the cavity, replaces the tops and dusts them with sugar.

Zoe put the baby down twenty minutes ago for her nap. Leah drags a chair from the table to the counter and scrambles up. Zoe left the beaters and empty mixing bowl in the sink. Leah steals one of the beaters. Holding it like a lollipop, she licks off the cream.

Zoe is shaking powdered sugar over the cream puffs when the telephone rings. "Get that, honey?" Her hands are coated with sugar. She wipes her dusty hands on her apron, rinses them under the faucet, dries them on the seat of her sweats.

"It's Grandpa," Leah says, handing the phone to her mother.

Don't, Zoe thinks, as she takes the phone. *Don't you dare tell me you're not coming.*

Zoe slams the phone on the hook, dropping the dishtowel she'd been using to hold the sticky receiver. Sorry, her father had said. Didn't realize she invited them for lunch. Her mother was out all morning …running errands. Just this minute returned. Zoe closed her eyes. This very minute, he repeated, as though reading her mind. Her mother has plans for this afternoon, tickets to a concert in Boston. He's terribly sorry. Zoe's throat aches. This is just an excuse. Her mother could have changed her plans. Turned the tickets in, exchanged them for a different show. She doesn't feel like driving to Hudson today. She wants to spend the day with Zoe's father—alone.

Zoe slumps into a chair, head in her hands. Fingers splayed, she massages her neck, the tender spots in front and back of her ears.

Leah tugs at her leg.

"I'm sorry, sweetie. Mommy wasn't paying attention. What did you say?" Zoe pushes the chair back, spreading her knees, draws her daughter into the empty space between her legs.

"What Grandpa say?"

Zoe takes her daughter's face in her hands, tips her head back. "Grandpa says they'll come another day. He says tell you he loves you. They'll see you real soon."

"Oh," Leah says, nodding.

With her fingers, Zoe combs the hair out of her daughter's eyes. Leah had been looking forward to her grandparents' visit. Zoe wonders if she's disappointed. She gathers her daughter into her arms, lifting Leah onto her lap. "My sweet baby," Zoe murmurs, holding her daughter close. "Mama's precious little girl."

Leah pulls away before Zoe is ready. "Do trot, trot?" Leah pleads.

Trot, trot is a baby game, but Zoe goes along anyway. She turns Leah around, so they're facing one another, slides her daughter backward, takes hold of her hands.

"Trot, trot to Boston," Zoe chants, bouncing Leah on her knees. *Trot, trot to Lynn. Better watch out or you're gonna*—holding Leah's hands tightly, Zoe opens her legs, dips her daughter down, close to the floor. *Fall in.*

Breathless, Leah begs Zoe to do it again. "Again, Mommy. 'Gain."

"Trot, trot to Boston," Zoe repeats. Again, again.

Finally, Leah has had enough.

"Sweetie," Zoe says, out of breath herself. "Check on your sister? See if she's asleep."

Leah shakes her head and hops down.

When Leah returns, Zoe makes her daughter a peanut butter and jelly sandwich. Zoe is due for her period. She winces, her uterus contracting, the pain intense, like the phantom pain people feel in an arm or leg after an amputation.

When she opens the cabinet to fetch a glass for Leah's milk, she eyes the bottle of Percocet, wedged in the corner. Her breathing is labored. She blinks against the sudden shooting pain in her womb. Just one more, she thinks. Or two. Two would help a lot. She pours a glass of water to wash down the pills, rinses the glass. She fills it with milk and hands it to Leah before she takes a seat at the table across from her daughter and watches her eat.

When Leah finishes her lunch, she climbs back into Zoe's lap, twiddles a lock of her mother's hair. "Your hair is pretty. I wish I had pretty hair like you," Leah says.

"Your hair *is* pretty, honey. You have Daddy's hair. Very pretty."

Leah grins, pleased to be told she resembles her father. Yawning, she drops her head, nuzzles Zoe's chest. Zoe strokes her daughter's hair. Leah smells of the outdoors, as Zoe imagines a baby robin might smell—of the trees, the grass, the air.

Leah falls asleep in her mother's arms. Zoe stands, cradling her child. She carries Leah to the den, lays her on one end of the sofa, and tucks a pillow under her head. Then she settles on the couch, opposite Leah, her daughter's bare feet are tucked between her shins.

Within minutes, Zoe's asleep.

In the dream, Zoe is rowing a canoe in the middle of the ocean. A swell washes over her, tipping the boat, and Zoe is treading water. She tries to swim, but the current is too strong. The tide carries her to a saltwater river. A party boat passes, so close she can almost reach out and touch it. Zoe cries out, but no one hears. Suddenly, she spots Leah floating toward her. Zoe kicks her feet, harder, harder, propelling her body forward. Leah reaches, grabs onto her neck. *No, Leah. We'll both drown. Take my hand, baby. My hand.*

He's dead, Mama. He's dead. Leah tugs Zoe's hand.

"What?" Zoe says, somewhere between waking and sleep. "Baby, what's wrong?"

Leah is shrieking, her face blotchy, contorted. Zoe raises herself to her elbows. Her tongue is cotton, her ears full of liquid.

A haze has fallen over the house. She searches for the clock.

The room blurs. Zoe thinks she might vomit. Leah tugs harder. She is trying to pull Zoe—where? Reaching backward, using the arm of the sofa for leverage, Zoe drags herself up.

"Mommy, listen," Leah cries. "You're not listening, Mommy."

Zoe floats toward the stairs, Leah zooming ahead. Her joints ache, the soles of her feet burning as she presses one foot then the other to the hardwood floor, sheer will propelling her forward. She wishes she could go back to sleep. She could sleep forever, she thinks.

Sleep forever.

"Mommy," Leah calls, from the top of the stairs. "*Hurry.*"

"I'm coming, Leah. I am."

Zoe holds onto the banister, the stairs moaning under her weight. Leah has drawn stick figures with black magic marker on the walls inside the stairwell. Zoe's temples throb, blood draining from her head into her chest.

Mommy. Come, Mama. Hurry.

What has she done? *My God*, Zoe thinks. What have *I* done?

"I did it, Mommy," Leah cries. "I killed him."

Zoe's breath catches. "Who, Leah?" For one horrific moment, the world goes still. Then Zoe is shaking her daughter—"Who, Leah? *Who did you kill?*"—terrified of the answer.

Suddenly, the baby is wailing.

"I wanted to make him pretty, Mommy. I hadda hold him. I holded him nice. I did. I tied the ribbon around him and he stopped breaving."

She sees the hamster now, in Leah's open palm, a pale blue ribbon cinching its waist.

Zoe blinks, catches her breath. Holding Leah's free hand, she guides her daughter back to the bedroom, removes a shoebox from Leah's closet, and lays the hamster to rest. Taking Leah by the hand, she goes to Justine. After she changes the baby's diaper, the three of them will take the hamster outside and bury him in the backyard. They'll say a prayer, sing a song. Afterward, Zoe will read the Genesis story, from Leah's *Bible for Children*. She will take her daughter into her arms, tell her she mustn't blame herself. All creatures die. Death is part of God's plan. Don't be afraid, baby, she'll say. Death, she thinks, afflicts only the living.

When Leah looks up, Zoe will read in her daughter's eyes the faint stirring of comprehension. And she will hold her tightly, Leah's powdery, baby-soft cheek pressed to her heart, protecting her child while she still can, from the long blue ribbon of earthly disappointment.

Six

Sisters I, Goblins and Ghosts

Justine was sitting on the vanity braiding her hair when the first trick-or-treaters arrived. Her father had rigged the doorbell to play Beethoven's Fifth. *Dat, dat, dat, da*...The music was annoying. Justine couldn't understand why her family always had to be different, why they couldn't have a normal doorbell, one that buzzed like everyone else's.

"You getting that, Leah?" she hollered. Their parents had gone to dinner, then to a party in Boston, and wouldn't be home until late. Leah was grounded again for doing poorly on her progress report. Since she had to be home anyway, she'd promised to give out the candy.

Justine was wearing the Pippi Longstocking costume she'd worn the previous year—a plaid farmer's shirt and blue overalls. When she finished braiding her hair, she opened the wings of the mirror, turned her head left and right, examining the path in the back, to be sure it was straight.

"What do you think, puppy? I look okay?" The braids stuck out like rods from the sides of her head. Exactly like Pippi's. *Sweet.*

With her mother's Burnt Maple lip liner, she gave herself freckles.

The doorbell rang again. Now they were knocking. Justine hopped off the vanity and dashed downstairs, Dog at her heels, to answer the door.

A plastic cauldron, brimming with candy, sat on the floor beside the front door. Their mom had bought the right kind of treats this year: miniature Reese's Cups, Mallo Bars, Milk Duds. Their mother avoided candy. Carbohydrates made her gain weight. She seemed to forget that, for kids, popcorn wasn't a treat. Year after year, the treats at the Tyler house were the worst on the block. Popcorn, oranges, peanuts. Once, they'd given out raisins. On the bus the following morning, the Tyler raisins had been the topic of discussion. Justine had wanted to crawl into her backpack. This year, the kids would be happy.

She scooped a Mallo Bar out of the cauldron, tucked it into her pocket, and opened the door. The three trick-or-treaters standing on the doorstep gazed up at her expectantly. Justine couldn't bring herself to hand out singles, as most people did. Instead, she offered the cauldron to let the kids pick what they liked. The first child, a cheerleader dressed in a blue and gold uniform, the Cortland school colors, chose a Mallo bar, thanked her politely, and took a step back.

"Here you go." Justine handed her a Reese's Cup and a box of Milk Duds. "Take a few."

The next child, a pirate, helped himself to three Mallo Bars, taking the candy bars one at a time, glancing at Justine each time for approval. Justine waited patiently. Smiling, she offered the cauldron to the last child, a pintsized ghost. The ghost peered up at her brazenly. A hand darted out from under the sheet, plunged into the cauldron, and surfaced with a fistful of candy.

"Hey," Justine said, pulling the cauldron back. "I said a few. Not all those."

The ghost tossed the loot into his pillowcase and ran off, signaling the others to follow.

Too bad Leah hadn't answered the door. She would have said something. Leah complained constantly about the kids in the neighborhood, how spoiled they were, how disrespectful.

"But they're only little," Justine would say, whenever one did something—threw leaves at her sister, for instance—that set Leah off. Now Justine realized how naïve she had been. She couldn't wait to share the news.

"Leah," Justine called. "Leah?"

Justine went to the kitchen, Dog on her trail, thinking maybe Leah was in the half-bath in the back hall. As she passed the kitchen window, Justine saw her—outside on the deck, smoking a cigarette.

Justine's heart sank. She'd noticed the ashes in the ceramic hand on Leah's bureau, but she'd refused to believe they were Leah's.

Justine pulled open the slider, Dog settling inside by the door.

Leah stood in a shadow cast by the porch light, her back to the railing, the cigarette dangling between her index and middle fingers, like the sticks the girls used to hold when they were little, pretending to smoke. Leah brought the cigarette to her lips, took a long drag, let the smoke filter out through her nose. She was wearing jeans, an olive V-neck tee-shirt, and her UGG sandals. She had to be freezing.

The oak and birch trees in the backyard had lost most of their leaves. Their gnarled branches curled skyward like witches' fingers.

Justine shivered, hugging herself. When she was younger, she'd been afraid of the dark, of the tickle lady who swooped down from the ceiling. Justine was still frightened, but of other things now. She was afraid of murderers, thieves, the coyotes lurking in the woods, the mating cats outside her window, their howl like babies crying at night. She was afraid of the way the full moon turned the water in the pool below their deck an eerie shade of purple. And she was afraid of the way her sister was standing here now, alone, with her eyes closed, smoking a cigarette.

"Leah?" Justine ventured.

Leah looked over and smirked. "So, gonna tell on me or what?"

Justine dropped her eyes. How could her sister ask such a question? Imply that Justine couldn't be trusted? At times, Leah hurt Justine's feelings more than Justine could ever explain. Her sister would look at her a certain way, talk to her in a particular tone of voice, and Justine would feel useless—no, worse than useless—*dumb, stupid, invisible even*. Other times, just being around her sister made Justine feel special.

Take last month for example, the week after school started, when Matt Mattiveo made fun of her, calling her names. Justine refused to cry. The whole way home on the bus, she'd choked back the tears. Afterward, there'd been no holding back. Tears clogged her throat and nose, spilled out of her eyes. Justine's parents, home from work early that day, were sitting in the breakfast nook, drinking coffee. Justine slinked by, covering her face, too embarrassed to let anyone see her. But Leah had seen.

Leah was lounging in the family room watching TV—practice, she'd said, was called off for the day. She'd followed Justine to her room, lain beside her, forever it seemed, rubbing Justine's back, Leah's silence comforting until Justine was ready to talk. Leah had listened, eyes narrowed in concentration, until Justine had finished her story.

Matt Mattiveo, the boy Justine had loved since the second grade...Justine had no idea how he'd found out.

Maybe he'd caught her staring, Leah suggested.

Possible, Justine said, but she didn't think so. That very afternoon, on the bus, he'd sat beside her. He likes me, she thought. *He likes me.* Exactly the opposite, it turned out, was true.

"Look at that hair," he'd said, pointing at Justine's arm. "You look like a monkey." *A monkey.*

"What's wrong with me, Leah?" Did she really look like a monkey?

"Nothing's wrong with you, Jus," Leah had answered. "He likes you. Don't you see? That's how boys your age act when they like a girl. Immature." Her response was so different from any Justine's mother might have offered. "Ignore him, Justine," her mom might have said, something Justine could never, ever have done. Or, "It doesn't matter, sweetie, you're beautiful just the way you are. He doesn't see yet, that's all. But he will." Or worst of all, "Matt's a jerk, Justine, forget about him." But Leah understood.

Now Justine's feelings were hurt, though she tried not to show it.

"No," she said, shaking her head. "You know I don't tell."

Leah shrugged; it was an offhanded gesture Justine interpreted as "thanks." She cupped her hand around the cigarette, turning the filtered edge to Justine. "Want to try?"

Justine looked at the cigarette, and cast her eyes toward the floorboards. Justine would never smoke. Not after what had happened to Grandma Chandler.

"No thanks," she said, shaking her head.

"Won't rat you out." Leah crossed her index finger over her lips.

"That's okay. Thanks anyhow."

Leah's eyes looked glazed, as if she were coming down with a fever. The flu was going around. Justine hoped her sister wasn't getting sick. "You okay?" she asked. "Want me to stay here?"

"Nah," Leah said, in a tone that made Justine feel like a pest.

"Are you sure? Because I—"

Leah ran her hand over her head, twirling her hair. "I'm fine."

Justine watched her sister take another long drag from the cigarette. "Leah?"

Her sister peered at her.

Justine crossed and uncrossed her feet. She'd been practicing the runaway arm, a trick she'd made up for her sister, to make Leah laugh. Justine lifted her right knee, pulling it into her chest, and wound her left arm. "Look," she cried, winding, winding, her arm spinning, spinning, out of control. "The runaway aaaarrmmm."

When they stopped laughing, Justine said, "Can I ask you something?"

Leah brought the cigarette to her lips, her eyes squeezed into slits. "If you want," she said, through a mouthful of smoke. "Can't promise I'll do it."

Stop smoking, Justine wanted to say. "It's not anything big. I don't want you to take me anywhere or lend me anything or anything. I just want you to—" Justine felt like a six-year-old, talking too fast, tripping over her words. "Want you to—"

"Spit it out." *Shpit*, it came out.

"Stop smoking," Justine blurted. "Cancer runs in the family. I'm scared you're gonna get cancer, like Grandma." *And die*, she thought. *I don't want you to die.*

"Don't get liver cancer," Leah rolled her eyes, "from smoking."

Of course you don't get liver cancer from smoking. Justine was not a moron. It was the predisposition to cancer she worried about. Her honors science class was doing a section on genes. Their grandmother dying of liver cancer, she'd learned, put them at risk. Justine didn't say that, of course. She would feel like a geek. Instead, she said, stupidly, "You sure you're all right?"

"Uh-huh." Leah took the last drag from her cigarette, flicked the butt onto the grass, then spread her arms wide, both hands on the rail, and tipped her head back. Making an *O* with her lips, she blew rings of smoke into the air.

Justine watched the smoke rings spiral upward. A cricket chirped and the wind blew a low whistling sound that made her uneasy. Justine located the North Star, the first star of the night. *I wish I may, I wish I might...*

Justine traced an imaginary path from the point of Polaris to Cepheus to Cassiopeia.

"Pipster," Leah said, after a couple minutes. Her hips swayed, as though she were dancing. "Sleeping at Holly's, right?"

"I could stay home," Justine offered again. "If you want to go to bed. Or go out, I mean. With your friends or something."

"S'okay. By the way, Teenie," she said, using the nickname she'd made up when Justine was a baby. "Cool costume you got there. 'Zactly like Pippi."

"Honest?"

"Yep." Leah said, massaging her arms. "Have fun," she called as Justine turned away.

After Justine left, Leah switched off the porch lights and all the lights in the front of the house, and skipped upstairs to change into her party clothes—a gold sequin sweater and a flirty black skirt.

Todd would be here soon to drive her to Hope's. Hope was hosting a Halloween bash tonight. Hope had totally outdone herself. She'd even hired this cool band that a friend of Lupo had started. The band wasn't signed yet, but they'd recorded a CD and posted their songs on YouTube, and they'd sold almost a hundred copies already.

At eight on the dot, the doorbell rang. Leah scooped the bag of lollipops she'd bought, grabbed her purse, and pulled on a sweatshirt.

"Hey." Todd peered around Leah. "Coast clear?"

"It's cool." Leah waved to Lupo in the driveway, sitting at the wheel of his '94 Lincoln, and followed Todd out the door.

Justine had stopped at Holly's house two doors down from her own, and the girls slogged through the neighborhood, stopping at the six houses on their street, dropping the candy they collected into their brown paper lunch bags. Younger kids passed in their own costumes, toting pillowcases, carrying flashlights, waving glow-in-the-dark sticks. Their parents, in clusters, straggled behind. Justine tried to act upbeat, but her face felt like plastic.

"What's wrong?" Holly kept asking, but even if she had wanted to, Justine couldn't have said.

They were turning onto Old Orchard Road, on their way to the next block, when a dented black jalopy careened past, a Bloodbath decal on its bumper. The driver honked as he swerved around them.

Jerk, Justine thought. "Slow down," she hollered after him.

"This stinks," Holly said. "Want to go to my house?"

Leah felt as if she'd fallen into a rabbit hole in the frenzy of motion and color and sound. The living room rocked, music blasting out of speakers in all four corners of the room, the dancers writhing, disjointed.

Leah waved an arm, her glow stick flickering. Todd twirled her around and pulled her to him, the white-hot music swirling around them.

All of a sudden, Leah felt weird. She'd swallowed half a tablet of Ecstasy at her house, the other half on the way to the party. She couldn't think straight, her head jumbled, and her arms were itchy.

Her heart raced. Sweat dripped down her back. She wished she could take off her shirt. Trembling, she pulled Todd off the dance floor.

"You okay, babe?" he asked. "What's wrong?"

"My—" *arms*, she meant to say, but her mouth had gone dry. They were everywhere, skittering across her flesh.

"Come on," he said, and led her into the kitchen.

A girl in a pleated skirt and white button-down blouse sat on the floor by the slider. The girl rolled up her sleeve and tied an elastic band around her arm. To her right, kids were playing beer pong.

Todd filled a plastic cup with beer. Leah gulped it down in two swallows. The beer cleared her throat, but the bugs were still there.

"Get them off," Leah cried, swatting her arms.

"What?" Todd gave her a look of genuine concern. "Get what off?"

The bugs were crawling up her sleeves, inching toward her neck.

"Babe?" Todd said. "Look at me. What's going on?"

"Noth…noth…the bugs. Get them *off*," Leah squealed and took off at a run, shaking her arms. "Get them off me. Get them *off*!"

Justine followed Holly to her room and sat next to her friend, watching politely while Holly logged into Justine's Facebook account.

"Oh, my God," Holly squealed. "Jackie Hall wants to friend you. What a loser!"

"She's not a loser," Justine said, annoyed. "She's nice."

"Nice?" Holly looked appalled. "You obviously don't know her."

"Do, too. She sits behind me in algebra."

"Whatever." Holly tore open a bag of peanut M&Ms. "She's a freak. So Clay Gomez, right? He saw her Frenching some kid at a party."

"Clay's a jerk," Justine countered. "He always lies about girls."

Holly clicked over to Jackie's Facebook page. "See, she's only got fifty friends." Holly giggled. "Look at her wall. Told you she's a freak."

Jackie's poems were dark, all about depression, hinting at suicide.

Justine took the mouse from Holly and clicked through the pictures in Jackie's photo album. Every single photo was a picture of her family—her brother and sister, her sister's two kids. Maybe she did French kiss some kid at a party. She was still a nice girl.

"I'm gonna say yes."

Holly shrugged. "Sucker. I wouldn't add her to my list."

You don't have a list, Justine considered pointing out, but that would be cruel. It wasn't Holly's fault her parents forbade her being on Facebook. Holly hated being excluded. They went through the silly routine every time Justine accepted a new friend. Justine didn't blame Holly for feeling left out. Luckily, Justine's parents trusted her.

Justine tried to focus, but she couldn't get her mind off Leah. Justine felt horrible for leaving her alone. She'd looked so pale. What if her illness had gotten worse? If her fever had spiked? No wonder Leah hated her. Justine was a horrible sister. The worst sister *ever.* A blight on sisterhood.

"Justine," Holly said, rattling Justine's arm. "Wake up."

"I've got to go," Justine said, standing. "My sister needs me."

Justine stared at Holly's long, dark driveway. Wind rustled through the trees. For all she knew, an axe-murderer was hiding in the woods. *Baby, baby, baby,* Leah would have sneered. *Time to grow up.*

Her sister would have been right. Justine was being a baby. Breathing deeply, she worked up her courage, and took off.

In the cul-de-sac, she pulled up short. A strange car was parked beside their mailbox. An ancient black Lincoln with a dented front fender and rust on the driver's door. Justine's knees went soft.

A thief! This was his getaway car. She had to call the police. She looked around, frantic, trying to figure out the best place to go. Maybe she should run back to Holly's house. She swung around. What if the car didn't belong to a robber? What if there was no robber? If the car belonged to somebody's guest? She would look like a fool. Really, she thought, working up her courage, she ought to investigate first.

Justine blinked as she entered the circle of light. Rays from the street lamp fell over the windshield. The car looked empty. Edging closer, cupping her eyes, she peered through the driver's window.

A leather jacket lay on the seat. Empty cups littered the floor. Soda cans. Crushed papers. A lamb's wool sheath covered the steering wheel.

She walked around the car, hoping for clues. As she passed the trunk, she caught sight of the sticker on the rear bumper. *Bloodbath. The guy from Old Orchard Road.* He'd been here all along! The guy was a maniac. What if he was doing something awful to Leah?

Justine tore down their driveway and across the front lawn.

The house was dark. Leah hated being alone in the house. She would never turn off all the lights. Something terrible had happened. Justine felt it in her bones. Holding onto the doorframe, she wriggled out of her shoe. Shook her sneaker. The key? Where was her key?

Heart pounding, she rushed down the walkway to the garage. The side door was unlocked. She patted the wall next to the door, felt the switch, flicked on the light, and sprinted across the garage, crashing head-on into the dog. Poor Dog yelped.

"I'm sorry. I'm sorry." She scratched Dog's head. "It's okay, girl. Okay," she said, and tripped up the steps to the back hallway. On the top step, her overalls caught on a nail jutting from the riser. She heard a rip as the hem tore.

She barely touched the knob. The door swung open, and she lurched forward, stumbling over the threshold, losing her footing. She landed on her knee, pushed up, dashed down the side hall.

"Leah," she called, her eyes adjusting to the dark. "Where are you?" She checked the half-bath, the laundry, looked out the window at the deck. *Please, God,* she prayed. *Don't let that guy be here.*

Justine scrambled through the shadows to the kitchen, tore open the drawers, open, open, open—a knife, she needed a knife—ran her hand over the counter, located the wooden butcher block, snatched the knife at the top, a long, thin carving knife with a razor-like edge.

Thump...thump...thump...

Footsteps. Upstairs.

She skidded down the hall, around the corner, up the stairs. The lights. She swiped the wall, missing the switch. Up the steps, two at a time, her heart pounding. *Hail Mary full of grace...please, please, please,* she prayed, gripping the knife's sleek wooden shaft.

At the top of the stairs, a hand reached out of the dark.

Duck. She held the knife over her shoulder, poised to strike.

With the opposite hand, she made a fist, protecting her face. *Tight. Left hook. KIA-HA. Out and back. Quick.*

"What the hell are you *doing*?"

A hulking figure loomed over her.

She waved the knife. "Get back," she ordered. "Or I'll kill you."

The monster edged closer.

"Get away from me," Justine shouted, kicking. Left foot. In and out. Connected. *Thwap.* Heard a thud. All at once, he was falling.

"What the *fuck*?"

The lights went on, the sharp beam blinding her for an instant.

"Hey." A blonde-haired boy materialized. "It's me. Todd."

"Get back," she shouted, brandishing the knife.

The boy flashed a smile. Blonde curls cascaded over his forehead.

The other boy, bigger, darker, was slumped on the floor near the bathroom, his back to the wall, his thick legs spread in front of him. The kid's head was shaved. A Band-Aid partially covered a menacing cut over his right eye. Silver hoops ran the length of his left brow.

Justine stood her ground.

The bald boy glared at her. "Who the *fuck* is that?"

"Her sister. So shut up."

Justine waved the knife at the kid on the floor and swung the blade, pointing at the boy who'd claimed to be Todd. Liar. What would Todd be doing here? Their father would ground Leah for life if she allowed boys in the house when their parents were gone.

She didn't trust these two for a minute. If they'd hurt her sister, she'd kill them. Plunge the knife right into their hearts.

The kid on the floor pushed himself up.

"Get back," she hissed. Or she'd slice his ugly face into pieces.

"Put the knife down," Todd urged.

"Where's my sister?" Justine demanded.

Todd pointed at the knife. "Put it down first."

"What are you kissing her ass for? That bitch tried to kill us."

The Todd imposter turned to his accomplice. "Shut up, Lupo."

The big kid hurled himself at her, his black eyes driving Justine backward. The kid was bigger than her father and burly. Todd yelled at Lupo and Justine backed up again. Todd reached. She batted him away, her windmill arms whipping in circles, the knife swinging this way and that, Todd dodging the blows…*get away, get away.*

Todd advanced and Justine pulled back, overstepping, her feet slipping out from under her. Her left foot slid off the landing.

The wall. Where was the wall? She saw the foyer. The floor.

Todd grabbed her hand and yanked.

Justine yanked back. "Let go," she screamed, kicking her feet.

Todd jerked her onto the landing, catching her in a stronghold.

"Leah," she called, struggling, desperate. "Where is she? What did you do to her?"

He squeezed her wrist until the knife fell from her hand. Lupo, seizing his opportunity, lunged at the knife.

Todd, elbowing the other kid, ordered him to stay put. "What's with you?" he asked Justine, gripping her upper arms. "What are you trying to prove? Somebody's gonna get hurt."

"Let go of me."

Todd dropped his hands. "What's wrong with you?" he asked again, quietly now. "You trying to kill somebody or what?"

Justine swallowed. *Baby. Don't cry.* The other boy, Lupo, hands thrust in the pockets of his oversized chinos, was blocking the door to Leah's room. "What did you *do* to my sister?" she asked.

Lupo laughed, a deep hawking guffaw.

Justine glared at him. "Where is she?"

"In there," Todd said, thumbing Leah's room. "See for yourself."

The other boy shot Justine a contemptuous look and stepped aside.

Her sister appeared to be sleeping. She'd been acting strangely earlier. Justine had been right all along. Her sister was sick. Leah probably hadn't realized it yet. Sometimes you don't until it's too late. She'd probably gotten worse—Justine cringed—maybe thrown up. Desperate, she'd called the boys so there would be somebody here to give out the candy. Justine felt like a fool jumping to conclusions again.

"Does she have a fever?" Justine whispered.

"I don't think so," Todd said. "Check, if you want."

Justine's eyes passed over the familiar forms: the piles of clothes on the floor, the revolving black light on Leah's desk, Paddington Bear at the foot of her bed, the net filled with stuffed animals, suspended from the ceiling in the corner of the room. Justine tiptoed inside. Her sister's head was propped on a pillow. Justine laid her hand on Leah's forehead. Leah must have taken some aspirin. She didn't feel hot. Leah moaned and rolled on her side. Justine squeezed Leah's shoulder, to reassure her, and backed out of the room.

"See?" Todd said, on the landing. "What did I tell you?"

Lupo was downstairs, standing by the front door. "Corbett," he called. "Let's get out of here. Before their old man gets home."

Todd held up a finger.

"I'm sorry," Justine said. She hoped he'd forgive her.

"Forget it." Todd wrapped her in a brotherly hug. Releasing her, he shook the curls out of his brilliant crystalline eyes. When he smiled again, she noticed an adorable gap between his front teeth. Justine saw exactly why her sister was hooked.

Lupo opened the door. Todd told him to hang on.

Yeah. Hang on. When Todd turned back to her, she asked what had happened.

Before he had a chance to respond, Lupo cut in. "She took some bad shit, man," he said from downstairs. "What d'ya think?"

Bad shit? Like drugs? The kid was nuts. Her sister got in trouble from time to time, for dumb things—sassing their mother, coming home late—and, yes, her sister smoked cigarettes. Leah would never do drugs.

Last year, an eighth grade boy at her school was arrested. The principal, acting on a rumor that a student had brought marijuana onto the premises, called the police. The police spent the entire morning searching lockers. That afternoon, they led a boy out in cuffs. Justine felt bad for the boy. Only kids from the worst families used drugs. Certainly not someone like Leah.

Justine turned to Todd, relying on him for the truth.

"Asshole." Todd turned an apologetic face to Justine. "Sorry. Big Mouth down there don't know when to keep his trap shut."

His response confused her at first. Then it hit her. *Lupo was telling the truth.* Justine's pulse throbbed; her brain reeled, fighting to keep pace with the churning inside her head. There had to be a logical explanation.

In a made-for-TV movie Justine had seen, a teenage girl had been drugged at a party. When she turned her back, a boy slipped a Rohypnol tablet into her soft drink. That had to be what had happened to Leah. This afternoon, probably, before she came home.

"Where did she get it? Did you know what she took?"

"Beats me." Todd headed downstairs. "But I'm gonna find out."

Seven

Eyes Open Wide

When Leah opened her eyes, a sliver of gray-blue light peeked under her shades. Her head throbbed. She squeezed her eyes shut, pulling the covers to her neck. She remembered swallowing the second hit of E, recalled dancing in Hope's living room. Within thirty minutes, her heart was racing and she'd been sweating profusely, her hair drenched, her shirt stuck to her chest and her back.

She saw a blurry image of herself running in circles waving her arms, shouting. Something about bugs, an army of spiders. She vaguely recalled Todd chasing her, heaving her over his shoulder, carrying her to Lupo's car. After that, she drew a blank.

Leah would never hear the end of this. Once the goody-two-shoes at her school, tools like Cissy Hanson, caught wind of her behavior last night, Leah was doomed. Last year at a party, a freshman downed a pint of vodka, climbed onto a table, and flashed her boobs. On the way out, she barfed, a trail of Pepto-Bismol pink puke that went from the doorstep, down the stairs, and onto the lawn. For months when she walked down the halls, the boys leered, and the girls made vile hawking noises and laughed. Leah's stunt blew that girl's sideshow away. Leah rolled onto her belly and pulled the pillow over her head. If she got lucky, maybe she would die in her sleep.

Next time she opened her eyes, her sister was stroking her hair.

"Hey, sleepyhead," Justine said.

"Hey," Leah yawned groggily. A blade of light shot through the gap between the windowsill and the lower rail of her shade. She blinked, rubbing her eyes. "What time is it?" It had to be close to noon.

Justine consulted her Mickey Mouse watch. "Five after one." She crossed to the wall and switched on the lights. "You okay, Lee? You were crying."

"One?" Normally, Leah had trouble sleeping past seven. She pushed herself to her elbows. "Fine, yeah. Must've been dreaming." She felt a little better. Her head ached, but the throbbing was gone.

"What's up, Jus?" Her parents couldn't possibly know what had happened last night. Leah was almost positive Todd had driven her home. Her parents had planned to be late. He'd have been gone long before they got home. "Dad's not in one of his asshole moods again, is he?"

Justine shook her head. "Lee?" she said, meeting Leah's eyes. "I need to ask you something."

"Where's Dad? Did they have fun last night? What did he say?" If she was in trouble, she might as well know it. No point in spending the whole day in a knot, wondering when the ball would drop.

"Dad's at the hardware store. Lee? What happened last night?"

"The hardware store?" Leah swept her hair out of her face. She was wearing a baggy tee-shirt she'd filched from her father's bureau drawer one day when she ran out of clean shirts. Someone had changed her out of her clothes. Hopefully Todd. She threw off the covers, a putrid odor wafting out of her bed. She sniffed her armpit, wincing. She smelled as if she'd worked out for three days without bathing. "What's he doing at the hardware store?"

"Mom asked him to fix the shelf in their closet. The one that fell down?"

"Oh, yeah." Leah rooted through her laundry pile, hunting for her flip-flops. Giving up, she slid into cheap leather thongs she'd owned since the eighth grade, the stiff leather chafing her toes. Turning her back to her sister, she stripped off the tee-shirt, tossed it in the general direction of her laundry pile, plucked a cotton camisole off her floor, held it up, checking to be sure it wasn't too dirty, and pulled it over her head, smoothing the fabric over her boobs. Shutting her closet door, she examined herself in the mirror. She looked like crap, her skin flaky, mascara smudged ghoulishly under her eyes.

"Come on, Lee." Her sister crawled to the foot of Leah's bed. "I was worried about you."

"Huh?" Leah brought her face close to the mirror. Squinting, she picked at a zit.

"You can tell me. I'm not gonna rat you out."

"What are you talking about?"

"You know."

Leah spun to face her sister. "No, Jus. I don't know."

Justine stared at her feet. "I came home early. You were asleep."

"What time?"

"Ten thirty."

Leah wasn't sure how to handle this. "Must have fallen asleep waiting for you."

"The boys were here."

"Oh." Leah took a seat beside her sister. "What did they say?"

Justine shrugged. She said the Lupo kid claimed Leah had been doing drugs. "I didn't believe him," she said, and massaged Leah's arm. "He's a big loser. What really happened, Lee?"

"You're right," Leah said. "Don't listen to him."

"Did you get roofied?"

Roofied? Seriously? Justine wasn't *that* naïve, was she? She was staring at Leah, her face hopeful, those earnest brown eyes open wide.

Leah considered fessing up. Justine had come home early last night because she was worried. She was sitting here now because she cared about Leah. Leah owed it to her sister to tell her the truth. Only who knew how Justine would react?

"Yeah." Leah stared at her hands, unable to meet her sister's gaze. "I'm so stupid." She'd left her cleats in her locker; this random kid offered to hold her Gatorade bottle while she ran to the gym to fetch them. "I was gone for like a minute. Must have been him."

Justine threw her arms around Leah. "I *knew* it," she cried, and hugged Leah tighter. Leah felt odious, a tsunami-sized wave of shame washing away any relief. "Were you scared?" Justine wanted to know. "Do you know the kid's name?"

Leah forced herself not to stiffen. She should have been psyched. She'd done something supremely stupid and gotten away with it for once. The more Justine sympathized, the worse Leah felt. Finally, she told her sister the truth. Well, almost the truth. She omitted the Ecstasy. She claimed it was weed in pill form.

For an instant, the light in Justine's eyes dimmed. Then her face brightened, and it occurred to Leah her sister had made a conscious decision to trust her.

"I won't tell," Justine assured her, on one condition: that Leah promised—"swear to God, Lee. Cross your heart and hope to die"— she would never, ever do it again.

Eight

Up and Away

"Who gave you that shit?" Todd demanded. The E from Halloween night, he meant.

It was a dazzling November day, the sun radiant in an azure sky.

Leah ran her fingers through her spiky blonde hair. She couldn't believe she'd cut it. The other day, as a joke, she'd shown her mother a picture in *Star* of some British model with this hideous, gelled-up hair.

"My new 'do," she said, assuming her mother would laugh.

"Nice. You'll look like a punk," her mother had snapped, leaving Leah no choice except to go through with it.

"I want to know where you got it," Todd pressed.

With her toe, Leah swirled the sand under her feet. She and Todd were hanging out on the swings at the elementary school playground. The place was deserted. A male teacher exited the building and crossed the tarmac, briefcase in hand, with nary a glance in their direction.

Todd had surprised her by showing up at the high school. She'd been about to lead the girls on a five-mile training run when she spotted the Wrangler. Todd worked in Ayer, at this hole-in-the-wall used CD shop called Music Head. On Tuesdays, he worked until six.

She'd practically choked on her spit when she saw him. He hadn't called in days—since that fiasco on Halloween. Clutching her stomach, she'd told the girls to go on without her. It was an emergency; she'd catch up in a minute. Her teammates jogged to the top of the drive. As soon as the dawdlers rounded the corner, she'd sprinted to the truck.

A bee circled drunkenly in front of her nose. Leah fanned the air, chasing it away. The interrogation annoyed her. Taking the E was stupid. Agreed. She had no intention of doing E again. She had no intention of doing any drug again, *ever*. So why fight about it?

"Come on, babe. Fess up. Tell me where you got it."

As if. He'd go ape shit if he knew Hope hooked her up.

"Can't be doing that shit." He veered toward her, twisting the chains on his swing. "What," he pressed, "do you think would happen if your coach found out? I was a wide receiver in high school," Todd reminded her. Athletes who used drugs had been banned from the team.

"So—" Leah paused, letting the word hang to achieve maximum dramatic effect. "What did your *boss* say when you left work this afternoon?" She emphasized the word "boss" to taunt him. She meant Jamie, the owner. Leah knew that if Todd asked his permission to leave for any decent reason, Jamie would grant it.

On the nights Todd worked, she and Hope often visited him at the store. Usually, she and Jamie wound up talking while Todd waited on customers and Hope thumbed through the CDs. Jamie had scared her at first. He reminded her of an aging rock star, with his craggy face and sour expression. Once she'd gotten to know him, she'd found him interesting and surprisingly easy to talk to.

"What did he say?"

"He said, 'Tell your girlfriend that shit's bad news.'"

"Liar." She gave him the stink-eye. He wouldn't *dare* tell Jamie.

"Ask him," he said with an annoying downward tilt of his lips.

What a *loser!* She could never face Jamie again. If it were any later, she'd force her boyfriend to drive her home. She couldn't go now. If her mom came home early, she'd know that Leah had ditched practice.

On impulse, Leah swept sideways, as though swinging a bat—
—and swatted.

"Hey!" Todd lunged, shielding his head. "What are you doing?"

Figure it out, she told him telepathically—and swatted again. This time, her chop landed smack between his shoulder blades.

He grappled with the chains, his toe catching on a partly concealed rock, and toppled off the swing, landing in the dirt, yelping.

She covered her mouth, trying to hide the fact she was giggling. Sulking, he brushed himself off. "Bitch," he said irritably.

Bitch? She hopped off her swing and stormed off, swinging her arms. Feeling him behind her, she pumped her arms, her stride faster and faster, until she was practically running. Let him try to catch her. He was gaining ground. Furious, she broke into a sprint.

He shot past her, breathing hard, and circled back, stopping two inches from her. "What's...up...with...you?" he asked, between hiccupping breaths. "Didn't...say...nothing...to Jamie."

"Yeah, right." She was sorely tempted to hit him again.

Sweat dribbled down his face. With his forearm, he wiped it away. "I'm telling you, I didn't say nothing."

Leah abhorred lying, especially by people you were supposed to be able to trust. "Then how come you said you did?"

He sidled up to her, draping an arm over her shoulder. "Lighten up. What if me and Lupo weren't around?" They'd given her two Valium pills they'd found in Hope's medicine cabinet to calm her down. The Valium had knocked her out. "Why'd you do it? Talk to me, babe."

She kicked at the overgrown grass. How was she supposed to know that shit would bug her out? She'd never done Ecstasy before.

On the playing field, the Pop Warner coach was directing position drills, the boys, maybe seven or eight, running willy-nilly. Leah envied the boys. It was hard to recall the last time she'd played a game, the last time she'd had any fun. Soccer wasn't a game; it was a job. She wished she could turn back the clock, be a kid again, young enough so she didn't have to think all the time, didn't have to apologize, didn't always feel bad. Young enough so she could just *be.*

"This is serious, babe. You coulda got hurt."

"Yeah, well. Let's get out of here." She spun on her heels and made a beeline for the jeep. "I shouldn't be here, anyway," she said petulantly. "I'm not allowed to see you, you know."

"Huh?" He reached for her hand. "What are you talking about?"

"My father hates you. I'm not supposed to go near you."

"Me?" He shook his head in disbelief. "What did I do?"

Um, duh! You quit high school? You used to deal drugs? "Who knows? Don't worry. He hates all my boyfriends at first. He'll come around."

Will was perched on a barstool at Marcus, a brass and mahogany watering hole near his hotel, nursing a spicy October lager, wishing he were back East. This business with Leah tore him apart. His daughter was a good kid. Her involvement with Corbett confounded him. He and Zoe had made mistakes, sure—what parents didn't?—but they loved their kids. They worked hard to provide a stable environment, give their daughters a good life.

Growing up, neither he nor his wife had much in the way of material things. They wanted their kids to have a shot at being decision makers, among the select few who were in charge of their own destiny. Leah had been well on her way until that scumbag Corbett derailed her. Will wanted to be at home with his wife and kids, where he belonged. What use was he three thousand miles away?

He'd been out here since Sunday. The trip to San Francisco was a last-ditch effort to pump some life back into the Micronics project. The V. P. who'd brought Will in had left Micronics in August, replaced by a stiff named Cushing, a tight-ass MBA-type in his thirties. He should have arranged to meet Cushing here, where they could've discussed the project over a few beers.

His jacket lay over the back of his chair. He rooted in the pocket, dug out his cell, and dialed Cushing's number. Reaching voice service, he left a vague message—"I've got an idea to blow by you," he said and asked Cushing to give him a ring.

After winning the contract for a six hundred million dollar project for his faltering firm, he should have been a hero. Instead, he felt like the company schmuck. NAC couldn't afford to walk. They were two mil over budget on the site work alone and sinking fast.

Usually, exhausted after a long day on the job, he ordered room service or ate in the bar at his hotel. Occasionally, he'd take in a movie. He'd finished early today and hadn't felt like hanging out in his room, so he'd asked the concierge at the Marriott for a recommendation. The food at Marcus was decent, the concierge had told him, and they served some interesting microbrews, which had caught Will's attention.

The ambiance played to a professional crowd in their thirties and forties: dark paneled walls, Tiffany chandeliers, and a brass-accented marble bar. From Thursday to Sunday, they brought in jazz bands. Too bad it was Tuesday. He'd have enjoyed hearing a band.

Will downed the dregs of his beer and peered down the bar, attempting to catch the eye of one of the bartenders. The two guys on duty were setting up for the evening crowd, one checking inventory, the other replenishing the wine rack under the counter.

Frustrated by the slow service, Will fished for his wallet. He'd no sooner laid his credit card on the bar when a third bartender, a perky redhead, strolled out of the kitchen. All three wore the same uniform: tuxedo trousers, black satin vest, starched white shirt, and a red, white, and blue tie. One of the guys said something and she shook her head, laughing, and pulled a menu from a pile by the cash register.

In her late-twenties, Will figured. Her biceps suggested membership at a gym. She had an upturned nose, nice chin, warm green eyes. She reminded him of Nicole Kidman's sexier, less regal little sister.

"Hi." She extended a small freckled hand. "I'm Kyra. You are?"

"Will." Why did women insist on shaking? It always felt forced.

"So, Will. Beer? Or something different?" She flipped the menu, and pointed to a list of mixed drinks. "We're known for our martinis."

"Sounds good. Let's see." He scanned the menu. "I'll try this 'Gold.' Stirred. Extra-dry. With Ketel One, if you have it."

"Dirty?"

He smirked. "Any chance of three olives?"

"Sure." She laughed easily. "With blue cheese? You'll like it."

After she left, bored, Will doodled on a napkin, sketching ideas for a proposal he could sell Cushing, trying to work his way home.

———⊗———

Rumbling rock music pounded out of speakers standing like mini towers in all four corners of the room—quadraphonic sound, Todd called it—some kids dancing, others leaning against the wall, drinking beer. A bunch of kids sat in a circle on the living room floor, passing a joint, the entire scene enveloped in a thick cloud of marijuana.

Hope's mom, Mindy, gave their cat the run of the house. The sofa and chairs were covered in hairballs. Leah wondered if anybody cleaned the place, *ever*. If you swiped your finger across the top of the table, you'd probably catch hepatitis or AIDS or some other vile disease.

Leah couldn't believe her boyfriend had brought her here. He didn't actually think she enjoyed being the only one sober, watching him and his friends swill beer and get high? When he asked what she wanted to do, she'd told him, "Whatever." Any nitwit should realize that "whatever" did not translate into "take me to a party at Hope's."

She was proud of herself for resisting the temptation to drink. Still, it was weird, being at a party and being the only one sober. She felt like an outcast. Also, Leah was bored. Everybody thinks they're hilarious or brilliant when inebriated, but they're not. She was embarrassed for them.

Leah scooped a handful of barbecue chips from the bowl on the coffee table. A dark-haired girl waved her cell phone, pestering them to smile, to pose. Who did she think she was? Ansel freaking Adams?

Leah backed up, turning her face away from the camera. If she were caught on film, she'd be toast. According to MIAA rules, any high school athlete caught in the vicinity of alcohol or drug use was automatically suspended for twenty-five percent of the season, sixty for a second offense. She'd caught a break: Coach Thomas hadn't heard about the Halloween party. She wasn't about to test her luck twice.

Leah winced. The pounding music was giving her a headache.

Across the living room, Hope was bitching out a party crasher. Hope was right in the girl's face.

"What's wrong, babe?" Todd asked, through a mouthful of smoke.

"What do you think?"

"What do you say we go outside where we can talk?" Cell Phone Girl was still snapping away.

Leah shrugged. "I guess," she said. "I've got to be home by six, you know. Otherwise, my mom will have the cops out looking for me."

"They don't trust you," he said flatly.

"Not anymore."

"Don't worry about it. I'll get you back."

With the slider closed, the piercing music faded away. She'd intended to ask Todd to drive her home. She was tired; she also had homework to do. Now that she had him to herself, she changed her mind.

Todd had mentioned his roadie days, but he'd never offered details. Curious, she asked what it was like on the road, traveling with a band.

He gazed at the woods behind Hope's house. "The roadies were tools," he said finally. "The musicians were talented dudes. The band shoulda been huge." It was tough to make it today. Record companies would rather invest a fortune in some lame American Idol than risk a dime on an unproven band, no matter how talented they were. In the sixties, his old man worked for an indie label in Boston. It was different back then. They cared about music. "Today it's all about the denari."

They spent a few minutes scoffing at consumerist greed, the idiocy of spending your entire life working to accumulate material things. "Life ain't worth shit if you live like that," Todd declared. "It's gotta be *real*."

Leah sighed. "Seriously, I could live in a cave."

A chipmunk skittered across the grass.

Following the rodent with her eyes, she spotted a trampoline at the far end of the yard. She and Justine had a trampoline when they were kids. In junior high, one of Leah's friends competed on an elite gymnastics team. The girls had spent hours on the trampoline, practicing back-flips, tucks, you name it.

"Is it Hope's?" Leah asked, certain that he would say no. Hope's mom probably did daycare or something. "I know it's a kid's thing and all."

"Hope's a kid." Todd blew out his cheeks. "A *big* kid."

"*Nas*-ty." Leah whacked his arm. Giggling, she jogged to the trampoline and hoisted herself up. She bounced a few times, and threw her arms, gaining height, up, up, up—and flopped on her knees.

"Hey—" Todd sprinted to the trampoline. "You're gonna get hurt."

"No I won't," Leah shouted, bouncing again. This time she landed a tuck. "Come on up," she said, harassing him until he climbed on.

"Like this." She bounced, her knees bent. "It's all in your legs. You've got to push off."

They bounced, holding hands, Todd surprisingly agile. They flipped like a synchronized team. Leah let go of his hand and jumped, throwing her arms and legs, tucking as she caught air—rising, rising—double-flipped, landing in his arms, and they collapsed onto the trampoline.

Leah lay on her back, her head tucked under his arm. "I'm sorry," she said, about the Ecstasy she meant. "Will you forgive me?"

"Sure, babe," he said. And, for the very first time, he told her he loved her.

Nine

Stormy

A week passed in their normal bustling confusion, which for Zoe meant a period of relative peace. Both daughters seemed to be moving in the right direction: no rude outbursts, no undone chores, no "courtesy calls" from the high school, informing her Leah's grades were dropping or she was falling behind in her work.

Of course, with teenagers you never *really* knew what was happening inside their heads. Just when you thought you understood your child, the instant you decided that you'd figured her out, the moment you began to believe you knew what to expect, she would change. Or be kidnapped by Martian invaders. This morning, Zoe's daughters had been replaced by two sullen teenagers who looked like Justine and Leah.

At three thirty, Zoe's five o'clock patient called and left a message with the receptionist, canceling her appointment. Every therapist Zoe knew required a twenty-four hour cancellation notice; if a patient failed to show, the therapist charged for the hour. Zoe posted a cancellation policy in her office, but she rarely enforced it. Most families she counseled lived barely above sustenance level; she didn't have the heart to charge for missed appointments or last-minute cancellations. It was a source of tension between Will and she, especially since they were nearly broke. Most patients appreciated and respected her generosity. Every so often, someone took advantage.

Turning out of the lot behind her office, she fastened her seatbelt and switched the radio on, adjusting the dial to ZLX, a classic rock station that helped her relax. She was glad for the chance to leave early.

Leah had given her grief this morning, *again*, about school. "It's a waste of time," Leah whined. She could not care less who'd fought which war or where battle lines had been drawn. Who cared about books written before her great-grandmother was born?

Until last winter, both girls had been straight-*A* students. Last spring, Leah's grades had slipped; this semester, she was barely squeezing by, her progress report littered with *C*s. Two weeks ago, Zoe had logged onto the Website for the U.S. Bureau of Labor and printed out statistics comparing the income of college graduates to people with high school degrees, a difference of nearly a million dollars over a lifetime.

"Look—" She'd handed her daughter the printout. "—the average salary for a high school graduate is twenty-eight thousand dollars a year." On that salary, a single person couldn't afford to pay the rent on a decent apartment in Boston.

"Twenty-eight thousand?" Leah exclaimed. "A year? I could easily live on that."

Miraculously, Zoe had managed to keep her tongue in check.

Zoe recognized the opening chords of a song from *Evita* and turned the radio up, singing along with Madonna. When the girls were little, they'd begged Zoe to sing. She had a dreadful singing voice, totally tone deaf. Her daughters, if they'd noticed, didn't seem to mind. She would sing their favorite songs: "Over the Rainbow," "A Spoonful of Sugar," "Edelweiss." After the first verse, the girls would join in, their exuberant songs rocking the car. If Zoe dared to sing now, Leah would probably pull her coat over her head.

What troubled Zoe most were the mood swings. For a day or two, Leah would be the ideal daughter, sweet, helpful, attentive. Zoe would drop her guard, convinced Leah's recent conduct was a fluke, a glitch, a temporary stage. Then, out of nowhere, Leah would explode, her daughter's outbursts followed by periods of glowering silence that frightened Zoe more than the fits. It would be easier if her daughter acted out all the time. If she and Will knew what to expect, they could plan an effective response.

As it was, Zoe tiptoed around Leah, constantly afraid of setting her off. All the tiptoeing, never knowing what was in store, frazzled Zoe's nerves. Though it shamed her to admit it, there were days when, if she knew that her daughter was there, she would do almost anything—paperwork, errands that could easily wait—to avoid going home.

A half mile out of the town center, she passed the Cortland Exchange, a converted mill that housed the Post Office, a Thai restaurant, a florist, a yoga studio, a hair salon, and La Mode, the day spa where Zoe occasionally treated herself to a manicure or pedicure.

She turned into the Exxon Station down the street from the mill. Filling her tank, she remembered that she'd run out of face cream. She paid for her gas and doubled back to the spa.

Limestone pebbles embedded in the asphalt glittered in the sun. Zoe walked briskly across the lot, her purse tucked under her arm, high heels clicking, loose cotton skirt swishing around her legs.

The day spa was on the first floor, its rear windows overlooking the parking lot. Last time she was here, Zoe had been with the girls.

Through the spa's French door, she saw Nora, the manager, at the reception desk. She scowled at her computer screen, her left shoulder cradling the phone. Nora ran a hand over her spiky, green-tinted hair.

Two women stood by the desk, waiting impatiently, one studying her bill, the other watching Nora, rolling her eyes. A pretty, light-haired woman Zoe had never seen before stood by a table in an alcove to the right of the reception desk, selling jewelry.

Nora waved as Zoe entered and mouthed a "hello." The clients nodded, sizing Zoe up.

Zoe's stomach churned. As always, she found the spa's affected atmosphere unnerving—the hushed voices, the cascading fountain by the archway leading to the back rooms, the New Age music, synthesized sounds of wind and rain. She felt as if she'd invaded a private club, its cultured clientele more refined than she.

Gradually, she settled into the rhythm.

The metal racks lining the walls displayed a dizzying array of skin care products: night creams, day creams, eye creams, lip balms, astringents, exfoliating masks, bath beads, as well as pre- and post-shower lotions. A block of soap with flecks of yellow and green sat on a shelf on the back wall, a carving knife by its side. Another rack was devoted entirely to candles—rosewood, sandalwood, lavender, vanilla. Zoe wondered how Nora tolerated the warring smells.

They'd moved the anti-aging lotions to a round, triple-tiered display case at the center of the floor. With the weather turning cooler, Zoe needed a stronger moisturizer than she'd been using. She selected the jar with the most enticing label and studied the ingredient list. She'd read an article in *Vogue* recently, touting some new wonder ingredient. Beta hydroxy? Vitamin C? She returned the jar to its designated spot, picked up a lime-green tube the length of her middle finger. Glycolic acid? She glanced at the reception desk, hoping to catch Nora's eye, to ask for advice.

Nora was still on the phone.

"Can I help you? I'm not an esthetician, but I can tell you what I like."

"Hi," Zoe said, turning to face the woman she'd seen in the alcove. From a distance, the woman was pretty. Up close, she was gorgeous. She wore a scoop-necked tank and black chiffon skirt, a wide belt cinching her tiny waist, and black ballet shoes. *I could never pull that off,* Zoe thought, embarrassed of her dowdy outfit.

"Thanks," Zoe said. "I'm just waiting for Nora. I love your bracelet." The woman turned her wrist. The small beads shimmered like sea glass. "It's striking."

"It's called Greta Garbo. All my bracelets have an identity. Here, let me show you." Zoe followed the woman to her table. "They're made with vintage buttons, dating between eighteen ninety and nineteen sixty. I find the buttons at antique stores, flea markets. It's a ball. I'm Dorothy Klein." She extended her hand. "It's lovely to meet you."

A printed sign on the display tree said, "Ruby Slippers Design."

"They're gorgeous." Zoe ran her finger over a deep blue bracelet. "Like pieces of art."

"Here—" Dorothy slid three bracelets off the wooden bar, and handed the blue one to Zoe. "That one's made of Bakelite. I call it 'Stormy.' It's part of my mood collection. Try it on?"

"'Stormy,'" Zoe mused, and slipped the bracelet over her wrist.

"I'd go with this one," Nora said, peering over Zoe's shoulder.

Zoe returned the blue bracelet and pushed the second one Dorothy offered over her hand, rotating her wrist. The yellow in the alabaster buttons brought out the gold in her skin.

"'Liz Taylor,'" she read from the note card that came with the bracelet. On the bottom right corner of the card, she saw the price written in pencil. A hundred and twenty dollars. "Thank you." She handed the bracelet back. "It's exquisite."

Zoe set the jar of vitamin E cream on the counter and handed Nora her credit card. Leah looked stunning these days. *She'd love that bracelet,* Zoe thought. The bracelet was special. Leah would know Zoe had been thinking of her. Her birthday was only a few weeks away.

While Nora awaited authorization from Visa, Zoe bought two bracelets, the dark blue, "Stormy," for Leah, and the gold, "Liz Taylor," for herself, paying Dorothy by check.

———⊛———

Justine entered the empty house through the garage, opened the door to the mudroom, and kicked off her Nike sneakers. Leaving her shoes on the rug by the door, she went to the kitchen, dropping her new ergonomic backpack on a barstool. She opened the fridge, scanned the contents, looking for something filling and reasonably healthy to eat.

On the bottom shelf, she found a Tupperware bowl with leftover beef stew. She ladled stew into a soup bowl—beef, potatoes, noodles, picking around the turnips and carrots—put the bowl in the microwave, took a spoon from the dishwasher, and rinsed it off. When the buzzer sounded, she took her stew out of the microwave and carried it upstairs.

The two hours after school, with her parents still at work, her sister at practice or a game, were Justine's favorite time of day. She loved the stillness, the quiet, the sounds—water running through the pipes, the tick of a clock—that otherwise faded into the noise and busyness of the house. Her mind wandered, free to think and imagine and daydream.

Dog hopped off the bed as Justine opened the door.

Justine set her stew on her desk and bent, scratching the pup's ears. Crouching, she gave Dog a hug. Dog whimpered in her embrace.

"Hey, puppy—" Dog licked Justine's face. "What's wrong? Let's see, baby," she said, pushing Dog to her feet. "Is it your hip again? Here, puppy. Treat?" She opened the bag of liver treats she kept by her computer and fed one to Dog. "Another one? Okay. Here you go."

The prednisone treatments the vet had been giving the dog were a joke. Poor Dog was in pain. There had to be something better.

Justine logged onto her computer, Dog settling by her feet.

A Google search of Labrador Retriever arthritis and treatment turned up a list of possible options: anti-inflammatory drugs, acupuncture. *Here's one*, she thought—*Pulsed Signal Therapy.* "PST is non-surgical and pain free," Justine read, "with no known side effects…a top treatment choice for arthritis." *Perfect,* she thought and copied the article into a Word document, then forwarded it to her mom.

Justine checked the time on her computer: three fifteen. She had nearly two hours to kill before her mom came home. At CCD class last Sunday, Justine learned that she had been chosen, from among two hundred and fifty kids in her class, to present the speech at their Confirmation in April. Justine hadn't told her family yet—not even her mom. She planned to talk about *them*, her family, and wanted to surprise them with a draft.

She opened a new document and began typing, jotting down notes. Their family had problems, of course—everyone did—but they loved one another. What else mattered? She had an amazing sister, parents who loved and protected them. Through the lens of her family's love, she'd caught a glimpse of God's transcendent, all-powerful love.

I've learned what it means to be part of God's family, she wrote.

Zoe never heard the siren until the cruiser was right on her tail.

In her rearview, she watched the cop stroll back to the cruiser. His height and compact muscular structure suggested a military background, ditto the buzz cut. He favored his left leg. An accident, she mused: he was a chaser, this guy, all self-righteousness and gusto.

The cop reminded her of a policeman in Boxborough, the rural town north of Cortland where she had grown up. Once Zoe's mother reached a certain state of inebriation, she had an ugly habit of cutting herself. One particular cop, Officer Regan, seemed to respond to every nine-one-one call Zoe or her father placed. The cop bandaged her mother's wrists with the efficiency and detachment of a military medic. Though he never looked directly at her, Zoe always felt judged, as though she were to blame for her mother's drinking.

A car whizzed by, the teenage passenger eyeing her, gloating. Zoe flinched. The cruiser's blinking light made her feel like a criminal. Zoe flipped open her cell phone and dialed the landline at home.

She let it ring into voicemail and dialed again. Justine was probably online. Zoe and Will ought to set a rule for using the computer. Limit her to an hour after school, an hour at night. Justine was twelve. She ought to be outdoors, riding her bike, getting exercise instead of sitting all day, staring at a computer screen. When

Leah was that age, she'd played on town softball and basketball teams in addition to playing soccer all year. Justine had no interest in sports. She'd taken karate lessons when she was younger and quit after earning her first degree black belt. If not for that silly heavy bag in her room, she'd get no exercise at all. No wonder the child was on Zantac. All that nervous energy and nowhere for it to go.

Zoe swung backward to check on the cop. She'd been waiting ten minutes. This was ridiculous. She had to get home, make dinner, feed the kids. Later, she had to tackle the mountain of paperwork in her briefcase. She didn't have time to sit here while the cop played his power game. She had a mind to get out of the car, trot on over, and ask what the heck was taking so long. *In fact*, she thought, *I will.*

As she approached the cruiser, the cop looked up, pulling a face. *God, they were getting young.* He looked about twelve.

His window slid down. "What do you think you're doing?"

"Excuse me," she said, offended by his tone. "I'm in a hurry."

"Yeah. Everybody's in a rush," he barked. "Get in your car."

She was outraged. Who did the cop think he was, taking that tone with her? *The one writing the ticket*, she thought. Unless she wanted him to double the amount, she'd best keep her mouth shut.

"Officer, please," she said, trying a different tack.

"I said, 'get back in your car.'"

"Damn cop," she muttered, glancing back at the cruiser as she opened the wagon door. *What was his problem?* In the car, she tried calling the house again. The line was still busy. She looked in the rearview. *This was such a waste of time.* She had to get home.

At last, the cruiser door swung open and the cop climbed out. He handed her a slip of paper, along with her license.

"Sorry." She tucked her license into her purse. "I didn't realize I was speeding," she said and instantly felt stupid. He obviously didn't care. All he cared about was his stupid ticket, making his daily quota.

"Slow it down," he said gruffly. "Before you kill somebody."

Zoe replied with a dispirited nod.

Before driving off, she checked the ticket, hoping he'd cut her slack, charged a hundred bucks instead of two. As the Explorer pulled away from the shoulder, she rechecked the ticket. A warning. The possibility of a warning had never crossed her mind. She took in the vibrant blue gift bag on the passenger seat. She thought about the beautiful bracelets wrapped inside, Leah's dazzling smile when Zoe presented her with the gift. This warning was a sign, a gift from the universe, letting her know that the worst was behind them.

Their lives were finally turning around.

Ten

The Rules are the Rules

Today's was the final game of the regular season. Cortland was fourteen and one, a game ahead of Westford, the next best team in the Hillside Division. A win would clinch the league title. Leah wasn't playing. Coach Thomas had dropped her name from the roster. Coach didn't have the decency to tell Leah herself.

A freshman, of all people, the sister of one of the seniors, delivered the news between classes. Leah wasn't sure she believed the girl. Why would Coach Thomas bench her best player? Leah had scored more goals this season than the rest of the team put together. According to the reporter from the *Gazette*, she *was* the team.

Infuriated, she skipped art, her last class, stomped to Coach Thomas's office in the gym, and demanded an explanation.

"I'm sorry," Coach Thomas said. "It's out of my hands."

Leah rocked on her heels. This couldn't be about skipping practice last week. Last Friday, after the bell rang and while the girls changed into their sweats, Coach Thomas had called Leah into her office. "You're either part of this team or you're not," Coach Thomas had said.

"I didn't feel well," Leah had replied. "My mom picked me up."

"In a black Wrangler?" Coach Thomas demanded that day, and launched into a boring dissertation about responsibility, commitment, teaching the younger kids by example. Leah *was* a good example. An example of how to behave like an adult, how to take control of your life instead of being led around like sheep. But it had been in her best interests to keep her mouth shut. So she'd stood in Coach Thomas's office for forty-five minutes, shuffling from foot to foot, her legs falling asleep, while Coach reamed her butt.

Afterward, Coach Thomas had given her a hug.

Leah had been the model player since then. Running five miles a day. Motivating the younger players. Doing extra drills. Dropped from the roster? On game day? What had she done to deserve that?

Coach Thomas, it emerged, had heard about the party at Hope's last week. "Mr. Minihan saw it during a routine Facebook check."

For real? That idiot Camera Girl must have posted her pictures.

"Nothing I can do," Coach Thomas said. "You have to sit out two games."

Two games? One a playoff game? This would kill her chances of making the *Globe* All-Scholastic team. "I didn't even drink." She'd been the only sober kid at the party. "Doesn't that count?"

"You know the rules, Leah."

What about the girls? Her teammates depended on her. If their team won today, they'd win their division. "I can't sit out." She had to play. She had to help the team win. "Please?" Leah begged.

Coach Thomas appeared to be thinking. For an instant, Leah thought she might reconsider. Then she opened the file drawer in her desk and thumbed through the folders. Leah knew exactly what her coach was looking for: the pact Leah had signed at the pre-season captain's practice, promising to steer clear of alcohol and drugs.

Coach Thomas produced the paper, held it out for Leah to see. "This *is* your signature?"

Leah could have argued. She could have claimed that she was coerced. Why fight a battle she couldn't win? Instead, she issued an ultimatum. "If I can't play," she said, "I'm quitting the team."

She was stunned when Coach Thomas agreed.

When she left Coach Thomas's office, Leah called Todd. She stood by the gym door, waiting for her boyfriend to pick her up.

Bored, she toyed with the button bracelet her mom had given her last week. It was supposed to have been a birthday gift, her mother too excited, too impatient to wait.

Figures her mom would buy her a bracelet called *Stormy*. Though Leah had to admit, she sort of liked being thought of that way. She rotated her wrist, a fiery blue button catching the light.

Stormy, she mused. *Tempestuous. Wild. Raging. Intense.*

The gym door swung open, startling her, and the soccer team marched out with Cissy leading the pack, her callow brown eyes focused straight ahead, as if Leah weren't even there. *The bitch.*

"One, two, three, four," Cissy chanted. "Who we gonna win for?"

"Cortland! Cortland!" the team responded in unison.

A bus pulled alongside the soccer field. Fuming, Leah watched the opposing team disembark. For an entire week, she'd been on her best behavior. Twice, she'd made dinner. She helped Justine with her algebra homework. Offered to wash and wax her father's car—he hadn't let her. But still. She did her homework every night, whether she felt like it or not, had even turned in several old assignments, ones she'd ignored or neglected to finish. She'd received the only *A* in her entire class on the biology exam. At Hope's party, even though she'd wanted to drink, even though she'd wanted to smoke, she'd been the model kid, resisting every temptation. What good had it all done?

Thankfully, her father was in California. Otherwise he'd be here. He insisted on arriving twenty minutes early for games. The warm-ups, he said, gave him an opportunity to observe the opposing players, size up the competition. Leah wondered if Coach Thomas had called her mom yet, or if she'd wait until after the game. If she'd called, Leah's mom would have immediately called Leah's father, on the job site.

If there was anything worse than her father hearing bad news, it was hearing it when he was at work. Once, when Leah was ten, she'd broken a metatarsal bone, an injury that had sidelined her for most of the season. Her dad was in Chicago. Her mom called from the hospital, interrupting a meeting, and her father had caught the first plane home. He hadn't yelled at her, but he had not been pleased. With her luck, he was probably already in the air.

Leah kicked backward, hitting the steel door with the sole of her shoe. She had to pinch herself to prove she was here with all the other losers, outside the gym, waiting for a ride. Her father was going to kill her. He talked incessantly about that dumb All-Scholastic award. If she made Player of the Year, she *might* have a shot at redeeming herself with the Harvard coach. Now, she'd be lucky if the coaches in her league voted her onto the All-Star team.

She could hear her father when she broke the big news: "This is the last straw, Leah Marie. Quitters never win." Meaning she was a loser. Wouldn't surprise her if he kicked her out of the house. To hear him, he had plenty of reasons. She was disrespectful. A liar. A lousy example for Justine. He and her mother were sick of her antics. *Shape up or ship out.* Well, she hadn't shaped up.

This was it: time to ship out.

Leah wondered where she would go. To Todd's. Or maybe to Hope's. Hope was cool; she didn't strike Leah as the type who would mind. Leah would have to find a job, of course. She'd probably waitress. She'd never waited tables, didn't know the first thing about food service. Really, how tough could it be? Maybe she could crash on Hope's couch until she'd saved enough money to move someplace nice, where she actually wanted to live. Forced to choose now, she'd pick New York.

She'd been to the city with her parents a few times when she was a kid to visit her father's uncle on the Upper West Side. A nice one-bedroom co-op with a doorman had to cost at least five hundred a month. She was not about to rent a place with cockroaches or rats. Maybe her uncle would help her find an affordable place in the Village. She pictured herself in a sidewalk café, serving seeded organic bread, wearing flowery secondhand clothes. Or maybe she would move to southern California where the weather was always sunny and warm. She had never been to the West Coast, but she knew from all the movies she'd seen that she'd feel right at home.

By the time her boyfriend arrived, the game was in progress. Cortland was up, one-zip. But it was early. Plenty of time to lose.

"Where were you?" Leah snapped. She hoisted herself into the truck, tossing her pack on the rear floor. "I've been waiting forever."

"Work," he snapped back. "Want me to get fired?"

"Like Jamie would fire you."

"You think he likes it when I cut out early?"

"He wouldn't fire you for that."

Grunting, Todd stepped on the gas. The Wrangler jerked forward. "He accused me of stealing fifty bucks from him this morning."

Leah shot an accusatory look in his direction. "Did you?"

"Steal money out of the register? Hell no."

"Good," she said, relieved. She'd be mortified dating a thief. Never mind a thief who stole from his friends. "That's not like him. What did he say?"

"Nothing." He lowered his voice. "I told him I'd pay it back."

Leah bolted upright. "So you did steal the money?"

"I said I'm paying it back. Could we get off this already?"

"Fine," she muttered, too exhausted to argue.

He slid a CD into the changer. "Don't you have a game today?"

Leah shrugged. She didn't feel like talking either.

"So, what's up? I got worried when you called."

What's up? Where was she to begin? She'd lost her sense of direction. Her boyfriend, she'd just learned, had stolen fifty dollars from his employer. She'd quit playing soccer, the only thing in the whole world she was good at or truly knew how to do. The kids at school gossiped about her constantly. Her parents were on the verge of disowning her. Did that count? Being disowned by your parents? She was about to be thrown out of her house, with no place to go. Life as she'd known it for sixteen years had ended, and she had no idea what would come next.

"Nothing," she lied. "I missed you." Since her answer seemed to satisfy him, she left it at that.

Will polished off his martini and ordered a second. The Micronics deal was unraveling fast. Last week, the project manager had blown him off. Tuesday afternoon, three days ago, Cushing's secretary had called, all apologies. Cushing had presented Will's proposal at their project meeting that morning and wanted to meet with Will the next day.

Refusing to accommodate the jerk was not an option. Will had flown back to San Francisco that afternoon for a meeting that lasted exactly six minutes. Cushing had arranged for Will to meet with the architects today, at noon, to go over the details. By Thursday morning, a friend in NAC's marketing department produced and posted, by Federal Express, an audio-visual presentation detailing Will's shear wall proposal.

At today's meeting, two minutes after he'd dimmed the lights, Will had caught the lead architect with his eyes closed. When the video ended, Will quizzed the architects, asking each in turn what they thought about the possibility of switching to shear walls. RCC walls were standard. Period. End of story. Wouldn't surprise Will if they'd called Cushing and advised him to bring in a competitor to re-bid the rest of the job.

Will's first inclination had been to drive to the construction site, confront Cushing head-on, and force him to deliver the news to his face. A mile from the site, he'd changed his mind—such an impromptu visit would kill the project outright, an outcome he could not afford. He'd tried phoning the airline to rebook his ten o'clock flight, struck out, and headed over to Marcus for a drink.

It was one thirty, the tail end of the lunch shift.

The restaurant was emptying out. The staff compared notes on their weekend plans as they cleared vacated tables, busboys ferried tubs of dirty dishes back to the kitchen and replaced the tablecloths.

Near the end of the bar, a kid not much older than Leah was talking with the manager, discussing the Brazilian jazz trio playing tonight. The band, Will gathered, was popular with the local crowd.

"Band sounds pretty good," Will said.

"Yeah," Kyra said absently, shaking his martini. "They are."

She poured his drink into a glass, speared two blue cheese olives, and laid the swizzle stick over the rim. Then she dropped three extra olives into a shot glass, and set both glasses in front of him.

Will raised the glass of olives. "Taking good care of me, Kyra."

"You sure you're okay? You look a little down in the mouth."

"Nothing earth-shattering," he lied. "Martini looks great."

"Hope it's cold enough. I like to keep the vodka in the freezer. Joe down there—" Winking, she tipped her head toward the bar manager. He was making his way toward them, washing the counter, his rag moving in neat circles. "—insists on leaving it out."

"So the customers can see it." Joe tossed the rag in the sink. "Folks don't order—"

"What they can't see." She rolled her eyes, laughing. "I know, Jo-Jo. I know."

Joe untied his apron, draped it over one arm. "You're good, Kay, right? Ray ought to be here shortly to help you get ready for happy hour. It's my day with my girl."

"Single dad," Kyra explained after he'd left. "He adores that little girl. She's sweet. Too bad more guys aren't like him."

Kyra had mentioned a daughter last week, but she'd said only that the child had just started school. Before Will had a chance to ask about her, the kid at the end of the bar came over to settle his bill.

While Kyra was at the register, her back turned, two fortyish women wandered into the bar, gabbing, distracted. She took their orders and poured drinks—Coors Light, a glass of Merlot—set their drinks on the bar, and opened their tab. An upscale bar was the perfect place for people watching. He got a kick out of seeing how they interacted, the games they played—who talked over others, who moved, or didn't move, their stool to make room for a newcomer.

One of the male bartenders switched the TV station to classic baseball—the Boston Red Sox versus the Cincinnati Reds, 1975,

Game Six in the Series. It was the most competitive World Series in history.

Will had gone to the game with his dad. Until his retirement, Will's father had managed the janitorial services at the Philadelphia City Hall. Mayor Rizzo had given him the tickets. From the time Will was old enough to understand the game, the Sox had been his favorite American League team. The night his father showed him the tickets, he had not slept a wink. The next morning, Will and his dad boarded a train to Boston. They sat behind the Sox dugout, close enough to hear Yaz psyching his teammates up between innings, to smell the cigarettes the players were smoking. That game, those three days in Boston with his dad, had been the highlight of Will's youth.

An inning went by before Kyra returned. With the rag Joe had left in the sink, she cleaned the puddle of beer under the tap.

"Baseball fan?" Will asked, gesturing toward the TV.

"Oh, yeah." She pushed a curl out of her eyes. Normally, Will preferred long hair on women. The cropped style fit Kyra. Soft auburn curls framed her heart-shaped face and brought out the blue in her eyes.

"I love baseball," she said. "That was an amazing game. Boston against the 'Big Red Machine.'"

"I was there."

"You live in Boston, I thought."

"I grew up in Philly, outside the city. I went to the game with my dad."

"One sec—" She held up a finger. "Sorry. I've got to see this."

The door opened, sunlight glaring across the screen.

Will squinted. He's fourteen. There he is, behind the dugout. *The pitch.* His forehead breaks out in a sweat. They're on their feet. Morgan slams a line drive into deep right. Evans sprints back, back, crossing the warning track—

"Yes!" Kyra pumped her fist. "I've seen that catch a dozen times. It still gets me."

Will released a breath he hadn't realized he'd been holding.

"You believe the Sox lost the Series after that catch?" Kyra shook her head. "And Fisk's twelfth-inning homer?"

A guy at the end of the bar lifted a hand to get Kyra's attention. When she didn't jump at his signal, the guy snapped his fingers.

"Asshole," Will groused. "Pardon the language."

"It's okay." She pushed a curl behind her ears. "I'm used to it." Kyra waved to let the guy know she was on her way. "Be right back."

Will turned back to the TV. A Nike ad came on. The girl in the ad reminded him of Leah. *Damn.* She had a game today. He checked his watch. Two o'clock, five at home. This Micronics business had turned his brain to mush. The game had slipped his mind. If Cortland won, they would capture the league title. He couldn't believe he'd forgotten to call to wish his daughter luck.

On the fourth ring, he reached her recording, and left a message, saying he was sorry he couldn't be there. "I'm thinking about you, honey."

After leaving the message for Leah, he dialed Cushing again, reached an automated voice, and tried Zoe. Last night when they spoke, he'd asked Zoe to videotape the game so he could watch it at home over the weekend. If he got lucky, he'd catch her as she was leaving her office. If she'd forgotten the camera, she would have time before the opening kickoff to drive home and get it. Another recording. He left a message, saying he loved her, asked her to wish Leah luck for him.

"Tell the girls I miss them," he said, and then turned his phone off and put it away.

On her way home, Zoe stopped at the supermarket for staples: butter, napkins, toilet paper, a package of string cheese for Justine, a bag of Macintosh apples. She'd also run in to the cleaners. She set the groceries on the island counter and laid the dry cleaning bags over a stool. When Will called last night, he'd asked her to do something important. For the life of her, she couldn't say what. Because her notepad was not in the secretary where she normally kept it, she'd neglected to write it down. Eventually she would remember.

Justine was upstairs in her bedroom. Zoe could hear the shush of Justine's feet as she skated across the hardwood floor, the *thwap, thwap, thwap* of her punches, connecting with the regulation sized punching bag hanging in the corner of her room. Zoe used to tease the girls when they were little, telling them they weren't allowed to grow up.

"You're gonna stay six," she would say, "like Christopher Robin—forever and ever." *Wouldn't it be nice,* Zoe mused, *if you could keep your children innocent forever? Prevent them from turning into surly teenagers who frustrated you and scared you out of your wits?*

Oh stop, Zoe scolded herself. *Don't be a drama queen.*

After she put the groceries away, she set a kettle of water on the stove and lit the burner. From the dishwasher, she retrieved her favorite blue mug and fetched a ginger chai teabag from the pantry.

More than a week had passed without an outburst from Leah. If anything, her behavior had been too good, Stepford daughter good. Was this polite, helpful teenager really Leah? Zoe had been waiting all week for the bomb to drop, one of Leah's foul moods to erupt, her daughter to say or do something to shake Zoe back to reality. This time, as naïve as it sounded, things truly seemed to be turning around.

Zoe couldn't wait to talk with Will tonight. He'd promised to call on his way to the airport. She'd meant to call him this afternoon, see how he'd made out with the architects, but her phone had died.

If Leah's team made the national championship tournament—everyone thought they would—maybe the family could fly to Phoenix for the game. She'd earned nearly a thousand dollars from her last seminar, enough for three tickets. The town would cover the fare for the players. After the game, they could stay a few extra days. They'd explore the city, maybe drive to the Grand Canyon. Their last family vacation had been to Disney World when Justine was eight. It would be good to get away, spend time together, with nobody angry or fighting.

The phone rang. Justine answered before Zoe could pick up.

Zoe fixed her tea and headed to the family room to relax for a few minutes before starting dinner. As she was setting her mug on the coffee table, she happened to catch sight of the window on the far wall, and noticed that it was getting dark. She checked her watch. Ten past five. Leah should have been home by now. Normally, practice ended by four. Zoe didn't recall her daughter having asked for a ride. She hoped Leah hadn't been trying to reach her on her cell phone.

She was standing at the foot of the stairs, about to holler up, ask Justine if she'd heard from her sister. As if on cue, Justine's bedroom door swung open and her younger daughter appeared on the landing.

"Hey, Mom." Justine leaned over the banister, one foot poking between the balusters. She'd changed out of her school clothes into jeans and a tee-shirt. She'd pulled her hair into a stubby ponytail. Her socks, Zoe noticed, were filthy. "I didn't hear you," Justine said. "I was talking to Holly."

"That's nice, honey."

"Did you have a good day?"

"Do you know where your sister is, sweetie? It's awfully late."

Justine's face clouded. "She's not home yet."

God, Zoe thought. *What's wrong with me?* Shortchanging Justine, implying she wasn't important. What a message to send. "Something to eat, sweetheart?" she asked, scrambling to rectify the slight. "A cup of hot chocolate?"

"Doesn't she have a game today?"

Shoot. The last game of the season. By now, it would be just about over. "Come on, honey. We've got to go. I can't believe I forgot."

⟡

The Lansdown place was depressing. It was late afternoon and the house was dark. No one had bothered to turn on the lights. The CD Todd had put on the stereo, some eighties head banger band, was annoying. If only she could go home, climb in bed, snuggle under her cozy down comforter, and fall asleep. Forget this day ever happened.

Todd cut lines of coke on the coffee table. He rolled a dollar bill and snorted a line. Sniffing, he offered the bill to her.

What was his problem? If she'd told him once, she'd told him a hundred times. She had no interest in coke.

He snorted another line and tucked the bill in his pocket. "What's up with you?" He patted the sofa, hunting for the clicker.

"What are you talking about?"

"What're you being such a bitch for?"

"Screw you," she said, struggling to stay calm.

"Fuck you, too, if that's how you want to be."

"You, *too*," she mumbled, fighting back tears.

She should have been happy. This was what she wanted, wasn't it? She hated soccer. She was tired of carrying the whole stupid team on her back. If she were not such a coward, she would have quit ages ago. Only, she'd wanted to quit on her own terms. In her fantasies, when she announced her decision to quit, she was standing on a bench in the locker room, towering over her teammates. The sobbing girls begged her to reconsider. They couldn't function without her, they cried. Coach Thomas implored her to stay. "What can we do to change your mind? Anything, Leah. You're in charge. You don't have to practice anymore! No more drills!"

Leah never dreamed Coach Thomas would accept her resignation without a fight. Her coach was supposed to question herself, ask where she'd gone wrong. The team was supposed to stand in allegiance; her teammates were supposed to quit if she wouldn't play. It wasn't supposed to happen like *that*.

Todd flipped through the stations, watched two MTV videos, and switched the television off. "What's up, babe?" he asked, politely this time. "I hate seeing you like this."

"Noth—" Leah burst into tears. "Coach…Thom—"

Todd moved closer, pressed her head to his chest. "What?" he whispered, stroking her hair. "Coach T. say something?"

Leah shook her head. "Not," she said, gulping back tears. "Team…any…more."

"She kicked you off the team?"

Sobbing, Leah nodded. Earlier, in Coach Thomas's office, then afterward, cleaning her locker, she had been incensed, rage burning in her arms, her fingers, her hands. Her fury roiled, pounding her skull, attacking the walls of her chest. She kicked her locker, pretending she was kicking a person—Coach Thomas, her parents, her teammates— and whacked it again, harder. Gradually, her anger subsided, her fury shifting to self-pity, then to indignation. Coach Thomas had no right to treat her this way. Who did Coach Thomas think would replace her? Surely not Cissy.

Now the tears flowed as she thought about all the games she would miss: sectionals, regional playoffs, states, possibly nationals. For the first time in school history, Cortland was ranked. She thought about all the people she had let down. Her teammates, her coach. Her parents. The news would crush her father. Leah would never play soccer in college, not at Harvard or anywhere else. She'd also disappointed herself. That part of her life was finished.

"It's over," she cried. "My…whole…life has been soccer."

Todd cupped her chin, kissing her forehead. "Don't cry, babe." With his thumb, he wiped a tear from her cheek. "It's okay."

"What's up?" Hope asked, emerging from the kitchen.

Leah wiped her eyes with a balled up napkin. Any other time, she would laugh. Hope and Lupo stood in front of the coffee table— Hope's faded flannel shirt unbuttoned to her waist, exposing a ratty pink bra, Lupo's bushy eyebrows bunched in a mock angry scowl.

"What's up?" Hope asked again. "What are you crying about?"

"Jealous." Lupo winked, clucking his tongue. "Am I right? 'Cause you ain't getting it on."

"Cut the shit," Todd said. "This is serious."

"Sor-ry." Hope rolled her eyes. "Gonna let us in on the secret?"

"Don't you *get* it?" Todd's blue eyes flashed, electric. "She don't want to talk."

Hope licked her middle finger and flicked it at Todd.

Leah blew her nose into the napkin. "I got kicked off the team."

"You shitting me?" Hope said. "You were, like, the best they had."

Were being the operative word. "Because of your party."

"No way." Hope threw up her hands. "You were the only straight one there. That's bullshit," Hope said, her voice turning livid.

"What a bitch," Lupo said.

"Shut up, Lupo," Hope cut in. "You never even met her. What a *bitch.*"

Leah stared at the blank TV screen. Nothing she could do.

"You used to play," Todd said to Hope. "Can't you talk to her?"

Hope's gaze slid from Todd to Leah and back to Todd. "Guess so," she said, probably recalling how, freshman year, Coach Thomas had caught her smoking in the locker room and thrown her off the team. "Sure," she said defiantly. "I'll give that bitch a piece of my mind."

"Me, too." Lupo leapt into a boxing stance, his beefy hands curled into fists. "Let me *at* her," he said, the Cowardly Lion on steroids. "Let me *at* her."

"Thanks," Leah said. "You guys are awesome. But I'm all set."

Leah laced her fingers through Todd's. These were her friends. She pictured her teammates as she left Coach Thomas's office, whispering behind their palms, Cissy passing her, pretending Leah didn't exist. For the first time in her life, she understood the true meaning of friendship. Friends helped you cope; they lifted you up when you were down. True friends didn't judge you when you did something they disapproved of or make you feel like a loser when you made a mistake, as if you'd purposefully intended to hurt them.

"So, dude," Lupo said, turning to Hope. "How 'bout I open that JD I got in the car?"

"Sounds like a plan." Hope looked down at Leah. "You good?"

Leah laid her head on Todd's shoulder, grinning at Lupo and Hope. No, this wasn't the end of the world. Soccer was one part of her life. If that part was over, so be it. Why prolong the inevitable? She'd learned a valuable lesson today. She couldn't control her teammates' behavior, couldn't force Coach Thomas to trust her or believe in her again. If her teammates abandoned her, if her coach had lost faith in her, why did they matter? Why be involved with people like them? In a way, it was good this happened. At least she knew where she stood. Sometimes you need a push in order to change and adjust.

The three of them were watching intently, awaiting her response.

"I'd love some JD. Time to get this party rolling," she said, with all the hope and enthusiasm of a girl whose world had just opened up.

Eleven

Another Bad Day

Jerry was on his way to the town forest to break up a teenage party when the dispatcher radioed. "Juvenile. Requires medical assistance. Six Lily Farm Road. Ambulance dispatched."

He was exhausted. He hadn't slept a full night in three months, not since the birth of the twins. It had taken over two years for his wife to get pregnant. The morning the test stick turned pink, she'd leapt into his arms. To celebrate, he'd taken the day off from work and they'd driven up to Hampton, New Hampshire, and had a picnic on the beach.

The birth of his sons had been the most exciting, awe-inspiring moments of his life. The miracle of birth, the sight of their tiny heads, reduced him to tears. Now, at times, though he adored his sons, he wondered why they'd been so desperate to have children. Maura's anxiety had spiked soon after the birth. When he tried to help, she pushed him away. She looked past him, her eyes vacant. He wondered where she had gone, what had happened to his loving wife.

He took a shortcut over the railroad tracks, drove a mile, and turned left, crossing a suspension bridge, and took a right onto Old Orchard Road, a winding street flanked by stone walls. He sped past a fallow cornfield, the transfer station, the last working orchard in Cortland. The grade steepened. Downshifting, he stepped on the gas.

It was rare for Jerry to be summoned to the east side of town. Cortland was a quiet suburb of fewer than four thousand people, a town where young hooligans smashed mailboxes or occasionally broke into a car, offenses cops in bigger towns were sometimes forced to ignore. In Cortland the police took a smashed mailbox seriously, even prosecuted sometimes.

Like many old New England towns, Cortland was divided by a river. From the west, Jerry's side of town, it could take twenty minutes to reach the nearest highway. The houses in West Cortland were older and smaller than people built today, the undeveloped land, primarily forest or scrub, isolating the neighbors as opposed to providing views.

When people on Jerry's side of town called the police, the call often arose out of helpless desperation. An elderly woman hadn't answered her telephone in three days, a family member was drunk or out of control. If you were new to the area, driving west to east and landed here, you might wonder if you'd accidentally crossed the town line.

East Cortland hugged Route 2, providing easier access to Boston; here the subdivisions were not neighborhoods; they were "estates." Residents typically called the police to report some minor inconvenience. A lockout, a lost pet, at times a dead deer in the road. Not that wealth liberated people from personal problems. Rich people had their share of trouble, as Jerry could attest.

He entered the Lily Farm development through the mouth of a pompous stone wall, took his first left, and proceeded up a mildly graded hill, past several huge contemporary colonials with multi-gabled roofs and chimneys housing multiple flue pipes. The houses set on level two-acre lots with sweeping front lawns. At the end of the cul-de-sac, he slowed the cruiser, switched off the siren to avoid causing a disturbance, and eased down the driveway marked "Six."

The house was enormous compared to the fifties-style ranch where Jerry and his family lived. He used to envy these guys, with their fine breeding and private school pedigree. Next to them, he'd felt like a loser. Ten years on the force had taught him never to judge from the outside. He'd be impressed by the size of a house, its custom design and manicured lawn; inside, he'd discover a cavernous shell.

He parked by the lantern post nearest the garage. The weather was changing, the nights colder, his breath visible when he exhaled. A brick walkway, illuminated by discreetly placed landscaping lights, led to the front entry. He hurried up the steps, hoping he wasn't too late.

A big man, over six-three, Jerry was dwarfed by the entrance. A brass knocker hung below three stalks of Indian corn. He knocked, waited a few seconds, and rang the bell.

The rooms at the front of the house were dark. He rang the bell again, waited a few more seconds, and scooted down the steps, around the garage, to a deck at the rear of the house. He took the steps two at a time, tapping the kitchen window as he passed, rapped on the slider, waited, and turned the handle. Locked. A light burned in a room off the kitchen. Someone had to be home. He heard voices inside and knocked again.

Finally, a dark-haired woman in jeans and a bulky Irish-knit sweater opened the door. The woman he'd pulled over last week, the one who got out of her car. Zoe Tyler. Not many people had the nerve to do that. They were too afraid that he'd up the ante on their ticket. It was dangerous and showed impatience, neither of which he approved. The spirit he admired, the warning a discreet way of letting her know.

"Jerry Johnson," he said. "I'm responding to a call."

———◆◆— –

Kyra set Will's sandwich—roast chicken on wheat with lettuce and onion—on the bar, with a bottle of Evian and a glass.

"Water's on the house," she whispered. "Don't tell my boss." She winked and untied her apron. "I've got a short break. Okay if I sit with you for a few minutes? There's a table over there." She pointed to an empty table near the band. "I hate sitting at the bar. I feel like I ought to be working."

Will had been at the bar for five hours, the time inching toward seven. Considering how little he had eaten, he was surprisingly sober.

Minutes after Will and Kyra took seats, the band went on break. The musicians impressed him, their music a far cry from the watered-down bossa-pop the record companies put out. The classical guitarist, a virtuoso by any objective standard, was accompanied by a flashy, supremely accomplished American kid on drums and a sexy Latina vocalist in a red sequined gown with a plunging neckline. Her throaty confidence reminded him of Linda Ronstadt in her glory days.

"So..." Kyra dunked a steak cut fry in a ramekin filled with ketchup. "Have you been out to the prison?"

Alcatraz. "The Rock. Sure. Tough place."

"My grandfather knew the Birdman."

"Robert Stroud. The guy who studied canaries."

"In Leavenworth. They didn't let him have his birds here."

"Right. Because of the still." Imagine—a guy in federal prison, trying to bootleg. "I always wondered how he got away with that."

She shrugged, grinning. "He didn't." She dunked another fry.

"No." He grinned back. "Guess not." Kyra was young, beautiful. He had no business sitting here with her. It was a slippery slope, adultery. He knew it, and he knew, or thought he knew, he'd never go there again. That made his behavior all the more despicable now. But he needed to talk, needed company, so he convinced himself it was okay.

She pushed her plate aside and leaned forward, crossing her arms. "My grandfather was a prison guard before the war. After Japan, he went to college on the GI Bill. He had a soft spot for the Birdman. They used to write."

Will scratched his chin. He needed a shave. "So they were pen pals."

She arched her brows. "You're mocking me."

He laughed. "I'm not. It's interesting."

"I've always thought so. My mom, not so much."

"Probably scared her. Stroud was a psychopath."

"Maybe," she said thoughtfully. "Wasn't like he'd ever get out."

"He killed a guard in Leavenworth. You know that, right?"

"Of course. He and Grandpa talked about it. People felt comfortable with my grandfather. Later in life, he became a minister. Every Thanksgiving, we'd go around the table, naming things we were thankful for. One year, Grandpa said, 'Stroud.' The family stared. Mom's jaw dropped. I got it, you know? I totally got it. Befriending a guy like that changes you. In a way, Stroud made him who he was."

Fascinating woman. She reminded him of Zoe. Similar mannerisms. His chest ached. He hadn't realized how much he missed his wife.

With the band on break, drinking had picked up. The queues were three deep along the length of the bar. "Better get back," Kyra said. "Inmates are getting restless."

He had to go, too. He had a plane to catch. He followed her to the bar to settle his bill, stood back, waiting for the crowd to disperse.

When a space opened, he slid into it.

Kyra set a bowl of bar mix in front of him and asked how he thought the Sox would do next year with their GM and manager gone.

"Francona,"—the manager—"got a raw deal," she said. "I get that he should have taken control. Can't have guys boozing in the clubhouse. But he did a lot for that team."

"Tell you the truth," Will said, "I'm more of a fair-weather fan these days." When he was a kid, players considered it a badge of honor to spend their career with one team. There was no loyalty today. "They're like all the rest of us, for sale to the highest bidder."

She opened the tap, poured a local micro beer into a tall glass imprinted with the Marcus logo. A hand, reaching from behind Will, handed her a five-dollar bill in exchange for the beer.

"So I was right," she said. "I pegged you as a romantic."

Interesting. He wondered what she saw that he'd missed.

They talked for a few minutes. She showed him a picture of her five-year-old, Rachel.

"Quite a kid," he said, and she was. A tiny spitfire blonde with her mother's red curls and deep-set eyes, she looked a handful.

He showed her school photos of the girls. While she studied the pictures, he flipped through the credit cards in his wallet, found his American Express, and laid it down.

"Gorgeous." She handed him the photos. "Time to go already?"

"Ten o'clock flight." He had to stop at the hotel for his things before he left for the airport. "I'll need time to return the rental car."

"Okay." She glanced at her watch. "I'll take care of this then."

While she rang up his bill, he calculated the time it would take to get from here to his hotel room across the street and drive to the airport. Eight fifteen. He'd make the flight, but it would be close.

She returned his credit card a few minutes later, wrapped in a napkin. "Call next time you're in town. I'll give you the *real* Alcatraz tour."

Zoe smiled, but her eyes were tired. "Officer Johnson." She inched the glass door closed, the metal frame dividing her slender body in two. "I'm sorry to have bothered you. I overreacted."

A dog growled from inside. Jerry stepped back. He'd been attacked once by a Doberman Pinscher owned by an elderly woman. A neighbor had called, said she hadn't left her house in a week, asked if they'd check on her. When she opened the door, the mutt charged. He'd needed twenty-five stitches to close the wound on his calf.

"Don't mind her." Zoe grabbed the dog's collar. "She's a big old wimp."

Noticing the Lab's weathered face, Jerry relaxed. He ruffled her ears. "Mind if I come in, check things out? Won't take long."

"Of course. Sorry." She opened the door, stepping aside. "Good girl," she said, nudging the dog out of the way. The Lab shuffled to the rear of the breakfast nook and settled on the floor under the window. "If my husband were here, this wouldn't have happened."

Embarrassed for her, he averted his eyes. The place looked like the models in the *Better Homes and Gardens* magazines Maura stored in the wicker basket in their bathroom. Ten-foot ceilings, cherry cabinets with a mile of granite, a wine cooler the size of his fridge. All that, plus a knockout for a wife—yet the guy couldn't stay home.

"It's easier when there are two of you, I meant. I panicked."

"No problem," Jerry assured her. "That's what we're here for."

He followed her into the kitchen. He caught a whiff of garlic, a hint of sage. He wondered what Zoe had been cooking.

"She's in here." Zoe pushed her sleeves over her elbows.

An arched doorway with fluted columns led to a sunken great room furnished with two oversized chairs, upholstered in red and gold plaid, and a coordinating pillow-back sofa flanked by a pair of antique end tables with turned legs. A family portrait hung above the stone fireplace. An open laptop and several magazines sat on a glass coffee table in front of the sofa. As he took in the room, his eyes skimmed Zoe's slender bare feet, her nails painted a startling pink.

A cute girl, eleven- or twelve-years-old, in jeans and a tee-shirt, sat on the floor at the foot of the sofa. She fixed him in a wary gaze. Things didn't add up. She looked fine. Everything appeared to be in order.

Zoe, sidestepping the coffee table, set a hand on the girl's shoulder.

Jerry smelled the alcohol before he saw the older girl curled on the sofa, a bed pillow under her head. The angle had cut her out of his line of vision. He pictured her with a gang of teenagers gathered around a bonfire, passing a bottle of rum. Damn shame. She had everything a kid could want. Why do this?

Zoe crossed her arms, one hand at her waist, the other at the base of her throat. "She was hyperventilating. I couldn't calm her down. I was afraid she'd stop breathing."

He rubbed his hands together to warm them and checked the girl's pulse. Sixty. *Good.* He laid a hand on her forehead—no fever— and pulled the blanket over her shoulders. "Color's good. Pulse's normal. Ambulance'll be here shortly. We'll get her checked out."

Zoe flashed a weak smile. "That won't be necessary."

"It's no trouble. They're on their way."

"No, really. But thank you."

He unclipped his radio. "All right then. Let me call. Tell them we're set. If you don't mind, I need to take some information." His back ached, his sciatica flaring again. He shifted his weight.

Zoe touched his arm. "Please. Have a seat." She showed him to an overstuffed chair and sat across from him, crossing her legs.

The younger girl stayed parked on the floor by her sister.

Forcing his eyes away from Zoe's feet, he radioed the dispatcher and gave her a rundown. "All set," he said, opening his notepad. "Would you like to tell me what happened?"

Zoe and the younger girl exchanged a troubled look. "She had a big game today." The mother shook her head, as though silently scolding herself. "By the time I got there, it was over."

Jerry nodded, encouraging her to go on.

"I figured she'd gone home with Cissy. Hanson. Her best friend—former best friend, I should say." Zoe paused, grimacing. "I don't think she ever went to the game. Leah, I mean. I don't know why her coach didn't call. Or maybe she did. The battery died in my cell, and I haven't checked my messages yet. Oh, God. I'm babbling. I can't think straight. I'm sorry."

Cissy Hanson. He scribbled the name on his pad. "The girls, were they together?"

"I don't think so. No, definitely not." She leaned forward, her left hand massaging her right shoulder. "Anyway, around seven thirty the doorbell rang. I was on the phone trying to figure out where she was. By the time I got there, they were pulling out of the drive." She glanced at her younger daughter. "Justine recognized the car."

"It's this kid's," the little girl said. "Lupo."

"Lupo?" Jerry wrestled the emotion out of his voice. "You sure?"

The Lupo kid was bad news. Jerry tried his best to avoid judging kids. He'd been a punk, too, at that age. The summer before senior year, a neighbor caught him stealing his chainsaw, called the cops, and Jerry found himself facing robbery charges. In exchange for a clean record, the judge, a wise older man, had sentenced him to a "work-study program."

That summer, while his buddies were out raising hell, Jerry had worked. He mowed the judge's lawn, weeded his gardens, cleaned his attic and basement, and painted the picket fence in front of the judge's rambling Dutch Colonial house. Jerry had hated every second; he'd cursed the judge and his wife for treating him like a slave. In adulthood, it occurred to Jerry the judge had probably paid his regular crew extra to clean up his mess. He'd spent his entire working life trying to repay the debt.

Antonio Lupo made Jerry look like a saint. Assault and battery, drunk and disorderly, three DUIs. Last March, the kid held up a Mobil station in Ayer—with a water pistol, it turned out—every charge dropped or dismissed. The kid's father, a labor attorney, was constantly pulling strings to get his kid out of trouble. If her daughter was tangled up with Lupo, Zoe had a heap of trouble on her hands.

"I saw the sticker on his bumper," the younger girl said.

"They just left her there, on the stoop." Zoe dropped her hands in her lap. "She was a mess. She couldn't even stand up."

He underlined the words *couldn't stand up* and closed his notepad.

He wanted to say they'd arrest the punks. That's what he'd want to hear if he were the parent. Unfortunately, dumping a drunken girl on her doorstep, however thoughtless and cruel, was not a crime. Underage drinking, he could take care of, if, *big* if, she agreed to testify against her friends in court—doubtful—or he caught Lupo drunk or with alcohol on him.

He stood, favoring his left leg. "I'd be happy to take her to the hospital. Have them check her out."

"No, really." Zoe rose. "I shouldn't have called. My mother drank." She dismissed her words with a wave. "I work with kids. I don't know. With your own it's different, I guess."

"Teenagers are tough," Jerry said. She had guts, this woman. She was a survivor. Everyone hid at times. The difference was the strong acknowledged what they were up against, and they came out of it swinging. "Glad mine are babies."

"You have children?"

"Twins," he said proudly. "Three-month-old boys."

"How sweet." This time her smile lit her eyes. "Can I get you anything? Sorry. I should've asked. Would you like a drink, Officer?"

"Jerry."

"Jerry? Tea? Coffee?"

Coffee. With Zoe Tyler. Or a glass of red wine. He pictured himself selecting a bottle from the cooler, heard the clink of glasses.

"Thanks," he said, locked in a prison of competing desires— pleasure, decency, relief. She'd had a harrowing night. He'd be taking advantage. There were spouses to think of. "Got to write up a report."

"Thank you." She touched his forearm, her fingers electric. "You're a kind man."

Or stupid, Jerry thought, and followed her to the door.

Twelve

Chase the Blues Away

He couldn't get Kyra out of his head. He heard her voice, pictured her compact body, the bounce in her step. He'd almost forgotten how it felt to be at ease with a woman, to talk without editing his words, worrying that she'd read into something he'd said, misinterpret his tone or be offended by a look he was not even aware he had made.

As he approached the hotel, the bellhop opened the door and an elegant older couple emerged, holding hands, him in a tuxedo, her in a strapless black gown, her silver hair pulled in a twist. In his future, he'd always seen Zoe beside him. Without her, life would be empty. These days, the likelihood of growing old together felt increasingly slim.

They met in Berkeley, in the spring of '88. For two years, he'd bounced from bar to bar, playing a night here, two or three there. He'd finally landed a long-term gig at one of the few bars in the Bay Area featuring folk singers. Most nights he drew an older crowd—aging hippies who wanted him to sing covers so they could pretend they were young. The gigs tired him out. That night, it was different, his connection with the audience intense, their energy feeding him.

He felt invincible.

Midway through his second set, four coeds strolled in, jabbering, took a table at the back of the bar. Now and then, one would glance at him, whisper into another girl's ear. They'd quiet down; soon, they'd be yakking again. Infuriated, he did something he'd never considered doing before—put down his guitar.

"Thanks," he said to the stunned audience. He unhooked his mike. "You've been great."

In the back alley, leaning against the bar's blemished stucco wall, smoking, he watched the crowd file out. Three years down the tubes. Maybe it was for the best. He'd been kidding himself thinking he had talent. Time to go home, find a real job, settle down.

"Excuse me? Will? That's your name, right? Will?" The girl touched his arm. "Sorry. I tried to get them to shut up."

He took a long drag on his cigarette. "They always like that?"

"Not really. Do you mind?"

He handed her the cigarette.

"Actually—" She turned to let out the smoke. "They are." They both laughed.

Will made it to the airport with time to spare. The airport was dead. In no time, he was in and out of Hertz, the rental car returned and checked in, and aboard the shuttle heading to the Delta Terminal. He set his bag on the luggage rack and took a seat by the door, closing his eyes.

On the way to the terminal, he drifted in and out of sleep.

Workdays, he was too busy to notice the jetlag; as soon as he stopped moving, it hit him, his body heavy, his muscles aching.

He felt a hand, and reached, yawning, thinking it was his wife.

"Sir." The driver nudged Will's shoulder. "This is your stop."

Groggy, Will departed the bus.

Partway down the ramp to his gate, he spotted a vending machine. He rooted in his pocket, digging for change to buy a candy bar and a Coke. With the handful of coins, he pulled out the napkin Kyra had given him. He scanned the area, searching for a trash can, and stuffed the napkin in his pocket, planning to dump it at the gate.

He found his gate, and took a seat near the podium.

Within three months of losing his job, Zoe had graduated college and they were living together in a cheap apartment on the water. She encouraged him to stick with his music. For a few months, he continued to audition. But his desire was gone. He'd lost his drive to perform. It wasn't the girls. He could handle hostile crowds. He'd begun to think vaguely about marriage. Not immediately, but in the future, when he found a job that paid well enough to support a family.

Adjusting to life outside of music was tougher than he imagined. Occasionally, he'd try his hand at writing a song, recording the lyrics in a spiral bound notebook he stashed in his underwear drawer. After he and Zoe married, he played for his family, the girls dancing around the living room, singing along. If they forgot the lyrics, they'd improvise, substituting their own words for lyrics they couldn't remember. Their lives grew fuller with work, household chores, activities for the kids. One day, he realized he hadn't played his guitar in over a year, and his notebook was gone.

Before Zoe, he'd never believed he would marry. Zoe was different from other women he'd dated. Maybe because she was curious, constantly questioning, always pushing to do more, to grow. She didn't bore him and never had. A disconnect had prompted his one, as he thought of it now, inconsequential affair. Thirteen years later, thinking about his infidelity still produced a sharp pang of guilt.

Zoe had undergone a medically necessary abortion. Afterward, she'd curled into herself. Her depression confused him. She seemed to blame herself, punishing her body as if it had failed her somehow, punishing him. He spoke with her physician. Rationally, he understood his wife's grief. On a gut level, it made no sense. If she'd allowed the baby to go to full-term, the pregnancy could have killed her, leaving two young kids without a mother and him without his wife. He tried to reach her, console her. She pushed him away.

He and the other woman had been casual friends in high school. They met by chance at Logan airport. He was headed to Boulder, she on her way home from a meeting in Boston. The plane was almost empty. When the last person had boarded, he moved to the seat beside hers. Before the plane touched down at Denver International, they'd exchanged numbers. Because their jobs required traveling, it was easy to meet.

In two months, they'd slept together a half dozen times in hotels all over the country. He was never in love. When it was over, he confessed the affair to his wife.

"I had a feeling," Zoe replied, a strange impassiveness in her voice. She'd forgiven him unconditionally, a munificence he did not deserve. The anguish in her face had torn him apart.

His plane was about to board. He pulled his cell from his briefcase and called home to let Zoe know he'd made his flight.

"Were you asleep?" he asked. His wife's voice sounded raspy.

"You didn't get my messages? I've been calling."

He squeezed his temples. His blood pressure rocketed. He'd kill the bastard who left his daughter on the stoop. "Is she all right?"

"Yes. But she needs counseling. We should all go."

"Zo?" The chink in her voice told him that she'd been fighting back tears. "You okay?"

"I'm fine," she said, eerily calm. "I'll make the appointment."

"It's late. Try to get some sleep." He'd be home by ten the next morning. "We'll get through this," he vowed, with all the conviction he was able to muster.

PART TWO

IN LEAH'S WAKE

Thirteen

Meeting Coach Thomas

In their noon session with the family counselor, Leah admitted to having quit the soccer team. Quitting at this point in the season made no sense. What was Hillary thinking? Why the hell would the coach allow her best player to quit? Leah was a kid. If she was having problems, it was up to the coach to get her on track. If Leah performed well in the playoffs, scoring her normal two or three points a game, the *Globe* All- Scholastic award was a lock. That she was tired, her feet hurt, she'd lost interest in the game—Will understood. For months, she'd devoted hours a day, every day, to soccer. If not on the field, practicing or playing, she was in the gym lifting weights. Late season exhaustion was normal. Even the pros suffered fatigue.

They were on the way home. Leah, visibly hung-over, was sitting beside Justine in the backseat of Will's BMW sedan with her eyes closed, her head propped against the window.

"It's only a few more weeks," he said. "You can hang in there."

Zoe touched his arm. "Please." The counseling session had gone well. "Let's try to maintain the momentum."

"What are you talking about?" he whispered. He'd agreed to turn the drinking and boyfriend issues over to Molly. Soccer was his department. Their daughter had worked too hard for too long to flush it all down the toilet. "She's too young to make a decision like this."

"Will?" His wife's hand fell to her lap. "Please, just wait."

Wait? They'd already waited too long. "If we'd confronted this head-on instead of procrastinating, we wouldn't be facing a crisis now."

His wife sighed and turned to the window.

"You can handle a few more weeks," he said, and gave his daughter a pep talk on the rewards of hard work, honor, and commitment. "You're not like everyone else. You're a leader. You've got to show 'em what you're made of."

To gauge her attention, he considered asking her to repeat the key points. Instead, he caught her eye in the rearview and said he'd talk to her coach. "I'll tell her you made a mistake. Everyone's entitled to a mistake, right? We just have to show her you're serious."

"Whatever." Leah stretched her neck. "She won't listen."

The door to Coach Thomas's office was closed. Through the plate-glass window, he saw her, bent over her desk, working on a game plan.

She made a notation in pencil and then erased it. A plaque designating her Coach of the Year for the Hillside League hung on the wall behind her desk. He gave her credit: she'd overcome a rough start to her tenure in Cortland. She'd come on board Leah's freshman year after a string of losing seasons. After assessing the talent, she'd decided to rebuild. The parents of the older girls were enraged. It was unfair for freshmen to get more playing time than experienced upperclassmen, they griped, and accused Hillary of favoritism. They wanted their kids on the field where college coaches would see them.

From the sidelines, Will had watched the battle unfold. Hillary made some unpopular calls, yes. In her defense, Leah was the only natural talent on the team. His daughter had a monster season that year, especially for a freshman. She'd won Cortland High MVP and made the league All-Star team. When the season ended, the disgruntled parents brought their complaints to the athletic director, demanding he fire her. The A. D., who'd admired Hillary since her days as a high school star, requested a hearing with the school committee. Hillary had surprised a lot of people, Will included, by hanging tough, refusing to be run out of town. Every year, her team had improved.

She looked up when he knocked. Gesturing, she invited him in.

Hillary was built like Leah, tall and well toned. When Will met her five years earlier at a coach's meeting—they'd both coached town teams—he'd been surprised by her youth. He'd figured her for her twenties. In fact, she'd been thirty-five, just a few years his junior.

She still looked young for her age, her complexion dewy and clear, but her eyes and mouth showed the strain of the past several years.

"Hillary." He proffered a hand. "Do you have a minute?"

"Have a seat." Hillary showed him to the chair by her desk.

On the drive over, he'd rehearsed this moment. With conflicts, it was best to be direct, get right to the point. He planned to ask outright why she'd allowed Leah to quit and what it would take to get her back on the team.

"How are you?" he asked. He hadn't seen her in a few weeks.

"Pretty well. You were away, Leah said. Trips good?"

"All right." He gestured at her plaque. "Took long enough."

She shrugged. "They spelled my name wrong the first time."

"Hillary?"

"Thomas."

"Ridiculous. Why didn't they ask if they weren't sure?"

"Good question." She glanced at the window. In the locker room, on the other side of the window, the girls were gathering for a pre-practice meeting.

"Big game Tuesday," he said. As a courtesy, because he was a former coach, as well as the father of her star player, she often showed him her game plan. "It'll be tough. Games get serious at this level."

She rotated the sheet. "We're playing Avon."

"I heard." He pulled the paper closer, scrutinizing her diagrams.

"Heavy on D. Good." Without Leah, relying on defense was her best option. "They've got that stud, Silva. Otherwise, their offense is weak. Good plan, Hill." He'd underestimated her ability to make such a facile adjustment. Still, to win big games, they had to score.

"Thanks. I hate to rush." She glanced at the window again. "Practice starts shortly. How's Leah? I assume that's why you're here."

He leaned back, crossing his legs. "She's all right."

"I'm glad. We were devastated to lose her. Puts us at a serious disadvantage."

He couldn't tell if she was making a point, letting him know his daughter had let the team down or feeling him out, trying to gauge his intentions. "If you feel that way, have her play," he said.

"If I could, I would."

"Why can't you?"

"I think you know why." The rosacea that often plagued her in games spread from her chest to her neck. "She broke an MIAA rule."

"You've got to be kidding. This is because of a *rule*?"

Someone knocked. Amy Randall, a sophomore, poked her head into the office. Hillary told the girl she'd be out shortly and asked her to have Cissy start the conditioning exercises. "Have her do fire drills first." The girl groaned, pleading for mercy. "Go on, Amy. Five minutes."

Hillary waited, presumably until the girl was out of earshot, and said, "Leah signed a pact. She knew the consequences of violating it."

"That's bullshit. And you know it." A Cross pen, a gift from the team, stood in a silver holder at the edge of her desk. He read the engraving—*Coach Thomas, 2009*—and put the pen back. "I don't get it. She's your best player. Why the hell would you do this?"

"Why would *I*? Excuse me? Your daughter quit the team, Will."

"After you sat her. She's a competitor. What did you expect?"

"I don't know. Common courtesy? Leadership?"

For Christ's sake. His daughter had devoted two years of her life to the talent-starved team. Thanks to her, Cortland High owned a winning record. Hillary was the frontrunner once again for Coach of the Year. She owed Leah for that. "Do you have any idea what this will do to her? It'll blow her chances for a scholarship."

"Look, I don't want to argue." She put the game plan in a manila folder. "It wasn't my decision. Every athlete at that party was benched. If I didn't sit her, I'd have lost my job."

Ah, the puzzle came together. "So this is about your job?"

"No, Will, this is not about my job. You want the truth? Your daughter's been a problem all year."

"All year?" He felt as if he'd been slapped. He'd attributed Leah's constant grumbling to frustrated jock talk. Whenever he'd reached the boiling point in football, he'd threatened to quit. Until college, he'd never followed through. "What do you mean 'all year'?"

"I mean she's been a problem all year." Laughter bubbled outside the window. Scowling, Hillary went to the door. "Let's go, ladies, *now*," she barked. To Will, she said, "If you think I like this, you're wrong."

"I'm sorry. I'm missing something. What exactly has she done?"

"Let's start with the fact that she missed practice last week." A redhead opened the door and attempted to ask a question. Hillary dismissed her with a wave. "She's constantly challenging me. Doesn't want to do drills. Running is a joke. I ask her to take the girls for three miles; they're back in ten minutes. What kind of message do you think that sends? Anyone else would've been gone long ago."

Will didn't want to believe her. His gut, and Leah's steady decline in performance, told him he was hearing the truth. "I'll talk to her."

"Wait." The coach held up both index fingers. "We're not done. Her slacking is disrespectful. I almost had a mutiny on my hands."

Will winced. "She's seeing a therapist." He rubbed his knuckles.

"Good," the coach said. "I'm glad to hear it."

"She's a good kid. You know that. Let her prove she deserves to be on the team. That's all I'm asking, Hill."

The coach deliberated for a long, nerve-wracking moment. "All right. If she's serious, agrees to follow the rules, we'll talk. How's that? No promises. Leah's got to want this, Will, not you."

Will nodded, relieved. Leah was a smart kid. He'd sit her down, explain the stakes. After the season, he'd have a year to work with her, help her get her head back on straight. "Thanks, Hill. I owe you."

"One more thing," she said, as he was leaving.

He turned.

"I've given her captainship to Cissy."

Leah would have a fit. "What about next year?"

"If the girls vote for her, sure. She can have it back next year."

"Fair enough. Thanks again. I'll have her stop by tomorrow."

"I'll be here," Coach Thomas replied. "Tell her I'll be waiting."

Fourteen

Sisters Redux

Coach Thomas could keep waiting. She could wait forever, for all Leah cared.

Leah laid in bed, doodling on the wall, a swish, swish, swipe of black magic marker across the pale violet paint. She couldn't believe she was grounded again. She was supposed to go to the Ani DiFranco concert tonight. Todd had surprised her with tickets.

Furious, she drew stick figures of her parents, and crossed them out. After the meeting with her coach, her father had acted all nice and understanding, pretending to listen, as if he actually cared how she felt. When she informed him and her mother she would not keep her second appointment with that dorky shrink, he'd freaked out.

"You ought to be glad I'm not as bad as other kids," she'd spat.

"I don't care about other kids," her father had shouted. "I care about you. You'll keep that appointment. Is that clear?"

Uh, no.

Leah got up and put an Oasis CD in the player.

Leah drew a tiny star, other stars circling around it. Up close, the rotating stars looked like a galaxy. From a distance, you saw an explosion.

She set the marker on her nightstand. With a pen, she drew a three-dimensional square, a theater peopled with stick figures, the kids she couldn't stand anymore, Cissy Hanson, the girls on the soccer team, on one side, her new friends, Hope and Lupo, on the other. At center stage, she drew Todd, his arms outstretched like a messiah.

"Champagne Supernova" came on, Leah's favorite song on the CD. She bobbed her head to the music. Noel Gallagher was a genius: people really did change—Cissy. Coach Thomas. Leah's parents. Her mom always used to pester Leah to share her problems, "verbalize" her feelings. Now her mother couldn't be bothered. Just the other day, she'd knocked on her parents' bedroom door. She was upset about Cissy being named captain. She'd wanted advice, wanted her mom to tell her what to do, how to handle the situation graciously. Her mother was on her computer, working on a Website to market her seminars.

"Can I talk to you for a minute?" Leah had asked, the request purposely vague, so she could determine whether her mother actually wanted to help.

"Can't you do whatever it is yourself, Leah?" her mother replied. "I'm busy right now."

If she could do it herself, she wouldn't have asked. "Sure," Leah had said. "Thanks anyway."

What did her parents think they would accomplish, cutting her off from the world, unplugging her landline, taking her cell phone, removing her computer? Did they really think isolating her would change her behavior? Convince her to go crawling back to Coach Thomas? Force her to dump Todd? Her soccer days were behind her. Period. And she had no intention of dumping Todd. She was a different person than she used to be, stronger, more independent. She refused to follow orders. Her parents might as well get used to it.

The telephone rang. On instinct, she scrambled to answer. Then she remembered, her father had taken the phone out of her room.

"Jus?" Leah tapped the wall between their bedrooms. "Who's on the phone?"

"Nobody."

"You sure?"

———⋘⋙———

Of course, Justine was sure. Why would she lie?

Justine snapped her science book shut and patted her mattress, signaling for Dog to jump up.

"Here, girl," she said, taking hold of her dog's paws. With Justine's help, the old yellow Lab hauled her hindquarters onto the bed, and wheezing, snuggled next to Justine.

Justine felt bad for her sister. Their parents were overreacting, grounding her, forcing her to see a shrink, treating her like a loser. Sure, her behavior had changed. Leah was sneaky and secretive now, and she liked different things. In the past, except for Cissy and a few other friends, soccer was all Leah cared or even thought about, really. Now she claimed to hate soccer, wanting nothing to do with her old friends.

Justine understood their parents' concern—she didn't want to see Leah hurt, either—but the changes were not all bad, as their parents believed. Certain aspects of her sister's personality had improved. Leah was starting to tell her things now, for example. Not big things, not yet; she refused to say what she and Todd did on their dates. But she told Justine she'd played hooky a few times, admitted to stealing a toe ring last time she went to the mall. Leah was testing her, trying to see if she was a snitch. Justine had not breathed a word.

Justine dialed the phone. Hope's mother answered again and Justine hung up. Hope Lansdown was bad news. She was the real reason Leah was always in trouble. Even the junior high kids knew about Hope, the wild parties at her house, her weird, disgusting mother. Supposedly, Hope's mom got the boys high and took them into her bedroom. Though Justine would never say it to Leah, her sister's friendship with Hope embarrassed her. The kids at school had started whispering. She couldn't be sure they were discussing her sister, but they shut up whenever Justine moved into their circle.

Hope made Justine so...so...so *mad.*

Justine punched Star 67, so her number wouldn't show up on caller ID, and dialed again.

Justine enjoyed pulling pranks on people. Normally, she and Holly worked as a team. They would dial a random number. When the person answered, they would ask a question such as, "Do you have Prince Albert in a can?" Riddles that had been around for decades, the same ones their parents had probably used. Sometimes when the girls were in the mood to be mean, they pretended they were calling from the IRS. "We're calling about your recent tax statement," they would say. Or, "We're calling to schedule an audit." But only when they reached an adult. Kids couldn't care less about taxes.

The phone rang...five, six, seven. Finally, someone picked up.

"Speak," said a cranky voice on the other end of the line.

"Is this Hope?"

"Who wants to know?"

"Good. Here's a hope, Hope. Hope you go to hell," Justine said, and clicked off. "Yes," Justine squealed, high-fiving herself and then Dog.

"How's that, girl? I *got* her. Leah." Justine tapped the wall between her room and her sister's. "Guess what."

"Go away," Leah said. "I'm tired."

Her sister was lying. Justine could hear the stereo blasting out of the tiny Bose speakers on top of Leah's bureau.

———◦◦———

Leah *was* tired. Tired of her life. Tired of living in this crappy house, in this crappy neighborhood, with crappy parents who didn't appreciate her. Parents who did nothing but pick, pick, pick at her all the time. Plus, her sister was a pain. Why couldn't Justine be a normal eighth grader instead of a precocious wannabe genius? Leah heard a popping noise and rolled her eyes—Justine pretending to be Buffy the Vampire Slayer again, whacking that ridiculous punching bag.

"Cut it out." Leah pounded the wall. "You're giving me a headache."

She rolled onto her back. Nearly all the phosphorescent stars she'd tacked to her ceiling had fallen. She had a half a constellation left. The Big Dipper was gone. She'd have to buy a new pack of stars next time she went to the mall. She got up, popped the Oasis CD out of the player, put in a Rage Against the Machine disc she'd borrowed from Todd.

Leah heard a weird scratching noise and turned down the music.

"I want to tell you something," Justine hollered.

"Go away, I told you."

Didn't the little geek have homework to do? Work on her science project? The project was getting way out of hand. Justine was constantly conjuring new ideas, more complicated schemata. Originally, she'd talked about constructing a papier-mâché model of the Milky Way galaxy. As far as Leah could tell, the project incorporated the whole universe now. Pictures of celestial phenomena—planets, nebulae, star clusters, red giants—photographed from every conceivable direction, cluttered her sister's desk. Amazingly, Dog hadn't destroyed anything yet. You'd think the dog would have a heyday in there when Justine was at school. Somehow, Dog had an instinct for protecting anything that belonged to Justine.

Had to be hell being Justine, always holed up in her bedroom, doing schoolwork, working on her project, or playing on the computer, her only friends their dog and the girl down the street. Holly wasn't bad. She just wasn't cool. Didn't Leah's sister get bored? Being grounded bored Leah silly. To pass time, she listened to music and doodled on her walls. Above her desk, she'd scrawled aphorisms. *F—the world. Drugs rule. Party or die.* By her bed, she'd drawn hundreds of hearts, with arrows piercing their centers.

Leah lit a stick of sandalwood incense, tapped a cigarette out of the packet on her nightstand, and went to her window. If she reached outside, she could touch the branches of the oak tree next to the house. The tree was practically bare, a few stray leaves clinging to the branches. Leah missed the robin that used to live in the boughs of the tree. Once, the robin landed on Leah's windowsill. She'd wanted to capture the bird, touch her feathers; she'd wanted to bring her inside. Leah wouldn't cage the bird the way people caged parakeets or canaries. She would fashion a nest from a shoebox. Feed her lettuce and worms. She would keep her bedroom door closed, so she couldn't escape and get lost in the house. In the end, she didn't have the heart.

Leah dragged her futon to the window and knelt on the cushion, elbows on the sill. An icy breeze blew in. Soon winter would be here. Todd had promised to teach her to snowboard this year. His stepmother owned a cabin somewhere in Maine—near Bangor, she thought. In January, when the cottage was empty, they planned to drive up. Leah couldn't wait to go. Every Christmas, she asked her parents for skis. Every year, they denied her request. A broken leg would end her precious soccer career. *Ha.* The joke was on them. Soccer was over.

She lit the cigarette, brought the butt to her lips, and inhaled deeply. Her parents would kill her if they caught her smoking. Which was also a joke. They'd already grounded her. What else could they do? Lock her in her room and throw out the key? Send her to boot camp? She wished they would. Any place would be better than here.

Not that she was worried. Her parents rarely stepped inside her room lately. Her mom had stopped making her bed. Leah dumped her dirty clothes in the laundry chute in the bathroom; a day or two later, her mother left a pile of folded clothes outside her door. Her parents had no more desire to venture into her room than she had to invite them.

A knock at the door caught her by surprise.

"Wait a sec," she called, fumbling with the screen. *Come on. Open.*

Finally, the screen popped. She snubbed her butt on the shingles, flicked it away, tugged the screen, pulling it too far inside the frame. She righted the screen as best she could, and yanked down the sash. Grabbing her perfume mister, she sprayed by the window and around her bed.

"Oh," she said, breathing hard as she opened her door. "It's only you."

———◆———

Only her? Justine's heart sank.

"You didn't have to get rid of the cigarette, you know. I wouldn't have told."

"Yeah," Leah growled. "I know."

With the heel of her bare foot, Justine pushed the door closed and hopped onto Leah's bed. Leah's room had undergone a dramatic change, the Nike poster at the foot of her bed the only memento left from before.

Leah's old soccer schedules, which she used to tape to her walls, were gone. In their place, she'd plastered the walls with posters of arrogant hip-hop artists and moody rock stars. There was a glossy picture of Sugarloaf, skiers gliding down the lush, sun-dappled mountain, a poster of a fat lady sitting on the toilet reading the paper.

Justine crossed her legs Indian style. A package of Marlboro cigarettes lay on the nightstand. Justine wondered what her sister would do if she filched one. Justine was tired of being Queen Dork. She didn't want to be a goody-two-shoes anymore. She wanted to be like her sister. Fun and exciting and brave. Leah didn't feel obliged to follow rules. She smoked in the girls' room at school, she drank and smoked marijuana, and she had a cool boyfriend, one their parents didn't approve of. Leah was her own person. She wasn't afraid to stick up for herself, give adults a piece of her mind. No one pushed Leah around. Justine was sweating profusely, her shirt glued to her back. It was time to make a stand, time to grow up. Time to earn some self-respect. *Today*, she told herself. *Today is the day.*

Justine rose, went to the window. "Is it okay if I open it?"

Leah shrugged. "Whatever."

"Leah?" Justine said, faltering. Why was she so nervous? So what if she wanted to smoke? Leah smoked. What could her sister possibly say?

"Can I ask you something?"

Leah shrugged again.

No. That's what Leah could say.

"You want me to call that kid you like? What was his name?"

Justine stood alone at the window, shaking her head.

———◈———

Justine tried Leah's patience. Leah couldn't stand when people beat around the bush. Why not just ask for what you wanted? Be direct. Justine was a baby. That was the problem.

Leah cleared her throat, a hint for Justine to hurry. "Well?"

Justine turned from the window, fanning herself. "Are you hot?"

"No. I'm not hot. Look, Justine." Leah put her hands on her hips. "If you want me to do something, ask. Okay?" She wasn't an ogre. She'd probably say yes. Unless her sister wanted help with her homework. "You're doing algebra, right? I can help with that. Science, forget it. I mean, I would, but I'm lousy at science."

Leah picked a satin camisole off the floor, held it in front of her. Violet used to be her favorite color. She would never wear purple now. Too girly. "Want to borrow something? Is that it? A shirt? You can, but my clothes are probably too big."

Justine hedged. "Could I—"

"What? Spit it out already."

"—try one of your cigarettes?"

Cigarettes? No way. Justine was a geek. Even Todd had noticed. *What,* he would ask, *is the little geek up to these days?* Or, *how's the little geek doing today?* Leah had misheard her sister's request. Justine would never smoke. She was always nagging Leah to quit. She was scared of cancer. And heart disease. And all the other diseases smoking supposedly caused. If Justine were anyone else, Leah would think this was a trap. Justine was too honest. Leah doubted the girl could tell a lie to save her own life. Can I *throw out* your cigarette, she had probably said.

"Can I have a cigarette?" Justine repeated, confident this time.

Leah swiped the pack of Marlboros from the nightstand, tucked it in her pocket. This was absurd. Leah's sister was sweet and naïve, if a little pathetic. Leah could never allow her to smoke. Sure, she'd offered a couple times, but that was only to tease. She'd never have asked had she thought Justine would say yes. Their father was wrong. Leah would never corrupt her sister. Leah had taken a different path from the road her parents had chosen. She was glad she'd gone her own way, didn't mind that she was always in trouble. She was proud of her choices. Proud of herself for being an independent thinker. Those same decisions would spell disaster for most kids, particularly an innocent girl like Justine. So what if Justine was a geek? Geekdom was good for her. In certain arenas, geeks had the advantage.

"Please?" Justine pleaded.

Leah couldn't believe this. Justine? Wanting to smoke? Yet the poor kid was so earnest. Maybe Leah should play along, let Justine see for herself why she shouldn't start smoking.

"All right," Leah said finally. She reached into her pocket, retrieved the package of cigarettes, and tapped one into her outstretched palm. "Go for it, if you want."

―――◈◈―――

Justine was a dope. No, *worse* than a dope. For thirty minutes, she'd obsessed over the idea of smoking. Wanted to prove to her sister, prove to herself, she was mature, she wasn't a baby. Naturally, the second Leah agreed to let her smoke, the urge vanished. Justine could name a hundred reasons why smoking was a lousy idea. Yet she'd made such a production, practically begging. If she chickened out now, Leah would think she was a ninny. Justine wouldn't blame her. She couldn't believe she'd gotten herself into this mess.

Leah was still offering the cigarette. It was hard to tell if she was annoyed or amused.

"Maybe this isn't such a good idea after all," Leah said, closing her fist around the butt. "Let's skip it, okay? Pretend you never asked."

"No," Justine insisted. This was her chance; she had to try. "Will you light it for me?"

―――◈◈―――

Leah did not feel at all comfortable with this idea. Lighting a cigarette for her sister. Letting a twelve-year-old smoke. Maybe their father was right. Maybe she *was* evil. He hadn't said those exact words, but that was what he meant. Yet even evil people had limits. She could not be responsible for leading her sister astray.

Justine was staring up at her.

If the little geek wanted to smoke, Leah should probably let her. Who was she to judge? She could advise Justine not to smoke;

ultimately the choice belonged to Justine. Her sister had a right to decide for herself. Besides, she'd already said yes. Only cowards went back on their word.

Leah opened the window to draw the smoke out of the room, went back to the bed, and sat beside her sister, their thighs touching.

"Watch," she said, placing the cigarette between her lips. She lit it, took a long drag, and turned the filtered end to Justine.

Justine took a tiny puff, immediately blew out the smoke.

Oh God. She's an even bigger geek than I thought. Leah couldn't help laughing.

"What?" Her sister looked wounded. "Did I do it wrong?"

"You're supposed to inhale," Leah said, forcing a straight face. "Like this." Leah took a long pull and handed the cigarette back to her sister.

Justine brought the butt to her mouth, pursing her lips, mimicking Leah. Eyes closed. Sucking hard. Suddenly, she was—

—doubled over, coughing.

Leah swooped, rescuing the cigarette before it fell and burned a hole in her rug. "Take it easy," she said, patting Justine's back. "You all right, Jus? That's it for today."

———◆◆———

Justine wanted to die. Here she was, trying to prove she was grown up, she deserved her sister's affection, her sister's respect, and what did she do? Made an idiot of herself. Throwing a coughing fit. Practically starting a fire in Leah's bedroom.

Think you're so cool, she scolded herself. *Look at you. You big stupid nerd.* She stared at her fat stubby feet, afraid to meet her sister's eyes. She knew what Leah was thinking. *Baby, baby, baby.* No wonder Leah didn't like her. Justine didn't like herself very much, either.

Finally, she gathered the courage to look up.

"Don't feel bad." Leah took hold of Justine's hand. "Same thing happened my first time."

"Really?"

"Really. You should've seen me and Cissy coughing. I almost barfed." Leah opened her arms, drew her sister into a bear hug. "Sure you're okay?" Leah asked, when they both let go.

"Sure," Justine replied. "I liked it, sort of."

Leah ruffled Justine's hair. "Liar."

Justine giggled and Leah got up, slipped a disc by the artist 50 Cent into her CD player. "The song's called 'Candy Shop.' Like it?"

Justine detested rap. The repulsive chauvinistic lyrics and violent downbeat made her feel small. On the other hand, if Leah thought rap was good, then it probably was.

Leah slid her hands through her hair, her body pulsing.

Leah was talented enough to dance professionally. Music flowed through her like waves of electricity or heat. Justine had no sense for music, no timing, no rhythm, no feel. She was all arms and feet. She stood in the center of the room, her sister dancing circles around her.

"Come on, Jus," Leah said. "Move your shoulders."

Justine's shoulders twitched.

Her sister laughed. "That's the idea. Let's try to time your moves with the music." She stopped dancing. "Listen for the boom. The first boom starts the phrase. Hear it now? One, two, three, four," she said, snapping her fingers, her arms and shoulders and hips moving as one.

She took Justine by the hand and twirled her around.

"One, two, three, four," Leah sang. "One, two, three, four."

When the CD ended, Leah said, "Could you do me a favor?"

"Sure," Justine said. *Anything.*

Leah looked Justine in the eye. "Swear to God you won't tell?"

Justine drew an *X* over her heart. "I never tell."

"I know you don't, Jus. I'm sorry." Whispering, she said, "Ani DiFranco concert tonight. If I went, would you cover for me?"

Was that it? Was that all Leah wanted?

"Sure." Cupping her hands, Justine whispered in Leah's ear.

"*Great* idea," Leah said, laughing. "I owe you, big time."

Fifteen

Not a Little Girl

After dinner, Justine clattered back up the stairs. When Leah opened her door, her sister handed her a DVD of *The Princess Bride*, snagged from the video library in the family room.

"You still like this one, don't you?" Justine asked.

Definitely, Leah said, and turned the movie over to read the credits. She loved this movie. The princess reminded Leah of herself, with her fair skin and pale blonde hair. Also—she hadn't shared this with anyone yet—Leah had been dreaming lately of becoming a bride. She glanced at Justine, lying on the bed, tiny feet crossed at the ankles, waiting for the movie to start. The wedding would be smaller than it might have been if Leah were older. Justine would be her maid of honor, of course. For attendants, that left only Hope. Todd was an only child. He would ask Lupo, and possibly Jamie, if Jamie hadn't fired him yet. She didn't know of anyone else.

Her TV sat on a small wooden table at the foot of her bed. She plugged the movie into the DVD drive, hit *play*, pulled her spare pillow from the shelf in her closet, and climbed onto the bed next to her sister, rolling the feather pillow and tucking it under her head.

Her room was warm and inviting, her mattress comfy. A patchwork quilt lay at the foot of her bed. She unfolded it, covering herself and her sister.

It might be nice to stay home with Justine. Her sister was getting a charge out of the movie, giggling, her face alight. Her sister's enthusiasm was contagious. She'd missed out on a lot, Leah thought, by dissing Justine. Staying home would keep them both out of trouble. Only, Leah couldn't stay home. Todd would never forgive her if she backed out. Also, she wanted to see the concert.

Todd and Justine had ironed out the arrangements. Todd was to wait at the end of their street, set to fly when Leah showed up. She checked the clock on her nightstand: five past seven. The concert started at eight. In ten minutes, Todd would turn onto their street.

Leah hauled herself up. "Time to get going," she whispered. She snatched her Cortland team sweatshirt from her laundry pile.

Justine rolled on her side. "Are you excited?"

Leah, nodding, brought her index finger to her lips. "Wicked," she mouthed. She zipped her sweatshirt and laced up her boots.

Bending, Leah kissed her sister's forehead. "Wish me luck."

"Want some help? With the window?'"

"I'm good. I'm a little nervous about climbing back in, though."

"When I go down to say goodnight, I'll unlock the back door."

Leah squeezed her sister's hand. "Cool, Jus. Thanks."

Belly to the sill, Leah slid under the sash and, catching hold of a hefty branch, pulled her body out the window. With her legs wrapped around the branch, she inched her way to the trunk of the tree.

So far, so good. She squatted, steadying herself. Her mistake was looking down. The drop was a good twenty feet. She thought she might vomit. Her room beckoned, awash in soft yellow light. Justine lay in bed, laughing. Leah could easily crawl back inside, tell Todd her parents had caught her sneaking out, guarded her for the night.

Only she couldn't disappoint him. He was probably at the street corner right now, waiting impatiently for her to arrive.

Do it, Leah told herself. *Don't be a baby. Just do it.*

Concentrating, ignoring the fear pounding in her skull, she dropped her right leg, her foot feeling for the next lower branch.

The branch. Her foot sliced the air. *Where was the branch?*

Finally, she hit something solid. She dropped her left foot and slowly lowered her body.

At last, she reached the split in the trunk just above the bole.

She set her foot in the *Y* and leaned back, breathing hard. Perched on a low branch, five or six feet above ground, she could see her mother in the family room, curled on a chair by the fireplace, reading. Her father lay on the sofa watching TV. A commercial came on; her father, rising, peered at the window.

Breathing hard, she pressed her spine to the trunk. *Please don't let him see me.*

Her mother said something. And her father moved toward the kitchen. Leah let out a breath. *If you're up there, God, thank you.* She scanned the yard, searching for a safe place to land. *One,* she counted. *Two.* On three, gritting her teeth, she jumped.

From the foot of the tree, she monitored the movement inside the house, waiting for the right moment to split. Her father strolled back to the family room, a glass of white wine in one hand, a beer in the other. He set the glass on the coffee table, his back to the window. *Run for it. Now.*

Leah sprung out of her crouch, dashed across the lawn, her head down, arms pumping, toward the woods at the edge of their property.

Safely under cover, she paused to catch her breath, and then walked down the street, hugging the curb. Midway down the block, she spotted Todd's jeep and sped up to a jog.

"You made it," he said, leaning across the seat to kiss her.

———

Jerry was on duty tonight. He'd agreed to cover for Larry Hollingshead, who'd come down with the flu. He backed the Explorer into the vacant lot at the intersection of Blanchard and Old Orchard Road. Lately, Jerry often found himself parking here, in the spot where he'd been parked the afternoon Zoe Tyler's Volvo whizzed by. Coming here, Jerry told himself, had nothing to do with Zoe Tyler. Old Orchard was a treacherous road, flanked by towering oak and maple trees. People drove as if the sparsely populated road were a freeway, gathering speed as they sailed downhill.

A few years earlier, a souped-up T-bird, carrying four teenage boys, spun out of control and crashed into the oak tree at the foot of the hill. Three boys died on impact. A fourth boy was trapped in the backseat, crying, pounding on the window. When Jerry arrived, two men were struggling to open the jammed door. The T-bird had caught fire. Jerry, shouting, gesturing, ordered them back. He was ten steps away when the T-bird exploded. For months, he'd had nightmares. He'd wake, drenched in sweat, cursing his incompetence for having let the boy die.

Friends of the dead boys nailed a cross festooned with carnations to the base of the tree, a shrine whose implications were lost on the kids who'd left them. For a month, the kids paid attention, drove slowly; soon they were speeding again. This time of year, the road slick under a blanket of leaves, speeding was deadly. *That* was why he was here.

Yet, even as he sat here, certain parking in this particular spot was unrelated to Zoe Tyler, he saw her—green eyes and olive skin, her bewildering smile—and his imagination tormented him with images of the two of them in New Hampshire or Vermont, engaged in some strenuous activity: hiking, riding a bike, climbing a mountain. In his fantasy, she wore shorts and a tank top, and he watched from behind, her hamstrings straining against the exertion, shoulders glistening, her hair pulled up, exposing the graceful curve of her neck.

Jerry blinked the image away. His wife and sons needed him and he loved them. Eventually, Maura's energy and zest for life would return. Until then, he had to be patient. He owed as much to his wife.

To kill time, he ran the tags on vehicles that went by. He recognized most of them already. A white Jetta rounded the corner, sputtered uphill. Maggie Whitefield, nineteen, sensible kid, judging from her cautiousness in the car. Black Honda Civic: Wayne Wilson, head of janitorial services for the high school. Dodge Caravan, blue: Rhoda McCabe, retired, self-appointed Cortland historian.

A purple Taurus blew by. Jerry switched on his siren and lights.

Leah snapped her fingers, bobbing her head.

"*Ani,*" they shouted, a whorl of hands and hips and feet. "*Ani.*" The audience impatient. Opening act come and gone, a reggae recording pounding out of the speakers. "*...Ani...Ani.*"

Leah's shoulders pulsed, her body rocking to the rumbling noise. "*Ani...*" Suddenly, the canned music died. Matches flickered.

Leah reached for the stage, the tips of her fingers barely visible. As a roadie adjusted a speaker, Todd handed Leah the joint. Exploding lights washed the stage in a rainbow of color.

From the wings, Ani appeared...*there she is*...a tiny girl, in tan chinos and a plaid flannel shirt, dwarfed by a giant guitar.

An eerie quiet descended.

Ani stared into the audience, the sea of faces willing her on...

"*Ani,*" someone shouted. "*Ani,*" the crowd joined in. "*Ani, Ani.*"

She tipped her head, gazing up at the lights.

The elf-girl threw her head forward and back, and plunged into her song, the energy real and sizzling and raw.

Pausing, mid-song, she ripped off the flannel shirt, stripping to a snug black camisole, her shoulders sinewy, lithe...tuned her guitar and then she was playing again, her presence expanding. Music flowed from the core of her body, filling the stage, the arena...now Leah was on her feet, a raindrop in this raging river of music.

She took the joint, sucked hard, handed it back...

...up, up, up the notes rose...

Todd propped his feet on the back of an empty seat. Leah squeezed his hand. "Can you feel it?" she asked. "Can you feel it?"

He rolled another joint...pulled her to him...the notes full and strong and real, reaching into the depths of her body...she felt his tongue in her ear...his hand on her thigh. And now she was up there, too, on the stage. She climbed onto her chair, pulled him up with her...her body swaying in the swirl of sound and color and light...

"Oh, my God," Leah said. "She was *amazing*."

Todd, holding her hand, led her across the lot behind the arena, where he'd parked the truck. The temperature had dropped, the sharp wind chafing her face. She should have worn a jacket. Her lightweight sweatshirt provided little protection against the elements. Normally, she'd be frozen. Tonight, she was not the slightest bit cold.

Leaving the arena, he'd asked if she'd enjoyed the concert. She'd replied with a terse nod, unwilling to release the music whirling in her head. Now, as they approached the jeep, she was ready to talk.

"Oh, my God. Wasn't she, like, incredible on guitar?"

Todd smiled a noncommittal response. He rooted through his pocket, digging for the keys.

She wished she'd taken him up on his offer to buy her a CD. In the concourse, they'd stopped at a table displaying Ani's recordings, her latest as well as the older records, all of which Ani had produced herself under her Righteous Babe label. Leah was dying to hear the recorded version of the songs Ani had played. Also, it would have been nice to add an older disc to her collection. But she'd felt uncomfortable accepting a CD after Todd had spent so much on the tickets.

The lot was a nasty tangle, vehicles battling to get to the exits. Todd swore under his breath and pushed a jazz CD into the deck.

As they inched toward the exit, an awesome idea popped into her head. She and Todd could form a band, a boyfriend and girlfriend or a husband and wife team, like Jack and Meg White or John and Christine McVie. Or maybe she'd go solo like Ani and hire Todd to manage her act. According to the bio on her Website, Ani had left home when she was Leah's age, moved to New York, lived with friends. If Ani could be a huge success after all she'd been through, there was no reason why Leah couldn't be a star, too. She strummed her air guitar. She would give anything to play as well as Ani DiFranco. She wondered how long it would take to learn.

"Todd? Think you could teach me to play? You know. Guitar?"

"Sure. You can use my old guitar, if you want."

She pictured herself on stage, performing before a packed house for her adoring fans. "Think I could ever be as good as her?"

"Who?" he asked, appearing perplexed.

"Ani. If you taught me, I mean."

Todd's eyebrows curled in dissent. "Don't get me wrong. She's got great energy and all. But her guitar playing's kind of simplistic."

Ani DiFranco—simplistic? Leah shifted sideways, scooting away from her boyfriend. He probably thought the noise he'd put on was good. "Vital Transformation," he said it was called, by some weird seventies band, Mahavishnu Orchestra. Who named a song "Vital Transformation"? Her boyfriend seriously annoyed her at times. He fancied himself this big music expert just because his father had worked for Rounder Records for a few years. He didn't even *know* his father. Leah wagged her foot. Obviously, Todd wasn't all that smart if he didn't appreciate the brilliance of a talented musician like Ani. *She*, on the other hand, knew good music when she heard it.

"I think she was wasted," Leah said, once her anger abated and she felt somewhat amorous toward him again. "She seem it to you?"

Todd grunted and hit his blinker, signaling left.

"She was totally wired. She used to do acid, you know."

"Actually, babe, I was paying more attention to you."

Leah pecked her boyfriend on the cheek. "I loved the concert," she said. "It's so cool you got the tickets."

Todd grinned. "Look at this traffic," he said, gesturing at the parade of taillights.

Route 2 was a long, dark stretch of tarmac. The road of tears, her mother called it. The jeep's headlights caught the heads and arms of the makeshift crosses lining the grass alongside the shoulder. Leah wondered aloud who they belonged to and Todd told her a story about a friend of a friend, drag racing on Route 2.

"It's up here," Todd said, pointing to a small wooden cross nailed to the stump of a tree.

When they reached 495, Leah's boyfriend picked up the pace.

Sixteen

The Arrest

Jerry was sitting in the lot with his window rolled down, listening to the wind sweep through the trees and enjoying the crisp night air on his face when Corbett's truck careened around the bend. The jeep was traveling erratically, one minute skidding along the shoulder, the next nosing over the center. Corbett had to be drunk or on drugs. The last thing the Cortland PD needed was some punk townie, on probation for dealing, back on the scene.

A head bobbed on the passenger side. So Corbett wasn't alone. Antonio Lupo, no doubt, Corbett's sidekick. Lupo scared the hell out of Jerry. The Corbett kid had a conscience. When the El Paso cops arrested him, Corbett had bawled, or so he'd heard. The Lupo kid, on the other hand, was like the coyotes. Over the last ten years, land development had driven the coyotes out of their native habitat. At first, they'd lurked at the edge of the woods. Now they slunk through neighborhoods in broad daylight, brazen and fearless. Unless they were rabid or posed a clear threat to human life, there wasn't much you could do but chase them away. Like Lupo, they were protected.

Jerry switched on the strobes, light bouncing off the truck. Finally, Corbett pulled over. Jerry eased onto the shoulder behind him.

The wind cut across the cruiser as he opened the door. His sciatica was bothering him again. Pain shot down his leg. When the wind died down, he stepped tentatively out of the truck and onto the road. He shook his right leg, wincing, and turned on the flashlight.

While he waited for Corbett to produce his license and registration, Jerry shined the flashlight around the inside of the truck, checking for contraband. The cab was littered with paper, candy wrappers, empty cigarette packs. If he looked, he'd probably find wads of chewing gum tacked to the underside of the seats. He worked his way across the rear bench, over the seats, to the front of the truck.

The passenger shrank away, shielding his eyes. *Her* eyes. Jesus. She wore a blue sweatshirt, her lower body covered by a blanket. What was wrong with parents today? Jerry would cuff his daughter to her bed before he'd allow her to go out with a hoodlum like Corbett.

"Open it." Jerry flashed his light on the glove compartment.

"Nothin' in there," Corbett grumbled.

"Yeah, sure. So humor me then."

"There's nothin' in there," Corbett said, pulling it open.

"Is there a problem, Officer? If not, we'd like to get going."

He recognized the voice. *The Tyler girl.* She sounded just like her mother. Maybe he should spare Zoe the embarrassment, let the kids off with a warning, making it clear he intended to watch their every move. In the long run, letting them off would do more harm than good.

Somebody needed to set this girl straight, before she hurt herself or did something stupid. A good scare might wise her up.

"Can't detain us without reason." She clapped the door shut.

The little smartass was right. He couldn't hold them without justifiable cause. Jerry ignored her. No law against bluffing. "Out of the car," he ordered. "Both of you." An open beer can or a few twigs of marijuana would be enough to haul these two down to the station.

Jerry reached for the handle on the driver's door. "Today."

"Coming," Corbett growled. "Gimme a minute."

Arresting teenagers depressed him. Kids that age ought to be home under the protective wing of their parents. They were too young to put their lives and future at risk. They had no conception of consequences. Jerry's back ached. He should have told Hollingshead to find someone else to cover for him tonight, begged off, claimed he was needed at home. A coyote howled a desolate cry.

On nights like this, he hated being a cop.

Wind lashed the jeep, the cab vibrating. Peering inside to see what was taking so long, Jerry caught Corbett with his ass lifted, zippering his jeans. *Christ.* That was why she was under a blanket. As Corbett climbed out, he saw the Tyler girl kick a can under the seat.

———◦◦———

Leah sat beside Todd in the backseat of the cruiser, arms crossed indignantly. Officer Johnson—she remembered him now. He'd given safety presentations at her elementary school. One stupid joint and he'd found it. He'd seen her accidentally kick the Coke can under the seat, giving him "reason" to search.

Fine, she'd thought. *Go for it.*

He'd found nothing in the truck. There was nothing to find. Leah could tell he felt bad for harassing them. She was all set to accept his apology when he decided to pat them down. Todd was clean. They'd smoked everything they'd brought, except for one teensy joint he'd given her to smoke before bed. She'd forgotten all about it.

The cop didn't force her to spread her legs or anything, but he made her empty her pockets. Still, he wouldn't have found the joint if he hadn't insisted she turn her pockets inside out. She tried to divert his attention, planning to dump it. The cop was a bloodhound.

He radioed ahead, told his dispatcher to expect them shortly.

The cop would not get away with this. It was illegal to search people without a warrant. It was called entrapment or something. She couldn't wait to tell her father he'd tricked them. Her father would hire a good lawyer, and get *Officer Johnson* kicked off the force.

The whole experience was surreal. She'd had an awesome night. She'd seen Ani DiFranco! Now this? She wondered if her parents knew she'd snuck out of the house. She hadn't seen them since breakfast. If they'd gone to her room to check on her, kiss her goodnight, they'd have noticed her empty bed. Which meant they knew.

Relax. They wouldn't have bothered.

Worse than her parents killing her, her name would appear in the police log, and everybody would know she'd been arrested. Sweet. One more thing for the jerks in this ridiculous town to gossip about.

His laptop blinked. Once, she and Hope had seen a patrol car parked near the store where Todd worked, the cop playing video games on his laptop. She wondered if that were standard procedure.

There had to be a way out of this mess. Searching for a way to open a conversation, she spotted a photo taped to the dashboard. "Are those your kids?" she asked sweetly.

"Yep."

Great. One word response. "Adorable. How old are they?"

"Three months."

Don't give up, she told herself. *He'll come around.* "Boys or girls?"

"Boys," he answered, and raised the volume on his CB.

Murder One. She could see the headlines already. Irate father hacks rebellious teenager to death. Fine, so her parents might not kill her. But they *would* ground her for life, a fate worse than death as far as she was concerned. This was all Todd's fault. How could he do this to her? If he hadn't brought the weed, they wouldn't have smoked, she would not have been giving him head, and he would not have been driving like an idiot. And the stupid cop would not have pulled them over. Swear to God, if she managed to get out of this, Todd was history. She planned to break this relationship off.

Please God, she prayed. *I'll be good. So good, you won't even recognize me.* She would dump Todd. She'd play soccer again. It was too late for this year, but she'd talk to Coach Thomas anyway. She'd respect her parents. She'd help at home, earn better grades in school. And. And. *I'll start going to church.* Every week. Whether she felt like it or not. She folded her hands in her lap and sat back, closing her eyes, waiting for God to perform one of His miracles.

Fifteen seconds elapsed. Twenty. Twenty-five. Her stomach was on fire. She'd probably developed an ulcer already. If she cried, maybe the cop would take pity on her. Release her right here. She'd walk home, if necessary. Tears burned hot and raw in her throat.

Grow up. She toyed with her button bracelet. *Don't be a baby.*

Face it: this wasn't Todd's fault. She was the one who'd begged him to bring weed. What fun was a concert if you didn't get wasted? Why was she worried? She was totally overreacting. So the cop found a joint. What could he do? Send her to jail? For possession of a joint? She'd never so much as looked cross-eyed at a cop, let alone broken the law. If she didn't live in such a backward state, she wouldn't even be in this predicament. In California, marijuana was legal. For medicinal reasons, but still. They were bound to legalize it for general use soon. Another reason to move there. California had sensible laws.

At the head of the rotary in the town center, the cop slowed. Leaves swirled across the great lawn. The whole town appeared to be sleeping, the lights out in the shop fronts, the only illumination cast by the streetlamps. A ten-speed bike, chained to a banister, stood on the porch of a battered Victorian, a rooming house now.

The cruiser rounded the rotary and turned onto East Main Street.

A cellar light was on in Cooper's Funeral Parlor, just outside the center; the undertaker was probably preparing a body. Too bad she wasn't on the slab. Better that than the misery of seeing her parents.

She laid her hand on Todd's thigh. The thought of dying freaked her out. She needed contact with the physical world, to touch someone *real*. After death, it sometimes took a while for the mind to catch up to the body. She wanted to be sure she was alive. Her heart slammed into her throat. She was alive, all right. In the backseat of a cruiser. About to be booked on drug charges.

Please let her be dreaming.

You'd think her boyfriend would hold her hand, provide a teeny bit of solace. Oh, no, he just sat there, comatose. She poked his thigh.

Come to think of it, he hadn't said a word since the cop discovered their weed. She couldn't imagine why Todd would be worried. His mother couldn't care less what he did. He could rob a bank and shoot all the tellers; if he said he was innocent, his mother would believe him. His mother bought any lie that was reasonably plausible.

Oh, no. Oh, my God. She wrapped both hands around his forearm, the realization suddenly hitting her. *His probation.*

"Don't worry," Todd whispered, "everything's cool."

The cop eased the cruiser into an empty spot close to the station's entrance. The concrete structure reminded her of the boarding school in *Jane Eyre.* Although the outward appearance was different, the building was every bit as depressing. It was easy to imagine cruel prison guards depriving their inmates of decent clothing and food.

Officer Johnson guided Leah and Todd toward the entrance, his hands on their shoulders. Leah hugged her chest. She hadn't noticed how bitter the night was. Or how dark.

When they reached the double glass doors, the cop cut in front of them and held the door open, a gust of wind swelling his jacket.

Leah stepped inside, squinting against the harsh prison light. She wondered how long it would be until her parents arrived. If her father had his way, he'd let her stay here and rot. Todd had spent the night in jail after his first arrest. In the morning, his mom flew down and posted his bail. Wasn't too bad, he'd told Leah. The cops were okay once he answered their questions. The cot was lumpy, so he'd had trouble falling asleep. And prison food sucked. Otherwise, he had no major complaints. He'd slept in worse places, he'd told her.

The cop led them to the reception area, and disappeared.

Leah stood beside Todd, before a wide, bulletproof window. Computers surrounded the desk behind the window, the displays blinking. She could hear muffled voices. Odd, no one was back there.

Flyers for a benefit basketball game lay in a bin on the metal shelf in front of the glass. Another bin contained applications for firearm and motorbike permits. Leah shivered. *If only I were here for a permit.*

She folded her hands, lacing her fingers to keep from shaking. In a back room, people were talking, probably deciding which charges to press. She ached to hold her boyfriend's hand, feel the comforting weight of his arm on her shoulders. Only she was too scared to move.

"Don't worry," Todd whispered again. "It'll be okay. I promise." Leah stared at her shoes, shifting her weight from foot to foot.

When she looked up, a towering black woman was looking down at her, glowering. According to an article in the *Globe*, the prison matrons in Boston searched the body cavities of girls the cops arrested. Leah had never heard of any strip searches in Cortland, but that was hardly something the cops would advertise. A wave of nausea swept over her. She'd been arrested for possession. What if they thought she was hiding other drugs? If they decided to conduct a body search? No way would Leah strip for this horrible female cop.

Thick glasses magnified a pair of fearsome brown eyes. "Name," the woman demanded.

"L-Leah," Leah stammered.

"Full name please."

"Tyler."

"Could you speak up?" The matron stopped typing. "Can't hear you, honey."

"Tyler," Leah repeated. "Leah Tyler."

While they awaited booking, the matron recorded their credentials. "L-e-a-h?" she said, punching Leah's name into the computer.

Officer Johnson reappeared a few minutes later, accompanied by an older guy, a former athlete, Leah thought, with a bulbous nose and beetle black eyes. The Chief of Police. She recognized him from photos in the *Gazette*. Officer Johnson opened the door to the inner office and spoke to the matron. The chief, wheezing, cupped Todd's elbow.

"Let's go," he said, and escorted Leah's boyfriend away.

"Wait," Leah cried, as Todd disappeared around the corner.

"They just have some questions for him," the matron told her. "They're sending you home, honey."

Leah burrowed into the sleeves of her sweatshirt. "What are they going to do to him?"

The matron stepped down to the reception area. "Officer Johnson called your folks. We've got a room in back. You can wait there."

"Will they keep him?" Leah pressed. For violating his probation, she wanted to say. But she kept her mouth shut. For all she knew, the Cortland police were in the dark regarding his last arrest. "Ma'am?" "Can't tell you that, honey." She was only the dispatcher. "It's not my place to say."

Leah followed the older woman down a long corridor, their footsteps echoing through the cavernous hall, to a dank room no bigger than Leah's bedroom, lit by a rectangular fluorescent light. A round table sat in the center of the room surrounded by six rigid plastic chairs. A filing cabinet, pushed against the left wall, was stacked with newspapers.

On a metal desk at the back of the room, a computer idled, its low hum like the buzzing drill of a woodpecker.

"Here you go." The matron pulled a chair away from the table. "Shouldn't be too long."

Leah slumped into the chair. "What's gonna happen to me?"

The matron lowered herself onto a seat and clasped Leah's hands. She smelled of honey and almonds, her scent warm, reassuring. "Officer Johnson? Trust me. He's a good guy."

Leah's heart beat in her throat. "My parents are gonna kill me."

"Well, I'd be steamed, too, if I was your mamma. But they'll get over it. They're your folks, right? They love you. I got kids myself, honey. Believe me, I know." The matron squeezed Leah's shoulder. "I'm Millie," she said. "Need anything, you come get me. You hear?"

Seventeen

All a Big Lie

The telephone jerked Zoe out of a deep sleep.

"Oh, God." She clapped her mouth. "Is she all right? What happened?" *Impossible.* "She's here," Zoe argued, knowing even as she spewed the words that she was deluding herself. "She's in bed."

She listened for a few minutes, trying to wrap her head around the arrest, sorting details, and hung up the phone. Will was sitting at the foot of their bed in an undershirt and jeans. He pulled on a Grateful Dead tee-shirt, Jerry Garcia's face in living color on the chest.

"Will. *Please.* That shirt. They'll think we're white trash."

"What the hell do you want me to wear?" He yanked the shirt over his head. "A tux?"

"Slacks and a sweater," she snapped, "will be fine."

He flung the tee-shirt on the bed and tramped to their closet.

She heard a clunk followed by cascading thuds, as if an entire shelf had come down. Flinching, she worked her nylons over her hips, pulled on a skirt, and went to the bathroom to brush her teeth.

Stay calm. We haven't heard the whole story, she reminded herself. The police had decided to release their daughter for a reason.

"If I see that Corbett," her husband ranted, jerking her to. He stood in the doorway, waving his socks. "I'll kill the son of a bitch."

She spat her mouthwash in the sink. "You just about ready? We've got to go."

"When I'm done with him, he'll wish he never met this family."

"Please. Stop." She fished the antacids from the medicine cabinet. "I told you"—she handed him the roll—"they're not pressing charges."

"I've had it with this shit. We're done pandering to her."

"Damn it, Will. You think I like this any better than you?"

He stomped to the tub. "I'll call Delaney in the morning," he said, pulling on his socks. "At least he won't screw us."

"We don't need a lawyer. Officer Johnson said—"

"Johnson? Isn't that the guy who responded to the nine-one-one call?"

She nodded. Her husband was trying her patience.

"And the warning?"

She smiled indulgently.

"What's the guy, stalking us?"

"Oh, for Pete's sake. Don't be absurd." She nabbed her keys.

Zoe inched Justine's door open and crept into the room.

Justine lay across the bed, bathed in moonlight, one arm draped over the dog, the bedclothes in a bunch at her feet. Zoe set her hand on Justine's forehead. Her daughter's hair was damp. "Be back shortly, sweetie," she whispered and kissed the top of her head.

Dog opened her rheumy eyes and peered up at Zoe. "Good girl," Zoe said, ruffling the dog's ears. "You take care of her, Dog."

Dog nuzzled Justine's chest. Groaning, Justine rolled onto her belly.

On her way out the door, Zoe set the burglar alarm.

In the garage, she nearly tripped over the box of clothes designated for Goodwill. Two weeks ago, she'd asked Leah if she would like to add anything. She was still waiting for Leah's contribution. How had the situation with their daughter come to this? How had they raised such an irresponsible kid? Leah rarely followed through on anything. She'd quit playing soccer right when her team needed her most. Skipped school. Managed, God knew how, to be arrested tonight. Nothing worked with her. Reasoning was useless. Zoe could beg, scream, threaten, cajole. Her pleas fell on deaf ears. Worse, Leah would agree—*sure, Mom, you're right*—and then do as she pleased.

A year ago, if someone had predicted a call from the police, their daughter arrested for drug possession, Zoe would have scoffed. *You're out of your mind*, she'd have said. Yet here they were. Leah had been lucky this time. Colleges looked poorly upon applicants with a criminal record. If the acting out continued, she'd destroy her future. They had to find a way to reach their daughter, get her on track.

Only, how?

---⟨⊕⟩---

Will pressed the button on his visor, ducking instinctively as he backed out of the garage. A garage door had hit him once at their old place in Hudson. The door nicked his shoulder, knocking him off balance. He'd fallen backward, his head missing the steel beam by an inch, a tricycle breaking his fall. The door snapped shut. He adjusted the mirrors, backed into the turnaround, and headed up the drive.

"Warm enough?" He spiked the temperature to seventy-five.

"Fine," his wife replied, "thanks," and flipped up the vents.

This situation with Leah was driving him crazy. That one of his children might someday be arrested had never crossed Will's mind. Cortland was supposed to be safe. He'd paid fifty grand extra for a house in this town so their kids would be shielded from trouble.

On the drive to the police station, he tried to regain control of his emotions. It was embarrassing enough that his daughter had been arrested. No need to make a fool of himself, too. When Leah was a toddler, his mother, among the most levelheaded people on the planet, told him that childrearing was a bittersweet enterprise.

"Your children will bring you the greatest joy in your life," she'd said. "And they'll break your heart. You've got to accept the good *and* the bad."

He'd listened and done his best to put her advice into practice. When Leah was in eighth grade, Judy Hanson had caught the girls sneaking cigarettes behind the bushes in her backyard. He and Zoe had sat Leah down, explained the dangers of smoking, exacted a firm promise from her to quit. In October, when she refused to study for the SAT test, he'd allowed her to put the test off until spring. Even the soccer fiasco he'd managed to rationalize and accept. An outsider messing with his daughter's mind? Screwing with her life? Sorry. Not on his shift.

"What do you think?" he asked, as they pulled into the station. "How do we handle this?"

"I think we need to hear her out," his wife said quietly.

He withdrew the key from the ignition. "Figures you'd say that."

---⟨⊕⟩---

Leah had a sick feeling the police had discovered Todd's criminal record. If so, they'd probably transport him to the maximum security prison at MCI Concord. She didn't know what she'd do in that case. This was all her fault. She hated herself.

A door opened and closed and she heard her parents' voices. The jig was up. Maybe she ought to confess. Tell the truth—about everything this time. Skipping school. That she'd tried Ecstasy once. That occasionally, her friends smoked meth. If her parents forgave her, she'd do everything in her power to live up to their expectations. She'd take up where she left off last week, only this time she would do better. Work harder in school, help more at home. Study, *honestly* study, for the SATs, take every practice test in the program. She couldn't live this way, constantly at odds with her parents. If they would give her one last chance, she'd prove that she could be trusted.

They were headed this way, the volume of their conversation increasing. She recognized the measured click of her mother's heels, the impatient squeal of her father's leather-soled loafers. The third set of footsteps belonged to Officer Johnson. Any second, they would be here.

Leah felt naked, exposed. If only she had somewhere to hide. She covered her face, pressing her knees together, hugging her chest.

Leah felt a hand on her shoulder, caught a whiff of her mother's perfume. She looked up through splayed fingers. Her mom met Leah's eyes briefly, and took the seat next to her. Officer Johnson, acknowledging Leah's presence, slid onto the seat beside her mother. Her father stood with his arms crossed, refusing to meet Leah's gaze.

Officer Johnson cleared his throat. "Leah?" Three sets of eyes converged on her. "Want to tell your parents what happened?"

"Don't they know?" she stammered.

Her mom coughed, covering her mouth. "We'd like to hear it in your own words, Leah."

"You can start with why you snuck out," her father interjected.

Her mother shot her father an exasperated look. The cop cleared his throat again. Leah wondered if he was coming down with the flu. Maybe she should warn her mother to sit farther away.

Her mom touched Leah's arm. "Tell us what happened, honey."

Leah tucked her hands in the sleeves of her sweatshirt. She wanted to tell her mother the truth, but she didn't know where to begin. The words caught in her throat. Instead, she stared at the table, studying the scratches in its scarred wooden top, chewing her lower lip.

In her peripheral vision, she saw her father cast a withering eye at the door. For one irrational instant, she thought he would leave. Her heart leapt. Then she realized he was gathering momentum.

"She's sixteen, for God's sake. I want that asshole in jail."

Jail? "Mom?" Leah said, expecting an ally against such outrage.

"As long as possible," her father growled. "Let him rot in there."

Rot? Her father was nuts. Leah burst out of her seat.

Her mother snagged Leah's wrist as she attempted to flee, and turned to Officer Johnson. "My husband and I are exhausted," she said. "We never expected this." Shifting her attention to Leah, she said, "The truth, Leah. Were you smoking marijuana?"

"For God's sake." Her father's blistering eyes lit on her. "Of course she was."

"Sir," Officer Johnson said, "if you don't mind me saying—" To his credit, he ignored her father's rage. "We're all set." He stood, his face flushed. "Why don't you go on home?"

Pressing her hands to the table like an old woman, Leah's mother pushed herself out of her chair. "Thank you," she said, extending her hand to Officer Johnson. "We appreciate this."

"Your daughter's got herself tangled up with the wrong people," Officer Johnson said. He glanced at Leah, as if to say, *you know who I'm talking about.* Lupo, she figured he meant. Officer Johnson ushered them out of the interview room, he and her mom walking ahead, her father following at a clipped pace, Leah lagging behind.

"By the way," the cop said, before they left. "Your boyfriend told us the truth."

Her father slammed his car door. "That kid's bad news."

"That's so unfair," Leah complained. "It wasn't his fault."

Her mother stretched her arm across the back of her seat. "You've had your chance to talk, Miss. Now it's our turn."

Slouching, Leah stared at the window, a black hole opening into a vast, empty universe. She fidgeted with the buttons on her door. *Blah, blah, weed*, her father said. *Blah, blah, disappointing. Blah, blah, Todd.* Was her father a moron? Covering for her was the coolest thing, *ever*. Her boyfriend could end up in jail because of her. She imagined herself as the loyal girlfriend, trekking to the prison with a razorblade, or grapefruit spoon, or paring knife baked into a cake.

Her father was still harping on Todd when he pulled in the drive. He slapped the steering wheel. "I can't believe this."

Can't believe this. Cannot believe that. How many times did he plan to repeat himself? Every shred of remorse Leah felt earlier had vanished. Her parents were disappointed. Too bad. She was disappointed, too. In them. How they treated her. How they shat all over her boyfriend.

She was sick of hearing how she'd hurt them, what a crappy daughter she was. She had more important things on her mind—such as determining what had happened to Todd.

"We'll look for a new therapist," her mom said. "One you like."

Leah rolled her eyes.

Her father hit the button on his visor, ducking as the garage door rumbled up. Ordinarily, he pulled in and out of the garage three or four times, aligning the car perfectly, parking far enough from the wall so that you could open the doors without scratching the paint. Tonight he shot inside, the tires screeching, and cut the engine.

Leah kneed her door open, carefully avoiding the wall.

"Hold it," her father barked. "It's about time you apologized."

Apologized? Was he out of his mind? The whole way home, he'd attacked her, attacked her boyfriend. She'd never apologize now.

"Your father's right," her mom said. "You owe us an apology."

"And by the way," her father snapped. "It's over."

Over? Leah must have missed a link. "What's over?"

"Have you paid any attention at all to us? Tell her, Zoe."

Her mother twisted toward the back seat, her face drained. "He's not good for you. It's an unhealthy relationship. You need to end it."

Her father's eyes flashed in the rearview mirror. "I see that kid anywhere near you, I swear to God, I'll—"

Kill him? Not if he kills you first.

"Leah?" her mother interrupted. "You're not saying anything."

"What's *wrong* with you two? The 'kid' stuck up for me. He could end up in jail. You *owe* him. You ought to be kissing his ass."

Her father snorted. "That guy's a piece of shit."

"Shut *up*," Leah cried.

"Stop," her mother pleaded. "Both of you."

"If not for that asshole, none of this would've happened."

This is it, Leah thought. She wanted nothing more to do with her parents. They made her sick. She rammed the car door open.

"Goddamn it, Leah Marie. What the hell—"

"What?" Leah sneered. "Your door?"

"Apologize," he ordered. "Now."

She squeezed between the seats. "Come on," she taunted, jabbing her check. "Hit me. You know you want to."

Her father stared at her hard, and looked away.

Leah jerked backward. "You pathetic *fuck*," she hissed, booting his seat. Then she scooted out of the car, her parents gaping at her in shock.

Eighteen

The Blame Game

At dawn, Justine heard her sister moving around and got up. Their father's nylon duffel bag lay on Leah's bed. Leah was dressed in her nightclothes, a blue tank top, and flannel Teddy Bear bottoms. She tossed a tee-shirt and a pair of jeans on her bed. She looked exhausted, purple moons under her eyes, her cheeks pale.

"Hey," Justine said, trying not to worry. "Was the concert fun?"

Leah stuffed the tee-shirt and jeans in her bag. "It was awesome," she replied, without looking up. She slogged to her bureau, rooted through the top drawer, dug out a lacy black thong and matching bra.

"I'm out of here," she said, stuffing the panties and bra in the bag. "I'm not sure where I'm going. I don't care. As long as it's not here."

Justine's heart sank. Last night, after Leah left, she'd tiptoed to her own room, surfed the Internet until the movie ended. She'd found a great astronomy site packed with information she could use for her project. At nine thirty, she'd gone downstairs and kissed her parents goodnight, exactly as planned. Their parents had seemed a little distracted, not at all suspicious. "I didn't say anything. Honest."

Leah pulled a white tee-shirt from the laundry pile on her floor, sniffed, and tossed it back on the pile. "It's not your fault, Jus."

"Lee?" Justine twiddled the hem of her pajamas. "Don't go."

"I'm sorry, Jus." Leah squeezed Justine's hand. "You'll be okay." Leah eyed Dog on the floor by Justine's feet. "You've got her."

Dog climbed on the bed, wheezing, and nuzzled Justine's leg. Justine loved Dog, but no animal could ever replace her sister. When they were small, she and Leah were best friends. They'd played together—school, doctor, store—Justine always in the subordinate role: the disruptive student, the long-suffering cancer patient, the obtuse customer demanding merchandise Leah's store didn't stock. When Leah entered middle school, their relationship changed. Leah wanted nothing to do with Justine. *Go away*, Leah would say, whenever she'd invited a friend to the house and caught Justine loitering by her bedroom door. *Find your own friends.*

Leah couldn't leave now, just as they'd finally grown closer again. Didn't Leah say, just yesterday, Justine was cool? A good kid? She could be trusted? Hadn't their parents taught them their family would be there for them always? Love conquers all? *With people you love, you find a way to work through your problems.*

"I'll help you," Justine pledged. "I'll do whatever you want."

Leah yanked a padded bra and two more pairs of panties from her top drawer. With her elbow, she pushed the drawer shut. "It's them, Jus. It's not you. I can't be here anymore. I hate them."

"Lee? What happened? Tell me?"

Leah's cell phone rang. Last night, Justine had snuck the phone from her mother's secretary and put it on Leah's nightstand. Leah answered on the first ring. "Okay. I'll be there."

From the tenderness in her sister's voice, Justine gathered that she was talking to Todd. She wondered how long until he arrived, how much time she had to talk her sister out of leaving. *Please, don't let him be here.* Ten minutes. Ten measly minutes was all she'd need.

Leah dressed quickly in low-slung jeans, a ribbed tank top, and baby blue sweatshirt. She combed her short blonde hair, parting it unevenly, and swiped the mascara wand over her lashes. Her cheeks were flushed, her lips pale pink. Her sister was the prettiest girl Justine had ever seen. The house would feel deserted without her.

Justine fought back the tears.

"I'll miss you, Teenie." With her thumb, Leah wiped a tear from the corner of Justine's eye, and gave her a hug. "Try to understand."

"But—"

Leah zipped the duffel bag. "Hey." She took hold of Justine's hand, pulling her up. "Why don't you come? We can leave together."

Justine struggled mightily to mirror Leah's smile. She wanted to go with her sister, badly. But run away? Her parents would hate her. She'd get behind on her science project. She'd miss school. Who would feed Dog? She was the only one in the house who regularly remembered. If she went, she thought, brightening, she would be with her sister. If Leah needed her for anything, to do her a favor, to talk, Justine would be there. Living away from home might be good for her. After all, she had to strike out on her own sometime.

"Sure," she said, and asked Leah for five minutes to pack. "Awesome."

"I'll call Todd," Leah said, "and ask him to wait."

When Justine emerged from her room, wheeling her tweed suitcase, her sister was waiting on the landing.

"I'm ready," Justine said. "We can go now. We better hurry up."

Leah shook her head miserably. "I can't do this to you, Teenie. I just have to teach them a lesson. I'll be back. Sister's promise," she said, hugging Justine as if she'd never let go.

Leah had taught her parents a lesson, all right. Here she was, alone on this smelly hide-a-bed in Hope's living room, the springs poking into her back, wishing more than anything else in the world she was home, in her own room, in her own comfortable bed. She missed her little sister. She had no one to talk to, no one she could rely on. She was all alone here.

Hope's response to her arrival this morning had been lukewarm. "I *guess* you can stay," Hope had said. "I'll tell my mom it's just for tonight, so she doesn't think you're moving in or anything. You'll have to sleep on the couch." As if Leah had planned to confiscate her room.

Strangely enough, Leah missed her parents. Hope's mom was cool, but she was not Leah's mother.

Now she could never go back. After the scene in the car, she could never face her parents; she could never look them in the eye. What was wrong with her? Why couldn't she keep her stupid trap shut? Her parents hadn't disowned her exactly; she'd seen their disgust, the revulsion in their eyes. They were probably glad she'd left; glad to be rid of her. Not that she blamed them. She'd disappointed them—again. She'd disappointed everyone. Her mother, her father. Coach Thomas. The girls on her soccer team. The high school dean, who, "for the life of me, Leah," could not understand why such a bright girl would skip class or let her grades slide. She'd alienated her teachers. Withdrawn from old friends. When she approached, the kids turned their heads or walked away. Worst of all, she'd disappointed Justine.

Leah's eyes welled when she thought of her sister on the landing, Justine begging her not to go. When Leah asked her sister to run away with her, although she was obviously scared, Justine had been willing to join her. Leah pictured her sister, all phony smile and fake animation, towing that big tweed suitcase stuffed with all her earthly belongings.

Her parents were right. She was a loser. A worthless, no good loser. If only she could disappear. Fall asleep and never wake up.

Leah's duffel bag lay on the floor by the sofa with Hope's cat curled inside. The cat arched its back, rubbing its sour odor into her jeans. Leah tried shooing her away, but the cat was too stubborn to leave.

Leah suppressed an urge to throw the dumb cat at the wall. Feeling bad, she picked the cat up, stroked her back. The cat lay on Leah's belly, mewling, and then scampered away. Leah stretched her legs, pressing through the soles of her feet, and stared at the ceiling.

Outside, a car skidded around the corner, its brakes squealing. Leah swallowed the bile in her throat, and rolled onto her side. In the next room, Hope's mother had tuned in to a sitcom. Leah felt the vibration from the laugh track. She wondered how her sister was holding up. Leah pictured her, curled in her bed, hugging Dog. How would Justine manage without her? Leah wanted to call, hear her sister's voice. But it was eleven o'clock. Justine would be asleep. If her parents answered and realized that it was Leah on the line, they'd hang up. The people on TV were laughing again, a low rumbling yowl that shook Hope's sad little house. Leah dug her toes into the space between the cushion and arm of the sofa and covered her ears.

———⊕———

Zoe and Will had had a harrowing night. That morning, they'd both overslept. When Leah didn't show her face at breakfast, Zoe figured she was up to her usual antics. Any other day, she would have engaged, called from the foot of the stairs. If Leah didn't get up, she'd have marched to her room, stood over her bed, pestering until she opened her eyes. This morning, she'd been too angry to fight. She felt betrayed, less by Leah's arrest than by her daughter's insolence, her lack of respect. She'd showed not the slightest remorse. Instead of an apology, which Zoe and Will had every right to demand, she'd flown into a rage, taunting, kicking the seat, swearing at her father.

Zoe was glad Leah had stayed in bed. She didn't want to look at her daughter this morning. She and Will were by no means perfect. God knew they'd made plenty of mistakes. Their intentions, however misguided, had always been good. She and Will worked hard to provide a good home for their daughters. Zoe prepared elaborate dinners to celebrate birthdays and special occasions. Since the kids were in Pre School, they'd opened their home, welcoming their daughters' friends. She and Will encouraged Leah in her pursuits, supported most decisions. Will had devoted countless hours to Leah's athletic career. This was how she behaved in return? Leah could sleep the day away, for all Zoe cared. It was high time Leah assumed responsibility and accepted the consequences of her behavior.

While Justine dressed for school, Zoe set out a bowl of Raspberry Crunch cereal and a slice of wheat berry toast. Leah, depending upon her mood, could be impossible to feed. At age three, she'd subsisted on hotdogs and macaroni and cheese. Zoe had tried every trick in the *Mom Book* to convince Leah to eat. She tried the airplane trick—*zoom, zoooom*, the spoon in Leah's mouth before she knew what was on it—baiting—*Mmm, yum, mmm, good*—bribery—*eat this teensy piece of chicken, Mama will make you a yummy hotdog.* She even snuck shredded ham in Leah's macaroni and cheese. Leah ate the macaroni and picked out the ham. With the exception of goat's cheese or lamb, which Zoe rarely served, her younger daughter ate anything set in front of her.

This morning, she'd picked at her cereal and left her toast. Zoe offered something different—oatmeal, French toast, eggs. Justine shook her head and opened a book. Zoe should have known something was up. Instead, she'd rationalized. Justine was about to hit puberty; mood swings were normal. After breakfast, Zoe did a perfunctory sweep through the kitchen, ran upstairs, pressed her ear to Leah's door to see if she'd begun to stir, and left for work.

Under the circumstances, her day at the office had gone reasonably well. Still furious about last night, she'd evaded the issue, too frightened to consider the possibilities, contemplate the future. Busyness put the arrest out of her mind. When her two o'clock patient cancelled, rather than taking advantage of the time to catch up on paperwork, she'd called her other patients and shifted her schedule forward an hour. Before she'd worked fulltime, she and Justine spent all their time together. It had been ages since they'd tackled a project. Tonight, they'd make dinner together. Justine would enjoy that.

Anticipation, moving forward, thinking positive thoughts, energized her and the day passed quickly. Between appointments she searched for recipes on the Web. By two o'clock, she'd designed a perfect menu: butternut soup, roast chicken with sweet potatoes and *haricot verts*, and chocolate lava cakes for dessert. Before leaving work, she compiled a grocery list and tucked the list in her handbag.

Why hadn't she done this sooner? For months, she'd been preoccupied with Leah. Every day brought a new problem, it seemed. Corbett, then soccer, now *this*. Justine had always been stable, her problems less urgent than Leah's. Zoe had pushed her aside, focusing on the problem at hand, oiling the squeaky wheel. She'd been lucky. Justine hadn't rebelled. Zoe was not about to lose another daughter.

At four, Zoe packed three new patient files in her briefcase—if she had time, she'd look them over before bed—and gathered her handbag and coat. In the grocery store lot, she remembered she'd forgotten to lock her office door. Over the past three weeks, four offices in the building had been robbed. At the tenants' request, the property manager had installed surveillance cameras. Somehow, the thief evaded them. An inside job, the manager opined. Zoe considered leaving the door unlocked. What was the worst that could happen? Her patient information was safe, her files backed up on the server. The thought of someone violating her space, fingering her photos, touching her books, pawing through her personal belongings, unnerved her enough that she took the time to go back.

Her phone was ringing when she opened the anteroom door. "Yes," she said, breathless from the short sprint to her office. *Mindy Lansdown?* Zoe struggled to place the name.

"Hope's mother?" the caller prompted. "Hope Lansdown? Your daughter's friend?"

"Your house?" Zoe said, repelled by the caller's coarse voice.

In the family counseling session, Leah had admitted to having been at a friend's house the night she'd been drunk. She'd been tightlipped regarding the name. This Hope person must have been that friend. The "friend" who'd dumped her, drunk and hyperventilating, on the doorstep.

Who was this woman? Any decent adult with a shred of common sense would have sent Leah home. Throughout their brief conversation, Zoe forced a tight smile. As soon as the Lansdown woman paused for a breath, Zoe thanked her profusely for giving her daughter a safe place to spend the night, hung up, and called the police, using her credentials as a child therapist to gain information. The Lansdown house was a drug den, the police chief informed her, a hangout for every two-bit criminal west of Boston. For a month, the narcotics unit of the Ayer PD had been trailing a coke ring. Last week, they'd observed one of the prime suspects, an acquaintance of the Lupo boy, leaving the house. Insufficient evidence for an arrest, but they were 'closing in.' When she admitted her teenage daughter had run there, he said they could press charges against Mrs. Lansdown for aiding and abetting a runaway.

"It would give the drug investigation a boost," the chief pointed out. They'd have reason to search the house.

"Absolutely not," Zoe told him. Her daughter would not be a pawn in a drug bust. Besides, sending the police after Leah would only exacerbate the situation. Zoe had counseled dozens of runaway kids. Returning home had to be *their* decision; otherwise running would always be an option. At the first sign of a threat, they'd take off. No, better for Zoe to drive over, talk to Leah herself.

Zoe resisted the urge to call her husband. He'd insist on confronting the woman. If she and Will showed up on the doorstep, issuing threats, something ugly might happen. Zoe booted her computer, looked up the address, and printed directions from *Map Quest*. One of these days, she'd buy a GPS or get a new cell phone.

In the car, she checked and rechecked her directions. North Cortland was a wasteland, four miles west of the center, a remote section of town. No shops, no gym, no dance studios. Only the people who lived in the area or came for riding lessons had cause to be here.

As she approached the Lansdown's street, she considered turning back. If Leah looked outside and happened to see the car, she might hide. Maybe it would be better if Zoe and Will approached her together. This was a plea for reassurance on Leah's part; she wanted proof that, despite her antics, her parents loved her—and of course they did. They'd always love her. *Always*. No matter what.

I love you, stinky face, Zoe thought, recalling a line from the girls' favorite board book when they were babies.

The Lansdowns' squalid ranch looked every inch the drug den the chief had described. A tangle of rhododendron skirted the house, partially concealing a grimy picture window. A child trick-or-treating or selling Girl Scout cookies would be petrified to stop here, never mind knock on the door. A rusted chain, tied to a maple tree, lay in a coil in the front yard, a miserable square of pine needles and dirt. If the Lansdowns owned a dog, it was nowhere in sight. In the drive sat an ancient black Cadillac, a boat of a car—it should have had fins. Zoe parked behind the Caddy and got out of her car.

On the stoop, she cleared her throat, anticipating a verbal confrontation, and knocked on the door. She knocked again, a third time, and then she walked to the rear of the house and rapped on the slider.

She checked her watch. Justine was home alone. If she waited, she could be here for hours. Depressed, she returned to her car. On the Caddy's rear bumper, a sticker proclaimed, "Jesus is my Savior."

Save *her*, Zoe prayed. *Save my daughter.*

Two o'clock: Zoe jerked awake, her entire body trembling.

"Will." She nudged her husband's arm. They had to go to the Lansdown house. *Now.* They should have driven over earlier, camped out on the doorstep if necessary. They'd called the house a dozen times; no one picked up. Leah's phone was turned off.

They'd reached Hope's mother at midnight. She'd taken the girls to dinner and a movie, she claimed. *Dinner where?* Zoe wanted to ask. *What movie?* The girls had conked out, Mindy said. She'd hate to wake them. Poor kids were beat. Could they come for Leah tomorrow?

The Lansdown woman was a lunatic. What had possessed them to believe her? God only knew what they really were up to over there. Night was the most likely time for a drug bust. If the narcotics unit stormed the house, Leah would be caught in the dragnet.

"Will?" Zoe switched on the reading lamp. "Wake up."

Her husband moaned, reaching for her, and squeezed her thigh.

"Oh, for God's sake." She shoved his hand off her leg. "Would you listen to me?"

"Goodnight," he grumbled, and rolled away from her.

"Will?" She rattled his arm. "We need to talk."

Yawning, he patted his nightstand. "Jesus." He brought the watch closer to his face. "It's two a.m."

Zoe huffed to her bureau and put on panties. "We need to go."

"Huh? Where?"

"The Lansdown's." Was he dense? "Where do you *think*?"

Reaching backward, yawning again, he switched off the light.

"She's in trouble." Zoe switched it back on. "We've got to go over there."

"Tomorrow."

"So you're saying you don't care if you're daughter's involved in a drug bust?"

He rolled over, pulling a pillow over his head.

"Tomorrow could be too late."

Will propped himself on his elbow. "Roll over. I'll rub your back till you fall asleep. When you wake up in the morning, we'll go over. We'll both go."

"Damn you. *Do* something. It's your fault she's there."

"*My* fault?"

"Had to keep pushing," Zoe snapped, incensed by her husband's refusal to accept responsibility. "Admit it, Will. You fucked up."

"*I* fucked up?"

And round and round they went.

———⊛———

Justine's parents were at it again. Their bedroom suite sat at the end of the hall. Even with the doors to both bedrooms closed, she heard them. The digital clock on her bedside table said two o'clock. She'd been trying for hours to fall asleep. She'd counted sheep, tried thinking positive thoughts. Her roiling stomach kept her awake. To make the bus, she had to be out of bed by six thirty. She couldn't imagine how she would do it. Maybe she could play hooky tomorrow.

Justine lay in bed for a few more minutes, went to the bathroom, peed, drank two glasses of warm tap water, and climbed back in bed. She wanted desperately to talk to her sister. She'd tried to leave a message earlier. Stupidly, she used the phone in the kitchen instead of calling from her room, where she could have talked to her sister in private. Her mother saw her dialing and took the receiver.

"Her phone's off, honey," Justine's mom had said. "We've already tried. This is a delicate situation. We don't want to upset her."

Justine's head told her that her mother was right. Only her heart didn't always hear what her head tried to tell her. "Why can't I call?" she'd demanded.

Exasperated, her mother finally said, "If your sister wanted to talk, she'd call us, Justine."

"That's not true," Justine cried. "I'm not the one she's avoiding. It's you and Dad and your stupid rules, giving her shit all the time." Her mother raised her eyebrows at the word "shit," but said nothing. "You make her feel like a loser. And...and...and..." There was more. A lot more. If only Justine could think.

"Calm down, honey." Her mother lifted the phone out of Justine's sweaty palms and set it on the counter.

"No," Justine shouted. "I won't calm down. This is your fault. I hate you. I hate you both."

Maybe her mother was right. Maybe her parents were not the only ones Leah was avoiding. Maybe her sister was avoiding her, too. Last night, after her parents went to bed, she'd snuck downstairs as she and Leah had planned, and unlocked the mudroom door. At breakfast, when her father asked if she had any idea who'd unlatched the back door, she'd crossed her fingers behind her back and said, "No."

When Leah left to meet Todd, instead of racing after her as she desperately wanted to do, or waking their parents and telling them Leah was gone, she'd curled up at the back of her closet with Dog, and pulled the door closed, so their parents wouldn't hear her crying.

Justine slipped off her bed. Dog followed, easing herself to the floor. Justine had trouble recalling the last time she'd knelt to say prayers. Leah never prayed, as far as Justine knew. Her sister had stopped believing in God. God was a crutch for weak, dependent people, according to Leah. "You're a scientist, Jus. Scientists believe in logic and reason."

Justine listened politely and kept right on praying. In low moments, she had to admit, she wondered if her prayers reached God's ears, and it occurred to her that maybe Leah was right. Maybe there was no God. Or maybe, if He existed, God was not the loving father she imagined. Maybe He was inaccessible. Maybe He never paid attention at all. But, always, the instant she opened her heart and started talking to Him, her doubts disappeared.

"Oh, my God, I am heartily sorry," Justine prayed. She believed in asking God's forgiveness before deluging Him with requests. "For lying, being a jerk to my mom…"

Please, God, take care of my sister. Bring her back home.

Nineteen

Woodstock Mama

The next morning, Leah felt better. After the fight with her parents the night before last, she'd had trouble falling asleep; she'd dozed for an hour or two and woke before dawn. A good night's sleep had cured her anxiety. Her lower back was sore from the sofa springs jabbing her spine; otherwise, she felt refreshed, her head clear.

When she played soccer, it was an effort to get out of bed in the morning, her legs and feet protesting in pain as she took her first excruciating steps. Now, she swung her feet off the sofa, stood, and strolled breezily to the window. She was proud of herself. She'd survived an entire day and night without calling her parents, without caving in. Yesterday, she wouldn't have believed she could do it; now she had.

Hope's mother, an early riser, clattered around the kitchen, the tang of brewed coffee filling the house. Leah's stomach grumbled. The dinner Justine had brought to her room two nights ago was the last meal she'd eaten. She wondered what Mindy was preparing for breakfast—pancakes, she hoped, or Belgian waffles. Leah's mom made the best Belgian waffles ever, thick yet light, heaped with berries and cream.

Leah winced. *Waffles are way too fattening for breakfast.* Oatmeal and wheat toast would do. Leah shooed the cat out of her open suitcase, picked a black tee-shirt and gray sweats from the meager assortment of clothes, and carried her clothes to the bathroom.

The door was locked. Inside, Hope was singing a pop song Leah couldn't quite place, in a sonorous alto, missing the high notes.

When the shower went off, Leah knocked.

"Just a sec," Hope warbled. Evidently, she felt better today, too. Steam swirled out of the bathroom when Hope opened the door. Water dripped down her face. She'd wrapped herself in a threadbare terrycloth towel, the butterfly tattoo on her left breast peeking out.

"Hey," Hope said. "How's it going?" Hope often traipsed around the house with her shirt unbuttoned, exposing her bra. Still, seeing her practically naked was jolting. "Sleep good?" she asked.

"Yeah," Leah said, averting her eyes.

"Great. Mom's got breakfast," she said, and strolled to her room.

Leah set her tee-shirt and panties on the toilet, undressed, and climbed into the shower stall, cringing as she stepped under the icy water. Grit coated the floor. With the ball of her foot, she wiped a section big enough to stand on, adjusted the shower head, and turned up the spigot, raising the temperature by about five degrees. She picked a sliver of soap from the floor, washed quickly, rinsed and hopped out, her body covered in goose bumps. She wasn't used to cold showers. When her parents built the house in Cortland, her father had paid the contractor to install two heaters so they never ran out of hot water. Well, those were the breaks. If she wanted to live on her own, she would have to put up with certain inconveniences.

With a thin hand towel she found on a hook on the back of the door, she blotted her body dry.

"You look good," Hope said. "Cool shirt."

Leah stood in the doorway to the kitchen. She'd bought the black tee-shirt with fake pearls on the collar from the markdown rack at the Gap. She ran a hand over her head, her hair stiff from the cheap aerosol spray holding it in place.

"Liar," she said. "I look gross."

Hope's mother tapped the ashes from her cigarette into a coffee mug. Scary how much Hope resembled her mother. Mindy was several inches taller than her daughter and her face was wider, but their features—deep-set eyes, pug nose, rosebud lips—could have been cloned. Even their posture was the same: shoulders back, butts tucked, bellies slightly distended, like out-of-shape dancers.

"Pretty as a picture." Mindy winked. "Even in sweats."

"Really?" Leah's mother would have given her crap. *You're not leaving this house dressed like that*, she'd have said. *You look like a beatnik.* "You don't think I look like a beatnik?"

"A beatnik?" Mindy repeated, deep horsey laughter rising up from her belly. "Ain't heard that word since the Village."

"Greenwich," Hope said, rolling her eyes.

"You lived in Greenwich Village?" Maybe Mindy could give Leah some pointers, tell her where to find an apartment, suggest places to look for a job. "What was it like?"

"I'm a country girl. Never did take to the city." Mindy dragged thoughtfully on her cigarette. "I was at Woodstock, you know."

Hope made a looping motion next to her temple with her index finger.

"Woodstock?" Leah said, ignoring Hope's gesture.

When she was a kid, her father used to play an album recorded at Woodstock, Leah dancing around the room, pretending she was on MTV. As she grew older, she'd come to appreciate the gathering, the atmosphere—*open, alive*—the communal spirit, the peace, acceptance, and love. Today, if three hundred thousand kids gathered anywhere, a massive fight would break out. Leah often felt out of place in her world, as if she'd been born twenty years too late, into the wrong generation. She'd never met anyone who'd been to Woodstock. Her parents were too young.

"Really?" Leah asked. "You really went to Woodstock?"

"Sure. Hope never told you?"

Leah shook her head. "What was it like?"

"A ball." From a bag of potato chips on the counter, Mindy filled two plastic sandwich bags, and zipped them shut. She took another drag from her cigarette, deep crow's feet puckering the skin at the corners of her eyes. "Ever seen them pictures in *Life*?"

"Mom," Hope said. "She doesn't want to hear about that."

Thankfully, Mindy ignored her, otherwise, Leah would have spoken up. "Me and Hope's dad's in one of them. Way in back."

"They're butt naked," Hope interjected. "It's gross."

"I wrote a letter, you know, asking them to send me one. When Leo left, he swiped the original. So all I got now's this faded copy we made. It's on my bureau, if you want to go see it."

"That stinks," Leah said. "Sorry about your husband."

"That's okay. Me and Hope, we're better off without him. Right, sweets?"

Hope looked at Leah and shrugged, shaking her head.

"Oh, come on, you." Mindy waved her daughter's grimace away. "You know it's true. Hope was our love baby. I was forty-five when I had her. After she was born, her daddy pressured me to get married. Imagine? After all those years. He wanted to 'do the right thing.' Big mistake. Listen, sweetie," she said to Leah, "got to eat something, keep your energy up." Snack-sized cereal boxes lined the counter. "Have some cereal."

Leah selected Fruit Loops and opened the box. Hope used her box as a bowl. Leah's mom would never buy Fruit Loops. She fed them weird organic cereals from the Natural Grocer, or homemade granolas with names like Rainforest Crunch or Boysenberry Nut.

While the girls ate, Mindy stuffed paper bags with boxes of Hi-C and packets of peanut butter and cheese crackers, all the while humming the melody to a love song Leah remembered from a long, long time ago.

When Justine went to the kitchen, she found her father in the breakfast nook, sulking. The *Globe*, open to the sports page, was spread in front of him on the table. Her mother, feigning indifference, scooted around the kitchen, scrubbing counters, watering the potted ivy on the windowsill, her ratty purple robe fluttering around her feet.

"Look at this." Her father swatted the newspaper, as if it had done him some grave injustice. "They're talking about trading Youk."

"Kevin Youkilis?" Justine said, as though outraged. It was a pathetic attempt at commiserating. She had no idea what the implications of such a trade might be. She knew Youkilis played for the Red Sox. In *Moneyball*, the manager referred to Youkilis as "the Greek God of walks"—whatever that meant. If Leah were here, they'd be trading stats, arguing about the team's chances for making the playoffs next year without Youk, batting around names of players the Sox might receive in a trade.

"Toast?" Justine asked, lacking anything better to say.

"No, thanks." Her father blew air through his teeth. "They've got their heads up their asses. That Lucchino, he's the problem."

"I thought you hated baseball," Justine's mother chided.

Justine cringed. Was she the only one around here who realized fighting was a waste of time? That nothing positive ever came out of combat? Couldn't her parents pretend to get along? Just this once? What did her mother hope to gain by goading Justine's father?

Justine poured a glass of orange juice and buttered a slice of wheat berry toast. The sour smell of the butter nearly made her retch.

Justine cut her toast and fed half to Dog. The TV was on in the family room, the sportscaster discussing the possible Youkilis trade.

"Youk's got a .289 career average," said Justine's father, aping the sportscaster. "Who do they think they'll get that's any better?" Her mother scowled. "Since when do you give a damn?"

"For Christ's sake, Zoe." He folded the paper. "Get off my case."

"I'm just saying. You hate baseball, so why the big deal?"

"Mom?" Justine pulled a face. "I'm sick. Can I stay home?"

Her mother sighed and felt Justine's forehead. "You're not hot."

"My stomach hurts," Justine said. "I won't be able to focus."

"I'm sorry, Justine. You're going to school. We need to stick to our routine." In other words, forget Leah's not here. As if she could *ever* forget. "Don't worry, honey. She'll be home today." With her fingers, her mom brushed Justine's hair back. "I have a good feeling."

"Woo-hoo." Justine's father curled his fingers. "Your mother's got a feeling." He went to the pantry, shaking his head in disgust, and threw the newspaper in the recycling bin. "Stick to our routine," he said under his breath. "What the hell is that supposed to mean?"

"Don't pay attention to him." Her mother slammed the dishwasher door, startling the dog. "Your father's being a jerk."

Justine stroked Dog's ears. She couldn't decide which parent was less mature. So she'd make it to lunch without passing out, she forced another spoonful of cereal, and poured the rest in Dog's bowl.

"See you guys," she called on her way out the door. *Try not to kill each other today.*

<hr />

Leah's mood deteriorated over the course of the day. She kept feeling as though she'd lost something. She'd race back to her locker, only to discover the missing item in her arms. Between classes, she floated mindlessly through the halls, her eyes trained ahead.

In class, she hunkered down in her seat, avoiding the questioning eyes of her teachers. When Mr. Mulvany called on her in social studies class, she asked to be excused, slipped into the girls' room and hid in one of the stalls until the bell rang.

She had home economics the following period—the class was making frog pillows. Ick! The teacher, Mrs. Berman, had a nose for trouble. She'd stand over you, pretending to watch you sew, and pepper you with embarrassing personal questions. Normally, ditching class was easy: go to the nurse, fake sick, gag if you have to. Only the nurse might call Leah's mother—not a good idea today. Instead,

Leah went to the office to visit her dean. Dean Leahy's door was shut. His secretary said the dean might be a while. "You're welcome to stay if you like."

Leah sunk into the metal folding chair outside Dean Leahy's office, her mind wandering, waiting for some vaguely imagined change to take place, making her life different and better.

Their family used to be close. A memory of the Stoneham Zoo popped into her brain, Leah balanced on her father's shoulders, peering into the polar bear cave.

"How comes that one's so lazy?" Leah pointed to a fat white bear, sunning itself in the corner.

"That's the mama bear," her father replied.

The mama bear, her mother explained, was expecting a baby. "They'll be a family soon, sweetie. Just like us."

Leah pictured her sister standing in the doorway with her suitcase, ready to follow Leah blindly. Leah had never felt so lonely or displaced. She forced herself to picture the ride home from the police station the other night, the rage in her father's eyes, the disgust on her parents' faces when she climbed out of the car.

You're not their little girl anymore, she reminded herself. Life as she'd known it was over.

When the bell rang, she headed to the cafeteria for lunch.

The line snaked into the hall. Today's main selection was pizza, the only edible food served in this dump, the spicy tomato sauce odor fusing with the curdled tang of cheese. The usual hysterics, kids shouting, laughing, horsing around, overwhelmed her. She stood at the entrance, repelled by the swarm of gyrating bodies, searching for a place where she could be alone.

At last, she spotted a nearly empty table; three dorks sat at the far end, books open on the table, probably discussing their calculus homework. Leah took the aisle seat and set her backpack on the empty chair next to hers. She nibbled a chip, ignoring the kids passing by, carrying trays loaded with pizza, plates of salad or fries, cartons of milk.

A tray crashed, glasses and plates shattering. At the front of the cafeteria, two boys scuffled, fists flying. One fell and the other leapt on top of him. A crowd quickly gathered, the onlookers clapping, cheering them on. Scanning the faces, Leah spotted Cicely Hanson, who, at that very moment, caught sight of her. Leah lowered her eyes. She'd heard through the grapevine that Cissy wasn't allowed to hang out with her anymore. Leah couldn't care less about Cissy. She had no use for unsupportive, judgmental friends. That Cissy's mother thought her daughter too good for Leah, pissed her off. True, the girl didn't drink. Or smoke—she'd quit smoking cigarettes after she and Leah were caught. But she lied. And made fun of other kids. And plagiarized every essay she wrote, cheated on tests. Cissy was also a thief.

Look at her, in a hot-pink shirt and designer jeans. That outfit had to cost three hundred dollars. How did Cissy's mother think her daughter paid for those clothes? She gave Cissy twenty-five dollars a week, barely enough money for gas. Cissy had no job. She'd stolen her outfit from the Jeans Company, a boutique in Groton. Cissy had bragged about it for weeks. Evidently, Mrs. Hanson had no problem with her precious daughter's illicit activities. As long as her little darling never got caught.

Cissy strolled down Leah's aisle, surrounded by a posse of JV players. Leah swept her crumbs off the table and gathered her things. She didn't have the energy to fight.

"Hey." Cissy waved a spirited hand. "Look who it is."

The younger girls' eyes darted from Cissy to Leah and back.

Let it go, Leah told herself. *Ignore them.*

"You heard, right?" Cissy said, her posse giggling. "We won the division."

Leah's heart thumped. "Nice jeans, Cissy. Expensive?"

Cissy's face flushed. "So you know we're going to states," she said, pretending to pout. "Too bad you won't be with us."

The girl had no idea how close Leah was to punching her out.

From out of nowhere Hope materialized, fists clenched. "Hey," she said, her eyes squeezed into slits, challenging Cissy. "These jerks giving you trouble, Lee?"

Grimacing, Cissy dropped her gaze. The girls passed without another word.

Hope followed Cissy with her eyes to a table on the opposite side of the cafeteria. "What was that all about?" she asked when Cissy and her gang finally stopped gossiping and dug into their lunch.

"Nothing," Leah said.

"Lying sack of shit." She punched Leah's arm. "Spare a few chips?"

Leah gave her the bag. "What are you doing here?"

"Came to check on my bud." Hope nudged Leah's shoulder.

"You didn't cut trig again, did you?"

"Yup," Hope said. "Just for you." Hope crushed the empty chips bag. "You okay? You look a little pale."

"Sure," Leah lied. *No*, she wanted to say. *I'm not okay at all.*

"See that kid?" Hope indicated a redheaded boy in the lunch line, a tray balanced on his hip. "So I used to have really long hair. Down to here." With her fingers, she sliced her lower back. "I never cut it 'till I was like ten."

Leah had trouble picturing Hope as a child. In her mind, Hope had always been exactly as she was now: tall and plump, and, well, a bit rough around the edges. Leah had never seen a baby picture of Hope. The Woodstock photo was the only picture Leah had ever seen at the Lansdown's. Unlike her mom, who saved everything—every school picture, every costume, every project the girls had ever brought home, Hope's mother seemed indifferent to mementoes. Why did it matter, really? Mindy thought Leah looked pretty, even in sweats. Plus, she was cool. She'd attended the concert at Woodstock!

"So anyway," Hope continued, helping herself to the rest of Leah's crackers. "That kid, right? Sam Ridley? He was always pulling my pigtails. The whole class used to say shit. Like me and him were gonna get married." Hope pulled a face, underscoring the idiocy. "And he stunk. Swear to God, the kid rolled in dog turds."

Dog turds? Hope would say anything for a laugh. Leah couldn't help but oblige.

"Gotcha," Hope said. "What's up? The truth, babes. I'm your friend, remember? We're living together. We're practically sisters."

Sisters? Leah took in Hope's faded jeans, stretched taut over her massive thighs. Hope thought the jeans flattered her figure; in fact, she looked like a cow. If Leah were a real friend, never mind a sister, she'd tell her. Real friends looked out for one another. With Cissy, she'd never held back. If Leah couldn't tell Hope her clothes looked bad, which as a friend was almost her *duty*, how could she possibly say she longed to go home?

Twenty

Whirlpool

After school, Todd picked up Leah and they drove to Anderson Farm, an abandoned apple orchard. He turned onto a gravel road that cut through the orchard. Since the owner died, the property willed to his heirs, the place had been left unattended.

"Nobody'll know we're here," Todd said. "Nobody's ever here."

"Great." Leah rolled a joint, took a long hit, and held it for Todd, the liberating smell of weed electrifying the air inside the truck.

The jeep bumped along a dirt path strewn with decaying fruit, past a dilapidated mill where farm workers had once pressed cider. At the end of the path, Todd turned left, cutting across the rows of squat apple trees, and headed up a short hill toward an open field fringed by ragweed. The purple flowers swayed in the light wind.

"That spot looks good." Leah pointed to a clearing between two Macintosh trees at the outer edge of the orchard.

Todd parked the truck and they both hopped out.

Mist hung in the air and rain clouds scudded in from the west. She buttoned Hope's black sweater, leaving the top button undone.

"Look." Leah pointed to a tractor parked by a decaying shed, and skipped to the adjacent field, leaving Todd to spread their blanket.

She set one foot on the tractor's runner and mounted, grasping the seat. "Hey," she shouted, waving to her boyfriend. Leaning forward, she gripped the wheel. "I'm coming to get you."

"Get back here," Todd griped. "Help me."

She tapped the pedal, trilling like an engine. "Hey," she called again. "Look at me."

Holding the wheel for balance, Leah climbed onto the seat. Crouching, she extended her arms. Slowly, she straightened her legs. Standing on the seat of the tractor, she could see the whole world. She was a bird. Flapping her wings, she jumped—

—and crashed to the ground, landing on a rock, twisting her ankle.

"Ahhh!" she squealed. "Help me. I broke my foot! Hurry! It hurts."

She removed her shoe and massaged her ankle and foot.

"Let's see." Squatting, he lifted her foot, placing it gently on his knee. He turned her foot left and right. "Don't look broke to me." Evidently, her boyfriend didn't care that she was dying. He ran his fingers over her ankle and down her foot. "Can you move it?"

"I don't know." She examined her ankle for signs of bruising. Wiggled her toes. "I guess."

"Here." Todd put his arm around her. "Lean on me. I got you."

With her boyfriend's help, she limped back to their blanket under the apple tree.

Earlier, after a drawn-out debate, each parent fighting to be heard, Will and Zoe had decided to wait until after the high school dismissal to go to the Lansdown place. It was the right decision. Why disrupt a school day?

At noon, unable to concentrate, her mind fixated on Leah, Zoe cancelled her appointments, left the office, and drove around town for two hours, killing time.

At half past two, she stopped at Sullivan Farms, voted Best Ice Cream in Boston, by *City Magazine* readers, eight years running. From early March through mid-autumn, all eight windows would be open, lines snaking into the parking lot. While parents recited the ice cream flavors to their little ones, older kids raced from window to window, the teenagers behind the screens working feverishly to keep pace with the orders.

Bob was alone today, filling the tubs of ice cream.

Zoe had met Bob ten years earlier on the starting line of a road race on the Fourth of July. She'd run cross-country in high school.

That March, she'd started running in earnest again, hoping to lose the extra fifteen pounds she'd been carrying since her pregnancy with Justine. Her first time out, she'd circled the block three times; even that was a struggle. Her strength and endurance quickly improved. By late spring, she'd built to five miles a day and thought it might be fun to enter a road race. The Fourth of July race, a flat two-mile course, was perfect. Will and the girls were waiting at the finish. After the race, they planned to watch the parade.

The race director called the runners to the start. Zoe squatted to tighten her laces. When she stood, slightly dizzy from the dip in blood pressure, Bob was standing beside her. With his confidence and physique, he looked like a seasoned runner. She figured him to finish in the top ten. He introduced himself and they chatted for a few minutes. She told him it was her inaugural race, and asked him, jokingly, to hail the ambulance if she passed out.

The gun went off. Fired by an adrenaline rush, Zoe took off with the rabbits, ignoring every racing strategy her high school coaches had taught her. By the quarter-mile, she was sucking wind. Her lungs felt as though about to collapse. If not for Bob, she'd have dropped out. "You all right?" he'd asked. "Don't give up. I'll pace you."

"Hey, Zoe," he said brightly, bringing her back to the present "What's happening? Haven't seen you in ages."

Bob had a thin face and lively brown eyes she had instinctively trusted. He was shorter than Will with a distance runner's strong legs and lean torso. Although he had to be well over thirty, he could have passed for a college kid in his twenties. He wore a Sullivan Farms tee-shirt, Kelly green, the number thirty-three stitched on his sleeves.

An autographed poster of Larry Bird hung above the soft serve machine. Zoe pointed to the poster. "Still a Bird fan, I see."

"Even if he did sell us out." He laughed. "I know…diehard. What can I say?"

"How's business?"

Bob had a loyal following, his warm, easygoing personality nearly as big a draw as the homemade ice cream. "Not bad. Not bad."

"Run any races lately?"

"A half marathon last month. The Apple-Fest in Hudson. Been trying to talk Mary Ann into running Boston next year." He shrugged. One of these days, he'd convince her. "You? Still out there, I hope."

"Not anymore." She felt a surprising stab of regret.

"Too bad. You were tough. So, what can I get you?"

"Small coconut chip. Extra jimmies," she added sheepishly.

A news clip from last year's Fourth of July race hung on the outside wall between two screened windows. Bob organized the race now, having turned it into an annual charity event. In the clip, the winner was breaking through the ribbon, fists raised in victory.

A year ago, in their final game against Westford, in the last second of playtime, Leah had scored the winning goal, a rousing come-from-behind win. Zoe's daughter had jogged twice around the perimeter of the soccer field, the crowds cheering wildly, Leah's hands raised just like the runner's in the clip. Her teammates had carried her off the field.

"You okay?"

Zoe felt a cool hand on her wrist. Startled, she recoiled. "Sorry," she said. "How's Mary Ann? I didn't even ask."

Bob looked at her quizzically. "She's good. Sure you're okay? You look pale."

"I'm fine. Maybe I'll go for a run today. You've inspired me."

Bob smiled uncertainly, handed her a plastic spoon, and told her to "take care." She saw him at the window, watching her, as she pulled out of the lot.

From Sullivan Farms, Zoe drove straight to the Lansdown place.

Zoe turned into the buckled driveway, steering around a pothole, and pulled to a stop behind the Cadillac. As she cut the engine, she realized it was rude to block the drive and shifted into reverse, backed out, and parked on the street. She smoothed her hair, took three calming breaths, buttoned her trench coat, and opened her car door.

A black and white tabby sat on the front stoop. The cat hissed as Zoe approached, scooted down the steps, its tail whipping her shin, and darted behind the house.

Zoe brushed herself off. *Keep your cool,* she told herself. *No matter what happens, even if she cries or screams or tells you to get lost, stay in control.* She'd tell Leah she loved her, missed her. She'd ask her daughter to come home. She wouldn't press for a hug or any other outward display of affection. She'd give her space, wait until Leah was ready. If her daughter reached for her or cried and fell into her arms, well, she'd act accordingly.

Zoe knocked, waited a few seconds, and knocked again.

In her mind, her heart swelling with hope, she was already pulling her daughter into her arms. This was a wakeup call. In the grand scheme of things, nothing truly terrible had happened. The family had time to adjust. Having learned from this experience, she and Will could still shepherd their daughter safely through adolescence, into a caring, responsible adulthood. They'd been overprotective, controlling, reluctant to give Leah rope, afraid she'd hang herself with it. But wasn't that what growing up was about? How does a child learn and grow *except* by making mistakes?

Why was no one answering the door? She heard movement inside, a shuffling noise, the drone of a TV. Zoe put her ear to the door, listening for Leah's voice. As she balled her fist to knock a third time, the door popped open, a wave of secondhand smoke billowing out of the house.

Zoe drew back, clutching her purse, fending off the assault.

Across the threshold, a tall heavyset girl, with her hands on her hips, peered down at Zoe. The girl had nice features. She would be pretty if she tidied up—washed her clothes, combed her hair, and lost thirty or forty pounds.

A soap opera played on the TV, the voices fraught with drama.

"Hello," Zoe said, involuntarily cringing. "Hope? I'm—"

"Mrs. T." The girl studied Zoe's face. "Whoa. You're like *twins.*"

Zoe managed, she hoped, a believable, "Thanks." It pained her to think this hardboiled girl knew Leah well enough to make a familial connection. She considered pointing out that most people thought Leah resembled her father and thought better of it.

From inside, a husky voice asked who was at the door.

"Leah's mom," Hope yelled, over her shoulder.

"Be there in a jiff," the woman called back.

"It's all right, Ma. I got it."

Why on Earth had Leah run here? Why spend a minute in this God-awful place? With these *people*? Patients Zoe freely accepted. In general, she tried to avoid judgment. This was different. These people were harboring her daughter.

"May I speak with Leah please?" Zoe asked, with exaggerated politeness.

Hope shook her head. "Sorry, Mrs. T. She's not here."

On TV, a hysterical woman accused someone of cheating on her.

"Where is she, honey?"

"I don't know." Hope tucked a string of greasy blonde hair behind her ears. "Sorry. Want me to have her give you a ring? If I see her, I mean."

"Honey, your mom called yesterday." Zoe peeked around the girl, hoping to spot Leah. "I know my daughter's staying here. I'd just like to talk to her."

"Sorry, Mrs. T." Hope stared at her feet. "Wish I could help."

163

Or *would* help. "Honey, listen." She set a hand on Hope's arm. "I know you're trying to protect her." Uncertainty flashed in the girl's eyes. *She wants to do the right thing*, Zoe thought, *needs help sorting it out.* "You're a good friend. It would be better for her if you'd tell me where to find her. She belongs with her family. Don't you think?"

"I'm not lying, Mrs. T. I don't know where she is." Hope stepped aside to let her in. "You can come in, if you want. You're welcome to wait. Could be a while."

"That's all right," Zoe said. "I'll come back. Let her know I was here. I'd like to talk to her. Would you tell her that? Please?"

———&———

Squatting, Todd lowered Leah onto their blanket, shrugged out of his jacket, and draped it over her shoulders. The smell of decaying apples mingling with the musky odor of the damp earth made her feel bold and adventurous, like a mountain girl at the turn of the century. She pictured herself and Todd living in a log cabin, battling the elements. He'd shoot bear, tan the hides for warmth in the winter. For food, they'd fish. Or trap rabbits. Her stomach groaned from thinking about food.

"I'm starving." A weather-beaten wooden picker lay by the path. "Pick me an apple?"

"Too late," he told her. The apples had rotted. "Got some gum, if you want it."

She folded the stick of peppermint gum he'd offered and stuffed it in her mouth. "I love apple picking," she said. "We used to go every year."

Their mom would buy two large bags—"way more than we needed." She and Justine would skip up and down the dirt paths, Leah hunting for the ripest, most perfect apples on the trees. Her little sister—Leah laughed—would pick any old apple in reach, however misshapen, or wormy, or green.

"That orchard near our house. It's a development now. Why would anybody sell an orchard to a developer?"

"For the dough?" Todd suggested.

Leah stretched out on the blanket, laying her head in her boyfriend's lap, and looked up at the darkening sky, watching the clouds. The blanket was soft, like a broken-in sweatshirt.

Todd slid his hand under her head, massaged her neck.

She gazed up at her boyfriend. "So this one Halloween, we went to the orchard, right? They had all these pumpkins with candles inside. Like thousands of Jack-O-Lanterns, all lit up." She closed her eyes. "It's weird. I don't usually remember much about being a kid."

Todd lit a pipe. Leah sat, and he passed it to her.

When the pipe was empty, he pulled her into his arms and laid her on the blanket. Straddling her legs, he lowered himself onto her, his eyes clear and bright.

A hand slid under her shirt. Leah groaned, shifting slightly, helping him find his way under her bra. He kissed her gently. Kissed her again, his hands traveling to the small of her back. Her belly tightened. She spread her legs, felt him push against her groin. He was breathing heavily, his breath on her face, her body tingling.

Her entire life had been building to this moment. Often she'd imagined making love with a man. She touched herself, pretending her hand was the hand of a boy. She'd let a few boys feel her breasts. Only Todd had gone any further. For a lot of girls she knew, sex was just one more experience, like drinking or smoking. Leah couldn't relate. To her, it was special, a gift. To give herself over that way, she had to be ready. The timing had to be right, the boy special, someone she truly loved.

Last week, she'd asked Hope to drive her to the clinic for birth control pills.

I'm ready, Leah thought. *I'm finally ready.*

He fingered her belly ring, circled her belly button. "Beautiful," he whispered, and she *was* beautiful, to him, to herself, to the world.

Relax, she told herself. *Let yourself go.*

He pulled her up and she slipped out of her sweater and he pulled her tee-shirt over her head, the air cool on her shoulders, her chest, her arms. Reaching behind her, he unhooked her bra.

Her breath quickened. And he pushed the straps over her shoulders. She felt his fingers beneath the swell of her breasts, and she arched her back, feeling the release as he pulled the fabric away, her nipples hardening in the crisp autumn air. She shivered and he pressed her to the blanket, pushing against her, kissing her neck, her shoulders, her clavicle bones, kissed her belly…unzipped her jeans.

Closing her eyes, she felt her panties slide over her hips.

Twenty-One

Where Are You? Where Am I?

Dusk had settled by the time Zoe pulled into the garage. As she stepped into the mudroom, she felt an echo from inside the empty house. She hated this time of day—the witching hour, she'd called it when the girls were babies—darkness settling, both girls irritable and hungry. She flipped on the lights, the house eerily silent. Justine was nowhere in sight. Justine had been spending every spare minute at her friend Holly's house, working on her science project, she claimed. After dinner last night, she'd retreated to her room, closing her door.

Zoe tossed her keys on the counter. The TV was off, the family room dark. She went to the foyer, called upstairs, not really expecting an answer. She waited a few seconds and wandered into the living room. A photo of the girls sat on the end table. In the picture, the girls were clowning in a wading pool in the backyard of their Cape in Hudson, Justine in her one-piece orange bathing suit with blue stars, Leah in her ruffled pink bikini. Zoe drew a box around the girls, leaving a trail on the dusty glass.

Closing her eyes, she summoned a picture of her daughter. "Be safe," Zoe whispered. "That's all I ask."

Dejected, she headed back to the foyer. "Jus," she called from the bottom step. "You up there, honey?" Zoe called again, before trekking upstairs to see if her daughter had fallen asleep.

Dog lay at the foot of Justine's bed. She slid down and followed Zoe to the closet, nudging Zoe's legs. "Looks like nobody's home," Zoe said and closed the closet door.

She and Justine had painted the room two years earlier. For amateurs, their job had turned out surprisingly well. Fluffy cumulus clouds floated across the powder blue walls. She'd been hesitant to paint clouds; soon, Justine would outgrow the look, want something more sophisticated, better suited to a teen. But Zoe had been wrong. Two months ago, at Justine's request, she'd ordered a matching bedspread and curtains, pale blue spangled with bright yellow stars.

Zoe scratched the dog's neck and went to Leah's room. Leah's bedroom looked exactly as she'd left it, her drawers open, her bed unmade. Zoe stood in the doorway for a few minutes, feeling strangely out of place, and ventured inside, Dog at her heels.

The room smelled of Leah. Zoe ran a hand over her daughter's gnarled oak bureau, and pushed the top drawer closed. Leah's CD case lay on the nightstand. Flipping through, Zoe was shocked by how few titles she recognized. She studied the doodles on the walls, mildly surprised by her daughter's childlike scrawl, remembering the hearts pierced by arrows that had adorned the brown paper bag covers on Leah's elementary school books. Zoe stripped the bed, changed the sheets, and folded Leah's comforter and laid it at the foot of the bed.

Will had a meeting in Woburn this afternoon. When she asked with whom, he'd evaded her question. She had a hunch he'd called a headhunter. Last week, Micronics had terminated their contract, claiming NAC had failed to perform. The client owed NAC several million dollars for work Will's crew had completed, and they refused to pay. Supposedly, unscheduled construction delays had cost them a fortune. According to their project manager—"a royal asshole," to quote Will—the money Micronics had withheld barely recovered their costs.

"You do realize," Will said last Sunday night, "we've already been paid?" His boss was holding Will personally responsible for collecting the balance. NAC had paid his commission in good faith. He poured two glasses of Merlot, handed one to her. If he couldn't get the client to pony up, he'd be forced to return the twenty-five grand.

Twenty-five thousand dollars. When she deposited the check, she'd placed five thousand dollars in the savings account to hold them until his next commission check; the rest had gone to overdue bills. They had no way to repay the money. Refinancing was not an option:

they carried two mortgages already. With their debt load, no reputable bank would grant a personal loan. Maybe, Zoe's irrational side suggested, they could take cash advances against their credit cards.

Good Lord.

She called the Lansdown house and reached Hope. Leah still wasn't there. Depressed, she started dinner. She browned a pound of ground beef, poured a can of crushed tomatoes into the pot, added a large can of kidney beans, a bottle of medium hot salsa, two tablespoons of chili powder, and a dash of cumin. While she waited for the chili to come to a boil, she washed the counter and folded a load of laundry. Then she covered the pot, turning the burner to simmer, scribbled a note in case Justine returned while she was out, and changed into running clothes.

Todd and Leah sat on the ground, wrapped in the blanket, while he refilled the pipe. She felt stupid, sitting there naked, plus she was cold, but she was too flustered to suggest getting dressed. She'd never made love before. Maybe this was part of the deal.

She'd expected to feel, well, different after losing her virginity. She'd bled a little. She was a tiny bit sore. She'd gleaned no secret carnal knowledge. Shared in no deep, cosmic revelation. She'd crossed no boundary, felt no sudden immersion into womanhood.

Had she done something wrong? Todd was *far* more experienced than she. When he traveled with the rock band, they'd been surrounded by groupies—Band Aids, he'd called them. Skanks. He'd hooked up with a few, he'd claimed. She'd asked him, once, for a count. She had no interest in descriptions or names. She wanted a number.

"Ten?" she pushed. "Twenty? Twenty-five?" she'd asked timidly, hoping he'd respond with a far smaller figure. Todd only smirked.

"Was I okay?" She hugged the blanket. *Please don't say no.*

"Yeah, babe." He handed her the pipe. "I told you already. You were great."

"Thanks." She inhaled deeply, filling her lungs. And coughed up a lungful of smoke. "This tastes funny. What is it?"

"Weed." He brought the pipe to his lips.

"It tastes like plastic."

He raised his eyebrows, handed the pipe back. "It's only weed."

"How come it's this color?"

"*What* color?"

"Red." She tipped the bowl to show him.

"I laced it with opium," he finally admitted.

"Opium?" Todd knew very well that opium scared her.

"Chill out." He dragged on the pipe. When he handed it back, she pushed it away. "What? You don't trust me?" he growled.

"Of course I trust you," Leah replied.

"So then chill out already."

After they'd smoked a second bowl, Todd set the pipe on the ground, and climbed on top of her again.

"Stop." She giggled, scrunching her shoulders. His tongue tickled her ear. "Cut it out." Her voice sounded hollow, as if she were talking into a microphone that wasn't turned up.

A squirrel skittered past the blanket. She thought she heard footsteps.

"The farmer," she moaned, shivering. "I'm scared. He's coming to get us."

He loomed over her, his piercing blue eyes boring into her brain. "There's no farmer. What's the matter with you? There's nobody here."

Terrified, she pushed him off and wiggled out from under him.

Seething, he stood, his blistering blue eyes tearing into her skull.

Her head spun, the earth slanting under her.

He scooped up her clothes, tossed them at her. Suddenly, his penis shriveled. She tried to keep a straight face, but she couldn't help herself. He thought he was so tough. His penis betrayed him, the thick purple snake shrinking, turning into a tiny, baby blue *prune*.

Zoe stopped at the end of the street, stretched, and turned left onto Old Orchard Road. She loved running in this weather, the air damp and cool. It felt good to be out, breathing hard, pushing herself physically, her feet pounding the pavement.

In the dark, the road seemed to bank and shift. She considered returning for a flashlight, a reflective vest, and decided against it. Once inside, she'd find a reason to stay. The road sloped downhill. She hugged the shoulder, taking the hill slowly, finding her stride.

Finishing her first race on the Fourth of July had given her a shot of badly needed confidence. For a few years, she'd run a race nearly every weekend. At the end of a tough five-miler, she imagined herself finishing a marathon, chasing Joan Benoit to the finish.

Zoe pumped her arms. *Let go.* Breathed in through her nose, exhaled through her mouth. She was in a rhythm, picking up speed.

The image of Joanie morphed into a vision of Leah, racing up the soccer field.

Wait, Zoe thought. *Wait for me.*

A van blew by, honking.

"Watch it, asshole," the driver yelled, swerving around her.

Startled, she sprung onto the shoulder, hitting a mound of wet leaves. Her feet flew out from under her and she felt herself falling.

When she opened her eyes, she was lying in the road. Stupid, running after dark with no reflective vest. She rolled onto her side, pushing to a sitting position, brushed the pine needles off her jacket. Gritting her teeth, she tried to lift herself to her hands and knees.

Pain shot through her leg. And then Zoe passed out again.

"I don't friggin' believe this." Todd snapped the wheel, veering onto the dirt road, heading out of the orchard. He plugged a Nirvana CD into the player, an angry, frenetic rush of sound, and increased the volume, turning the music up, up, up.

Leah could barely think. She covered her ears, ignoring the tin soldiers inside her brain. In her hurry, she'd pulled her shirt on backward. She tugged her arms out of the sleeves, spun the shirt around. The music raged on, a strident march into oblivion. "Turn it down. Please?" She squeezed her throbbing temples. "I'm sorry."

For laughing, she meant. "I didn't mean it. Todd, listen to me."

Rain pounded the windshield. In the dense fog, the headlights were useless. Todd hit the accelerator, racing through the orchard, crashing over the ruts.

"Please," she pleaded, straining over the din. "Slow down."

He switched the CD. *Don't fuck with me bitch*, the MC railed.

"Do we have to listen to this? I hate rap music."

He pounded the steering wheel, the keys jangling. "The hell did I *do?*"

"Nothing," Leah lied. "You didn't do anything."

He lit a cigarette, sucked hard, and handed it to her. She pulled the scalding smoke into her lungs. He lit another, his hands shaking, and turned out of the orchard.

They were headed toward Main Street, a winding asphalt blur.

Trees, stone wall, field. She saw a herd of deer. A rabbit. A bird.

He swiveled to face her. She flinched and he overcorrected, swerving too far right. He wrestled the jeep back to its lane, the abrupt directional shifts flinging her about the cab like a rag doll.

She gripped the dash. "Slow down. Please?"

"Can't pull this shit," he snapped, spewing spit. "It ain't right." Her heart beat in her throat. "Please?" *He was going to kill them.* "Don't want to do it, fine, say so. No, you fucking *laugh* at me."

Rain hammered the windshield, the wipers sluicing, back and forth, back and forth, her brain drowning in a watery fog. She couldn't take this. She had to get out. Get away. Be alone. Think things through. She swung sideways, seizing the handle on her door.

"You *nuts*?" Todd lunged, pinning her in place. A pickup skidded around them.

"Let me go," she whimpered. Just let her *out.*

He turned on the defroster, the whir drilling into her skull. "Taking you to Hope's," he said, one arm strapping her down.

"Not crazy." Gulping back tears, she pummeled her thighs.

"Stop that," he croaked. "I never said you were crazy." He loosened his grip and Leah grabbed for the door. The jeep nosed into the gutter. "Don't do this," he begged. He rotated the wheel, his free hand holding her down. "I won't let you do this."

"Let me out of here," she cried. She was drowning, a whirlpool sucking her into its core. "Let *go.*" She punched his arm. "Not going anywhere with you." Pitching left, she took a swing at his face, kicking the dash. "Let me *out*," she wailed, wrenching free.

"Fine." He jammed the brakes, the Wrangler fishtailing. "I don't need this shit. Get out, if that's what you want. Suit yourself. Go."

Leah eased out of the truck. Limped down the street. Todd called. "Wait. Babe? Come back." She heard his feet hit the road. "Leah, wait."

She set one foot in front of the other, eyes focused ahead, refusing to listen.

"Leah," he called, his voice breaking. He called again, swore, and slammed his door shut. The engine roared and the truck skidded around her.

She watched the taillights shrink to pinpricks. A sharp wind cut past her, the frigid gust slapping her cheeks. Her head hurt, her ankle, her feet. *Move,* she thought, *a step at a time. One foot in front of the other.*

She stretched her arms. Leah barely recognized her own hands, ghoulish in the dim light. She wasn't herself anymore. Who was this crazy, lost girl she had become?

Twenty-Two

Wakeup Call

In Jerry's dreams, he and Zoe Tyler are at a campground. She's swimming in a lake, an ocean, sometimes a pond. He hears a cry, sees her floundering, and dives in to save her. He cradles her in his arms out of the water, lays her on the dewy grass. Her eyes are closed. Kneeling, he plants a deep kiss on her lips. That was as far as he'd ever progressed. Just as the dream heated up, someone or something always woke him. He slung an arm over his face.

"Jerry." He felt his wife joggling his shoulder. "Wake up."

"Huh?" he said, squinting. "What?" He'd fallen asleep this afternoon, around three thirty after a double shift. Now the house was lit like a circus and the curtains were drawn. "What time is it?"

"Six." She handed him the phone. "You got a call."

Jerry pressed the phone to his chest. "Who is it?" he mouthed.

"Station," she snapped and stormed into the kitchen.

Jerry listened carefully as Millie explained the situation. "Urgent," she said. "Tyler girl." She wouldn't let them call her parents and they couldn't get her to open up. They thought maybe she would talk to him. Before he'd clicked off, Jerry had mentally left for the station.

His wife was hovering over him. "You're supposed to be off," she complained. She'd put the boys down for the night. She and Jerry were supposed to have dinner together.

Maura stalked him to the bathroom and stood outside the door, whining. He ran the faucet, splashed his face and tamped the stubborn hairs at his crown, and then he took a leak, washed up, and brushed his teeth. He felt bad for his wife, but she'd married a cop. She knew what his job entailed. If he got an emergency call, he had to respond.

He opened the bathroom door, squeezed by, begging her pardon, and advanced to the coat closet by the front door, his wife looming over his shoulder. He reached inside for his bomber. Casual clothes would have to do. No time to hunt for a clean uniform.

"You're not leaving," his wife cried, blocking the door. "You can't do this to me. *Wait.* Aren't you going to change?"

"I've got to go. You know that," he said. "This isn't about you."

"We had plans," she whimpered. "You promised."

Ironic, he thought, after all the times she'd brushed him off. All the times he'd begged for companionship and found himself alone, sleeping on the couch. "I'll make it up to you, I promise," he said, and pecked his wife on the cheek.

"I don't want to be here alone again," his wife pleaded.

Aching for her, he nearly gave in. But he had a job to do, a responsibility to uphold. "Maura, please," he said. "I need you to move."

It had been raining earlier. Now the world was stagnant. He gazed at the cloudy sky, searching for some sign of life—the moon, a few stars. A gust of wind ripped the last of the sodden leaves from a maple tree and sent them swirling. He'd parked on the street, leaving the driveway open so Maura could pull her minivan up to the door. He felt a pinch of his sciatica as his foot hit the sidewalk.

They lived in the sticks. It was a pretty street neighbored by trees, though inconvenient as hell. This far out, they couldn't even get cable. Given a choice, he would live in a development closer to town, a neighborhood of young mothers with kids, less isolating for Maura. Choosing to stay in Cortland, opting to buy rather than rent, had left them no option; this was the only house he and his wife could afford.

Jerry wasn't sure how much help he would be. Meghan O'Leary had already tried. O'Leary was good with kids. She was young. The kids sensed genuine concern; they knew she cared. If she'd failed, Jerry doubted he could get through to the girl, but he'd give it a try.

Sounded like the Tyler girl had left the Lansdown place. That was a plus. Except in serious cases of abuse or neglect, kids fared best at home with their parents. Jerry had run away when he was a teen, so he knew.

After his arrest, his mother—his father passed away when Jerry was three—had banned Jerry's friends from their house. Incensed, he'd tossed three changes of clothes into a pack, rolled his sleeping bag, grabbed his tape deck, and hopped in his Mustang, heading west. He'd always liked horses, figured he'd land a job on a dude ranch. In Wyoming he slept under the stars. He'd never imagined the world to be so big—or so lonely. He'd lasted all of two weeks. He'd do his best to convince Leah to go home, try to work things out with her family. When he arrived at the station, Millie was sitting at her desk, surrounded by computers, taking a call. She looked over, saw him, and held up a finger.

"I recognized the girl," Millie said, when she hung up the phone. "Figured, since you let her off last week, maybe she'd trust you. Chief—" The older man had just emerged from his office. "—will fill you in."

"The punk dumped her on Main Street," the chief groused. "Pardon," he said, coughing, covering his mouth with a fist. A former nose tackle at Rutgers, he'd never lost the weight he'd gained playing ball, and the extra bulk put pressure on his airways; he was constantly wheezing. He coughed again. "Lucky some idiot didn't run her over."

True enough, especially in this weather. "Is she all right?"

"Shook up. Otherwise, seems fine."

"We get a name?"

"Corbett," Healy wheezed. "Get with the program, big guy. Spending too much time with them kids. Brain's turning to mush."

Something was off. Less than a week ago, Corbett had risked his neck for the Tyler girl. They could have sent him away for violating his probation. Tonight he intentionally dumped her out of the truck? Didn't add up. "We sure it was Corbett?"

"Getting soft, Johnson? Yeah, I'm sure."

"Any idea why? We get any details?"

"Who knows? Should've locked the punk up when we had him."

"I heard that," Millie said from across the room.

Unlike Jerry and his coworkers, Millie believed all suspects, regardless of the evidence stacked against them, were innocent until proven guilty. Though experience proved otherwise, Jerry respected her views. Her "liberal bullshit" galled the chief. "Easy for her to be liberal," Healy always said. *She* didn't have to deal with the fallout.

"That girl's in a load of trouble, hooked up with Corbett," the chief said.

Jerry might have argued, but he didn't see the point. "Anything else?"

"Talk to O'Leary," Healy said, and returned to his office.

Millie was on the phone again. Jerry attempted to catch her eye. He wanted her take. He trusted her instincts. She had an uncanny ability to cut to the heart of a matter and she often saw things the others missed. Rather than waste time waiting, he went to the mediation room, where he'd sat with the Tylers that night, to talk to O'Leary.

O'Leary was sitting at the desk with her back to the door. Like him, she'd studied criminal justice at Northeastern. She was young, bright, two years out of school. With her ambition and talent, she'd be off the street before long. Probably wind up in law school.

He tapped the door to let her know he was there. "Meg?"

She swiveled to face him. "Jerry. Hey. Glad you're here."

Normally, he'd ask how she was doing; he might crack a joke about her boyfriend, a rookie ADA assigned to the courthouse in Lowell. Tonight, he cut to the chase. "The Tyler girl? What happened?"

O'Leary looked puzzled. "We were hoping you'd figure it out."

Basically, she'd noticed Leah limping down Main, stopped, and offered to drive her home. The girl refused to give her name or address. For her own protection, O'Leary had brought her here.

"I put her in the tank, Jer. Sorry. She was in such a state. I gave her a blanket and hot chocolate."

"Thanks, Meg. I'll see what I can do."

"The mother's been in an accident." Healy had come up behind him. "You know that, right?"

The news sent Jerry reeling. "What happened?"

Healy spat in a tissue. "Hollingshead radioed. Looks like the Tyler broad got nicked by a truck. Bet it's that bastard from East Main," he said, referring to last week's hit and run.

"Witnesses?" Jerry asked.

"No, unfortunately." Healy was hacking again.

Jerry rubbed his neck. "How bad?"

"Fracture." Gesturing, Healy excused himself, went to the cooler, and returned, carrying a paper cup full of water. "Like I said, we'll know more once Hollingshead gets a statement."

"She say anything? Mention a make? A color?"

"Nada."

"Did Hollingshead get *anything* useful?"

"Relax already. If I didn't know better, I'd think you were doing her."

Jerry refused to dignify that ridiculous comment with a response.

"I told you, we'll know more once we get a statement."
Jerry did not find Healy's clap on the back at all reassuring.

Leah was sitting on the floor in the corner of the dank holding cell, her knees drawn to her chest, wrapped in the smelly blanket the female cop had given her. Stunned, she wondered what had happened, how her life had gotten so far off-track. The instant she saw Officer Johnson, she knew her troubles had only just begun.

"Accident," she heard the cop say.

The jeep's fishtailing lights flashed before her eyes. Leah covered her ears. She didn't want to hear about an accident. Todd had been driving erratically. He must have hit the stone wall. She pictured him ejected on impact, rocketing through the windshield. This was her fault. They'd been fighting.

No. This isn't happening. Wake me up. Please.

Officer Johnson stared down at her, his face pinched.

He wanted her to go to the morgue to identify the body. She saw it in his eyes. She couldn't. She would be sick. This wasn't fair. Her boyfriend was only in his twenties. Too young to die. Leah felt like a widow. She'd never stop grieving. Ever. Even if she lived to be a hundred.

The cop set a hand on her shoulder, his face blurred by her tears.

She watched his mouth working, the words oddly detached. The world around her had stopped. She was still breathing, but whatever part of her lived inside—her soul, Leah, *herself*—had gone flat.

The room twisted; the floor heaved. She couldn't get her bearings. Her ears rang. A strange sound—a school bell, a fire alarm—went off in her head, drowning everything else. If only this day would end and she could start over. Take today back. Everything would be different. Todd would still be alive.

The cop crouched beside her.

She clutched her stomach. She was going to vomit.

"Let's go," the cop said, taking her by the hand, helping her up.

"Where?" Leah squeaked. "Where are you taking me?"

His pity filled look told her more than she wanted to know.

"Where?" she asked again. She couldn't go to the morgue.

"Gum?" Jerry offered Leah a spearmint stick.

She folded the gum, said, "Thanks," and looked away.

The Tyler girl was sitting beside him in the cruiser, her head against the window. "Thanks," was the first word she'd uttered since they left the station. He was taking her to the hospital to visit her mother. For her own protection, given her irrational state of mind, he should have put her in flexible handcuffs, but he didn't have the heart. She'd taken the news hard. She'd misunderstood him at first, thought her mother was dead. He felt like a heel, scaring her. Although generally good with people, he was a disaster when bearing bad news. He never knew how to broach the subject or what he should say.

She shivered. He shouldered out of his jacket, laid it awkwardly over her legs, and turned up the heat. She pushed his jacket onto the console between them. What he had initially mistaken for shock, he realized now, was actually guilt. She'd upset her mother, running away. Emotionally, it was easy to link one event to the next. The accident had nothing to do with her. Her mother had been jogging, the accident a crime, if it turned out to be a hit and run. Not Leah's fault.

"I have a niece your age," he said, floundering. "My wife, I mean. It's her niece. She has a nephew, too. I have a sister. She doesn't have any kids." *I have a sister, she doesn't have any kids.* This would not be nearly as easy as he'd hoped.

Leah tugged at her ear. A trail of silver hoops ran from the helix to the base of her lobe. "That's a lot of earrings there. Did it hurt?"

"Not really," she said, barely audible.

"I know how you feel," Jerry said. "She's your mom. I get it."

A call came in over the CB, Millie deliberately speaking in code.

Leah fiddled with the automatic button on her window. Up, down, up, down.

"Mom's doing good," he said when Millie signed off. "They think she broke a bone in her shin."

"Is it bad?"

"Didn't sound too bad," he told her. "She'll probably be on crutches for a while. Getting around might be a pain in the neck."

The heat had fogged the windshield. Jerry turned on the defroster and windshield wipers. At the intersection, he noticed her watching him.

"Don't worry, kiddo," he said. "We'll find him."

She turned back to the window.

The temperature was dropping, the visibility decreasing. He pumped the brakes. "All right?" Poor kid was scared out of her wits. Broke his heart. "You're not too cold?"

She answered with a barely perceptible nod.

As he turned into the entrance to St. Michael's Hospital, Leah broke the silence. "Are you sure my mom is okay? Really sure? Positive?"

He hadn't seen the medical report and didn't know the full extent of her injuries, but he had no reason to believe otherwise.

"What's gonna happen? To the guy who hit her?"

Nothing, Jerry thought. The bastard would probably get off scot-free. A fine for driving to endanger, if they caught the son of a bitch. Even if they did, it would be hard to get a conviction. According to Hollingshead, Zoe claimed she'd fallen, and she was sticking to her story. Poor kid had been through enough for one night.

"I think we've got enough to go on," he said, that small comfort all he could offer.

---⊙⊙---

Knowing the cops had information scared Leah out of her wits.

Now that she knew her mom was okay, she was tempted to press the cop for details, see if she could figure out what they knew about the hit-and-run. Only if she asked too many questions, she'd raise his suspicion. If Todd was at fault and they caught him, well, she'd have to live with the outcome. She was not about to rat him out. She'd have to play the cop, let him think she wanted to see the guy caught.

"Officer," she said sweetly, and then lost her nerve.

This morning, despite having slept on a lumpy sofa, she'd felt alive and refreshed. She was, proud of her gumption, pleased with herself for proving she could get by on her own, that she didn't need her parents' support. She'd eaten a decadent, unhealthy breakfast of Fruit Loops, listened eagerly to Mrs. Lansdown's wild stories about Woodstock. Years seemed to have elapsed since the morning.

The parking lot was jammed. Accidents, Leah surmised, caused by the rain and fog. The temperature must have dropped twenty degrees over the last two hours, the brittle air cutting right through her. Shivering, she hugged herself.

"Take it," he said, draping his jacket over her shoulders. "Please."

"Thanks," Leah said quietly. She pulled the jacket closed. "That's nice of you."

An ambulance screamed by, siren wailing. It pulled to a stop in front of the emergency entrance. Its rear door opened, an attendant hopped out, and then the gurney emerged. As the paramedics lowered the gurney, a medical team rushed out to meet them, several people barking orders at once.

"When I was your age," Officer Johnson said. "I ran away, too." He was trying to establish a bond, but his story depressed her.

Leaving the security of her parents' home had been the only interesting aspect of running away. Plenty of teens ran away, but they usually hailed from marginal families, families any intelligent person would leave. Among kids like herself, from solid middleclass backgrounds, she was a leader, she'd felt. Other than Todd, Lupo, maybe Hope, Leah did not know a single person brave enough to strike out alone. Listening to Officer Johnson, one of the most average people she'd ever met, talk about running away, forced her to face the painful truth: she was totally ordinary. Nothing special at all.

"You're limping," Officer Johnson said. "What happened?"

Leah shrugged. The accident was dumb, not worth talking about.

"I broke my foot once," he told her. "Jumping off a roof."

"Off a roof," she repeated.

Today was the worst day of Leah's entire life. She felt disloyal, assuming Todd hit her mother. Somehow, it all made terrible sense: Todd had dropped her off less than a mile from where her mother was hit. He'd been driving like a maniac. According to the police, she'd been hit by a truck. Obviously, if Todd was involved, their relationship was over. How could she ever forgive him? But it would break her heart. Seeing her boyfriend sent to jail would destroy her.

When they reached the revolving door at the ER, Officer Johnson stepped aside, gesturing for her to go in. His prompt stopped her in her tracks. Alone? It had never occurred to her that she'd be forced to face her parents alone. She'd been focused ahead, worrying about her mom, wondering about Todd, wondering what the future would bring, where they'd all end up. She'd skipped right over the present.

———— ❦ ————

Jerry set a hand on her shoulder. She looked like a frightened child. He thought she might run.

"Family can be tough," he said, putting his arm around her. "Hurtful words, misunderstandings, you let them slide, they take on a life of their own. Pretty soon, it's like you're on opposite sides of a valley, you know? Like there's a mountain between you." He pictured his wife, watching from the living room window as he'd climbed in the cruiser. "You build up too much distance; you tell yourself you've got no choice but to—"

"Run," Leah said softly.

"Try to patch things up. Might not seem worth it. It will be in the end." Leah offered a weak smile. "Your folks are crazy about you," he said, pulling her into a fatherly hug. "They'll be glad to see you."

When they released, she said, "Thank you," and pulled off his jacket.

He took the bomber, shook it out, and draped it over her shoulders. "Hang on to it," he said. He'd swing by in a few days. She could return it then. "Here. Before we go in." He handed her his card, with the phone number and e-mail address where he could be reached. "Call me. Day or night. Even if you just want to talk."

At the intake desk, he spoke with a wary administrator. It took three tries, the words arranged three different ways, to convince her that Leah was neither a convict nor a danger, his intent simply to reunite the child with her mother. Finally, he got through to her.

A few minutes later, the triage nurse came out of her office to greet them.

Jerry and Leah followed the nurse through automatic doors to the heart of the ER. Nurses and doctors in scrubs were congregated around the central desk, discussing cases. Others inside the U-shaped station sat in front of buzzing computers, entering test data, recording patient information. The triage nurse spoke briefly with a doctor and led Leah to Room Six, where Zoe lay behind the curtain, awaiting care.

Jerry watched Leah weave through the bustling staff, dodging the rolling gurneys. The triage nurse pushed aside the curtain. Leah dropped her head, and he noticed the staccato tic of her shoulders.

Will Tyler sat on a rotating stool, feet apart, his hands between his knees, staring at the heart monitor beside his wife's bed. He nodded when he saw his daughter, rose, and touched her shoulder. Leah tiptoed to her mother's bedside, pecked her mother timidly on the cheek, as if she were afraid of hurting her, afraid of getting too close.

Zoe squeezed her daughter's hand. Now she and Leah were crying. Leah's father drew her into a hug, as Jerry had done just a few minutes ago. In an hour or two, once Zoe had been treated and bandaged, they'd ride home together, a family again.

A wave of depression swept over him. Then, oddly enough, Jerry felt better.

Leah was a good kid. Decent head on her shoulders. Good family. Compared to most kids he dealt with, she had a leg up. He thought about his own youth, the headaches he'd given his mother. Adolescence was trying for all involved, teens as well as the parents. It took patience, enormous patience, but they would get through it. Someday, they would look back on all this trouble, and realize it was only a bump in the road.

Twenty-Three

In Leah's Wake

According to the emergency room doctor, Justine's mother's injuries were relatively mild. The following morning, Leah told Justine their mother had joked about how dumb she had been, jogging in the dark. Her leg hurt, she'd said, but it wasn't too bad. In a few days, everyone agreed, she would be up and around.

By that afternoon, when Justine arrived home from school, her mom's knee had swollen to the size of a small beach ball and she could hardly talk, her face pale, gaunt. Justine burst into tears. When she was ten, Justine had fallen off the jungle gym at her school, spraining her ankle, and she remembered clearly how much pain she had been in.

Her mom, it turned out, was in worse shape than the ER doctors had realized. The orthopedist Justine's father consulted the day after the accident ordered an MRI. The test confirmed the original diagnosis: a hairline fracture of the tibia bone, a minor injury, requiring a cast for four weeks. She'd also strained the anterior cruciate ligament in her knee. Freak accident, the orthopedist said. Unfortunately, there was no quick fix. For now, he preferred to watch it.

Surfing the Net, researching ligament injuries, Justine learned that if her mother lost the stability in her knee, she might need surgery. Until her next visit with the orthopedist, her mother was to stay off her feet and elevate the leg. Her doctor prescribed OxyContin to help her manage the pain, and told Justine's father to order a wheelchair.

Three days after the accident, at six o'clock in the morning, her dad's administrative assistant sent an e-mail informing him of a companywide management meeting their boss, Mr. Jackman, had called to address the Micronics debacle. Her father had no choice but to attend. The visiting nurse he'd hired to care for Justine's mom during the day didn't start until the following week. If they'd let him know a day earlier, he could have arranged for a neighbor to stay at the house.

Reluctantly, at her insistence—she wanted to take care of her mom—he allowed Justine to stay home from school. Holly promised to deliver Justine's assignments for her five honors classes. Justine was glad to be home. She never could have concentrated today, with her mom incapacitated and Leah isolating herself in her room.

Justine was sitting with Dog on the family room floor by the sofa where her mother lay, dozing, half watching cable TV, half daydreaming. She'd made the first major decision of her life today. When she grew up, she would be a physician. Since the accident, Justine spent all her spare time on the Internet, surfing medical Websites. Her initial research on ACL injuries led her to a site hosted by the Yale Medical School's anatomy department, where she learned the quadriceps and hamstring muscles stabilized the knee.

The site provided detailed pictures of the human body and its systems. The human body, Justine discovered, had six hundred skeletal muscles. Muscles worked in pairs, one stretching while the opposing muscle contracts, and were attached directly or indirectly to bones. So far, Justine had learned the names and functions of fifty of the body's six hundred skeletal muscles, but *that*, she bragged to Dog just as the doorbell rang, was only the start.

She was vaguely surprised to see Officer Johnson on the stoop.

"Hello," the policeman said. "How are you today?"

"Fine," Justine replied uncertainly. "Can I help you, Officer?"

"If she's here, I'd like to talk to your sister, see how she's doing."

"I'll get her," Justine said—if, that was, she agreed to come down. Her sister had been holed up in her room for two days, ever since their parents returned from the orthopedist's office with the bad news.

Justine found her sister curled in the corner of her bed in black silk panties, washed to translucence, and a rumpled blue tee-shirt, her button bracelet encircling her wrist like a handcuff. The policeman's jacket lay over her legs, the grimy soles of her feet poking out from under it.

Justine nudged Leah's shoulder. "Lee? That policeman's here."

Leah's foot moved, ever so slightly. "Go away," she mumbled.

"What should I tell him?"

"Nothing. Leave me alone."

"I have to say something." Justine shook her sister's foot.

"Here." Leah snatched the jacket and hurled it, the bomber slapping Justine in the chest. "Now tell that fucking cop to get lost."

The policeman thanked her and left, but the incident left Justine off balance. To clear her head, she took Dog outside. To Justine's delight, Dog raced around the yard, darting in and out of the woods, full of vim and vigor, almost as if she were a puppy again.

As soon as Justine came back inside, she checked on her mom. Her mother lay on the sofa, her head and feet propped on down bed pillows, a small pillow rolled under her knees. She blinked, motioning for the bottle of pills on the coffee table. Justine pushed a pill into her mother's mouth, and brought a glass of water to her lips. Her mom swallowed and closed her eyes again. Justine covered her with the mohair blanket, switched off the TV, and went to the kitchen to fix a sandwich for her sister.

"Leah?" She knocked once and opened the door. "Hungry?"

"Go away," Leah croaked, burying her face in a pillow.

Justine set the plate on her sister's nightstand, went to the window, and lifted Leah's shades, letting some daylight into the room.

"Oh, my God. Look at *Dog*," she said, amused. "You've got to see this, Lee." Dog raced across the backyard, chasing a squirrel. "She's going nuts."

"Come on, Lee. You've got to eat." Justine swiped a potato chip from her sister's plate and popped it in her mouth. "At least drink the Pepsi," she said, lowering herself to the floor by Leah's bed. She crossed her legs Indian style, took a handful of chips, and began talking—about nothing, really. The weather: cold again. Her algebra teacher: kind of a dope. *Silas Marner*, the book she was supposed to be reading for English.

"It's so *boring*, Lee. I hate it. Why can't they assign fun books? Like *Harry Potter*. Or *Lord of the Rings*? I'm not finishing it," she announced.

Leah rolled onto her side, shielding her eyes. "Why are you *doing* this?"

"What?"

"Bitching. You're like a reading machine."

"I want to pick my own books. I hate being told what to read." Leah pushed onto her elbows. "Get used to it," she said. "They never let you pick your own books. Hey, can I have that Pepsi?" Justine unscrewed the cap. "Mom seems a little better," she said, hoping she might draw Leah out. "She watched TV for a while."

Leah sipped the Pepsi and set the bottle on her nightstand. "I can't do this, Jus."

"What do you mean?" Justine asked, alarmed by Leah's tone.

Leah picked at her thumbnail. "I shouldn't have come back."

"Because of Dad?" Their father had been cool toward Leah, his silence worse than anything he might have said. "You know him. He'll get over it."

"It's not just him, Jus." She hated fighting with their parents, Leah said, always walking on eggshells. But that wasn't all. "The accident. It's my fault."

Justine climbed onto her sister's bed. "It was an accident, Lee. Nobody's *fault*."

"You know as well as I do. She was out running because of me."

"That doesn't make it your fault."

"I broke up with him," she mumbled. "I couldn't sleep."

"Oh, Lee." Justine wanted to hug her sister, but a hug was clearly not what Leah needed. She needed a sympathetic ear.

"I've got to pull myself together," Leah said. Time to get her life on track, she went on. As long as she was with Todd, nothing would change. She'd called him this morning, before he left for work. They'd talked for over an hour. "He kept repeating himself. Saying he loves me." He begged her to change her mind. "He cried, Jus. It was so *hard*." Justine squeezed her sister's hand. "I can't stand this, you guys hating me. I can't live like that. I just want things to be back how they used to be."

Justine's eyes welled. She'd be lying if she didn't admit to being angry with Leah—for running away, abandoning her, all the trouble she'd caused—but she heard the catch in Leah's voice and she understood the toll all this had taken on her sister.

"I could never hate you," Justine said, her own voice breaking. "I just want to help you." Justine convinced Leah to talk to their parents, apologize, tell them she'd broken up with Todd, and ask if they could start over. "I know they'll say yes."

Leah twiddled her belly ring. "The truth, Jus. Think it'll work, really?"

Will spooned the leftover cod in a Tupperware bowl and put it in the fridge. His wife had barely touched her dinner. He felt bad for her. He'd twisted his knee in college, his injury far less extensive than hers, so he could imagine how much pain she was in.

The phone rang. He picked up on the first ring.

"Excuse me?" He must have heard incorrectly. "Who is this?"

"Todd," said a low voice on the other end of the line. "Corbett."

What the—

"Just, uh, calling, you know, to apologize."

"Apologize," Will repeated. Give him a break. "Is that right?"

"I guess, uh, you probably heard I got busted. In Texas."

Will flung the towel over his shoulder and drummed the counter.

"I just," the kid stammered, "want, uh, you know. To let you know I changed."

"You changed," Will repeated in a monotone. "How's that?"

His wife had fallen asleep on the family room sofa. She'd been drifting in and out for the last hour.

"I ain't like that no more. I mean, I cleaned up. I just want you to know that."

"All right." Will released an audible breath. "Thanks for the call."

"Mr. Tyler?"

Will waited.

"Sorry about your wife. I hope, you know, I hope she's okay."

The remorse in Corbett's voice sounded genuine. Maybe he deserved more credit than Will had given him. Corbett was a kid, the wrong one for his daughter, but still a kid. It took balls to call your girl's father, apologize—big ones. "Thanks," he said. "I appreciate it."

"Tell her I hope she feels better?"

"Sure," he said, moved. "I will. Good of you to call."

"Mr. T? Sir?" Corbett said, as Will was about to hang up.

"Yes?"

"I love her."

"Excuse me?" It took an instant for the outrage to sink in, and then it hit full force. The son of a bitch had been playing him.

"Your daughter. Me and her—maybe you could—"

Will clicked off, infuriated, and flung his towel in the sink.

---◈---

The phone was ringing as Justine scooted up the stairs to Leah's room. One ring. Strange. It must have been the wrong number.

Her sister had changed into jeans and a clean white tee-shirt, the words "Sexy Babe" in sparkling blue script across her chest. She was sitting on the edge of her bed, staring at the floor. Justine's heart sank. Her sister had lost her nerve. She'd decided not to follow through on their plan. Who could blame her? Apologies were risky business. Adults were rarely satisfied with a simple apology. To grownups, receiving an apology was like a victory, license to pile on.

Leah tousled Justine's hair. "Don't be so paranoid. I was just thinking." She'd been rehearsing, psyching herself up. "You really think this'll work, Jus? They don't hate me?"

Justine gave an encouraging nod. "It'll be good. You'll see."

"Really?"

"Really."

Leah pulled a face. "I'm scared." Leah took a deep breath. "Okay. Let's get this over with." With her baby finger, she hooked Justine's pinky. "Wish me luck."

Justine followed her sister downstairs and sat in the breakfast nook, her hands folded nervously in her lap. Her sister approached their parents respectfully. Leah asked, quietly, if they could please talk for a minute. Their father turned off the TV.

Justine breathed a sigh of relief. They were off to a positive start.

"I told you," Leah argued.

What had happened? Justine leaned forward, listening.

"I broke it off," her sister said "Isn't that enough?"

Justine breath caught.

"You expect us to believe that?" their father demanded.

"It's true. Swear to God. I'm telling the truth."

Her father must have turned his head. Justine missed his answer.

"*What?*"

"You heard right," their father barked. "I want it in writing."

In writing? Justine clapped her mouth. *Please don't do this.*

"I'm sorry," Leah pleaded. "What more do you want? Why can't you trust me?"

"Because you proved you can't be, that's why."

Their mother, through her stupor, objected. "Not a war tribunal," she slurred. "Family...trust each other...good's a piece of paper?"

"Jesus Christ, Zoe." Their father's voice rose. "Trust. Want to know who just called?"

"Todd?" Leah sounded shocked. "Called here? What for?"

"Called, um, you know, um. Changed. Um, um, called to apologize," their father said, mimicking Todd. "Asshole. What's he think? I'm a moron? Like he gives a damn how your mother's doing." Justine covered her ears. Still, the voices churned.

"I hate you," Leah cried, kicking something—a table, a chair, the wall. "I hate you." She kicked again. "I wish you were *dead*."

Silence descended over the house. Then Leah hurtled upstairs.

Every year, from the time Justine was a toddler until she was eight, her family rented a summerhouse on Squam Lake. Justine and Leah spent the weekdays with their mom in New Hampshire, while their dad was working in Massachusetts. The owners of the cottage moored an outboard motorboat by their dock. Their mother never unlatched the boat. She was not a strong enough swimmer, she said. If there were ever an accident, how would she save two little girls?

Weekends, their father would unmoor the motorboat and take the family for long, fast rides on the lake, the boat crashing over the waves, the water spraying like rain. Leah begged to steer, her bright orange life vest slipping off her shoulder, her bikini bottoms riding up over her butt cheeks.

Justine never wanted to drive. She'd kneel in the stern, watching the blades cut through the glistening water, the waves churning. Justine felt sorry for the fish, their habitat all agitated, roiling. She wondered how they survived. Now here they were, in Leah's wake. She had no idea how to make things right. No idea what to do. No idea how they would survive.

Twenty-Four

Sisters III

With their mother laid up, Justine went into overdrive. She did her own chores as well as her sister's, kept her mom as comfortable as possible, and took care of the house. After school, when the bus dropped her off at the end of the street, rather than hang out with Holly until dinner, she went directly home, started supper, washed and folded the laundry, cleaned the kitchen and bathrooms, damp-mopped the floors.

She didn't mind, at first, that no one noticed. Helping her mom, covering for Leah, helped maintain some semblance of peace in the house, and peace was worth double the effort. It would have been nice if someone thanked her on occasion. If her mother tried to wean herself off the pills. If her father came home from work on time for a change so they could eat dinner together. Instead, she put his food in the microwave. In the morning, she'd find his dish in the sink, and he would be gone.

A week after the accident, Justine's father hired a carpenter to build an office over their garage. He called a plumber to install a bathroom. Justine had seen him browsing the Internet, looking at shelving, hardware, flooring materials. Last week, he'd ordered a cot.

Leah's birthday, the twenty-first of November, came and went with little ado. Their father gave her four CDs, which Leah immediately exchanged, an iPod with headphones that she wore morning and night, and a gift card for iTunes. No one bothered with cake. Technically, Leah was living at home, but she was rarely around. Justine suspected she was spending her time at Hope's. On the rare occasions when her sister *was* home, she moped around the house, acting all angry and hurt, refusing to talk. Justine often heard Leah, alone in her room, crying. She wanted desperately to console her, let her sister know someone cared. When she knocked on Leah's door, her sister shooed her away.

Two days before Thanksgiving, Nana and Poppa Tyler called and offered to drive up from Philly to spend the holiday with them. They would arrive on Tuesday afternoon, they said, and stay through the following week. Nana would cook dinner. Poppa, who'd taken up baking after he retired, would bake the holiday pies. After her father hung up the phone, he and Justine went to the grocer's to purchase the supplies on her grandparents' list. At the Natural Grocer, they bought a twenty-five pound free-range turkey and an assortment of vegetables and fruit. While her father organized the pantry, Justine washed the linens and made the bed in the guest room.

The night before her grandparents were due to arrive, Justine heard her parents fighting. Her father, in fit of frustrated anger, threatened divorce. The next morning, he called his parents, asked if they would mind postponing their trip until after the first of the year.

"My wife isn't up for company right now," Justine heard him say.

But what about us? Justine thought. *What about me?*

Thanksgiving was a disaster: dry turkey, "freaking waste," her father muttered, "four bucks a pound"; boring mushroom and artichoke stuffing in a casserole dish; limp string beans and lumpy mashed potatoes. They forgot the cranberry sauce. Her father insisted they eat at the dining room table. Justine's mom yawned, her eyelids fluttering, Leah pushed her food around with her fork, mashing it into a disgusting mush, and Justine and her father ate. No one said a word.

Justine's mother continued to rely on the OxyContin her orthopedist had prescribed. According to the nurse, Justine heard her dad tell her grandmother on the phone, her mom shouldn't need drugs anymore. After her father clicked off, her parents had their worst argument yet. Her mother, through tears, demanded to know why he'd spread those dreadful lies to his mother. Justine's father insisted it was out of concern.

He pounded the counter. "Time to snap out of it, Zoe." There was no getting through to her, though.

Soon, Justine tired of taking care of the house by herself. No one noticed all she had done; now, no one noticed all she left undone.

After school, she dragged herself to her room, spending afternoons and most of her nights at her desk with Dog at her feet, surfing the Web, researching facts for her Milky Way project.

Maybe I'll teach high school science, she thought. She'd given up on being a doctor.

The day after Thanksgiving, while Justine and Holly listened to music in Holly's bedroom, Holly's stepfather wound lights around the columns on their front porch and her mom put electric candles in the windows. Mr. Begley hung a red satin bow above their garage door. The Girl Scouts strung lights on the giant spruce tree on the common.

Gradually, twinkling holiday lights went up all over town.

In the weeks leading to Christmas in the past, the entire Tyler family had pitched in with the holiday preparations. Justine and Leah helped their mother shop and bake cookies and address holiday cards. Their father, in charge of the tree, trekked from nursery to nursery, traveling as far as New Hampshire some years, in search of the biggest, fullest tree he could find. He'd haul the tree home, secured by a bungee cord to the roof of his car, and drag it up the back steps, across the deck, and into the family room. He'd eyeball the space, making faces until he'd found the perfect spot to erect it. Every year, he chose the same spot: three feet to the left of the fireplace, so you'd see the tree as soon as you entered, however you approached.

The white lights her father always strung around the bushes outside were still packed. The staircase banisters, normally festooned with holly, were bare. They had no tree. Justine's father kept promising to buy one, but whenever Justine asked, he said he'd forgotten.

On Saturday morning, Justine took it upon herself to decorate. She carried the Nativity set, stored in a box filled with packaging peanuts, down from the attic. She unpacked the rustic wooden stable, set it on the family room mantle. She cut a brown paper bag into strips for straw, lined the stable's cracked wooden floor, and unwrapped the figurines. Over the years, the shepherds and Wise Men had vanished, leaving a miniscule Jesus, a cherubic infant lying in a manger the size of Justine's thumb, a seven-inch ceramic Mary in a sky-blue robe, her blue veil trimmed in white, and a featureless Joseph, carved from wood, two inches shorter than his dazzling wife.

Justine unraveled the artificial holly, wove the silk strands through the banisters in the hallway leading upstairs. Last year's ribbons were flat. She tugged the wire-reinforced loops, reshaping the bows, and secured them to the newel posts with garbage bag ties. When she finished decorating, she went to her room to check on Dog. Her dog lay at the foot of the bed, nuzzled on Justine's bathrobe. "Hey, baby," she said, offering a rawhide treat. "Hungry?" Dog lifted her head, took one lick, and settled back down.

As usual, her father had left for work early. Her mom and Leah were still in bed. Justine enjoyed the quiet, her mind wandering freely. In the kitchen, she prepared apples for crisp. When she'd finished peeling, she sliced the apples into a bowl, added cinnamon and sugar, and scooped the fruit into a buttered Pyrex dish. The apples looked skimpy. She peeled, cut, and added two more.

Maybe she and Leah could go to the nursery when Leah woke up. Leah didn't have her license yet. If they paid for the gas, maybe Hope could borrow her mother's car and give them a ride. They'd select the fullest, prettiest tree on the lot, a tree so magnificently tall, it would stretch, like the tree in the *Nutcracker*, to the family room ceiling. Justine had saved her birthday money and most of her allowance; she had three hundred dollars stashed in her bureau. If she had money left over, she would buy a wreath for the front door.

"Morning, sweetheart. Looks gorgeous around here."

Justine spun, startled by her mother's voice. It was barely eight thirty. For as long as Justine could remember, her mother had been an early riser. Justine, an early bird herself, would wake at dawn, find her mother in the living room, reading a book or staring into space, daydreaming. These days, her mom slept late, especially on weekends. Justine hadn't expected her for another hour.

"Thanks, Mama. I made apple crisp. Are you hungry?"

Her mother propped her crutches against the center island, and lowered herself onto a barstool. "Not yet. It smells awfully good."

Justine's mom set her elbows on the counter. She wore her old terrycloth robe, a washed-out violet, cinched at the waist. She looked different, though Justine could not put her finger on how. She'd combed her hair. Maybe that was it.

"How about some coffee?" Justine asked.

"Sure, honey. That would be great."

At half-past eleven, Leah clopped down the stairs. She'd borrowed Justine's baby doll pajamas. Two days ago, just as it had finally looked decent again, Leah dyed her hair a hideous rust-orange red. Her sister looked silly. The pink pajamas clashed with her hair.

"Aren't you cold?" Justine was wearing a thermal tee-shirt and a long-sleeved cotton turtleneck under her angora sweater, with fleece-lined jeans. Even in layers, she was freezing.

Leah finger combed her stubbly hair. "Never, little sis. I don't get cold. So what's up with Dog? How come she's not down here?"

Justine frowned. "Think it's normal for her to sleep so much?"

"How should I know? She *is* pretty old."

Dog wasn't old. She was only thirteen, a few months older than Justine. Ninety-one in dog years. Still, plenty of dogs lived longer.

Prancing across the kitchen, Leah flung open the pantry doors, plucked a box of cream of wheat cereal from the shelf, and turned the box on its side, inspecting the ingredient list. "Did you know cream of wheat's got thiamin mononitrate in it?"

Justine had no clue what thiamin mono—whatever Leah had said—even was. "Maybe that thiamono-nono stuff is a vitamin."

"Maybe," Leah said doubtfully. "I'm not eating this crap. I don't eat anything that isn't like totally, one hundred percent natural."

"Since when?" Leah always begged for Cocoa Puffs or Fruit Loops or Trix.

Leah set her hands on her hips, the cereal box angled away from her body. "Since now. I'm gonna eat really healthy from now on." She lowered her voice. "I quit smoking, you know."

"Seriously?" Justine could hardly contain herself. "That's awesome, Leah."

"Thanks," Leah replied, with a self-satisfied grin. "Starting today. Actually, I'm thinking about joining a commune. I found this really cool community on the Internet. Anybody can join. They're totally open-minded. It's in Vermont. You can come, if you want."

A commune? Communes were filthy, with all those people living under one roof. Besides, Justine was only twelve. "I don't know. Maybe when I'm older."

"Come on, Jus. You don't want to croak eating all this rotten stuff, do you? Know what I think? Why they put all this crap in our food?" Leah sent the cereal box sailing across the counter; it landed with a soft thud on the floor. "The Wall Street pigs, right? In the Senate and shit, the capitalists that run the big corporations? They want to get rid of the rest of us. So they can rule the world. You don't have to believe me. But I'm telling you, Sis, they're trying to kill us."

Leah returned to the pantry, reappeared a minute later, waving a box of Mallow Treats cereal. "Obviously *he* did the shopping. Bet Mom doesn't know he buys this crap. Wait a minute. *You* didn't tell him to get it?" she asked, in a tone Justine found insulting. "You don't *eat* this stuff, do you?"

Justine cringed, afraid of what her sister would say next.

Leah tugged Justine's arm. "Look." She pointed to the ingredient list. "Marshmallow, sugar, gelatin, artificial flavoring, *color* added. Maltodextrin. That's another kind of sugar, in case you were wondering. I don't know why they can't say it outright, so you know what you're eating. Look, sugar again. That'd be the real sugar. Partially hydrogenated soybean oil, salt, natural and artificial flavoring. What exactly is natural flavoring? Isn't that an oxymoron or something?" Leah clucked her tongue. "This shit's bad, Jus. I don't know which is worse, the artificial shit or all that sugar. Imagine what your intestines must look like?"

"Um," Justine said, nervous about the state of her innards.

"Whatever," Leah said. "I wouldn't trust anything that came out of a box.

"Want me to make you some eggs? Eggs are good, aren't they?"

"Cholesterol? Duh. I don't think so." Justine saw her sister's brain working. She hoped Leah didn't ask for some weird ingredient, like tofu. "Oh, why not," Leah said, finally. "Bacon, too. As long as it's not that turkey crap Mom used to buy."

When Leah finished eating, she and Justine cleaned the kitchen. Leah washed the pans. Justine scrubbed the stainless steel stovetop.

"What's she doing on the phone?" Leah flung the dishrag on the counter and shook out her hands. "Who's she talking to?" She cocked her head toward the family room.

Justine pricked up her ears. Their mother was talking about her knee. As long as her strength returned, she was saying, it didn't look as though she'd need surgery. Their mother lowered her voice. Justine winced. The conversation must have shifted to Leah.

"I don't believe this." Leah slapped the counter. "It's that *cop.*"

"No way," Justine replied. "Why would she be talking to him?"

"Yeah, it is. I heard his name. What's she talking to *him* for?"

"Maybe he's still investigating, making sure nobody hit her."

"Didn't they determine that already?"

Justine squirmed. She wished her sister would let it go. If Leah were around more often, she'd know that, in fact, her mom talked to him every day. Justine thought it nice at first; Officer Johnson's taking a personal interest in their family was welcoming. Now, almost a month after the accident, she'd started to think it was weird. Justine never mentioned the calls to her sister. Leah hated Officer Johnson. It was almost as if, because he'd sent her home, she blamed him for her problems with their parents.

"It's not him, Lee. It's one of her friends from work."

"Whatever. Where's the D-man?" Leah bent over the counter, scrubbing aggressively. "Something disgusting's stuck on here."

"Dad's at work."

"Yeah, right. On a Saturday? He's avoiding us, Jus. It won't surprise me a bit if they got a divorce. I've heard them both threaten."

A sharp pain shot through Justine's belly and under her rib cage. She doubled over, clutching her stomach. "He's working," she said, once the pain faded. "He had to return calls."

"You're so *gullible*, Justine. If he had to make calls, he could do it from here. He's got that stupid office over the garage." Leah rubbed the counter, set the steel wool aside and worked at the spot with her thumbnail. "Not that I blame him. She's addicted to those stupid pills. I bet she called that cop," Leah spat. "Phone never rang. What a jerk."

Please, Justine thought. *Stop*. "It did ring. I heard it," she lied.

Leah gave her a dubious look. "That isn't the point," she countered. "What's wrong with your stomach? You're not on that Zantac again, are you? Oh, my god, *I* know." Leah shook Justine's arm. "You're getting your period," she said, dancing in a circle around Justine. "You *are*. My baby sister's finally getting her period."

If only. She was one of the only girls in the entire eighth grade that didn't have it. Leah wouldn't let up. To distract her, Justine said, "We should get a tree today. If we wait for Dad, it'll be New Year's."

That got Leah off on a whole other tangent.

While Justine finished her math homework, Leah sat on a barstool at the island, laboring over a crossword puzzle and picking at the apple crisp. Their mother had fallen asleep on the family room sofa. Leah had called Hope to see if she'd drive them to a nursery to pick out a tree, but Hope was out for the day.

"Jus?" Leah scribbled an answer to one of the questions, crossed it out, and wrote a new answer above it. "Why do you think they hate him so much?"

Leah knew very well why their parents hated her ex-boyfriend. A) He'd encouraged Leah to run away. B) Since they began dating, Leah was constantly in trouble. C) The kid was defiant. He stopped by the house one day when Leah wasn't around, supposedly to visit their mother. He'd brought their mom a bouquet of assorted fresh flowers, asked a lot of questions about her injuries, how she was feeling. As soon as she'd dropped her guard, the wheedling started. He tried to talk her into permitting Leah to see him, told her how sorry he was, he'd never meant to hurt Leah. He pointed out all the ways he had changed. Her father happened to come home while Todd was still at the house. Todd refused to look at him, a tactic even Justine found offensive. Hardly the way to win their father's approval. All the same, their parents went overboard, blaming him for everything Leah did wrong. Her sister was seventeen, old enough to be responsible for herself.

It dawned on Justine suddenly: they were dating again. "You're not back together? How could you, Lee?" The day they broke up, Leah had told Justine what had transpired the night at the orchard. "After what he did to you?"

Leah sniggered. "We broke up for like two *days*. It was stupid. It was mostly my fault. I made him pull over. Besides, he said he was sorry." She picked a gooey apple out of the bowl. "They're crazy if they think they can keep me away from him. I'm stuck here right now. I don't feel like going back to Hope's and I don't have anywhere else to go. The second I turn eighteen, I'm out of here."

"You'd do that again? You'd leave me alone?"

"Alone?" their mother echoed. She stood awkwardly on her crutches, her shoulder leaning against one of the columns in the archway between the family room and the kitchen. "Did I hear somebody say something about leaving?"

"Hi, Mom," Justine said.

"So what's going on?" Leah sniggered.

"Justine?"

"Nothing," Justine answered. "Want us to take you for a walk?"

Her mother massaged her neck. "I have a headache. Maybe, though. Sure."

"You guys aren't seriously going outside, are you?" Leah thumbed the window. "We're supposed to get like six inches of snow."

The sky was gray and the wind had picked up. A gust shook the tiny dogwood tree their father had planted in the backyard last year, bending its trunk nearly in two.

"I wouldn't go out there. You might get caught in a snowstorm."

"It's not supposed to snow till tonight," Justine said. "Why don't you come with us, Lee? You could push the wheelchair."

"Great idea," their mother said. "We hardly see you lately."

Leah poked the cabinet with the nubs of her toes. "I guess so."

"Honey," her mother said, once Leah was gone. "Could you get my sweats? They should be in the laundry room. On top of the dryer." When Justine returned with her mom's sweatpants, her mother said, "Your father isn't avoiding us, hon. He's busy with work. That's all." Justine glanced nervously at the hallway. "I know."

"By the way, sweetie. Where's Dog? I haven't seen her all day."

"My room." Justine's mom untied her robe, and Justine helped her into sweatpants. "I tried to get her to come down. She wouldn't."

"Has she gone out today?"

For two seconds, Justine reported. Dog scooted to the trees at the back of the yard, ran right back, and sat on the steps, crying, until Justine let her in. She'd peed. Justine didn't think she'd had time for number two. "I don't know what's wrong with her, Mom. All she does is sleep. She won't even fetch when I toss her the ball."

"She's thirteen, honey. She's getting old."

Justine lifted her eyes, fighting tears. *Why does everybody keep saying she's old?*

"Why don't we take her," her mother suggested. "The walk will do her good."

Dog had been lying at the foot of Justine's bed for hours. Justine ruffled her ears, tugged on her collar. Dog lifted her head, yawning.

"Go for a walk, puppy?" Justine cooed and patted the mattress.

Dog hobbled off the bed. Justine stroked Dog's head, and holding her collar, pulled her gently toward the steps. It wasn't fair that animals had such a short lifespan. Parakeets lived only five or six years, goldfish just a few months. Even horses had a shorter lifespan than people. When they were little, Justine and Leah had hamsters. Their parents bought the hamsters all sorts of paraphernalia: mirrors and tunnels and exercise balls. They even bought a rubber mouse, so the hamsters would think they had friends. That made no difference. The hamsters kept dying and Justine's father kept buying new ones. One day, their mother insisted he stop.

"This is too hard on Justine," her mom said. "She gets too attached."

To be honest, Justine wasn't all that fond of the hamsters. She'd cried because crying, she thought, was expected. Dog was different. Justine scratched the old Lab's ear and Dog bounded down the stairs after her. Dog was her friend.

Justine's mom was sitting on a barstool when Justine led Dog into the kitchen. Her mother did reasonably well with the crutches. She could do almost everything now, except activities that required her to stand for long periods of time or needed two hands. She also needed help navigating stairs.

Leah was waiting in the back hall, snapping her fingers, reciting words to a rap tune. Justine did a double take. Her sister had changed into flannel pajamas that Justine swore belonged to Todd.

"Pajamas?" their mom said. "Isn't it a little cold for pajamas?"

Leah extended her leg. "What?" she asked, as if she truly did not understand. "They're no worse than the clown pants you have on."

Their mother let out a sigh and shook her head.

Justine helped her mom down the stairs to the garage, ran back up the steps and pressed the button, raising the garage door, and went to the back of the garage to fetch the wheelchair. She unfolded the chair and rolled it to the bottom of the stairs.

The wind had died down, the air brittle. Her mom drew a knitted black cap out of the pocket of her down vest and pulled it over her head.

It had snowed twice this week. A thin layer of frozen snow made the driveway slippery. Justine should have worn snow boots. Gripping the handles, she pushed the wheelchair up their drive, leaning into the grade. She was out of breath by the time they reached the cul-de-sac.

The Ridley girls were in their front yard. Justine waved and wheeled her mom down the street, Leah zigzagging ahead, dragging Dog with her. Leah dropped the leash and picked up the pace, swinging her arms like a speed walker.

"What's she doing?" their mom asked.

Who knew? "Hey," Justine called. "Lee? Wait up."

Leah spun around, arms frozen in midair. She looked comical in her goofy clothes, doing silly things to draw attention to herself.

Dog stood at the end of the Begley's driveway, sniffing the snow.

An engine rumbled. A schnauzer dashed out of the Begley's garage and chased Mr. B's car up the drive, Dog trailing after her.

"Leah," Justine hollered. "Get the leash. Dog's gonna get hit."

Leah crouched, coughing. "Here, Dog," she called. "Here, girl."

Dog skidded to a stop, planting her paws.

"Come on, Dog." Leah extracted a piece of cheese from her pajama pocket. "Come to Lee-Lee." Dog scooted across the street. As she closed in on the cheese, Leah jacked up her hand. Dog jumped, her snout missing the cheese, and flopped back down.

"Cut it out." Justine brought the chair to a halt. "You'll tire her out."

"What are you talking about?" Leah dangled the cheese. "Dogs are supposed to jump. It's like their job. Up," she ordered. "Jump." Dog jumped, wheezing.

"Justine's right," their mother said. "That's too much for Dog." Leah hid the cheese behind her back. Dog nudged her leg. Leah bolted, Dog at her heels, wheeled around, and skated back. As she neared the wheelchair, Leah hit a patch of ice and pitched forward, slamming into Justine.

Justine's feet slipped out from under her. She cried out, flailing, and landed on Dog's back, the dog yelping.

"You okay?" Leah grabbed Justine's hand, pulling her up.

"Yeah," Justine said, gasping for breath. The fall had knocked the wind out of her; otherwise, she was fine. She brushed herself off.

"Sure you're all right, honey?" her mother asked, twisting to face Justine. She offered her hand. "You took a pretty good fall."

Leah's eyes brimmed with tears. "I didn't mean it. I'm sorry."

"You shouldn't tease," their mother scolded. "Somebody could have been hurt."

"Sorry," Leah mumbled, downcast. "That was dumb."

Justine was fine. Her knee stung from hitting the ground. Their mom was making too big a fuss. Justine felt bad for Leah; her sister looked as if she might cry.

"I'm not hurt," Justine assured her. "Anyway, it was an accident." She stretched, arching her back, turning left and right. "Hey," she said, suddenly realizing her dog was missing. "Where's Dog?"

"Don't know," Leah said. "Did you see her, Ma?"

Their mother shook her head.

Justine scanned the neighboring yards. "Leah," she said. "Could you take Mom home? I'm gonna go look for her."

"Sure." Leah exchanged a look with their mother. "No prob."

"Dog," Justine called, her hands cupped over her mouth. "Dog?" Justine headed down the street first. No sign of the dog. Maybe she went home, Justine thought, switching direction. She'd fallen hard on Dog. She hoped she hadn't hurt her. The whole thing had happened so fast. Dog was in the wrong place. There was nothing Justine could do to avoid her.

Half an hour later, disheartened, Justine headed for home.

She was standing by the window in the breakfast nook when she spotted the old Lab, lying under the oak tree beneath Leah's window.

Justine snagged a blanket from the sofa, rushed outside, and covered her trembling dog. Dog's heart was racing.

Whimpering, Dog laid her head on Justine's lap. Justine stroked her neck, and Dog looked up, her red-rimmed eyes closing and opening again. "It's okay, puppy," Justine crooned, running her hand over and over Dog's head.

Dog licked Justine's hand. Justine picked a thorn out of the fur under her neck. "I'm gonna take you inside," she said, helping Dog to her feet. She tried to lift Dog, to carry her, but the Lab was too heavy for her.

"It's okay, my puppy," she said quietly, taking hold of her collar. "Justine will take care of you."

Leah and their mother must have argued. When Justine came inside, her sister informed her that she was leaving. She'd be out for a while, Leah said. Their mother, apparently realizing at the last minute what Leah was up to, called after her, demanding to know where she was headed. Leah just kept walking.

The front door slammed. Their mother, talking to herself, swallowed a painkiller and settled on the sofa, a Mozart concerto for the violin playing softly in the background. Ten minutes later, Justine heard Todd's truck in the circle.

After Leah left, Justine took Dog to her room and helped her onto the bed.

At seven, her father's car pulled into the circle. From her bedroom window, she watched the BMW roll down the hill, its headlights arcing over the lawn.

The garage door snapped up. Justine shuffled downstairs to the mudroom.

"Found a *great* one this year," her father announced as the door swung open. The buttons of his sports jacket were undone, his tie loose. His hair was damp, his face flushed from the cold. "Best ever, Jus," he said. "It was worth the wait, baby doll. Blue spruce. This big." He stretched, reaching for the ceiling. "It's in the garage."

"I was waiting for you." She struggled to get the words out.

"Mom asked me to stop for a tree." He patted her head. "You all right, sweetheart?"

Justine's lips quivered.

"What happened?"

She shook her head. Her throat ached.

"Wait 'till you see it." He headed toward the garage. "That'll make you feel better."

"Dad?"

Her father turned toward her. "Yes?"

"I need you to bury my dog."

Through all that had happened, their trials and travails, her mother's escape into the fuzzy world of her pain pills, her father's retreat, her family's dizzying fights, even while Leah was away, though Justine's heart was breaking, she had stayed strong. Now, the tears fell, releasing all her pent-up emotion.

Twenty-Five

Lonely Days are Here Again

Zoe's younger daughter had not been the same since Dog died. Justine moped around the house or sat in her bedroom in front of her computer screen, oblivious to her surroundings. After the accident, Justine had taken over for Zoe, cooking, cleaning, washing and folding the laundry. Justine was the one person Zoe could count on to keep her company, to cheer her up when she was down.

Depending on Justine as she had was unfair. She wished she could find a way to reach her daughter, to set things right. But the weight she'd placed on Justine's shoulders seemed to have caused some deep, irreparable damage. When Zoe spoke, Justine listened politely and accepted Zoe's apologies, her words accompanied by a disconsolate half-smile that broke Zoe's heart.

It was time for Zoe to go back to work. She could bear the pain in her leg now; she was able to get around, more or less, on her own. The family needed the money. Since the Micronics fiasco, Will had lost his drive and his sales had dwindled; his last commission check had barely covered their mortgage. Their savings would take them through January, if they were careful; after that, she didn't know what they would do.

The idea of returning to work overwhelmed her. It wasn't the workload. In her absence, a colleague had taken on Zoe's caseload, eliminating the backlog of appointments that otherwise would have been hanging over her head. Zoe dreaded the routine. She couldn't imagine spending eight or ten hours a day in an office, doing work she no longer enjoyed. Hard to imagine how she'd managed to do it for so many years.

On vacation, she'd always fantasized about quitting her job, buying a Bed and Breakfast in Vermont, opening an organic restaurant where she grew her own food. Within a day or two of returning to the clinic, she would be back into the swing of things, those silly notions of starting a new life set aside for another year. Having been away from work for over a month, with the clarity of distance, she realized the fantasies about quitting her job were not fantastic at all, but rooted in concrete desire.

If she had little enthusiasm for returning to her job at the clinic, she had even less for tackling the workshops. Exhausted, she'd made very few changes in her presentation since the summer. Initially, reluctant to face the truth, she'd rationalized the decreasing number of registrants. Fluctuations were a normal, if disquieting, part of the business. Besides, the local market was too small to support the program long-term. If she wanted to grow, she had to start traveling. A few days before the accident, at the clinic of all places, she'd overheard Molly discussing the workshops with a patient.

"Isn't she that soccer player's mother?" the woman asked. "From what I hear, she needs to get her *own* life in order."

Instinct told Zoe to confront the woman, demand to know where she'd heard such drivel, and she'd spun on her heels, about to stalk off in the direction of the voices. Fortunately, she'd taken hold of her senses. It irked her knowing people were judging her, boycotting her workshops because of rumors about her personal life. Plenty of professionals offered advice they themselves failed to follow. She was tempted to restart the workshops just to prove everyone wrong. But the thought of going through the process again, reestablishing a clientele, never mind explaining herself, overwhelmed her.

She'd tried umpteen times to discuss their work situations with Will. Her husband brushed her off. Couldn't she focus on something positive, for a change? Meaning, steer clear of anything important, skate over the emotional surface. Lately, his end of conversations involved one of two subjects. Sports: would the Red Sox sign a stud in the offseason? Too early to tell. And moving. He went on *ad nauseam* about moving, dropping out of the rat race, relocating to a healthier environment, which for him, included only the most desolate areas of the U.S.: northern New Hampshire, Maine, Idaho, Montana, Wyoming. Her husband didn't want to move. He wanted to hide. She often found herself wondering if she and Will spoke the same language. After Will's affair when the kids were small, Zoe had seriously considered divorce. In the end, she'd decided to stay because saving the marriage, she'd felt, was better for the girls. Her children needed a fulltime father, a constant force in their lives, not a part-time dad, an interloper they saw only on weekends. To maintain her sanity, in the calendar in her head, she'd marked off the days until Justine graduated high school. When the girls were grown, she would be free.

On Tuesday morning, five days before Christmas, Zoe sat in the oversized chair by the fireplace, flipping through a stack of law school catalogues, procrastinating the holiday shopping. The catalogues, ordered last week on a lark, were a silly distraction. On numerous occasions in high school, her social studies teacher had talked with Zoe about applying to law school.

"You've got such strong opinions," he'd remarked, "and you argue well." She'd be a superb attorney, he'd always said.

It was nice, but she'd had no interest in studying the law. Last week, a segment on *The View* about child pornography had fired her up. Her teacher's words echoing in her mind, she'd fantasized about becoming a lawyer, saving the children.

For two or three hours, ordering catalogues for schools around the country, she'd allowed her fantasies to reign free. A change in career seemed the perfect solution to her disappointments at work. Like so many people, she'd disregarded her true talent; instead, she'd taken an interest—psychology, in her case—and, finessing her abilities to suit it, turned it into a career. If she'd harnessed her strengths, she might have been a brilliant success. As she'd stressed in her workshops, it was never too late to reinvent one's self.

Until the catalogues arrived, she'd forgotten about those three hours in fantasyland. Returning to school was neither practical nor affordable. Nor something she actually wanted to do. It was an escape—intriguing, yes, an escape nonetheless. She piled the catalogues on the floor, planning to toss them, and opened her laptop.

While she waited for Windows to boot, the phone rang.

Nine twenty, too early for Jerry. Jerry's daily calls were her lifeline. Outside her immediate family, he was the only person privy to their current state of affairs. After college, her girlfriends had scattered across the country; she'd lost contact with all but her two closest friends, their communications limited to an occasional e-mail or birthday card, if they happened to remember. Nurturing a friendship required time and energy. With Will traveling, Zoe bore the majority of the responsibility for the house, the kids. Added to her work at the counseling center, she hadn't had time, *hadn't made time*, for establishing new or maintaining old friendships. Sharing intimate details with colleagues or acquaintances would have made her feel vulnerable. Jerry was different. With him, she felt safe.

"Hello?" she said. "Hello?" The line had gone dead. Probably a telemarketer—she'd somehow gotten onto their please-harass-me list.

She surfed a few Internet stores. Nothing appealed to her. Because it was easy, she logged onto *Saks*, ordered an Armani shirt from the sale page for Will, overpriced designer jeans and a cashmere sweater for Justine. Zoe had no idea what to buy Leah. Leah loved her button bracelet. She rarely took it off. Maybe a birthstone ring, Zoe thought, and hit the link for sale items in the jewelry department.

The rings on the first page were either too gaudy or too old for Leah. At the bottom of the second page, she spotted the perfect ring—a dazzling Topaz in a white gold setting encrusted with diamond chips. The ring cost two hundred and twenty-nine dollars—marked down from six ninety-five. The ring was gorgeous and a great deal at the price, although more than she'd planned to spend. She bookmarked the page and opened her e-mail.

At the top of the list was a message from Jerry.

"Hi," he'd written. "Thought I'd swing by this morning. Let me know if you'll be around. J."

A week after the accident, she, Jerry, and Officer Healy had gone over the events in detail. Jerry had stopped by once to let her know that they had closed the investigation. That had been the extent of their physical contact. Although they spoke every day on the phone and corresponded regularly by e-mail, they'd never gotten together in person. She hoped nothing was wrong.

"Sure," she replied. "Everything okay? Z."

Within minutes, she had a response. "Yes, fine. An hour?"

She answered two brief messages, one from a coworker, writing to say, "Hi," the other from a former workshop attendee, requesting the date of Zoe's next seminar. "No date yet," she typed, but she appreciated the interest and would keep her informed.

Zoe closed her laptop, hobbled up the stairs, and limped down the hall to her bedroom, frustrated by her sluggish recovery. She made the bed and threw the laundry into the wire hamper in their closet. Then she removed her walking cast and took a long hot shower, lathering her body with lavender soap, and washing and conditioning her hair. Afterward, she smoothed almond scented body butter over her arms and thighs.

Zoe stood in her closet, wrapped in a towel, waffling over what to wear. Black slacks? Too dressy. Chinos? Boring. Skirt? This was a friendly get-together, for God's sake. Not a *date*.

Zoe felt as giddy as a schoolgirl, her stomach in knots. Ridiculous. *Jerry's your friend.* The man was married, with infant twins. Even if he were interested in her, she was not attracted to him. He was too *earnest.* He had funny-shaped ears. And burred hair. And his hands were too big. Silly, criticizing his hands. Still, clunky hands bugged her. Will had elegant hands, his wrists graceful, his fingers slender and long. His hands were the first thing she'd noticed that night in the bar. She'd found it arousing, watching him pluck the strings, his deliberate fingers pressing the chords.

At ten thirty sharp, Jerry rapped on the sliding glass door.

When she opened the door, a rush of cold air blew through the loose weave of her scoop-neck sweater. She hugged herself. "Well," she said, squinting against the glittering midmorning light. She made a show of checking her watch. "Aren't we punctual?"

"Yeah, well." He stamped the snow off his shoes. "Had to drive around the block a few times." His nose and cheeks were flushed from the cold. "Didn't want to seem too eager."

She raised her eyebrows, teasing. "That right, Jerry?"

He laughed, and she stepped aside to let him in.

He handed her a small package wrapped in brown freezer paper. "It's sausage. I made it myself. I hope you like garlic and sage."

She turned the package over. "I love garlic and sage. Thank you." She pecked his cheek. "I can freeze it, right?"

"Sure. It should keep fine." He scanned the kitchen. "It's nice in here. Warm." His eyes traversed the length of her body. "You look great." He cleared his throat. "Feeling good?"

She felt herself blush. "A lot better. Can I take your jacket?"

He peered over her shoulder into the empty family room. "Thought it might be nice for you to get out, get some air."

"That's tempting," she said, stalling. Going out in public was a hassle. She felt awkward, bothersome, people constantly forced to wait for her, groups splitting as she approached, people moving right and left, kindhearted strangers holding doors that took her forever to reach. "Why don't I make some tea? Let me see what I've got."

She shuffled to the pantry. "We have blackberry," she said, sticking her head out of the pantry. "Or lemon. Or plain, if you'd rather."

"It would do you good to get out. It's a beautiful day. If you don't mind the cold. A great new coffee shop opened last month," he told her, "in Ayer. The coffee's incredible."

"I don't know." She felt uncomfortable going out with Jerry. "They roast their own beans."

The coffee shop occupied the lower floor of a newly renovated two-family house across from Ayer's town common. The shop was more sophisticated than it appeared on the outside. The paneled walls and honey-colored ceiling evoked the wistful feeling of a lazy weekend brunch or a Miles Davis song on a rainy spring afternoon. A fire crackled in a stone hearth on the far wall, the smell of the burning logs mixing with the heady aroma of freshly brewed coffee.

The shop was empty this morning. Behind the bar, a young woman in her early twenties was scooping beans from a small paper bag into the canister of a magnificent stainless steel coffee machine.

Zoe loosened her knitted scarf, tucked her gloves in the pocket of her suede jacket, and rubbed her hands together. "I wish I could do this with my feet." A thin athletic sock covered her left foot, inside her walking cast. "My toes are like ice."

"I'm impressed," Jerry said, cupping her elbow as they stepped down onto the wide-planked pine floor. "You're getting along pretty good." He let go of her elbow. "You don't need much help at all."

"Thanks." Though it felt too slow to her, she *had* made progress.

He led her to a wrought iron table in the corner and pulled her chair out. "If you tell me what you want, I'll order."

"That's okay. I'll go."

"Make yourself comfortable."

She dug in her leather hobo bag, pushing aside a notepad, her checkbook, her house keys, the keys to her office. She was hunting for her wallet, which she realized, *shoot*, she'd forgotten to bring. From an interior pocket, she produced a crumpled five-dollar bill.

Jerry set his hand over hers. "My treat," he said. "I invited you, remember?" She reluctantly put her money away. "So. What'll it be?"

Zoe studied the menu behind the counter: regular coffee, house blend, coffee of the day—Guatemalan Antigua today. They also served decaf, espresso, cappuccino, mochaccino, latte, plain, pumpkin, or vanilla.

"'Mocha Marvel?' What's the 'Marvel' I wonder?"

All the discomfort Zoe had felt when Jerry arrived had disappeared. In the car, they'd talked briefly about her accident. She'd surprised herself, telling him the accident had changed her life. How melodramatic, she thought, though in some ways it had. She felt like a different person, someone she was not sure she liked. She'd admitted her ambivalence about returning to work.

"I don't know what's gotten into me," she said. "I've never thought of myself as irresponsible."

She wasn't irresponsible, he'd told her. She was honest. "Most of us live on autopilot. Get up, go to work. Don't think about whether we like what we're doing or not. If we're good at it, even. You're lucky. You've had a chance to think."

"Thinking can be paralyzing," Zoe replied.

"And freeing," he'd said.

It felt strange talking philosophically with Jerry, the words stilted like a new suit or a hairdo she was trying on to see if it fit. As the conversation evolved, the words began to feel urgent and real, and she'd realized for the first time in a long time, she was talking about feelings, thoughts. Not about her family. Not about Leah. About herself.

"Mocha Marvel." Jerry set a tall paper cup in front of her, the coffee topped with whipped cream and sprinkled with cocoa powder. "Chocolate syrup swirled into 'vanilla-bean-*infused*-coffee,'" he said in a goofy, highfalutin accent. "Kills me when people talk like that."

They laughed, easy with one another. "Just kidding. They're good people, the owners. They're usually here. I hope you like cocoa."

With her finger, she scooped a dollop of cream. "I love cocoa."

He sat across from her, his hands on the table. His knuckles were chapped.

"So," she said, returning to the conversation they'd begun in the car, "what made you decide to be a cop?"

He looked at her thoughtfully, as though unsure how to respond.

It was a dumb question, too personal, too hard to answer without being glib. Consider her own choices: she studied psychology to satisfy her curiosity, find solutions to personal problems, maybe discover why her mother drank, as opposed to making a thoughtful decision based on her talents or strengths. Maybe she and Jerry were masochists, drawn to tough professions that offered fewer rewards than other jobs that might have suited them better. The thoughts flitting through her mind endeared her to the man whose large chapped hands were clasped on the table.

"I was a punk," he said finally. "My mother didn't deserve the crap I put her through." In high school, he'd been brought up on robbery charges. He chuckled, describing his feeble attempts at weeding the judge's garden. "I think I pulled up more flowers than weeds." One day, the judge pulled him aside. "He said I had promise. I could make something of myself. Or end up in jail. I took him up on the challenge." For five years, he'd worked fulltime as a night guard, attending school during the day. Eventually, he earned his degree in criminal justice. The judge passed away last spring. "Must have been a thousand people at his funeral. The line went around the block."

Several customers had wandered into the shop while Jerry was talking. Zoe edged her chair closer, so she could speak without raising her voice. "You're a good cop, Jerry."

He blotted her chin with his napkin. "Cream." He shrugged, grinning.

She let out a small, uncomfortable laugh, and backed up. "I'm such a slob. I wear whatever I'm eating."

"Seriously." He covered her hand with his. "I love what I do."

"I wish I could say the same."

He squeezed her hand. "You'll figure it out."

Zoe rarely allowed anyone outside her immediate family to touch her. She recoiled even from friends. Part of her protested, her legs uncomfortable, her thighs twitching. *Don't be ridiculous,* the other part said. This was the way friends interacted. She forced herself to relax.

"Is it always this slow?" she asked. How did they make any money?

"In the morning, the line's out the door."

He sat back and she wrapped her hands around the warm coffee cup.

The bells on the door jingled and a man entered—a construction worker. At the counter, he ran a hand over his head. She watched him flirting with the barista, the young woman basking in the attention.

She sipped her coffee and wiped her lips. "How are the boys?"

"Good." She lost him for an instant. "Getting big. Last time Maura—last time the kids were at the doctor's, they weighed almost eighteen pounds. That's huge for their age. Especially when you think, gosh, they were less than two pounds each when they were born." He opened a hand. They'd fit in his palm. "Blows me away."

"Kids grow fast," she agreed, "especially babies."

"And Leah? How's she doing?"

"So-so." She set her cup on the table. "She's still with Corbett." Jerry's concern registered on his face.

"I've never hated a kid. When I hear his name, I cringe."

"You're a good mother. You taught her right from wrong. She'll come around."

Zoe considered that. Her parenting had contributed to, maybe even caused, the problem. She had no respect for followers, people who couldn't think for themselves. When Leah was a baby, she'd made it a conscious goal to raise independent children. "I let her get away with too much. I didn't want to stifle her, you know? My father always told me to be careful what I asked for."

"I was a lot like Leah. Had to get it out of my system, I guess. Some kids just need to rebel. It's how they find their way."

"If we could just see ahead, you know? If I could see her at twenty-five and know she was okay, I wouldn't worry so much."

"It's tough. I'm glad mine are still babies."

She certainly understood why. "So they roast the coffee here, you said."

"Every Monday and Friday. Usually in the afternoon."

"Must smell good."

"It does." He covered her hand again. "On Friday, I'll pick you up. You can watch."

She slid her hand from under his, confused by the closeness she felt to this man who wasn't her husband, ashamed of having shared intimacies with him. He probably thought she was leading him on, and she hated herself for it.

"I've got to get back. Early release day."

On the way to the house, they talked about the weather. The forecasters were calling for snow again. Didn't feel like snow. "But look," Jerry said. "See the clouds coming in?" He pointed to the thermometer on the dash. The temperature had dropped. The sun slid behind a cloud, diffusing the light, the sky turning gray.

"It's too early for snow," she complained. If it were up to her, they would live on the equator. She'd gone to college in California. She'd loved the weather out there.

"Why didn't you stay?"

"Oh, you know. What about you? Ever live anywhere else?"

"I had a job offer in Houston after college." He signaled the turn onto Lily Farm Road. "Maximum security prison."

"Yeah?" She raised a brow. "You don't strike me as a hard ass."

"That right?" At the head of her drive, he pumped the brakes. "You'd be surprised."

She poked his arm playfully. "Tough guy. So what happened?"

"Stayed here." He backed into the turnaround, shifted into park, letting the engine idle. "I was tempted. Thought it'd be nice to see another part of the country. Maura didn't want to go."

"That must have been tough."

"I didn't blame her. Her folks would have gone nuts. Money-wise, it would've made sense. They paid pretty good. Better than a rookie cop." He stared ahead. "Couldn't do that to her, after she stuck with me through college. Figured I owed her that much. You?"

"What?"

"Any regrets?"

Regrets? She toyed with her wedding ring. A doe leapt out of the woods, a yearling tagging along. The deer bounded across the yard, their white tails lifted. "Sure. I guess. But I'm glad I came back."

She pictured gritty Fisherman's Wharf, the warehouses, the glittering water, Alcatraz in the distance. The harbor had changed since they'd left, Will had told her. They'd revitalized the Embarcadero, put in fancy restaurants, upscale shops. The development was good for the city, but change inevitably came at a cost.

"I miss it sometimes. San Francisco, especially. I don't know. I never felt centered out there."

"Do you now?"

Jesus. Yes, I feel centered. No. Maybe. Couldn't they stick with the weather? Simple and easy. "I don't know, Jerry. Do you?"

"Maybe." He studied her face.

Her breath quickened. Warmth radiated through her chest, her belly, her legs.

Zoe pulled back. She couldn't do this. However wrong her marriage felt at the moment, however badly she might want to escape. She couldn't plunge into adultery the way she'd plunged into a career, an impulse driving her into another man's arms. It wasn't fair to any of them—Will, Jerry, his wife, their children—to enter a relationship she wasn't ready for, a relationship she wasn't sure she even wanted.

"You're a good man, Jerry. A good friend," she said quietly, hoping he would understand, that she hadn't crossed a line. That they still had room to retreat. "That means a lot to me."

He wrapped her hands in his. "Me, too." He let go and she accepted a kiss on her cheek. And sad, flustered, angry with herself—but mostly relieved—she bid him goodbye.

Twenty-Six

You'd Better Not Cry

Leah got off the bus at the bottom of her street and walked home, alone as usual, dragging her feet through the gutter, kicking dead leaves with the toe of her boots. She was halfway up the hill when the cruiser blew by.

She did a one-eighty, catching the cop's face in the rearview. Johnson. What was *he* doing in their neighborhood? It wouldn't surprise her if he'd stopped at the house to tell her parents some juicy new tidbit, to see if he could get her in *more* trouble. Or else he was there for her mom. Which was worse.

"Screw you," she spat, and flipped him the bird. *Stay away from my house.* It felt good, flipping him off. Too bad he hadn't seen her.

The wind howled and it started snowing again. Big wet flakes stuck to her cheek. This weather was ridiculous. She wished her family lived in Florida, someplace where it didn't snow. She'd had enough snow for one winter already. She dropped her chin into the collar of her coat. Of all the years to have to ride the dumb bus. Only the nerds took the bus. Her father had driven her to school last year and the year before, when it would have been perfectly acceptable to ride the stupid banana. Now that she needed a ride, her father refused. Her parents were like that. They only wanted to do favors when it didn't matter. If you called them on it, they always had a gazillion lame excuses. Her school, her father claimed, was out of his way.

She stepped over a mound of petrified dog dung. Leah felt bad about Dog, although not nearly as bad as her sister. Leah was more pragmatic than Justine, more mature. Her sister had been unreasonable, naïve, thinking Dog would live forever, refusing to accept the inevitable. Leah had tried to tell her differently. Dog was thirteen years old, ninety-one in dog years. Nothing, after all, lasted forever. Not dogs, not hamsters, not people. Nothing, except mistakes. Mistakes lived forever.

The Ridley girls were singing: "Oh, you'd better not cry..." They danced around a tree, Sarah, the younger one, hanging on her sister's belt loop.

Santa Claus is coming to town. Humbug. Christmas was supposed to be a magical time of year, a time of kindness and generosity and cheer. What a joke. It was all a pretense, a big competition, a show. Nobody *cared* about anyone else. At the mall the other night, she'd been disgusted by the consumerism, bells jangling, shoppers tearing down aisles, shoving people out of their way in the process, zipping in and out of the stores. Real Christmas spirit.

Cheesy red and green decorations had taken over the world. Everywhere you turned you saw inflatable Santa Claus dolls, plastic reindeer, icicle lights. Everywhere except *their* house, that was. They had only those pathetic decorations Justine had put up. Their tree was in the garage, with the branches still bound. As far as Leah could tell, her mother hadn't bothered to shop. Leah had checked all the usual hiding places—the attic, under her parents' bed, behind her father's workbench in the basement. Nothing. Not a solitary gift.

"Hey, Leah," Sarah called, "wanna play snow fight?"

Leah shook her head and kept walking. At one time, she might have joined them. Leah had once done a lot of things she wouldn't do now. She'd hung out with Cicely Hanson, for instance. *Please.* They had nothing whatsoever in common. Leah was cool. Cissy was a tool. Leah laughed at her own stupid rhyme. Cissy *was* a tool, though. She was a follower. Not even the clothes stealing scheme had been her idea—you'd never know, listening to her. All her friends stole clothes. She only did it so they'd think she was cool.

Leah turned down their snow dusted driveway, trekked past the giant rock she and Justine had played on when they were younger. Once, when she was bored, Leah had drawn stick figures with black and red magic markers, swear words written in code underneath, across the front of the rock. When her father came home, he'd given her a bucket of soapy water and a brush and made her scrub it off. He used to be anal about the property. Now he didn't bother.

Leah picked up a stone lying in her path and tossed it in the woods.

Weird not to see Dog race out of the garage, skip up the driveway to greet her. Maybe her parents would buy them a new dog for Christmas. Something big, Leah hoped, a dog that would scare people off. A Rottweiler or a mean German Shepherd. Or maybe they'd get a cat. Hope's alley cat, Tabby, was pregnant. The kittens were due any day. Maybe if she asked permission, her parents would allow her to bring one home.

Right. Fat chance. Her father hated cats. Too finicky. Too stuck up. You had to work too hard to earn their affection. Of course, she could sneak one home under her jacket. The idea of hiding a squirmy kitten made Leah laugh. She pictured herself stealing past her parents, a tiny fur ball curled on her belly. She could probably keep the kitten a secret forever if she kept him in her room.

Leah entered the house through the garage. In the kitchen, she shrugged off her backpack and tossed her jacket in the general direction of the island counter. A light was on in the family room. And there was Leah's mom, on the sofa, her laptop balanced on her thighs, a pile of glossy catalogs on the floor by her feet.

"Hey." Leah stretched her lower back, sore from lugging her backpack. "What are you doing? I thought you'd be asleep."

"Answering some e-mails," her mother replied. "What do you mean, asleep? Come in here for a minute. How was your day?"

Leah shrugged. "All right." As she neared the sofa, she spotted a pile of catalogues on the floor. Yes! Her mom had been shopping after all. "Presents," she teased. "Can I see? "

Her mother ignored her, pushing the catalogues aside with her feet. "How was school?"

"Come on." Leah scrambled, pawing for the catalogues. "I just wanna see what you got. We can look together. It'll be fun," she said, wrestling a handful of—

—college brochures?

At first, Leah thought the catalogues were for her, which totally pissed her off. Then she realized they were law school brochures. "Mom?" And half the schools were located in other states. "What is this?"

"Honestly, Leah," her mother said. "Why can't you ever—"

"You're leaving us."

"I'm not leaving," her mother protested.

"Yes you are," Leah cried. "I don't believe this. Why else—?" she started, but she couldn't get the words out. She glared at her mother, shook her head, and stormed up to her room, ignoring her mother's pathetic pleas to come back.

Leah shut her door and turned the lock. She plucked a towel from her laundry pile, rolled it into a snake, and stuffed it into the crack under her door. Squatting, she reached for the mesh purse under her bed. She'd found the macramé bag in Hope's closet. Hope's mom had taken a seasonal job at the mall. Hope had told Leah to take the purse home; Hope had more new stuff than she knew what to do with.

Leah smoked the cigarette, pulling hard, holding the smoke until her lungs burned. Leah had finally done it. She'd driven her mother away. She'd never imagined either parent leaving the family and now it was happening, right before her eyes. There was not a thing she could do about it. She couldn't change the person she was.

Leah's mother hated her. Her parents despised her. They always had. After her mother's accident, she'd attempted to apologize to her parents for all the trouble she'd caused, hoping to set things right, hoping they'd give her a chance to start over. It had taken every ounce of courage she had to open her mouth. She was terrified her parents would think she was lying when she told them she'd broken up with her boyfriend, afraid they'd tell her they were finished with her, that she'd disappointed them one too many times.

"I'm sorry," Leah mumbled.

She'd been shocked to learn Todd had called their house that afternoon. He hoped, he'd told Leah later, to convince her parents to change their minds about him. If he could talk to her parents in person, he'd thought they'd realize he was good for her, he'd do her no wrong.

Leah's father had gone ballistic, insisting she sign some ridiculous contract. It was insulting. She shouldn't have to sign a contract to prove that she could be trusted. Her word should have been enough. Her parents should have believed her. That night, she'd phoned Todd to ask why he'd called. Within a few days, they were together again. She wondered if her parents realized that they'd pushed her into his arms.

Leah crushed the cigarette butt in the palm of her ceramic ashtray, and lit another, took one drag, touched the smoldering tip to her thigh and held it there, ignoring the pain, her breath quickening. Repulsed by the smell of burning flesh, she flicked the butt into the ashtray, and picked at her bubbling skin. Leah had made mistakes, yes. Still, she didn't deserve to be treated like a pariah. Not by her own family. Leah wasn't a loser. Not in her heart.

When she was little, her parents had forgiven her for botching things up. Once, when she was seven, she missed the bus and her father had driven her to school. Leah frequently missed the bus, sometimes twice in one week. Normally, he didn't mind driving her to school. That morning, he had a meeting with an important client and couldn't be late.

A mile from the elementary school, she remembered she'd left her spelling homework on the kitchen counter for the third time in two weeks. Her father had driven home to retrieve it. For the rest of the ride, he'd berated her for making him late. That night, at dinner, Leah presented her dad with a note. "DeEr Dad," the note read. "I diNT's mean A be late. I luv you. Hugs and kSSes, Leah Tyler." Her father, delighted, pulled her into a bear hug. Sometime between then and now, her parents had stopped forgiving her. They had no interest in apologies or excuses. They failed to see how tired she was of aiming for perfection. Leah wasn't perfect. She would never be perfect.

She retrieved a joint from the small wooden jewelry box hidden in her top drawer, under her panties. She changed the music in her iPod, switching from Nirvana to a Radiohead album called *OK Computer*, lit the joint and brought it to her mouth, tipping her head back, inhaling deeply, losing herself in the languorous strains of the music.

When it burned out, Leah removed her headphones, dropping them on the floor, and pulled the down comforter over her head, the room silent but for the soft hum of warm air blowing through the vents. Her breathing slowed. Soon, she was outside on the street, plodding through the snow, her backpack flung over her shoulder. The icy wet snow seared the pads of her bare feet and she began to limp. Worn out, she could think of nothing but sleep. She longed to lie down in the snow, like Sleeping Beauty, and close her eyes. She walked for miles, it seemed. Suddenly, a car whizzed by, an old black Cadillac, its window open, the driver whistled, calling her name.

Todd.

The car zipped around a corner and doubled back. He'd seen her limping, he said, and swept her off her feet, cradling her in his arms.

The radio was blaring. She gave her body over to the music. Suddenly, it was dark. Snow whirled in the beams of his headlights.

He stepped on the gas...*faster, faster*...the car morphed into his truck, the Wrangler speeding downhill.

Leah shouted, urging him on.

Faster, faster.

Out of nowhere, a deer…a jogger…"Oh my God," Leah cried—
her mother.

Todd twisted the wheel, turning it furiously. The disk snapped off the steering wheel column. He pumped the brake, his foot flat on the floor. Its brakes gone, the car spun out of control.

Leah woke, sobbing, her face buried in her pillow. That was her life—careening out of control. She had made terrible, unforgivable mistakes. And she had no way to make amends. No way to apologize. No way to turn back.

Twenty-Seven

And to All a Good Night

Christmas morning, Justine woke at dawn. Golden sunlight streamed into her room from the skylight over her bed. The second her eyes popped open, she got up and put on her slippers and robe. She couldn't wait to see the look on her sister's face when Leah opened her present. Selecting gifts for her parents was easy: a Brahms CD for her mom, weightlifting gloves for her dad—she overheard him one night, talking about joining a gym. Finding a gift for Leah was tough.

Last year, Justine had given her sister a Tim McGraw CD they'd heard on Country 98. Choosing a CD for her sister would be impossible now. Justine had no idea what Leah would like. Ani DiFranco? 50 Cent? Some indie band she'd never heard of? Last week, Justine and her friend Holly had wandered around the mall, poking in and out of stores, searching for the perfect gift.

"A shirt?" Holly suggested in Abercrombie and Fitch. "Sweatpants? A belt?"

Nothing felt right. Finally, in Wicks and Sticks, Justine found exactly what she had been hunting for: a wax figurine of Merlin the Magician.

Justine lifted her bed skirt, digging for the shopping bag she'd hidden under her bed. She set the gifts for her parents aside, lifted the candle out of its box. The magician was small enough to fit in her palm. He wore a pointy, star-studded hat, a flowing ebony robe. A crystal ball sat in his outstretched hand. Justine touched his eyes, sparkling sapphire glass, ran her fingers over the smooth black wax of his robe. This was the perfect gift, this magician. He would make all her sister's wishes come true. Justine laid Merlin back in his box and folded him inside the tissue.

With all they'd been through this fall, Justine was afraid her parents might forgo their Christmas celebration this year. Her mother, despite her physical improvement, spent the majority of her time in the family room.

Instead of watching TV or lying on the sofa listening to music, she surfed the Web or e-mailed friends at her practice. She'd stopped seeing patients, had postponed her seminars indefinitely. It was almost as if she were trying to figure out what she was supposed to do next.

Justine's parents hardly ever talked. When they did, they just ended up arguing. Her father went upstairs to his office before Justine woke in the morning, was there when she went to bed. He still worked at NAC, she believed. She had no idea why he didn't go into the office in Waltham, why he wasn't traveling anymore. Nobody said.

A few days ago, her parents had rallied. Justine overheard her mother and father talking about Christmas. One night, they'd even gone shopping together. The next morning, her father setup the tree he'd left in the garage nearly two weeks ago. Even Leah was unusually perky. At their mother's insistence, Leah had gone to their family practitioner, and the doctor had put her on Zoloft. The prescription seemed to help. At least no one was screaming.

The minutes dragged. Their parents insisted that Justine and Leah stay in their rooms on Christmas morning until they were called. Their parents liked to be the first downstairs, so they could see the girls' faces when they saw the tree, and their dad could videotape their reaction. Each year, while they were waiting for their parents to get up, Leah would sneak downstairs. Back in her room, she would describe for Justine what she had found. For Justine, the anticipation, imagining the brightly wrapped piles of gifts, was the best part of the day.

She knocked on Leah's wall. Leah wasn't budging today.

Justine curled up at the foot of her bed, under a blanket.

When she opened her eyes again, she heard someone in the kitchen. She hopped off the bed and hurried downstairs with her gifts.

"Merry Christmas, sunshine," her father said, greeting her. "Look who's up, Zo."

The family room shimmered. Her father had lit a crackling fire. In the corner stood a magnificent tree, trimmed in purple and gold, white lights twinkling. The floor was a sea of exquisitely wrapped gifts, silver and purple and green. Her mother wore a new white robe and she'd fixed her hair in a French twist. She even wore makeup.

Justine laid her presents on the family room floor. While her father poured coffee, she raced upstairs to rouse Leah.

Her sister had gone out last night, ignoring their parents' pleas to celebrate Christmas Eve with the family. Hope had picked her up at noon to go shopping. At four, when they'd expected her home for dinner, Leah had called from her cell phone.

"Coach Thomas is having a party," she'd said. "She asked me to come." She would be home by curfew.

Although they'd made light of it, they'd been disappointed.

Justine tapped on her sister's door. "Leah?" Tapping again, she opened the door.

Leah's room smelled putrid—a stew of stale cigarettes and rancid sneakers, masked by a syrupy floral perfume. Justine nearly tripped on a chunky black sandal. She stepped over the shoe and around a pile of dirty laundry.

"Wake up, sleepyhead," Justine said, shaking Leah's shoulder.

Her sister grunted and rolled onto her belly.

"Come on, Lee," Justine said gaily. "It's Christmas." She danced to the window and rolled up the shades, light pouring into the room.

Leah pulled the pillow over her head. "Go *away*."

Justine sat next to Leah, stroking her sister's head. "We're opening presents. You're gonna love what I bought you."

"You guys open." Leah rolled onto her side. "I'll be down later."

"Please?"

Leah flung her arm over her face. "Not now, Jus. I'm tired."

"Please, Lee." She tugged on her sister's arm. "Pretty please?"

"Fine," Leah grumbled, and pushed the covers aside.

Leah was naked, except for a lacey purple thong. Justine sucked in a breath, appalled by how scrawny Leah was. When her sister played soccer, her body had been strong and athletic. Now her sister's tiny breasts sagged. Her elbows were knobs and every bone in her body protruded, her hips, her ribs, all the vertebrae in her spine.

"You've lost so much weight," Justine gasped. "Are you okay?"

"Of course I am." Kneeling, Leah lifted her bed-ruffle, sending up a cloud of dust, and reached under the bed. "I know they're under here," she said, her cheek pressed to the box spring.

She dragged a pair of black satin slacks from under the bed, brushed off the lint. "Think I can wear these? They too dirty?"

"No," Justine lied. "They look fine."

Leah threaded a black patent-leather belt through her belt loops. She tugged, her slacks bunching at the waist, put on a blue silk blouse. "You know that cop was here the other day," she said, stuffing the tail of her blouse under her waistband. "Right?"

"He was? When?"

"When we had that half-day." Leah furrowed her brows. "I think she's doing him, Jus."

Justine rocked backward. How could her sister say something so outrageous? Their mother would never have an affair. "No way," Justine said, annoyed. "She wouldn't do that. Mom's not like that."

"Yeah." Leah smirked. "Sure." From a box on her nightstand, she removed a thin silver ring shaped like a serpent.

The ring was new—a Christmas gift, Justine suspected, from Todd. So that's where her sister had gone last night. Out with her boyfriend. What a surprise.

"So," Leah said, fingering the ring. "I pass inspection, or what?"

"You look great," Justine mumbled, and headed downstairs.

———⊗———

Leah could barely keep her eyes open.

Last night, before exchanging their gifts, she and Todd had smoked meth. She'd tried meth for the first time three weeks ago. It was a lot like coke, except it made her hornier and the high lasted longer. She'd liked it at first, a quick rush followed by hours of energetic euphoria. Now it agitated her and she had trouble sleeping. Flying, she'd accused her boyfriend of cheating. After they crashed, they'd had a long, heart-to-heart talk—about a lot of things, really. He'd reassured her, made her feel better.

She turned sideways, checking herself out in the mirror. She'd lost twenty pounds. She was down to a hundred and three—thin for five-seven.

Not too bad, though, Leah thought.

———⊗———

Justine rearranged her face, forcing a smile, before rejoining her parents.

When she stepped into the kitchen, her father thrust the video recorder in her face. Justine waved stupidly, clowning for the camera. A few minutes later, Leah appeared and stuck out her tongue.

The girls took turns opening their gifts, shirts and sweaters and jeans. Justine received a scarf and knitted hat and two new paperback books, and her sister a pair of mittens and a twenty-five dollar gift certificate for iTunes.

"There's something else," their father said. "Right, Zo?"

He turned the recorder, videotaping their mom. Smiling, she produced a small box wrapped in silver paper with a red satin bow. He moved in, capturing a shot of the box in her hand, and panned out, focusing on Leah.

Justine watched her mother, watching Leah intently.

Leah untied the bow and, sliding a finger under the tape, pulled off the wrapping. "Pretty." She turned the box toward the camera, displaying a gorgeous topaz ring in a diamond-studded gold setting.

"Your birthstone," their mother pointed out. "Did you know the ancient Romans associated topaz with Jupiter, the god of light?"

When their mom finished talking, Leah thanked their parents politely, and tucked the velvet jewelry box in a bigger box under a sweater.

Their mother glanced at the girls' father, and looked away.

Justine opened her final gift, a telescope for her room. She set the telescope aside and dove into her mother's arms, planting a kiss on her cheek, and hugged and kissed her dad.

"Oh, my god." To make up for her sister's blasé response, she pranced across the family room. "I love this, I love this, I love this," she sang, feeling off balance. "Thank you *so* much," she said, and settled uneasily on the floor.

Leah opened Justine's present last. She untied the ribbon. Justine held her breath as her sister peeled the shiny green- and gold-flecked paper away from the box.

"Thanks." Leah turned the wax figurine over in her hands. "This is really thoughtful. I love it."

"Really?" She'd worried the new Leah might hate it.

"Cross my heart. Only I feel bad. I didn't get anything for you."

Justine threw her arms around her sister. "You're here, Lee. That's the best present ever."

After breakfast, Leah asked what time they planned to have dinner. "Around four," their mom replied—and offered to bake an apple pie for dessert. Her sister had turned into a different person than the grumpy girl Justine had rallied.

Christmas, Justine thought happily, *is working its magic.*

By the time Justine's father pulled into the parking lot behind St. Theresa's, it was five minutes to twelve. The church was packed, the double doors propped open, the congregation spilling onto the steps.

On the exterior, St. Theresa's was an incongruous building, all angles and slopes. As Justine stepped inside, her heart swelled. The church, cool and dark like a cathedral, smelled of incense. It had vaulted ceilings and stained glass windows adorned with holly. Plaques along the walls told a harrowing story of the agony of Christ.

Justine and her father worked their way through the crowd, settling into a space near the vestibule door. Justine loved Christmas Mass, the majestic red and white poinsettias, the earthy smell of the pine wreaths and greens. She loved the scratchy sound of the brand new holiday outfits, families all decked out in new clothes, the fathers in suits, the mothers in festive holiday sweaters and skirts, little girls in smocked velvet dresses, boys in trousers, with a bowtie and vest. Even the typically bedraggled teenagers looked presentable today.

A girl from Justine's school sang "Silent Night," her high clear voice raising goose bumps on Justine's arms. The cantor gestured, urging the congregation to sing. Justine hesitated. Like her mother, she couldn't hold a tune. A scroll below one of the stained-glass windows read, "Singing is praying twice." God knew she needed the prayers. And so Justine sang, timidly at first, then gaining confidence.

A baby cried off and on throughout the sermon. Between the baby and all the people moving in their seats, Justine had trouble hearing the priest. After a while, she gave up, her mind wandering.

As she stood at the back of the church reflecting on all that had happened of late, it occurred to her that her sister had been teasing about their mom, testing Justine to see what she'd say. Justine was a terrible sister, always jumping to conclusions, assuming the worst. She wasn't much of a friend, either, her hasty assumptions a shortcoming, probably even a sin. At communion, Justine stepped aside, letting the others pass by.

———⊕———

After Will and Justine had left for church, Zoe and Leah cleaned the breakfast nook. Her daughter cleared the table and Zoe put the dishes in the dishwasher. It was nice, spending time together, working as a team. For a change, Leah was talkative, even pleasant.

"You don't like the ring," Zoe said. "We can return it."

Leah shook her head. "You don't have to," she said. "I like it."

"You're sure? I don't mind," Zoe said. "We can go together."

Zoe and Will had discussed buying skis for their daughter. For financial reasons, they'd decided against. Now, if only to prove she and Will listened—and cared—she wished they had.

"For real," Leah said, removing a bag of apples from the fridge. "I mean it."

While Leah prepared the apples for her pie, Zoe hobbled upstairs to shower. She changed into a tan sweater dress with a scooped neckline and a simple gold chain with a diamond chip at her throat. Passing the kids' bathroom on her way downstairs, she happened to notice a pile of towels on the floor. She hoisted the towels and tossed them in the laundry chute. A smarmy Hallmark card sat on the vanity counter.

Zoe had a feeling the card was from Corbett. She had no right to snoop. She'd made it her policy never to go through the kids' things. Trust was reciprocal; if she expected the girls to trust her, she had to trust them. Until recently, trust had come easily.

Zoe picked up the card, turned it over. Laid it back down.

Leah had left the card in plain sight. Maybe, on a subconscious level, she was trying to tell Zoe something, wanted her to read it. Zoe opened the card tentatively, feeling guilty.

You're the best thing that's ever happened to me, Babe. I will love you for the rest of my life.
Forever yours, Todd.

Forever? The card fell out of her hand. *The rest of his life?*

Good God. Zoe's daughter—her smart, talented, beautiful daughter—married to that trash? Did Leah have a clue what marriage to this Corbett would entail? What about school? College? A career? What about her life?

Reeling, she hurried, as quickly as her gimpy leg would take her, to Leah's room. Started digging, opening drawers, rooting through clothes, hunting—for what? Drugs. Paraphernalia. An incriminating letter. Any evidence she could use to prove to Leah, once and for all, that Todd Corbett was not, never had been, and never would be any good.

She rifled through Leah's nightstand, her heart pounding. Papers, tablets, books. She felt a small plastic container and pulled it out, figuring it was the missing case for Leah's retainers. Zoe's heart sank. Her daughter was on birth control pills. It wasn't the pills that bothered her. Thank God Leah was using protection. That she was having sex, sharing such deep intimacy with this...this horrible human being, drove Zoe out of her mind.

---⊕---

Leah peeled six Granny Smith apples, sliced them into a large plastic bowl, scooped a half-cup of sugar, poured it over the apples, and sprinkled a teaspoon of cinnamon over the top. While tossing the fruit, she remembered she'd promised to call Nana and Papa Tyler today. She washed her hands and ran upstairs to get her phone.

Leah's bedroom door was open. Her mom was standing in front of the nightstand, motionless.

"Mom?" Leah's gut clenched. "Everything okay?"

Her mother's shoulders rose and fell. She raised a hand, producing a round plastic case. *Leah's birth control pills.*

"I," Leah stammered. "I can explain."

"Explain?" Her mother turned toward Leah, glaring. "What's to explain?"

"It's not what you think—" Lame, yes, but true. Last night, when she and Todd talked, they'd agreed to stop fooling around for a while. She needed time to get her head together. Her boyfriend had not been psyched; for her sake, he had reluctantly consented.

"What I think is, you're having sex. With that boyfriend of yours."

The garage door rumbled and then the mudroom door popped open.

"That's not true," Leah argued. She wanted to say, *How could you go through my things? You're supposed to trust me. You've always said I should tell you if I have sex. You wanted me to be safe.* "We're not having sex," she said instead, because it was true.

"Damn it." Her mother shook the case. "Then what are these?"

Leah felt as if she'd fallen into a black hole, here but not here, her mind a jumble of disconnected thoughts. How had her life, her relationships, become so complicated? She just couldn't get it together. Even when she tried to do the right thing, it backfired.

That her mother knew she'd had sex with Todd mortified her. The flash she saw in her mother's eyes made her feel small—and dirty. Leah pounced, pawing for the case.

"Sorry." Her mother jacked her arm up out of Leah's reach. "I don't think so."

"Give them to me," Leah cried. "Why are you doing this to me?"

"To you? Why am *I* doing this to *you?*"

"What's going on?" Leah's father called from behind. "Leah? What's up? Zoe?"

Leah spun. Her sister stood behind their father with her mouth open. They looked like figures in a Norman Rockwell painting, all decked out in their church clothes, their faces strangely discordant. Leah shook her head idiotically, the floor heaving beneath her.

Her mother waved the case. "You know what this means, don't you?"

"Leah? What do you have to say? Let's hear it."

"She's having sex," her mother spat. "What else is there to say?"

"Leah," her father said sternly. "Talk to me."

"She's leaving us," Leah blurted. She stole a glance at her mom. She didn't really believe her mother would leave, not when it came down to it. The urge to defend herself drove her on. "I saw her law school brochures. And love letters to that cop in her e-mail."

Her mother's eyes blazed. "What were you doing in my e-mail?"

"Love letters?" Leah's father echoed, visibly stunned.

"She's lying. I never wrote any love letters."

"And what's this about law school?"

"Damn it, Will. I told you. She's lying."

"Mom?" Justine pleaded. With the back of her hand, she wiped her eyes. "Lee?"

"Those law schools," Leah cried, "they're not even in this state."

Justine's face pinched. Their father questioned their mother; naturally, their mother denied everything. *They don't believe me,* Leah thought. *They'll never believe me.*

"She's lying," Leah's mother insisted. "That's her M.O. It's a ploy."

A ploy?

Leah sank to the floor, sobbing. "Why do you hate me? What did I do to you?"

Their father crouched in front of her. "She doesn't hate you."

"Yes..." Leah said between sobs. "She...does."

"No, she doesn't." Her father pushed her hair back. "Leah, listen to me."

"For God's sake, Will. She's playing you."

"Damn it, Zoe," their father roared. "Would you shut up?"

"Quit coddling her," Leah's mom spat. "She knows I love her."

Leah struggled to her feet. "Do not," she cried, and tore out of the room.

"Lee?" Justine shouted, taking off after her sister. "Don't go, Lee. Wait."

What happened while they were gone? When she and her father left for church, her mom and sister were doing the dishes. Leah talked about making apple pie. Now this?

Not again. Please. She couldn't lose her sister again.

Their father brushed past her, chasing Leah, calling after her.

"Lee," Justine cried, racing down the stairs. "Don't go. Leah, wait. Please."

Leah glanced back, her eyes meeting Justine's, and ran out, slamming the door.

In the foyer, Justine skidded into her father, who was blocking the door.

"Lee," Justine hollered, her voice breaking. "Come back."

"Let her go." His hands on her shoulders, her father guided her gently away from the door. "It's okay. She'll be back. She just needs to blow off some steam."

No, Justine thought miserably. This time, her sister was not coming back.

Twenty-Eight

Silent Night, Under a Waxing Crescent Moon

Silent night, holy night...

Jerry and Maura each held one of the boys. The Tylenol the ER doc had prescribed for their ear infections had done nothing, or next to nothing, to alleviate the pain. The babies had been crying on and off for hours; now they sniffled, their backs rising and falling, barely perceptible spasms interrupting their rhythmic breaths. On Tuesday, they'd take the boys to see the pediatrician. For now, holding, rocking, and patting them were the only comforts Jerry and his wife could provide. The boys had been up all night last night and both parents were beat. And yet—

—look at them together, in the living room by the brightly lit tree, each with a twin over their shoulder, rocking forward and back, as if in an intricate parenting waltz.

All is calm, all is bright...

Leah's boyfriend reached across the silent truck and squeezed her hand.

"Sucks," he said. "I'm sorry."

"It's not your fault," she said, her voice flat. "I should've hid them better."

"She shouldn't go through your drawers."

She looked over at him, thought about it briefly, and said, "I guess. No. She shouldn't."

"Hope can hook us up if you need something," he said.

"Not tonight."

"Then what?"

"I don't know. I can't think."

And so they drove across the quiet town under a waxing crescent moon, a lunar phase of struggle and unyielding resistance—a phase that both horrified and, she thought, had come to define her.

Mother and child...

"Why?" Justine cried. "Why couldn't you leave her alone for once?"

"It wasn't a matter of leaving her alone," Zoe said. "It was—" She didn't know what it was, to be honest. An impulse had driven her, like the impulses driving her in the week before her periods, PMS devils that rose from inside and turned her into somebody else, someone she hated and couldn't control.

"It was what?" Justine demanded. "Why do you and Dad do this to her?"

"I don't know," Zoe said, sinking into a chair. "I don't know."

Tender and mild...

"It's beautiful," Leah said.

Her boyfriend had parked at the water tower. They reclined in the jeep at the crest of the hill, overlooking the town. The Christmas lights glittered with the promise of hope and rebirth. It was almost possible to forget the ugly argument with her mom.

Todd stroked her head. She yielded, and he pulled her into his arms.

Sleep in Heavenly peace...

Will opened his eyes again and scanned the street, searching for Corbett's jeep.

Leah had called shortly after she'd taken off. Someone had left the handsets in the downstairs laundry and bath, and they'd missed her call. She'd left a message, saying she was headed to Corbett's place. As soon as they'd retrieved the message, he'd driven over there. Now, he sat, parked across the street from the house, waiting.

He turned the key in the ignition, firing the engine to heat the car. He'd been parked here for hours. No sign of the jeep. He checked the address on his cell phone again, just to be sure. This was the place. The clock on his dash read quarter to two. He had no intention of leaving. He laid his head back and closed his eyes again.

The argument rang in Will's head.

"She hates me," his daughter had cried. "Why does she hate me?"

Zoe didn't hate their daughter. She loved Leah; they both did. Maybe too much, if it was possible—abiding love driving them to say and do stupid things. Yet Leah thought just the opposite—and wasn't perception nine-tenths of reality? If Leah believed they hated her, in his daughter's mind they did. The thought horrified him.

Why, oh why, *do we hurt the ones we love most?*

PART THREE

THE RUNAWAY LIFE

Twenty-Nine

Where There's Will There's a Way

"I'll pound the *piss* out of that kid if I see him." Will rammed his fist on the bar, a thick slab of polyurethane oak. His daughter was a good kid before Corbett got hold of her.

First his kid, mixed up with that piece of shit, Corbett. Now his wife. No, his wife wasn't mixed up with Corbett. His wife was involved, he'd learned last night, with that cop. Goddamn Johnson. Kill that son of a bitch, too, if the opportunity presented itself. Corbett was the responsible party. The punk had gotten the ball rolling.

"You okay?" the bartender asked. "Hit that hand pretty hard."

"Yeah, yeah. I'll have another one." *Nother 'un*, it came out, meaning a Bud. He'd traded upscale micro brews for the comfort of Bud, a step down on the beer drinker's food chain.

Will and his wife had been fighting since last night. He'd returned from Corbett's house at four this morning—without Leah—and fallen into bed. After a few sleepless hours, he'd gotten up and he and Zoe had resumed their Christmas night argument. Leah's leaving was his fault, it was Zoe's; their daughter's rebellion resulted from his relentless discipline, her laxity, a poor genetic combination. They agreed on nothing. They should drive to Corbett's to fetch her, they should wait, give her space. Cursing, arguing, assigning blame—Band-Aids they used to cover the gaping wounds of helplessness. And terror.

This afternoon, he'd dropped Justine at her friend's house down the street, taken another fruitless spin by the Corbett place, and landed here.

The bar, a dive he'd discovered off Route 40, was called Lahey's. The bartender wasn't a Lahey. Henry was a Hoight or a Holter or a Howler. Used to be a Hell's Angel before he moved east. Will knew all this history because the first time he drank here, he'd asked Henry about the mermaid tattoo on his forearm. He'd figured Henry for a weightlifter from those thirty-inch biceps. He didn't know who the hell Lahey was. He ought to ask. Ought to know. Ought to have all the pertinent facts.

"Hey, Henry," Will said, tapping out a melody on the bar. "Who's Lahey?"

Behind the bar, Henry was drying a glass. "Kid sister's old man." He swirled a paper towel inside the cheap crystal bowl, and wiped off the stem. "A real pain in the ass. You sure you're okay?"

"Just dandy," Will assured him.

Not all bars were created equal. This was an ace. Smelled all right, a little funky, depending on the clientele for the night. The wallpaper, an indifferent blue and green plaid, held the hostility down. Paneling under the chair rails. No neon. No neon was good. Henry dimmed the lights, allowing for a certain degree of anonymity, a plus in a watering hole. A string of colored lights blinked through the bottles behind the bar, twinkling in a way that struck Will as sad.

Christmas had come and gone; now, the day after, nothing had changed. People pinned too much hope on the holidays. Six billion bodies and counting. Couldn't all get what they'd wished for. Santa never could make it all the way around, the jolly old bastard just another eighty-percenter.

Will drummed the bar to catch Henry's attention. *What do you think of me, bruiser?* Will wanted to know, *had* to know. It was vitally important to know if Henry respected him or not. A good bartender could tell you a lot about yourself. If Henry had divined some dark secret deep in Will's being, he wanted to hear it. Maybe he'd figure out why his wife was screwing around.

The door bells jingled. *Jing-a-ling, jing-a-ling,* Will sang to himself, *hear them ring, hear them ring,* his mind alighting on a cartoon image from some Christmas special the kids used to watch. *Frosty the Snowman. A ve-ry hap-py soul.*

A pair of lowlifes in wool hunting jackets, coats unbuttoned, the hoods of their gray sweatshirts hanging over their collars, stamped their feet on the mat, kicking the sludge off their boots, swaggered to

the bar, and ordered Silver Bullets with a shot of JD. Henry served
their drinks and they strutted to the pool table, lifted cues off the wall,
and racked up the balls.

"The kid ain't worth it," Henry said, meaning Corbett. Without
Will's even asking, he'd produced another Bud. "Touch that kid, your
ass goes to jail. Hear me, Tyler? You ain't saying much tonight."

Will dug a twenty out of his pocket and laid it on the bar.

"Where you off to, buddy? All this yakking, you got me on the
edge of my seat."

"To take a piss," Will told him.

He'd left his cell phone in the car. He stood by the payphone in a
dark hallway that, if you trailed the overpowering odor of piss,
eventually led to the men's room.

Swaying, he fished through his coat pocket for the crumpled bar
napkin he'd been carrying around, Kyra's number scrawled in faded
blue ink. When he came home from California, he'd discovered the
napkin in a stash of receipts he'd collected on the trip. He'd meant to
throw it out; he'd accidentally put it in his armoire instead. This
morning, rooting through his underwear drawer, he'd found it again.
Almost like fate.

In the dark hallway, he could barely make out the numbers. He
dialed, got a recorded message. A male voice. Must have been four-
nine. Tried again. What the hell did he think he was doing? He
plunked the receiver on the hook and staggered back to the bar, said
goodbye to Henry, and left.

The lot was a sheet of black ice. He skidded, swearing, and
picked his way around the lot, hunting for his car. Some asshole must
have moved it.

Took another spin around the lot. Damn, the beamer was right
by the front door, where Will had parked it. Crazy ass must have
returned it when he looked the other way.

He fumbled with the lock, loaded himself into the car, turned on
the heat, and switched on the defroster. Squinting, he leaned into the
wheel, angling for a better view.

He drove aimlessly, along winding, poorly lit roads. He hung a
left onto a residential street, a horseshoe that dropped him a block
from where he'd started. After a while, he found himself on Main
Street, heading in the general direction of home.

Pointless to go home without Leah. If he could find her,
everything would change. They'd work on things, Zoe and him. He
missed his wife. He loved her. Fuck Kyra. He wanted his wife back.
Couldn't keep living this way. Had to bring Leah home.

First he had to find her.

He pressed a Springsteen disc into the changer. The Boss sang a haunting tune about a freight train inside his head. *Whoa-ho.* Pain rumbled from Will's skull into his temples. *Is he good to you, baby? Little girl?* She was his little girl. She was his baby.

After an hour in the car, he felt marginally better, his head clearing.

Up ahead, he spotted a cop. He'd parked his cruiser at the edge of a field behind a thicket, with only its nose exposed. Sneaky bastard. *Ha, ha. Not as sneaky as he thinks.*

Will veered onto a side street, heading west. The recession had hit the west end of town hardest, property values in the shitter. The homes, built before the yuppie influx—Capes, ranches, deck houses—were smaller homelier, and sturdier than the monsters they slapped up today. He passed a development of low income townhouses, their brick facades sandblasted to give the illusion of age.

He checked his gas gauge. Quarter of a tank.

A light flashed in his rearview. Corbett's jeep. *What the hell?*

The Wrangler signaled a left-hand turn. Will swerved onto the shoulder, did a *U*, tailed him into the development, and pulled into an illegal spot behind a Dumpster. The spot, out of Corbett's line of sight, afforded a clear view of the driver's side of the jeep.

"Let's go, Corbett," he grumbled. What the hell was he doing? Fixing his makeup?

After five antagonizing minutes, the driver's door opened—and a pair of orthopedic shoes swung out. Will slapped the steering wheel and backed out of his spot.

From there, he headed to the Corbett place, where he'd parked last night. The street, an off-shoot of the town center, was lined with pickups fitted with snow plows and old-model sedans the size of small trailers. The stately Victorian homes that once housed the bigwigs from the tannery had been converted to two- and three-family rentals.

The street was dark. For a second, he wondered if a transformer had blown. A third of the way up, he spotted Corbett's jeep under the lone operational streetlamp.

Hot damn, Will thought. *Pay dirt.*

The Corbetts had left the elaborate Queen Anne to rot. Since last night, someone had nailed a sheet of plywood over the broken window in the attic. The roof sagged. On the upper façade, scalloped shingles were missing or broken. The decorative spindles on the porch had been replaced by shapeless fiberglass columns, the balustrade warped.

In the front yard, an inflatable Santa Claus stood by a scruffy white pine sprigged with red and green bulbs. The same tacky lights blinked on the tree in the front window. The house was lit like a circus—surely, they were inside.

Will parked in an inconspicuous spot at the foot of the street, and slid into the passenger seat. He switched from the CD to "Sports Talk" on AM radio, the callers pulverizing the Patriots for giving up so many points, and settled in for the duration.

He surveyed the area, calculating the distances from the house to the jeep, the jeep to this side of the street. As soon as he saw movement, he'd slip out of his car. Corbett would never spot him; he wouldn't think to look this way. Barring shotgun reflexes—doubtful, seeing as how he abused his body—Will would be on him before he could react. He'd force Corbett to produce Leah and he would drive his daughter home.

The seconds dragged.

Thirty minutes. Forty. Maybe he should call Leah's cell phone, tease them out.

Better yet, he'd call the cops. Leave an anonymous message saying he'd witnessed a drug deal. He'd tell the cops his daughter was being held against her will. If she fought, he'd say Corbett had brainwashed her. Violating probation would get the boyfriend out of the picture. What difference did it make how he accomplished his goal?

He'd punched all but the final digit for the Cortland police when the front door of the Victorian opened and Leah trotted out, grinning ear to ear, followed by the asshole.

He cancelled the call and stuffed the phone back in his pocket.

Leah picked her way down the steps, holding onto the rail, her breath curling like smoke. Seconds later, the door opened again and a hulking, bald-headed kid stepped out.

At one time, Will could have handled these two punks together. He hadn't worked out in earnest for years. If he separated the boys, he might be all right. Generally, when an older guy raised his fists to a kid, it took the kid an instant to get it together, psych himself out of the parent-child role. That split-second hesitation would give Will an edge.

Will opened the BMW's passenger door, slowly, quietly.

He crouched behind a Buick directly across from the jeep, his adrenaline shooting into the stratosphere. He could see his breath and almost smell Corbett's bad vibes.

Corbett unlocked the jeep and the big kid climbed into the passenger seat. Leah pulled a face and looked back at the house, her shoulders hunched against the cold.

The door swung open again. And Will's younger daughter appeared.

What was she doing here? The shock of seeing Justine briefly immobilized him.

Justine slipped, landing on her behind. Leah skated over, pulled her to her feet.

He had to do something. *Now.* He couldn't let his daughters get away.

Corbett was outside the jeep, holding the door for the girls. The burly kid, inside, appeared to be playing with the radio. Neither was paying attention to their surroundings.

Will shot across the street, banking on the element of surprise.

As Leah stepped back to shepherd Justine into the jeep, she spotted him. "Oh, my God," she cried. "Todd, *look out!*"

Corbett wheeled in Will's direction, his eyes glinting.

The hulk popped the side door open, Mother Love Bone blaring from the stereo.

"Daddy, no." Justine rushed, slipping and sliding, toward him. "Daddy, wait."

"In my car, Justine," Will shouted. "Over there."

All at once, Corbett was on him, wrestling him into a stranglehold from behind. Will jerked backward, flicking him off. Corbett fell on his ass, fumbled in the snow. Will grabbed Justine's arm, and then Corbett was up, charging again, this time from the front.

"What do you want?" Leah waved her fists at Will, her features distorted by the shadows. "Justine," she shouted. "Don't listen to him. Come back here!"

"Get in my car, Justine," Will ordered again. "Go."

Justine started across the street, turned to look at her sister, and came back.

"He's *drunk*," Leah screamed. "He stinks."

Corbett swung. Will bobbed, dodging the flying fist, and landed an uppercut, knocking the kid backward again. Corbett slipped, got his footing, lowered his head and rammed into Will, head-butting his gut, knocking the wind out of him.

Any other day, any other opponent, any other stakes, and Will might have given up. Not now. Not with this asshole. Not when his daughters were involved.

Kicked into survival mode, his instincts took over. Connected. Right hook. Left. Upper cut—Leah behind him, slapping, punching his back, screaming for him to stop.

Next thing he knew, Corbett was down.

"Todd," Leah wailed. "Your *nose*. He's crazy. Call the cops."

Corbett swiped at his nose, blood streaking his cheek. Swearing, he lowered his shoulders, set to charge. The Lupo kid grabbed Corbett from behind, holding him off.

"Let's *go*, man," Lupo yelled. "You heard her. He's psycho."

The girls hesitated. Will grabbed Justine's hand. With his free arm, he hoisted Leah over his shoulder, his older daughter kicking, pummeling his back with her fists.

"Let's go," the Lupo kid said, waving a cell phone. "The cops are on their way."

Distracted, Will loosened his grip.

Leah jerked free, hands and feet hitting the pavement at once. "Come on, Jus." Clutching her sister's arm, she rushed to the jeep, ushered Justine into the idling truck.

"Jus," Will pleaded, a last ditch effort. "Come home with me."

Justine hesitated before climbing into the jeep.

"Well, Dad." Leah brushed herself off. "Looks like your *friends* are coming for you," she spat, and joined her sister inside the truck.

Will stood on the sidewalk, watching helplessly as the jeep pulled away.

It was not the police or the aftereffects of the beer or even watching his daughters leave with Corbett and Lupo that turned his blood to ice. It was the sudden realization that he was fighting a losing battle—no matter what he did or how hard he fought, he could not save his daughter this time. And that insight both terrorized and paralyzed him.

Thirty

Snow Angels

From Todd's house, the kids rode around town, the passenger's window rolled down, the song "Stardog Champion" pounding out of the stereo, blasting Justine's skull. Lupo rode shotgun, his elbow crooked on the lip of the window. Justine sat in the backseat with her sister, huddled under a blanket. Lupo lit a joint and passed it to Todd.

"You believe the fucker fell for that shit?" Todd guffawed. "The cops? What's he, stupid?"

"Shut up," Leah griped. "It's not funny."

Silently, Justine seconded the motion.

"What's with him?" Lupo asked for the third time. He turned his head, peering at them. *His* old man would never do something stupid like that. His mother had died when Lupo was four, he said.

"Pussy," Todd interjected. "See him floundering? Coulda had his ass if I wanted."

"That right, Corbett?" Lupo punched Todd's arm. "That's how come you're the one covered in blood."

Todd blotted his nose. His cheek had swollen and his eye was half shut.

Lupo sniggered. "What do you care? The goon was wasted."

"Was not," Leah said peevishly. "He was buzzed. Not wasted."

"Fucking psycho." Todd sucked on the joint, and then offered it to Leah who refused—wasn't in the mood, she said—and Leah passed it to Lupo. "Psycho," he said again. "That's all I got to say."

Justine felt like a traitor, sitting in silence, listening to the boys bash her father. She ought to stick up for him. Only it was impossible to defend what her father had done. What did he expect to accomplish, showing up at Todd's house unannounced, smelling as if he'd bathed in a vat of beer? If he wanted Leah to come home, why didn't he call her? Say he missed her? Tell her he loved her. Offer to smooth things over with their mother.

Justine and her sister had talked for a good hour this afternoon. Leaving home depressed her, Leah had said. Todd and his mom did their best to make her comfortable. His mom had even gone to the store this morning and bought her a toothbrush. No matter how they tried, this wasn't her home. She hated being alienated from her family. She wanted to sleep in her own bed, surrounded by things of her own.

"I miss you guys, Jus. I miss my room. Stupid, I miss Paddington Bear. I can't believe I'm saying this. I even miss *Mom*." But she couldn't go crawling home. She needed to be sure their parents wanted her back.

Todd had called earlier to invite Justine for a visit with Leah. He dialed Star 67. If her parents happened to answer, instead of Justine, they wouldn't know it was him.

"We'll pick you up," he had said. "She's scared to call you herself. Your sister thinks you hate her." They'd agreed to meet in forty-five minutes at the end of her block.

Justine told her parents that Holly's mom and stepfather were taking her to Boston and they'd invited Justine to join them. "I might be late," she had said.

Their father had no right attacking the boys. They'd done nothing wrong. They'd spent the afternoon watching *Reservoir Dogs*, one of the movies Todd's mother had given him for Christmas, drinking Diet Coke, eating stale chips. When they'd first arrived and she'd seen Lupo on the living room floor, propped on his elbows, playing Nintendo, Justine had been scared. On Halloween night, the only other time she had seen him, Lupo had struck her as evil. But she'd been wrong about Lupo. Sure, he was messed up—he *had* to be, to sell drugs—but he wasn't a bad kid. He was actually sweet, in a way.

She hated *Reservoir Dogs*, the awful people, not a redeeming character among them. She hated the violence. Lupo noticed her eyes closed, nudged her awake, and challenged her to a game of checkers. A lot of boys would be ticked, being beaten six times by a junior high girl. Lupo shook his head in awe and asked for her secret.

"Shut that window," Leah complained. "It's freezing back here."
"Want to go to my house?" Lupo asked out of the blue. "My old man's out of town."

Lupo lived with his father in a converted condo, on an estate property once owned by the Caldwell family from Boston's Back Bay—banking people, Lupo informed them. The main building, nestled on a knoll at the end of a winding drive, reminded Justine of a castle, with its airy portico and stucco walls. They parked in a pebbled lot in front of a ten-car garage. Lupo's apartment occupied the right wing of the estate. The apartment was as big as the Tyler's entire house, with a soaring entry, a sweeping spiral staircase.

The kitchen was equipped with the same restaurant-style appliances the Tylers had in their kitchen. "The old man," Lupo said, smirking, "fancies himself a cook."

Lupo's father never cooked for him. He cooked for his girl-friends, Lupo told them.

Lupo opened a huge refrigerator stocked with fifty or sixty bottles of white wine. He scoured the contents, scrutinizing the labels on the bottles, closed it, and opened the temperature-controlled closet on the other side of the room, pilfering a bottle of red.

"Rothschild," Lupo announced. "He'll never notice it's gone." He took four Wedgewood stems from the cabinet. "Careful," he said. "Suckers cost fifty bucks a pop."

The wine was "superb," evidently. Lupo and Justine's sister babbled, applying snobby words like *nose* and *tannin* and *complexity*, words their parents tossed around with their friends. Todd looked on, bemused.

Justine set her glass on the counter.

"What's the matter?" Leah asked. "You don't like red wine?"

"I do. It's—" Justine sniffed, and forced another sip. "Good."

Lupo offered her a slice of whitish-yellow cheese. The blue streaks running through it reminded her of Nana's varicose veins. "Gorgonzola." He gave her a hunk of French bread. "Try it with this."

The cheese smelled like B. O. "Thanks." Justine pushed it away. "I'm not hungry."

When they'd emptied the bottle of wine, Lupo opened another and led the three of them, expensive crystal glasses in hand, to a marble Jacuzzi room behind the kitchen.

Black and white photographs of Lupo and his father, shot in Jerusalem and Beirut, lined the marble-tiled wall across from the hot tub. After his mother died, his father had joined the army, Lupo explained. He'd worked as a lawyer for JAG. In a photo taken in

Kosovo, Lupo was sitting inside a tank. He appeared to be about seven or eight.

"Must have been scary," Justine said, picturing Lupo and his dad dodging bullets.

The question seemed to conjure some grave disappointment. "The war was over," he said.

Justine studied the photos while the others undressed.

"I don't have a bathing suit," Justine said when Lupo asked if she'd like to go in.

Leah shot her a look.

"S'okay," Todd said, pulling his tee-shirt over his head. When they arrived, he'd washed his face and iced his nose. The swelling had gone down significantly. "Don't need one."

Justine winced. Maybe *they* didn't.

"Don't be shy," Lupo said. "It's just us."

Justine shrugged without turning around. In the mirrored glass over the pictures, she caught a glimpse of the huge white moons of Lupo's butt. "These pictures are cool."

Justine watched her sister, reflected on the glass, unhook her bra, and slip out of her panties. Leah lowered herself into the tub, her nipples erect.

"Don't be a ninny, Jus," Leah said. "Least put your feet in."

Lupo was sitting in a corner, his arms spread. He turned in Justine's direction, treating her to a full view of his hairy chest, caught her staring, and laughed.

Mortified, she averted her eyes.

"Come on," Todd teased. "We don't bite, you know."

The bubbling water made a loud, gurgling noise. Reluctantly, Justine rolled up her jeans and took a seat on the edge of the hot tub. Gradually, she submerged her feet in the steaming water. Leah laid her head on the rim of the tub; her knees breaking the surface.

The boys splashed each other, soaking the marble walls.

Todd rose like a phantom, blonde hair in ringlets, water dripping from the hairs on his chin. He waded through the chest-high water, his shoulders hunched, his elbows crooked. *Quasimodo.*

"Weirdo," Leah shrieked. She dove, dragging him under.

"Hey," Todd crowed when he came up for air, and then Leah was under the water.

Lupo splashed and Justine splashed back. Justine's water-logged jeans stuck uncomfortably to her legs. She pulled them off, stripping to her panties and tee-shirt, and laid her jeans on the floor to let them dry out.

They stayed in the tub for a good hour. By the time they emerged, the skin on Justine's fingers and toes had shriveled. Shivering, their bodies covered in goose pimples, they pulled on their clothes and retreated to the living room, where there was a gigantic flat screen TV. The boys selected an old slasher flick from a floor-to-ceiling shelf.

The movie grossed her out. Justine watched for a few minutes, and fell asleep.

Justine felt her sister's hand on her shoulder. "Wake up. Time to get you home."

Justine yawned, blinking. "Are you coming, too?"

"Can't, Teenie. You know Dad. You're with him or against him. What if he saw me?"

"Please, Lee? Just for tonight? You can go back to Todd's tomorrow."

It took some doing, but Leah agreed, haltingly. "Just tonight. For you. But only tonight."

Todd covered the five miles from Lupo's house to the Tyler's in less than ten minutes. At the top of the circle, he lifted his foot from the pedal, and let the jeep roll down the drive. Rounding the bend, passing the stand of trees blocking their view of the house, they noticed the light from the living room lamp. The rest of the house was dark.

"Shit," Leah said. "Figures he'd be awake."

Justine wondered what he would do. Apologize for his embarrassing behavior? Or yell because they were late? *Well*, she thought with escalating dread, *we'll know soon enough.*

The girls waited in the shadows until the truck disappeared, opened the garage door carefully, and crept into the house. Getting to their bedrooms required passing the living room, where their father was waiting.

"I'll go first," Justine whispered at the head of the hallway. "Maybe he won't notice you."

Leah squeezed her hand. Holding their breath, they tiptoed down the hall. As they approached the French doors in the living room, they heard snoring, and Justine exhaled.

Their father had fallen asleep in his recliner, a book face down in his lap.

Justine shrugged. Leah made a face, her palms upturned.

That night, with her bare feet tucked between Leah's shins, Justine had the most wonderful dreams. In her dreams, she and Leah were little girls. They lay in the front yard, waving their arms, making snow angels. Holding hands, they stared at the deep blue winter sky, naming the clouds. In the last, long dream before she woke, Leah was pushing her on the swings. *Up, up, up,* Leah sang, the swing soaring over the grass, Justine giggling, pumping her legs. Justine hugged her pillow, holding fast to the dream.

When she opened her eyes, sunshine was pouring into the room.

Her sister was gone, her bureau drawers flung open, her closet stripped bare. A full bottle of Zoloft sat on the nightstand—the only indication that she had been home.

Thirty-One

The Waiting Game

Zoe had never dreamed it possible to feel so distant, so alienated from her own child. After their hideous blowout on Christmas night, Leah had run off to Todd's. The thought of their daughter escaping, enjoying the rest of the night, while she and Will sat at home in a funk, infuriated her. Enraged, she pressed Will to chase the kids down.

Once Will hauled their daughter home, Zoe had planned to force her to retract her absurd allegations. Leah had read a few friendly e-mail messages, which, for the record, she had no business opening: she'd been snooping in Zoe's Outlook account. Stupidly, Zoe had never bothered to password-protect her computer. There were no *love* letters.

Zoe lay in bed, half-thinking, half-dreaming about Leah, the morning noises burrowing into the outer reaches of her consciousness. This was her fault, Leah's running away. Her daughter and the Corbett boy had been together for several months. Of course they were having sex. It was naïve to think otherwise. Far better for Leah to be on birth control than, God forbid, risk an accidental pregnancy. A reasonable parent would have addressed the situation calmly, without recrimination, shared her concerns, pointed out the dangers of sexual involvement at too early an age. Told her daughter she loved her, offered her support. Zoe owed Leah that much. Instead, she'd behaved like a hothead, an immature child, driven by an irrational, gut-wrenching hatred of a boy she barely knew.

Their bedroom door opened. Suddenly, before Zoe was fully awake, Justine was hovering over their bed, screaming hysterically. Something about Leah. Something Todd. Something, something, *big jerk*. Justine was beside herself; she was making little sense.

Zoe rubbed her eyes. Justine had woken them for this? To tell them Leah was gone? Her sister left two days ago. "Justine, honey." It's early, she planned to say. Go back to bed. The fury in her daughter's face terrified her. "Sweetheart, what's wrong?"

"She took her stuff," Justine wailed. "Because of *him*."

Finally, Justine calmed down enough to tell Zoe the story. When she left the room, Zoe confronted her husband and Will confessed to a drunken escapade at Todd's.

"Idiot!" Zoe screamed. How could he? Had he made it a goal to push her away?

"Oh, and you're a saint? Do you think you deserve the peace prize for your little outburst on Christmas?" Generally, Will was not combative. Once in bulldog mode, he dug in deep and refused to relent. "You're a goddamn drug addict," her husband snarled.

"What a low blow!" she cried, seeing as how the day after Dog died, she'd flushed all her pills down the toilet. Enraged, she yanked on jeans and a tee-shirt and tore out of the room. "You're an asshole to boot," she shouted, slamming the door.

In a fog, she rushed downstairs to the kitchen, put on a pot of coffee, and pulled bowls, spatulas, measuring spoons out of the cabinets. She broke three eggs into a plastic bowl and beat them with the hand whisk, froth rising up the sides of the bowl. She defrosted a bag of blueberries in the microwave. With her teeth, she ripped the bag open.

Justine was in Leah's room with the stereo turned to full blast, the song's repetitive bass rattling the ceiling. Zoe winced. When had Justine started listening to rap?

She'd lit the stove too soon and the griddle overheated. She fed the first batch of pancakes, the tops raw, the undersides charred, to the garbage disposal. Zoe ladled six more onto the griddle, frying them to a deep golden brown. She flipped the pancakes onto a plate, folded one on top in half and stuffed it in her mouth, and ladled six more. She'd used all but a cup of blueberries. She couldn't refreeze them, and since she hated to waste perfectly good berries, she decided to make muffins, to freeze for later in the week.

As she slid the pan into the oven, she noticed the overripe bananas on the wooden tree by the sink, mixed batter for bread. While the banana bread baked, she whipped up a batch of chocolate chip cookies. As a special treat, she made a pecan pie, Leah's favorite.

By late afternoon, the house looked and smelled like a bakery, the counters lined with banana bread, fudge, chocolate chip cookies, lemon poppy seed cake, pecan pie.

"Who's going to eat all that?" Will asked as she pulled the pie out of the oven.

"*We* are." She tossed her towel in the sink and opened the fridge. "Who do you think?"

"Planning to drink that?" Will gestured to the Bud in her hand.

She handed him the bottle. "I don't know why I took it." She never drank beer.

He took a long pull, and then wiped his mouth. "Can we talk?"

She poured a glass of orange juice for herself and followed her husband into the family room. He moved the magazines fanned out over the coffee table, setting them on the end table by the arm of the sofa, and placed a log in the fireplace, prodding it with a poker. When the fire caught, he loaded a Keith Jarrett CD into the player.

"We should take down the tree," she said. The white spruce had been gorgeous when Will brought it home, deep green, full, and perfectly shaped. Now it looked like yesterday's news, the drooping branches losing their needles. If a spark from the fireplace landed on the dry needles littering the carpet the house would go up in flames.

"Okay. Tomorrow," he said. "I hate fighting, Zo. It's not right."

"Agreed." She hated quarreling, too. Besides, to bring Leah home they'd have to work as a team. "Thanks for driving over again," by the Corbetts' place, she meant.

He'd left forty-five minutes ago, without telling her where he was headed. He'd phoned from his car to let her know that they could relax: Corbett's jeep was still there.

While neither she nor Will approved of Leah's staying with Corbett, at seventeen their daughter was legally an adult. The local police had no jurisdiction. Leah had left their home voluntarily and they knew where she was, so she was not considered missing. Nor did state laws against aiding and abetting juveniles or harboring runaways apply. Unless they could prove their daughter was in danger, there was nothing the police could do.

"I tried calling this morning," Zoe said. "Nobody answered."

He swallowed the last of his beer. "Maybe they were out."

"Or maybe they recognized the number on caller ID and ignored it."

That they had no means of compelling Leah to return home frustrated them both. As a counselor, Zoe had put her heart and soul into helping teens, reuniting families. Yet when they had needed help, they were on their own. Unreasonably, it felt grossly unfair.

"We can initiate a suit," Will suggested. "Force them to do something."

"And then what? She'd be furious and we'd all be outcasts—more than we are already—for wasting tax dollars on a frivolous suit. Mind if I change this music?" The piano solo depressed her. In this gloomy weather, with so little natural light coming through the windows, the house felt like a cave. "It's dismal."

"Sorry. I thought you'd like it. Let me find something different."

She got up, motioning for him to stay seated, turned on the light.

Zoe scanned the CDs in the bookcase. Will had spent the morning organizing the shelves. Odd to see the bookcase, normally a mishmash of books and discs, look so neat. He'd placed the books on the bottom shelf; on the upper shelves, he'd alphabetized and arranged his CDs by genre, each genre subdivided by artist. She selected a Jan Garbarek disc, loaded the changer, and joined her husband again on the floor.

"I never thought I'd say this." She scratched a glob of batter off her arm. "It's a relief to know she's there." She balled the batter and flicked it away. "I mean, I'm not saying I like it. Obviously, I'd prefer she were here. At least we know where she is."

"We're in this together, Zo." He scooped a pillow from the sofa and tucked it behind her back. "We've got to remember. It's the only way we'll get through this."

"I just can't help feeling we're to blame."

"Maybe so. There's nothing we can do about that now."

Zoe slid forward, resting her head on the sofa. "She doesn't really think I hate her, does she?"

"Of course not. She's a kid. She's melodramatic."

"I can't stop thinking about it."

"You've got to let up on yourself. It doesn't help anybody."

"I know," Zoe said, and promised to try. She harped on the parents she counseled for the same thing. "Focus on your children," she told them. "It's not about you. It's about *them*." If she listened to her own advice, she'd direct all her thoughts and energy toward Leah. That would be too rational. Beating up on herself was easier, instinctive.

The toilet flushed. Then they heard a shuffling on the landing. Justine must have left her bedroom door open. A minute later, they heard her walloping her punching bag.

Thwap. Thwap, thwap.

"Listen to her up there," Zoe said. "She's killing that thing."

"Good," said Will. "She's getting the negative energy out."

Zoe reached for her drink. The quiet music had settled her. For the first time all day, her heart beat normally. "About the 'love letters'—she was lying, you know. I can show you."

"You don't have to show me."

"Jerry's a friend. That's it, Will. Nothing more."

"I believe you."

Zoe set her glass on the floor and held her husband's hand. "Him being here," she said tentatively, hoping to clear the air. "He did stop by one day. That's true."

"Shh." He kissed her knuckles, her fingers, the palm of her hand.

"We—" Her heart quickened. "Went for coffee—"

He pushed her hair back, massaging her neck, and she bowed her head, accepting his kiss. Pulling her into his arms, he kissed her forehead, her chin, the tip of her nose. Supporting her back, he lowered her to the floor. His warm breath, the musky smell of his body and hers erased the years, and he was the man she'd fallen in love with so long ago.

"Jus?" she whispered. "What if—"

"She won't."

For a few blissful moments, giving herself over to feeling, she forgot about their troubles. She accepted his love and she gave to him, violently, passionately, exquisitely.

Afterward, he said, "Should we drive by the house again?"

Nodding, she buttoned her blouse and tucked it into her jeans.

Justine had spent the better part of the day lying on her sister's bed, absorbing the heat of Leah's angry music. On fire, she returned to her own room, began slamming her heavy bag. *Leah.* She rammed the bag harder. *I need you.* Lights flashed. The hot lights bore down on her, and the audience went wild. She shuffled her feet. *Ladies and gentlemen, to your right, the one, the only, the incomparable— Cinderella Woman.*

Pow. She stripped to her panties and bra, her body glistening, *KIA-HA.*

Heart racing, she ripped off the gloves, whacked the bag with her bare fists, punching until her hands felt like stumps, her knuckles white, then purple, ballooning. When her hands gave out, she switched to her feet.

Justine collapsed onto her bed. Rolling onto her side, she reached for her phone and dialed Todd's number. Busy. She tossed the phone on the floor, lugged her aching body to the TV, and plugged in the DVD her father had recorded on Christmas morning.

Justine was sorry she had come home last night. She should have insisted on staying with her sister. If she were not such a coward, she and Leah would be together right this minute, at Todd's, playing a game or watching TV. Maybe they'd go to Lupo's again, swim in his Jacuzzi. She wouldn't be a ninny this time. She'd strip like the others.

Listlessly, Justine plucked her phone off the floor. This time, a woman answered, her voice gravelly, as if she'd been sleeping.

"Hello," Justine said. "Would Leah Tyler be available, please?"

"No," the woman snapped. "And stop calling here please."

———◦◉◦———

Leah picked through her suitcase, flinging underwear, tee-shirts, and jeans on Todd's bed. It was time to unpack. She'd moved into Todd's basement bedroom two days earlier—an arrangement Todd's mother had encouraged, once she realized Leah would be there for good. Despite their efforts to make her feel at home—"*La mia casa è la vostra casa,*" said Todd's mom, who had not a drop of Italian blood—Leah felt awkward, relying on her boyfriend and his mom. Problem was, she had nowhere else to go.

Hope's mom worked a second job now; mooching off her would be selfish. Leah had come here on Christmas to get away, so she could think. She'd needed to sort things out. She'd had every intention of going home. If not for dumb luck—she'd been walking on Old Orchard Road, trying to cool off when Todd happened by— things would be different.

Now she couldn't go home. The night her father showed up at Todd's house, the possibility of her ever going home had vanished. Her father had drawn a line, forcing her into a position she'd never expected to take and never would have taken: choosing between him and her boyfriend. Righteous indignation had forced her to choose Todd.

Inside the cup of a wireless bra, she found the wax figurine Justine had given her.

"Hey," she said, to Todd. "Look at this." She held up the figurine, the crystal head of her serpent ring catching the light. The serpent ring was a temporary engagement ring, Todd had told her on Christmas Eve. As soon as he could afford one, he'd buy her a diamond. Her boyfriend couldn't seem to get it into his head that Leah didn't care about diamonds; she had no interest in fine jewelry or gems. The serpent ring suited her perfectly. She swung the magician to and fro, making the figurine dance. "Isn't he cute?"

"Sure." Todd rolled his eyes. "Guess so."

She set the magician on the stereo speaker next to Todd's bed.

Todd had an incredible, top-of-the-line system, worth two thousand dollars. The stereo had been a bribe. After his mother bailed him out of jail, she'd offered to buy any stereo system he wanted if he would only agree to move home. She'd wasted her money, in Leah's opinion. It wasn't as if he'd had somewhere better to go.

After he moved in, they'd turned the basement into an apartment. Todd had done the work himself. The hardest part, he'd told Leah, had been moving the headboard and dresser from his attic bedroom down three flights of stairs. He'd painted the walls a cool midnight blue, bought a Persian rug from the Salvation Army, and hung a tapestry from the ceiling. *Voila*—a private apartment. It smelled weird, being in a basement and all. The pipes would look better painted. Minor details, considering he lived here rent-free.

"What do you think?" Leah waved the jeans she'd received from her parents for Christmas. She'd never heard of the brand, but they looked expensive. She was thinking about returning them for cash.

"Whatever." He tuned the stereo, pulling the bass forward. From a silver can in his bottom drawer, he extracted a plastic sandwich bag.

"What's your problem?" Leah hollered over the music. "Why're you such an asshole today?"

He shot a sour look in her direction, and reduced the volume on the stereo. "Your family's a pain in the ass, calling like ten times a day." He spooned powder onto a mirror. "Mom's sick of that shit."

"Five times," Leah corrected him. "In two days."

"We can't stay here forever," he said. "You realize that, right?"

"Why not?" Why couldn't they stay here? Until they'd saved some cash, this was a perfect arrangement. The apartment was *free*.

With his debit card, he cut the powder into lines.

"Fine. Don't answer," she muttered. *Think what you want. Doesn't mean it will happen.* Until she found a job and they'd saved enough to pay the first and last months' rent on a decent apartment, she planned to stay put.

Sniffing, he offered Leah the mirror. His dilated eyes scared her.

"I got to get a job," he said bitterly.

"You *have* a job." Pinching her left nostril, she brought her face to the glass, pushed the straw up her right nostril, and inhaled sharply.

"I got fired," he said. "Told you yesterday."

Fired? He'd mentioned something about him and Jamie having words. He'd never said the word "fired." *The serpent ring.* Leah sank onto the bed. He'd told her he'd borrowed the hundred dollars. She fingered the ring. "Did you tell him it was for me?"

If looks could kill, she'd have been on the express train to Hell.

His stepmother owned a cabin in Maine. "We could stay there," he said.

"Camden?" She wiped her nose, coughing. "Isn't it Bangor?"

"Yeah, well." He'd forgotten. He hadn't been to Maine since he was like twelve. Anyway, when he talked to his stepmother at Thanksgiving, she'd said she and her new husband planned to spend the winter in Southeast Asia. He knew where she kept the key.

"Might as well use it," he said. "It's just gonna sit empty."

"Maine?" Leah repeated. This was a lot to take in at once.

"I need a job," he reminded her. "Forget about a reference from Jamie. Be easier to find a job in Maine, where nobody knows me. Me and you could start over."

Start over. Leah's mind reeled. In Maine. *Four hours away.*

It took a few minutes for a solid picture to shape. Camden was a resort town on the water. They could work in a restaurant. In the summer, she and Todd could work the dinner shift and spend their days on the beach. They'd take diving lessons as soon as they could afford it. Once they learned to dive, they could trap lobsters and start their own lobster business. When she was little, every summer her family had driven to southern Maine for a special lobster dinner. Living in Camden would be fun, just like the old days.

Leah tossed the jeans back in her suitcase. "Maine," she mused, the movie of their brand new life already on *play.*

Thirty-Two

Lost

Week Two

Initially, knowing Leah's whereabouts had curbed Zoe and Will's apprehension. This was a temporary setback. As soon as she'd cooled off, Leah would come home. By the end of the second day, when neither they nor Justine had heard from Leah, anxiety assumed control. On day three, when Will drove by the Corbett place and discovered the jeep missing, they were frantic.

After several tries, they reached Corbett's mother, who confirmed their worst fear: the kids had left. After a great deal of prodding—and a pointed threat concerning her son's probation and recent drug use—Corbett's mother provided Will with a list of people that her son might try to contact. That afternoon, they filed a missing person report and they handed the list they'd received from Corbett's mother to the police.

The chief, Sergeant Healy, issued a statewide "Be on the Lookout" bulletin and registered Leah's name in the FBI's national database. "If an officer anywhere in the country runs a check, he'll get a hit, saying she's a runaway," Healy informed them.

The chief pledged the full cooperation of the Cortland PD. They'd do what they could. Unfortunately, resources were limited; despite the heartache to the families, law enforcement agencies didn't consider runaway teenagers to be critical missing person cases.

"She's an adult," Healy reminded them. "Running away isn't a crime." Her age made Leah ineligible for an Amber Alert. If the police located her, unless they caught her breaking a law, their only option would be to contact Zoe and Will.

"We can't send her home," Healy said. "Can't even detain her."

"We'd almost be better off if she'd been kidnapped," Zoe said dismally.

If they hoped to find their daughter, they should mount an aggressive campaign of their own, Healy advised. "In cases like this, that's where you've got your best shot."

Immediately after the meeting, Will called a colleague who put them in touch with a private investigator. The PI, a squirrely looking guy named John Dunham, had done undercover work for the FBI. Desperate, they borrowed the five thousand dollar deposit from his parents. They met him in a coffee shop two towns over, near Dunham's home.

"I'll start digging," Dunham said, typing notes into his laptop. With a portable scanner, he transferred a photo of Leah. "You might want to call around, talk to people, see what you can find out. You might be surprised. Be sure to keep me in the loop."

Together—Zoe from their home line, Will his office extension— they called every person they could think of who might have the slightest clue as to where the kids might have gone. They called relatives, friends. They contacted Coach Thomas, the Hansons. Zoe called Mrs. Lansdown and spoke with the daughter, who claimed to know nothing.

"Sorry, Mrs. T.," Hope said. "Wish I could help."

From a tracking service, Will bought the Lupo's unlisted number, called, spoke with the father. "Yes," the elder Lupo admitted, "my son knows Corbett. Tony had nothing to do with your daughter's disappearance." If he heard anything, he'd obviously pass the information along.

"Scumbag," Will said when he hung up. "The guy knows something. He's a liar."

Zoe stared at the palladium window in the family room, the gold buttons in her bracelet glittering in the sunlight. Justine lay on the sofa, reading. Will was somewhere in the house, puttering. Her husband and daughter were as lost as Zoe these days.

Leah had been gone for two weeks. They were no closer to finding her than they'd been the day she fled. All their efforts, every attempt they'd made to locate her, had failed. Zoe had filed her daughter's name with all the runaway hotlines. She'd alerted every halfway house and clinic in New England. She monitored Internet chat rooms, checked the files in all the family computers. She kept tabs on Leah's e-mail account.

By now, their daughter could be anywhere in the country—or, God forbid, out of the country. Some days, Zoe's anger consumed her. She wished the strength would return to her legs. Running would provide a modicum of relief. One morning after Justine had left for school, she'd tried punching the heavy bag. The bag barely moved when she hit it. When she tried to let go of the anger, without rage to fuel her, Zoe drifted into despair.

Since her accident, she'd gained ten pounds. She could barely zip her jeans.

She rested her elbow on the arm of her chair. The oak tree outside the palladium window had grown taller than the house. Ten years ago, the tree had begun to attain its girth, the low branches ten or twelve feet in length. Leah, seven then, begged for a rope swing. A rope swing was dangerous, they'd told her, knowing the instant Will hung one Leah would be climbing on the rail of the deck, leaping like Tarzan into the air. One of Leah's friends had a zip line; the line ran from their deck to a pole in their backyard.

Please, Leah begged. A rope swing would be *so* fun. *Way more fun than a zip line. Mom? Dad? Pretty please? With sugar on top?* Finally, they'd given in. The rope swing was dangerous. They should have stood their ground. Their waffling confused her; they'd taught her, essentially, she was in charge. With persistence, she could break them.

Zoe heard her name and turned, surprised to see Will with his guitar, the leather strap slung over his shoulder. He'd put it in the attic years ago. "You found your guitar?"

Justine looked up from her book.

Will lowered himself to the floor by the fireplace, positioning the body of the guitar in his lap. "I had an old song in my head," he said, strumming a chord. "I wanted to play it for you guys."

"Leah used to love when you played," Justine said. "Remember?"

Will smiled. "This was one of her favorites," he said, strumming a chord. *"Let me take you down..."*

"Strawberry fields," Zoe sang, and her daughter joined in, off-key, their voices faltering. By their second time through the song, they were laughing, singing exuberantly.

When Will stopped playing, Justine ran off to call her friend Holly.

"I miss her," Zoe said. "It's not the same without her. I miss her so much."

"I've always thought she'd do something great. Run the UN. Find a cure for cancer. All that energy." He grinned. "She'll be back," he said seriously. "I believe that."

"I hope so." Distracted by a shushing noise, she glanced at the window. Melted snow slid off the tree in a shower. "Remember the rope swing?"

"How could I not? Damn thing was a bear to put up."

"She was such a daredevil," Zoe said—and saw seven-year-old Leah, soaring over the yard, shrieking joyfully, her legs outstretched, one hand gripping the rope. "I was sure she'd fall and break her neck. Got to the point where I couldn't watch her play."

"And that big wheel. Remember how she used to stand on the seat?"

"No wonder she's the way she is." A strong-willed child, like Leah, needed solid boundaries. By giving in to her demands, they'd taught their daughter, in effect, her will was stronger than theirs. By pushing, haunting, she'd eventually get her way. Children aren't equipped to take charge. Predictably, she'd lost control. "We should've stuck to our guns."

Will laid the guitar on the floor, and got up.

"Where are you going?"

"Up to my office," he said flatly.

Sure, she thought, *walk away. Don't talk about Leah. Don't talk, period.* Pretend their daughter hadn't run away. Will had regained steam at work; he was selling again. Justine was fine, thank you very much. *If you don't want to talk, don't.* She did.

"I'm just trying to make sense of this. Listen to me," she said to his back. He didn't have to gush over her. "I expect common courtesy. Will, I'm talking to you."

He paused. His shoulders rose and fell in agitation. Or maybe it was resignation in his stiff posture and labored breath. Maybe rage.

"Damn it." She poked his shoulder. "Look at me."

He brushed her hand away. "What do you *want* from me?"

Want? Nothing. "I just want a friend."

He threw up his hands. "I *am* your friend."

"Like hell you are."

He squeezed by her, shaking his head.

She watched him shuffle across the family room. His jeans sagged.

"I thought you said you were going up to your office?"

He turned, and she noticed his sharp cheekbones, his hollow eyes. When had he lost so much weight? His jaw had gone slack. *My God*, she thought, *he looks old.*

"We should have stayed on top of her. That's all I meant."

He ran a finger across the top row of CDs, selected one, and held it up. "You like this one, right?" He loaded the Albert King CD and hit *play*. "I'll Play the Blues for You"— the title song.

She hugged herself, listening.

"Come here," he said, and reached for her hand.

She stepped back, crossing her arms. "I'm sorry. I can't."

"Don't do this to yourself, Zo. Don't do it to us."

"A kid doesn't just wake up a rebel. It happens a day at a time."

"Hemingway—'gradually, then all at once.' I know."

"That's all I meant."

"I knew what you meant." Taking her hands, he pulled her close, pressing her head to his chest, rocking gently.

When the song ended, they stood, holding hands. "It's not that I don't want to talk to you, Zo. I miss her as much as you do. I wish we could change things, too." He pulled her to him again. "I just don't see the point…"

"She's our baby," she said softly. "I can't let her go."

He stroked her head. "Tell me what to do, Zo. I'll do whatever you want."

"I just want—" She pulled away. "I just want her back."

———⟨◈⟩———

Justine lay in bed watching the Christmas DVD. She watched it all the time.

Singing with her parents had been fun, like the old days. But the fun never lasted. After she hung up the phone, she'd gone back to the family room, and found her mother alone, staring into space. Justine had been gone for fifteen minutes. *Fifteen minutes.*

That morning, she'd helped her father take down the tree. It had died a miserable death, the branches nearly bald, the skirt blanketed by dry needles. Justine removed the ornaments and her father unstrung the lights. Together, they'd dragged the prickly tree to the deck, leaving a trail of pine needles and dirt. While her dad vacuumed, she unwound the holly and untied the ribbons, packed it all away, and disassembled the Nativity scene. She laid the stable in a cardboard box, covering it with foam peanuts, and swaddled the figurines in tissue.

The forecasters had predicted snow for later that day. A dismal gray stratus hung over her skylight. Her room was dark, the air raw. Her sister's blue and gold Cortland High sweatshirt lay at the foot of her bed. Justine pulled the sweatshirt over her head.

Justine plodded to the bathroom, peed, and padded back to her room.

Earlier today, she'd been working on her essay for her Confirmation address. She turned off the DVD player, printed it out, and went to her mirror to practice.

As always, the girl in the mirror took Justine by surprise. She'd grown two inches since the fall. She wasn't chubby anymore, her belly flat, the clavicle bones visible at the base of her throat. Her features had matured; her nose was long and straight, like their mother's, her cheekbones defined. She curled and uncurled her toes. She wore a size six shoe now, a size and a half smaller than Leah.

Justine glanced at the paper, took a deep breath. "From my own family, I've learned—" She screwed up her face. "I can't do this," she said, wagging her finger at the girl staring back at her from the mirror. She would feel like a hypocrite.

Every night since her sister disappeared, Justine had gotten down on her knees and prayed for Leah's return. Every morning, she'd been disappointed. Maybe Leah was right. Maybe God was a figment of her imagination, her belief in a savior immature, the faith of a child looking for a father figure to take care of her, wash all her troubles away.

She crushed the paper, tossed it in the trash, strolled to her window, and raised the honeycomb shade. Spring was a long way away; the yard was empty; the trees were bare.

A rush of cold air streamed in under the sash. The air smelled of snow.

Justine pressed her hand against the cool glass, as she and Leah used to do on the windshield of their father's car, when they were small. *Stop*, he would scold. *You're smearing the glass.* She smiled, remembering how her sister used to love to egg him on.

She pulled her hand away from the glass, watched her prints disappear. Justine wished sometimes that she could disappear, too. *Poof*, just like the handprint.

Poof, just like her sister.

Thirty-Three

The Existence Period

Week Three

Leah's head throbbed. She remembered part of last night: the pizza shop, the shouting match on their way back to the cabin, Todd insisting they stay here until they'd sorted things out, Leah pressing to move closer to home. An eight-dollar bottle of champagne, uncorked in the secluded clearing in the woods where they'd parked Todd's truck. Bottles two and three in the cabin. Strip poker. As usual, she'd lost. She recalled peeing in the bed, Todd lifting her off the mattress, her head lolling like a rag doll's.

The rest of the night was a blur. She should have stayed on the Zoloft. She'd quit taking her meds because she'd missed the excitement, the highs and lows. "The antidepressant medication," her mother would say, "removes your affect." It made her feel flat. Now she just wanted to die.

Leah felt uncomfortable sleeping in Todd's stepmother's room. Initially, she'd had trouble falling asleep. A snapshot of Todd's father and stepmother, shot before the divorce, hung on the wall across from the foot of the bed. When she complained, Todd had lifted the photo from its hook, and laid it upside-down on his stepmother's bureau.

"Don't worry about it," he'd said. He hadn't heard from his old man in years and his stepmom would want them to make themselves at home. Besides, the loft was the safest place in the cabin. From up here, they'd hear an intruder before he found them.

Leah patted the nightstand, groping for the box of Hi-C.

"Hey," he said, the mattress sloping under his weight. "You're up."

She flung an arm over her head.

A cold metallic object touched her shoulder. Flinching, she turned onto her back, shielding her eyes. "Oh, my God." *A gun.* She pushed to her elbow. "Where'd you get that?"

"Found it last night, under the mattress." He turned the gun over and pointed to the engraving on the side of the barrel: *Colt .38.* "It's a .38 Special. She's a beauty, huh?" He caressed the six-inch barrel. "Here," he said, pressing the wooden grip into her palm. "Feel."

"Get that thing out of here." Guns terrified her.

Squinting, he pointed the gun at the wall.

"What are you *do*ing?" Leah slapped at his hand. "Don't shoot."

"Chill out." He pulled the trigger. *Click.* "See?" Fired again. *Click.* "She's empty."

"Put it back," Leah pleaded, and relayed a story about a widower her father knew. "Guns are dangerous. He killed his own son."

When her story failed to persuade him, she asked how his stepmother would feel if she discovered he'd stolen her pistol. "Isn't it enough, with us staying here?"

"Quit the fucking guilt trip. I'm going into town for some lunch." He stuffed the pistol in the pocket of his anorak. "Sandwiches all right? I'll get us some chips."

"Leave it here," she begged.

"Need anything?"

"Baby, please?"

After he left, she cocooned herself in the blankets, a pillow between her knees. She should have asked for Advil. Her cramps were killing her, sharp pain shooting from her abdomen to her lower back. Her period was all out of whack. The birth control pills regulated her cycles when she remembered to take them regularly. This month, she'd forgotten three times.

Holding her stomach, she felt her way to the bathroom. The master bath was slightly bigger than her bedroom closet at home. If she owned the cabin, she'd put in a double vanity, replace the fiberglass shower stall with a tub, and rip up the puke-colored linoleum floor. The skylight Leah would keep.

She rooted through the vanity drawers, hunting for tampons. In the cabinet below the sink, under a rusted plumbing snake, she found maxi-pads, the cardboard box limp from the dampness. Leah hated sanitary pads, the feeling like a towel between her legs. Since she had no supplies of her own, they would have to do. She peed, taped a pad to her panties, pulled on a tee-shirt and sweats, and headed downstairs.

The main floor of the cabin looked like an antique shop with teak tables and hand painted chests from all over the world. Todd's stepmother would die if she saw how they were destroying the place.

They'd dripped salsa on the tan carpet, scratched the wood floor. Todd had lit fires in the stone fireplace every day, the wood box now empty, the hearth coated with soot. A picture window looked out at the woods, the glass smeared with their prints. One of these days, when Leah had the energy, she'd have to do some serious cleaning.

She gathered their glasses and plates and carried them to the kitchen.

A phone with a rotary dial sat on the Formica counter next to an apple-shaped clock. Leah vaguely recalled drunk-dialing her sister last night. When Todd went to the bathroom, she'd snuck in here. She saw a flash of herself, dizzy from the champagne, leaning against the stove, shivering in her panties and bra. Her head bowed, her hands cradled the handset. On the fourth ring, her mother picked up. Leah had frozen when she heard her mom's voice.

She eyed the clock. One thirty. Justine was still at school. If her mother answered the phone and heard Leah's voice, she'd hang up. Depressed, Leah poured Hi-C into a goblet, wandered back to the loft.

Zoe lay on the family room sofa, half-asleep, dreaming of California. Last night, Hope Lansdown had finally come clean about Leah's disappearance. Leah "might" be on the West Coast, Hope had informed them. Apparently, Leah had mentioned California "a bunch of times." Leah, evidently, "digs the weather out west." Good grief, Zoe thought—*California.* How would they ever find her out there?

The phone rang, jangling her nerves.

For days, they'd been receiving prank calls, sometimes four or five in a day. Whoever it was always disconnected without a word. The police felt the caller was likely someone they knew, playing a practical joke. Zoe could not imagine being that cruel. If the caller ever stayed on the line, she'd give the jerk a piece of her mind.

Dialing Star 57 after the call ended was supposed to initiate a trace. Thus far, all attempts had failed. Apparently, some cellular and rotary phones fooled the tracking device. The police had also advised them to record all incoming and outgoing calls.

Trembling, she grabbed the cordless from the coffee table. "Hello?" she said, hurrying to the kitchen for the notepad. "Hello?"

A door closed and she heard Will scurrying down the hall.

"Who is this?" she shouted over the static. "Tell me who it is."

"Is it him?" her husband asked, breathing in her ear.

Apparently, her husband was talking to her again. Last night, after the conversation with Hope, they'd had an ugly row.

"You're the psychologist," he'd spat. If she'd managed to pry the information from the girl sooner, they'd have had the PI on Leah's tail, might have found her by now.

Pry? *Pry* it out of the girl? "For your information, therapists don't *pry*. Therapists listen," she'd said. "But then, you're not familiar with listening, are you? You never do."

"Static," she mouthed. She couldn't make anything out.

Just before she clicked off, she heard a voice on the other end.

"Sorry," Jerry said. "New phone system. How are you?"

"All right." She slouched against the counter, her knee sore. Last week, the orthopedist had arranged for her to start physical therapy. At the last minute, she'd cancelled the appointment. What she needed were pills to calm her nerves. Maybe she should go back, ask the orthopedist to refill her OxyContin prescription. Or, if she pleaded, maybe their family practitioner would hook her up with some Xanax.

"Checking in," Jerry told her. "Any idea who the caller might be?"

"No," she said. And the calls were driving her out of her mind.

"The PI? Anything there?"

Will lumbered to the fridge, pulled a Bud from the six-pack on the top shelf. He'd worn the same clothes for three days—his Harvard soccer camp sweatshirt, the sleeves pushed to his elbows, ill-fitting chinos, scuffed loafers, no socks. He twisted the cap off the beer bottle, shoved the cap in his pocket, and stood by the sink, staring out at the snow.

Zoe hobbled to his side, her knee tight. "Jerry," she whispered.

"What's he want?"

She shrugged. "Nothing new," she mouthed.

The wind howled, spraying snow crystals on the rattling glass.

"...have to be patient," Jerry was saying, as always. "Runaways are notoriously hard to find." This morning, he'd phoned a former classmate from Northeastern, now a trial attorney in L.A. "I asked him to put out some feelers. It'll take time." One of these days they'd catch a break. He hadn't given up hope; neither should they.

"What?" Will tossed the empty beer bottle in the recycling bin. Zoe raised a finger. Shivering, she buttoned her cardigan.

"He called a friend in California," she said when she hung up. "The guy's a lawyer, I guess. He promised to check their databases."

Will snorted. "Databases, my ass."

"Get off it." She limped to the refrigerator, scrounged up a tomato, a wilted head of iceberg lettuce, a hunk of Vidalia onion, set them on the counter. She sorted through the cheeses and deli meats, tossing several outdated packages in the sink, unwrapped a pound of pepper-roasted turkey, sniffed, and threw the turkey in, too. Rooting through the freezer, she came across the sausage from Jerry. "Hungry? I'll make sandwiches."

"How can you be hungry? We just ate."

She consulted her watch. "An hour ago."

"Think I'll call Healy, let him know what his boy's been up to."

"For God's sake. He's only trying to help."

"Help? The bastard's trying to move in on my wife."

She peeled the onion, her eyes watering. She should have kept her mouth shut. She'd hoped to clear the air by admitting to coffee with Jerry. Instead, she'd ratcheted her husband's suspicions. She wiped her eyes on her sleeve. With her elbow, she flipped the lever on the faucet.

"Look at me. Read my lips." She held the onion under the water. "We're *friends*."

Will, eyeing the sausage, took a reproachful slug of beer.

"Do you want a sandwich or not?"

Will blew out his cheeks and huffed away in disgust.

Zoe repackaged the sausage in a Zip-Lock bag and sealed the vegetables in a Tupperware container. She and Will had too much time on their hands. They needed to start working again. She was surprised NAC hadn't fired him. Since the Micronics fiasco last fall, he'd sold one job, six million dollars, netting twelve grand in commission. Paying a stack of bills this morning, she'd been unnerved by the three thousand dollar balance in their savings account—enough to last a month, if she juggled their charge cards. Luckily, Micronics had paid the balance on the California project, eliminating the twenty-five grand hanging over their heads. They still owed his parents the five they'd borrowed. God only knew how much more they'd rack up with the private detective. Unless she and Will got their act together soon, they'd be headed to bankruptcy court.

She brewed coffee, filled her mug, added skim milk and a teaspoon of sugar, and carried it to the living room. Will was immersed in a novel, *Independence Day*. The guy in the novel, Will had told her, reminded him of himself. She was afraid to ask how.

She cleared her throat. "We need to talk."

Her husband closed the book and set it on the windowsill.

Curiosity getting the better of her, she picked up his book and scanned the blurb on the jacket. *Frank Bascombe, in the aftermath of his divorce and the ruin of his career, has entered into an "Existence Period," selling real estate in Haddam, New Jersey.*

Sighing, she set the book down.

"Well?" he said. "Let's have it. Something's obviously on your mind."

A gust of wind sent a large branch sailing across their drive.

"I don't know how to put this nicely." She paused, weighing her words. Earlier, she'd gone up to his office to check on him. For ten minutes, she'd stood outside the door, listening for scraps of conversation, his keyboard, anything to suggest contact with the outside world. She'd heard only the click of electronic solitaire cards. "We need to get back to work."

He whisked the paperback from the sill and slapped it back down, knocking over the snapshot of the girls in their wading pool. He righted the photo. "What's that supposed to mean?"

She rubbed her neck. "Forget it. I'm sorry I brought it up."

He snapped his chair upright. "I'm going up to my office. I've got paperwork. If it makes you feel better, I was on the phone all morning. I've got appointments every day next week."

"That's great." Her knee ached. She reached for her mug, coagulated milk floating on the surface. "I'm glad to hear it. I really am."

Leah was cleaning the picture window when Todd returned from the store.

"Get your crap together," he ordered. "We gotta go. Hurry up. Let's go."

"What?" She spun to face him. "Go?" The wild look in his eyes stopped her cold.

"Got to get outta here," he said, his body tight, coiled, as though ready to spring.

"What's going on? Did something happen? You're scaring me."

He grabbed her arm gruffly, and pushed her toward the staircase. "Let's go."

"That hurts," she cried. "What are you doing?"

"I told you, we gotta get out of here. So move. Get your stuff."

Terrified, she followed her boyfriend's command.

He shadowed her up the stairs to his stepmother's bedroom, threw his clothes into his backpack, and flung the pack over his shoulder. "Hurry up. I'll go get the truck."

She tossed her things into her bag, stuffing the clothes inside with one hand, zippering the bag with the other. On autopilot, too scared to think, she just moved.

He'd driven over the snowy lawn, the truck idling by the front door. He hopped out, grabbed her bag, tossed it in the truck. As she was pulling her door shut, he took off. He drove at the speed limit, checking the rearview mirror every few minutes.

Leah stared at the window, the outside world a blur of trees and snow. She could barely breathe.

"The deli," he finally said, as they crossed the state line. "It just happened." Every time he went in, the old man asked his name—as if Jed Clampett was so tough to remember. When the old geezer failed yet again to recognize him, something had snapped, he told her. It was like opportunity knocking. "The old fart pissed his drawers when he got a load of the gun."

"The gun," Leah repeated. "You didn't—"

"Kill him?"

She nodded, trembling, too numb to speak.

"What the hell do you think I am?" He zipped up the heat. "Made him lay down."

In his wet pants. Good God. The poor frightened old man. Leah closed her eyes, too overwhelmed, too disturbed—too angry—to process any of this.

When Justine came home from school that afternoon, her parents were bickering again. All they did lately was fight. One of these days, they'd call her into the living room, ask her to have a seat, and tell her they were getting divorced. Parents all used that tactic to spring their divorce on their kids. It was the divorce notification M.O. They all read the same rulebook: *Sit your kids down. Say you've got something important to share. Say it isn't their fault.* Every time her parents mentioned a sit-down, Justine's heart lurched.

Tired of listening to them, she'd gone to visit Holly. Now, she and her friend sat cross-legged on Holly's bedroom floor, putting the finishing touches on Justine's science project.

Before the holidays, Holly's mom hired a decorator to renovate Holly's bedroom. The decorator, a weird lady with frizzy black hair, covered the walls with paper the shade of a leprechaun's hat, the accent color in the curtains and matching down comforter that same unfortunate green. If she were Holly, Justine would have freaked out.

The science fair was three weeks away. If she could, she'd retract her entry. That stupid fair was the last thing on her mind. The three and a half weeks since Leah left had been by far the worst in Justine's life. She couldn't eat, couldn't sleep. She had trouble concentrating in school. On Tuesday, her guidance counselor called Justine to her office.

"Your teachers are concerned," the counselor said. Justine had received a *C*-minus on her social studies exam. "That's not like you, honey. What's going on?"

Justine stared at her feet. The day before, her Honors English teacher had returned their book reports on *Wuthering Heights*. Justine had received an *A*-plus on the paper, the words "excellent job," scrawled in red ink. The *A*-plus was demoralizing. You'd think her teacher would be smart enough to realize she'd neglected to read the book, the paper based on a movie. Like everyone else, her teacher saw only what she wanted to see.

Justine scribbled her name on a crepe-paper star and taped it to the refrigerator box, on the floor between Holly and her. They'd painted the interior a swirl of blues and black to look like space, with glued-on sprinkles to represent stars, and suspended the planets from the ceiling, with pipe cleaners and string. Using iridescent puff paint, Justine had designed celestial phenomena: asteroids, supernova, nebulae, red giants. In a video, she described each heavenly body, detailing their unique characteristics.

Her project was baby work compared to what she'd originally hoped to produce. She'd envisioned a complicated scientific endeavor, something all-encompassing, grand. An analysis of the probability of life on other planets. A research project on Pluto. From an article in *Science*, she'd learned, after the Milky Way had formed, Pluto had shifted into the elliptical orbit it followed today. The finding posed fascinating possibilities about planetary movement. She'd planned to conduct further research. But she had lost interest. Maybe her mother *was* fooling around with that cop. If so, they could see a marriage counselor. Holly was miserable after her parents separated, never knowing whose side she was supposed to be on, constantly shuffled between the house she'd lived in since she was a baby and her father's tiny apartment. As soon as the divorce was final, Holly's mother remarried and Holly had moved with her mom and stepfather into this neighborhood. Holly loved their oversized house, the expensive things her stepfather bought, but she'd give it all up, she'd told Justine, if her parents would get back together.

"This is an awesome project," Holly said. "Think you'll win?"

"I don't know," Justine said, with zero conviction. "Could I have the sprinkles?"

Holly shook silver sprinkles onto her palm, testing the shaker.

The *Brady Bunch* movie played on Holly's plasma TV. The DVD case lay on the floor by Holly's knees. Holly worshipped the Bradys. Six perfect kids in a perfect family. What a joke!

Holly brushed the sprinkles off her arms. Leaning across the box, she handed the shaker to Justine, a pitying look in her eyes.

"What's *your* problem?" Justine snapped, and instantly regretted her tone. It wasn't Holly's fault Justine's family had fallen apart.

Thirty-Four

Misguided Angel

Week Four

Zoe and Will were in the family room, sitting on the edge of the sofa, studying the map spread out on the coffee table. At noon, Chief Healy called to let them know the Corbett woman had phoned with information about a cabin in southern Maine, owned by her son's stepmother. Why any parent of a missing child would retain vital information for a month Zoe could not begin to fathom. Was the woman a psycho or a moron?

The Cortland PD, in conjunction with the Maine State Police, had issued an All Points Bulletin. "If the kids are in the area," Healy had pledged, "we'll find them."

According to Corbett's mother, the cabin was located somewhere near Bath. She'd never been there herself, her descriptions of the house and surrounding area frustratingly vague. An hour ago, they'd learned from Dunham that the stepmother was out of town, whereabouts indeterminate. The woman and her current husband, both unemployed, lived in a high-rise in lower Manhattan. No one in the building had heard of an impending trip; no one Dunham contacted knew anything about a home in Maine.

A check of the county's Registry of Deeds also proved fruitless. When they spoke with Healy again, Will suggested they look for a deed in the stepmother's maiden name. Figured, Corbett's mother had no clue what the woman's maiden name might have been.

Corbett's mother was protecting her son. Zoe and Will agreed on this and detested her for it. For some inexplicable reason, the woman didn't want the kids to be found.

Zoe's right arm had gone numb. She rolled her shoulders, arching her back, and shook out her hands. *Unbelievable.* The Corbett woman was un-freaking-believable.

Will planned to leave for Maine shortly, to do some digging on his own. He had no faith in Dunham or the police. She and Will both felt the investigation was progressing too slowly. In fairness, Dunham and the cops had focused their efforts on the West Coast.

"If he can't turn up a stepmother, can't even locate the goddamn cabin she owns, what are we paying the guy for?"

"It's hard to find people who don't want to be found," she pointed out.

"Like Whitey Bulger. It took those hacks, what? Sixteen years to find him."

"Don't do this. It's not Dunham's fault. We're going to find her." At last, they had a solid lead. "This is great news. Let's not jinx it, okay?"

Will rolled his eyes. "I should pack." He had a four-hour drive ahead. It would be dark before he arrived as it was.

"Maybe we should give it another day. In case. What if they're in California?"

"Then I'll fly to California," he said. In the meantime, he'd nose around Bath. "Somebody's bound to know something."

"I want to go with you." They could take the Volvo. She'd bought new tires last fall. Why take the BMW when her car handled so much better in the snow?

"There's no point in both of us making the trip."

"Are you listening?" She rubbed her sore knee. She couldn't bear to stay behind waiting for news. Leah was as much her daughter as his. "I want to be there, too. We can stay at a Residence Inn. Jus can stay with Holly. She's always there, anyway. Or she can come, if she wants. I'll bet she'll want to come, if we ask."

"We can't rip her out of school every time we get a lead."

"I don't think you heard me. I said, 'I'm coming with you.'"

Will folded the map. "I heard you. Someone has to be home, in case Leah tries to reach us." He laid a hand over hers. "I'll keep you posted. I promise."

"If you hear anything, I mean *anything*, call immediately. I'll drive up. She'll need me, Will. I want to be there for her."

———⊷⊷———

"Well?" Todd demanded. "You coming or not?" He was headed into town to pick up a bottle of Jack Daniels.

"Go," Leah said. "And shut the door. It's freezing in here."

They'd been living in this dump for almost a week, a nineteen dollar a night room in a skanky motel called Northern Lights, one of those low-slung, chain-style jobs where all the rooms were connected. The sign out front read, "Vacancy. Free Colored TV." Not Internet. Not cable. Free *TV*. Leah swore she heard rats crawling inside the walls.

The town, a former logging community thirty miles south of the Canadian border, was a hellhole. Other than a filthy Mobil station, a Mini-Mart that could have doubled as a crack house, a boarded-up nondenominational church, and the doublewides squatting by the river, there was nothing for miles around. Just trees. Trees, trees, and more trees.

At the first town they'd come to in northern New Hampshire, they'd stopped at a hardware store and bought a hotplate, a tin pot, a set of plastic dishes, two coffee mugs, and a package of cheap aluminum utensils. Since then, she and Todd had been bouncing from one fleabag motel to the next, existing on ramen noodles and soup, eyes and ears tuned in to the news. As far as she could tell, the robbery had never made headlines.

Leah felt horrible for the old man. On principle, she'd considered ordering Todd to return the two hundred twenty-three dollars he'd stolen, the way her mother had forced her to return the cherry-flavored bubblegum she'd pinched from the rack by the checkout counter at CVS when she was five. "We're not a stealing family," Leah had informed the amused clerk behind the pharmacy counter.

Returning stolen money, saying you're sorry, didn't cut it for adults. Not even the most heartfelt apology released adults from responsibility for their crimes. For the sake of justice, someone had to pay. Todd would be caught, and jailed, and what would *she* do? She had made her own bed, as Nana Tyler would put it. Now she had to lie in it.

The jeep rammed into reverse and skidded out of the lot.

Her boyfriend exhausted her. A few short weeks ago, she'd been consumed by the prospect of marrying Todd. She'd planned their entire future. She'd imagined their house: a cabin by a lake. Named their children: Brittany, Taylor, Ashley, and Gina, four beautiful little girls with her silky blonde hair and Todd's piercing blue eyes. They had talked seriously about starting a band. Todd promised to teach her to play the guitar.

Now there were moments when Leah hated him. Inconsequential things annoyed her—his tapered fingers, constantly grasping at something, the cowlick at his crown, the space between his front teeth. The shape of her boyfriend's *head*—too narrow, she felt.

Leah hauled her body, a hundred pounds of dead weight, out of bed, and zipped the thermostat from eighty to ninety degrees.

She waited a minute for the heat to kick on before turning the knobs on the convector. She twisted right, left. Frustrated, she booted the casing, whacking the corner.

"Shit," she said, hopping on one foot. *Shit, shit, shit.* She'd probably broken her toe.

She swiped a Power Bar and a Coke from their stash on the desk and limped across the room. Sitting on the floor, she rummaged through Todd's backpack. She pulled on his long johns and heavy wool socks, then sat on the bed and put on her sweatpants.

A snowplow thundered down the street, the vibration rocking the motel's flimsy walls. Leah had never seen so much snow. It had been snowing since they arrived in New Hampshire, the roadside piles nearly six feet tall. At night, the plows kept her awake.

She had trouble remembering why she left home. At night, lying beside Todd, her brain replayed a continuous loop of home movies: afternoons in Boston, the *Make Way for Ducklings* tour their family had taken every spring when she and Justine were small. She and Justine climbing on the bronze ducklings in the park. Her family riding the swan boats, Justine sitting quietly on their mom's lap, taking everything in, Leah, enchanted by the sun-dappled water, leaning over the rail, her father gripping her ankles. Her parents were always there to support her, "especially your dad," her teammates always said. She and her father had flown to tournaments in Colorado, Arizona, California. She pictured her mom and Justine in the terminal at Logan Airport, waving goodbye.

Leah saw flashes of herself on her mother's lap, her mom reading stories from *Grimm's Fairytales* or Leah's *Bible for Children*. She remembered the day her hamster died. Though she was only four, she had been devastated, knowing she'd killed him. They'd buried the hamster in a shoebox in the backyard. Afterward, her mother held Leah in her arms, read her a story, sang her a song. Hammy's death was an accident, Leah's mom said. *Sweetie, it isn't your fault.* Sometime between then and now, she and her family had grown apart. The few times Leah had called home, her mother's voice had sounded so far away, like the voice of a stranger. Leah couldn't bring herself to speak.

She'd started at least fifteen letters to her sister, ripped them all up. She'd created bogus Facebook and e-mail accounts under fictitious names, thinking she could contact her sister, they'd communicate in code, and deleted them. It was too risky. Besides, if she contacted her sister, Justine would ask when she would be home. What would she say?

The plow disappeared over the hill beyond the motel. Leah went to the window and stared out at the darkness. Never in a million years would she have imagined herself holed up in a place like this. She'd never dreamed she'd be engaged to an armed robber, either. There were a lot of things she'd never imagined, Leah supposed.

Things she did dream about—the cabin by a lake, her pretty little girls, being a rock star—none of those fantasies would ever come true. Seventeen years old, and so much of her future was already decided, her life dictated by fate. Wasn't life strange?

From her iPod, Leah selected a Cowboy Junkies tune, "Misguided Angel," and put on her headphones. Yanking the musty blanket over the mattress, she fell on the bed.

Leah's heart ached. She wondered if her family missed her, too.

Since she and Todd left, she'd been combing the papers. She watched the morning and evening news. In all this time, she'd read not one article about herself. Never once heard her name. There was no missing person story. No Amber Alert. No FBI search. She wondered if her family thought about her at all. Or if, this time, she'd pushed them too far. If they'd forgotten all about her. If they'd simply gone on with their lives.

———◈———

Will's trip to Maine was a bust. He spent the first night in Bath, the second in Bar Harbor. Methodically, fueled by a fire of strong black coffee and rage, he hunted for his daughter and Corbett. He canvassed every shop, every restaurant, every real estate office.

Never in his life had he been so angry. Or so scared.

He strode down ice-covered streets, stopping each passerby, flashing a picture of Leah. Not one person recalled either the kids or the jeep. Nor had they heard of the stepmother. A photo would have been useful. They might have known her by face.

The third morning, he drove. In his hotel room, he mapped out a route, starting at the center of town, moving outward to the perimeter. He left at daybreak. Five miles out, five miles in, clockwise, like the hub of a wheel. Find the cabin, he'd find his daughter.

The first time, he followed the map precisely, no deviation. He repeated the course, turning down the dirt roads the second time around. The third time, parking his car at the side of the road, armed with a metal baseball bat, he searched the woods.

At dusk, he left in despair. All his life, he'd thought of himself as a fixer. A guy who took charge, ignored the fear in his gut, and made things right. Now, the only time in his miserable existence he'd undertaken a mission that mattered, he'd failed. On the drive home, he pumped up the radio. If not for the flashing number on the voice-activated monitor on his dash, he might have missed the call from his wife.

He lowered the radio, dreading the call. "Zo," he said. "I'm sorry."

"Will?" Her voice cracked. "Dunham called."

The private detective had located the cabin in a wooded area outside Camden. The kids had taken off in a hurry—skid marks by the front door. Last week, a deli in town had been robbed. As far as Dunham could tell, there was no suspect list, insufficient evidence.

"God help us," Zoe said. "Dunham said he'd do what he could."

"Jesus." Will slapped the steering wheel. "You're sure he said gun-point?"

"That's what he says."

"So they didn't get an ID?"

"The victim was old. He said the guy was 'male.' Where are you?"

"Coming up on the border," he said. "I'll be home in an hour."

⸺◈⸺

"No *way*," Justine hissed. "She'd never rob anybody."

"Jus—" Her mom reached for her. Justine backed away.

"How *could* you?" Justine demanded. "She's your daughter."

"Yes." Her mother swallowed. "I realize that."

"She was right. You don't love her. Probably me, either."

"Justine, please. That's not true and you know it. The police—"

"The cops suck," Justine screamed, and fled to her room.

Now that the initial shock had worn off, Justine realized that her sister and Todd probably had robbed the deli in Camden. Why else would they have left in such a hurry? Still, it didn't make her sister a bad person—did it? What if Leah had been motivated by hunger? Or she was sick? Needed money to get medical attention? Circumstances could turn *anyone* into a thief. Justine had always believed right and wrong to be absolute. She saw now she'd been wrong. The possibilities rolled round and round in her head.

Since Christmas, Justine had lost eight pounds. She could slide three fingers between her belly and the waistband of her old jeans. This morning, she'd snagged a pair of jeans Leah left behind. Justine found them rolled in a ball at the back of her sister's closet. Leah's jeans fit her perfectly through the waist and hips. She rolled up the hems. She wasn't stealing her sister's jeans. She was borrowing them until her sister returned.

She'd brought Leah's school picture into her room and set it on her desk, along with the ceramic ashtray she'd made for her sister. Justine pressed her hand into the palm of the ceramic ashtray, her long fingers curling over the edges. Hard to believe she'd made the ashtray herself. Hard to believe her hands had ever been that small.

Squatting, she lifted her comforter and, slipping her hand under the mattress, extracted the foil package. She withdrew a flattened cigarette and tapped it on her palm to reshape it.

That she'd conjured the nerve to buy cigarettes shocked her. She'd overheard kids at school talking about a guy at the Citgo station down the street who'd sell cigarettes to anybody, no ID necessary. During lunch period, she trekked to the station. Until she reached the counter and handed the attendant her money, she wasn't sure if she would go through with it. She'd thought she'd chicken out.

Opening her window to let in some air, Justine spotted a fox. When Dog was young, she loved to chase foxes. With animals her own size, she was a wimp. Whenever she saw a coyote, she cried. If they were walking, Dog would stop cold. Justine would kneel, her arms wrapped protectively around Dog's chest, until the coyote retreated.

Usually, Justine brushed away thoughts about Dog. It was easier to avoid thinking about the things you had no power to change. Thinking about Dog made her sad and what good did that do? Maybe that was why Leah had played soccer for all those years. So she didn't have to think. With sports, you have no time to reflect. You just *do*.

She lit the cigarette, took a long drag, inhaling deeply, and tapped the ashes into the palm of the ashtray. A breeze blew across her room, carrying a feint odor of burning logs. When she'd smoked the cigarette to the filter, she crushed the butt in the palm of her ceramic hand, and spritzed the air with Leah's cloying floral perfume.

Thirty-Five

Holding Pattern

Week Five

Will's wife sat on Leah's bed, facing the window, with an old snapshot of the girls in her lap. She wore a long-sleeved tee-shirt and black sweatpants, her curly hair uncharacteristically flat. She hadn't bathed in several days, and she smelled stale.

In the dark room, in the shadows, she looked like a ghost.

The room itself felt ghost-like. Since Leah ran away, they'd touched nothing. The Nike poster hung on the wall, the corner curled. Clothes and shoes lay on the floor and littered the unmade bed. Over the month, a layer of dust had settled over the room.

Through the barren trees, Will saw the streetlamps wink on. "Zo?" She blinked when he flipped on the light. "You okay?"

His wife was angry with him—again. He'd left toothpaste in the sink. Forgotten to pick up his socks. Turned his head the wrong way. If he was quiet, reflective, she pestered him to talk. If he talked, she wanted to be left alone. He was constantly gauging her moods, afraid of setting her off.

She'd been like this after the abortion. It scared him, watching it happen again. A few days ago, she'd overheard him on the phone, asking his mom for advice.

"You told your *mother* about me?" she'd demanded. "Why would you do that?"

The roots of depression were complex. Still, this was partly his fault. He'd known when Healy mentioned the cabin in Maine that the chances of finding his daughter were slim. In the first weeks after Leah's disappearance, Zoe's mood had deteriorated, but she'd managed to hang on, stay hopeful. Each setback had bitten deeper into her psyche.

By the time they received the tipoff about the house in Maine, she'd been close to a breakdown. He should have voiced his concerns. Instead, he'd taken the cowardly route, allowing her to believe in the impossible. Now she'd completely given up hope. Yesterday, Johnson stopped by to check on them. Zoe had stared at him rudely and sent him away. Later, when his wife was out of earshot, Will had called the cop to apologize.

Never before had he felt so helpless, so out of control. If Leah were desperate enough to participate in a robbery, she was scared. That image of his vulnerable child terrorized him. There was not a thing he could do to protect her or take her troubles away.

Zoe ran a finger across Leah's nightstand. "Should I dust?"

"If you want to, I guess."

"Remember this?" She flipped the photograph, showing him the shot of the girls in their wading pool. "I took it on her last day of first grade. She was always so happy when summer rolled around. I never understood why. She was such a smart kid."

"She didn't want to be trapped." He'd hated that feeling, too.

"Such a great student—straight *A*s every year. Whenever the teacher hung one of Justine's papers on the wall, Jus was ecstatic. It was the first thing she'd show me when I went in. Leah never cared."

"Speaking of Jus," he said, "we're going to a movie tonight. That sci-fi flick she wants to see. Why don't you come? It'll be fun."

"Not tonight." Her face clouded.

"Come." He squeezed her shoulder. "It'd be good for Justine."

She pulled back. "I don't feel well tonight."

"We'll keep the cell phone on. We won't miss a call. I promise."

"That's rude."

He cleared his throat. "We need to talk, Zo."

With her finger, she drew a circle on the photo, enclosing the girls.

"I think we should move." Moving had been on his mind for months. They didn't need this much house. The place was a money pit. In December, the oil bill was seven hundred bucks, the electric four-fifty, and winter had barely set in. In April, when property taxes came due, they'd owe the town eight grand, eight grand they didn't have and had no way of raising by then. "A change of scenery would do us all good," he said.

His wife got up and went to the window.

"We're leveraged up to our eyeballs." If they sold the house, their financial problems would disappear—he snapped his fingers—overnight. It would be a relief to unload this place, move forward again. He joined his wife at the window. He'd go anywhere—another town, another state. Hell, another country, if that made her happy. "Anywhere, Zo. Anywhere at all." He touched her shoulder. "You pick the place."

"That branch. If I opened the window—" She brought her face to the glass. "I could touch it. No wonder she got out so easily that night."

———◦◦———

Bored, Justine turned on the Christmas DVD—for background noise, not to watch. Seeing her family act all normal, like people with an actual life, pissed her off.

Her parents were in Leah's room. She heard her father talking.

The day her father returned from Maine without Leah, Justine's mother had called her doctor and wangled a prescription for Xanax. Justine's father was no better. He drove to the Corbetts' house every day and sat in his car, watching the house. A boy in her algebra class lived on Todd's street. He'd seen her father and told her about him. Neither parent worked regularly. For the first time in her life, Justine worried about money. *Soon,* she thought, *I'll have to resort to stealing.*

Justine wandered to her window, lifted her shade, punched her heavy bag a few times, and logged onto MSN Instant Messenger. Today was Holly's day with her dad. He was taking Holly to lunch, then to Cambridge to visit his mother. Holly had invited her to tag along. Holly's grandmother was sweet, but she was too nosy. Justine was in no mood to answer questions, or to talk or smile or be fussed over by anyone, not even a cute old lady with purple curls. When Holly signed off, Justine logged onto Facebook.

Last night, she'd received a coded message from Leah. Her sister had created an account under the name Elaine, her page set to private, with avatars instead of photos.

"I'll be at your fair," Elaine had written. "Promise. As long as I can. I miss you, Teeny girl." Elated, Justine had written a long note back, detailing all that had happened since Leah left, letting her sister know how very much she missed her.

Today, the Facebook page was gone.

Flipping through Leah's CD case, she located the 50 Cent disc, slid it into the player, and put on her sister's headphones. Closing her eyes, she listened for the beat. BOOM, boom, boom…She snapped her fingers, trying to feel the rhythm. ONE, two, three, four…

When the CD ended, she played it again.

In the second stanza of the fourth song, the lyrics drifted away from the instrumentation. *One, two, three, four.* There it was. *One, two, three, four.* She felt it. She finally felt it. *One, two, three, four—* Justine rolled her shoulders and danced across the room, feeling the music, energy dancing around her, almost as if her sister were with her.

———◦❦◦———

This holding pattern was destroying them, Will said. He refused to stand by and watch their marriage dissolve. Selling the house would give them freedom, a chance to make changes, a shot at a future. Once they were no longer strapped for cash, possibilities would open up. They could change careers, look for jobs they enjoyed. "Think about Justine. You don't want problems with Jus, do you? Have you seen her, lately?"

Of course she had. Their younger daughter listened to Leah's music. She wore Leah's clothes. Her grades had dropped. She'd lost interest in school. Yes, Zoe knew.

"Don't you see where we're headed, Zo? We can't let this happen. We've got to do something."

Zoe squared her shoulders, prepared for a fight. "I'm not moving."

"Why not?"

"Because we're not," she said, turning her back to him again. This was ridiculous. She shouldn't have to explain. Why did he think she wouldn't move? Because she loved living here? In a house they couldn't afford, reeking of misery, recrimination, and pain?

He circled around her, wedging himself between her and the window, and set both hands on her shoulders. "One reason. That's all I ask. One good reason."

"Jesus, Will." Zoe brushed her hair out of her face. "This is her *room.*"

"Okay, good. That's good. We're making progress. Look at this—"

He pointed to a creeping water stain on the ceiling, a snag in the carpet, Leah's chicken scratch on the walls. "She'll have a new room. A better room. *Much* better. We can paint. Any color she wants. Something vibrant. Buy a new bedroom set—white. That white furniture you always wanted to buy for the girls. She can have her own bathroom. A big walk-in closet. *A walk-in closet*, Zo. She'd go nuts over a walk-in. How about it?"

"No," Zoe croaked. The tree outside Leah's window was covered with snow. She heard a thump in the next room—Justine punching her heavy bag—and grinned. She hadn't heard that in a while. She'd begun to think Justine had abandoned the bag.

"So you like the idea," her husband said, misinterpreting her smile. "I knew you'd agree once you saw all the reasons."

"Are you deaf?" she hissed, glaring at him. "We're not moving."

"Huh? We're... What about Justine? You don't care about her?"

Zoe's lips quivered. "We can't move," she said again. "How would she find us?"

Thirty-Six

I Love You, Baby

Thursday Morning, Week Six

Leah was dreaming about soccer. Her high school team was playing in the state tournament, held in the Harvard stadium. Walking onto the field, she scanned the faces of the crowd, spectators two and three deep along the sidelines, searching for her parents.

Without consulting her, Coach Thomas had switched her position from forward to goalie. A buzzer sounded. Leah crouched in front of the net, shocked, paralyzed, trying desperately to remember the rules. The opposing team scored, and the crowd went wild.

Leah willed her body to move, but the balls kept coming.

In no time, the score was twenty-zip, the players taunting her. The crowd erupted in a chorus of boos, the mob jeering. "Get her out of there." "She stinks." A spectator lobbed an apple. Others immediately joined in. Leah flailed, dodging the rotten apples whacking her chest, splattering to mush. The infuriated fans waved their fists. "Tyler sucks!" *Splat*, another apple. Photo journalists from the *Gazette* and the *Globe* aimed their cameras—*splat, splat, splat*— the photographers closing in, the flashes blinding—

Leah blinked against the searing white light shooting into the room.

Her boyfriend was dragging the drapes across the grimy picture window, the drapery clips scraping the metal rod. "Time to get up," he chirped. "Rise and shine."

The room spun. For dinner, they'd split a large package of Reese's Pieces and a twelve-ounce bag of barbecue chips. They'd eaten their last real food at breakfast yesterday morning. After dinner, they'd polished off a bottle of JD, and she felt every last drop. This was it for drinking. Never again. Every bone and joint in her body cried out.

A plow rumbled by, the racket jarring her brain. She groaned and rolled onto her side, pulling her knees to her chest, shutting her eyes against the sudden wave of nausea.

"Let's go, babe," her boyfriend ordered, tugging the covers. "Time to get up."

"Go away," she said, squinting. He was standing at the foot of her bed, staring down at her. It was creepy. He'd already showered and shaved. His hair was still wet, a mop of damp blonde ringlets above his blistering eyes. He pulled on his black hoodie.

"Let's go." He circled his hands impatiently. "Time to get rolling."

"What's with you, all energetic? I feel like I'm gonna die," Leah whined.

"Yeah, well. We ain't all lightweights."

"I'm never drinking again. Swear to God. For real this time."

"Babe!" He yanked the sheet and blanket off the bed. "Get a move on."

Shivering, half-naked, she scrambled for the covers. "Get away from me," she shrieked, batting him with her bare feet. "Leave me alone. Can't you see I'm sick?"

"My old lady's loaning us five hundred bucks. I promised we'd go down."

"What? We can't—" Leah started, but the point slipped away.

"Hope's throwing a bash. Stay there tonight. Tomorrow, we go to my mother's."

"Are you out of your mind? Just because that old guy didn't remember your name doesn't mean he couldn't describe you. You went in there a lot. You'll get nailed." *We'll* both *be arrested*, she thought miserably. "It's a felony. You're looking at fifteen years."

"Nice." He snorted. "What'd you do? Look it up? You wishing it on me?"

"No, I'm not wishing it on you. Don't be stupid."

"Look, we need the dough. Come with me or don't. I'm going down."

Was that a joke? Twice, when Todd had gone into town for supplies, the pervert who managed this dump knocked on their door, under the guise of providing fresh linens, and tried to corner her. Last time, he succeeded. He had her pressed against the bathroom wall, his arms blocking her escape. Luckily, Todd showed up with the gun and scared him off. Staying here alone, overnight, would be an invitation for the psycho to rape her.

Another wave of nausea washed over her as she sat.

She vaguely recalled stashing a Power Bar in her suitcase, in case they ran out of food. Gingerly, stomach groaning, she lowered herself to the floor. Kneeling, she rooted through her clothes, squeezing each item. She slid her hand across the interior pocket.

"We're not taking money from your mother," she spat. If they planned to build a life together, they had to learn to rely on themselves. "Have some pride for God's sake."

"Pride tastes pretty good, I hear. We're broke, remember?"

"I don't give a shit. We're not a charity case," she sneered—and spotted a mouse, darting across the floor. "A rat," she screamed. She scooped up a shoe, and hurled it at the rodent as it skittered under the baseboard. The shoe ricocheted off the wall, knocking a framed picture off its hook, sending the cheap watercolor print crashing to the floor.

She gaped at the shards of glass, and looked up, stunned, at the silhouette on the empty wall where the painting had hung. "See," she muttered. "Told you we had rats."

He picked up the painting and replaced it on its hook. "This ain't Fantasyland, baby cake. Last I checked, money don't grow on trees. Time for the princess to grow up."

Screw him. She whisked her filthy jeans from her suitcase. If anybody needed to grow up, it was him. She flung the jeans on the floor. There was a Power Bar hiding in that suitcase. Or a Three Musketeers. She was sure of it. She pitched panties, ratty bras, unmatched socks, sweaters, a tee-shirt filched from Todd, clothes flying in all directions.

At the bottom of her suitcase, peeking out from under the folds of the nylon lining, she spotted the blue button bracelet her mother had given her. *Stormy.* Her heart broke as she pushed the bracelet over her wrist. Stormy—*wild, raging, crazy, intense.*

Thursday Afternoon

The seats in the icy jeep felt like slate.

"It's freezing," Leah grumbled, cranking the heat. "And I'm starving."

Todd wrested the blanket from the backseat and tossed it to her. "Found some change last night under the seat." He lowered the heat. "We can split a burger." He poked a cigarette in the lighter, offered it to her. "I'll stop in Plymouth. It's only two hours."

The acrid smell of the cigarette turned her stomach. She waved it away.

The landscape looked like tundra. A thick layer of newly fallen snow blanketed the roofs of the trailers, the farmhouses, the barns, and light glinted off the ice-crusted meadows and fields. In the forest and thickets, snow-capped pines bowed like supplicants to massive deciduous trees, their limbs sagging under the weight of the glittering snow.

A snowmobile ripped across the bank of a frozen river, airborne.

Leah put on her sunglasses and rested her head against the window, the icy glass searing her cheek. She wondered what the weather was like at home. For a while, she'd followed it on the weather channel. A few weeks ago, she'd stopped keeping track.

An image of the town center flashed through her brain—the great lawn, the stone wall covered with snow. *Stop.* Her throat ached. She rotated her bracelet. *Don't do this to yourself.*

It was insane, driving to Cortland. Even if they stuck to the back roads, as Todd promised, someone was bound to see them or recognize the jeep. There was something fundamentally, psychologically wrong with her boyfriend, always taking these risks.

They could have moved to Canada temporarily, found jobs in Montreal or Toronto. As long as they stayed out of trouble, maintained a low profile, they'd have been safe. They could have lived decent, law-abiding lives, gotten married, and started a family. In time, her parents would have forgiven her, and they could have gone home.

Instead, they were fugitives. Running from the law wasn't dangerous enough to satisfy her boyfriend. No, he had to taunt the police. Getting off after his drug bust in El Paso had led him to believe he was invincible. One of these days, his luck would run out.

She closed her eyes, lulled into sleep by the quiet rhythm of the jazz recording. She slept fitfully. In her flashing dreams, she ran and ran.

Next time she opened her eyes, they were pulling into a drive-way; through the snow flurries swirling in the headlights, she saw Hope's house. She yawned. For an instant, in her sleepy haze, she forgot what they were doing there, why they had come.

Hope's cat sat on the living room windowsill, pawing the glass. The colored lights around the front door blinked like a post-holiday welcome. An electric candle flickered in Hope's bedroom window. *Nothing has changed*, Leah thought, the stability comforting.

Todd opened his door, admitting a rush of frigid air. "Coming?"

"Yes," Leah said, and pulled on her warm woolen mittens.

Thursday, Early Evening

Todd rapped once, opened the front door, and walked in. "Anybody home?"

"Hey. Look who it is!" Hope threw her arms around them. "I missed you guys."

Lupo clapped Todd's back and drew Leah into a bear hug, lifting her off her feet. "Good to see you," Lupo said. "I can't believe you're here. It's so good to see you."

"So?" Hope spread her arms. "What do you think?"

She and Lupo had pushed the furniture against the walls. Bubbles floated out of a gurgling machine, a strobe lamp turning the bubbles into surreal iridescent lights. Two huge speakers stood on the side wall, positioned to pump maximum sound into the room.

"Remember the guys at Halloween?" Lupo arched his ring-lined brows.

"They were sick," Todd said. "They're coming tonight?"

"Yep, and they got signed," Hope boasted. "They're only coming because it's us."

"Cool," Leah said, struggling to remember the band. "That's awesome."

"Totally," Hope agreed. "They're like ready to hit the big time."

They followed Hope into the kitchen. On the counter, she'd set out huge plastic bowls filled with Tootsie Pops and chips, along with liter-sized bottles of Coke. At one end of the counter, they'd set up a keg. On the other sat a cut-glass punch bowl filled with a vodka and citrus drink Hope had concocted, a frozen strawberry ring floating on top.

Lupo opened and tested the keg. "Her old lady's gone for the weekend."

"She went up to the lake," Hope added.

"So we got the house all to ourselves 'till Sunday," Lupo said with a wink.

"Who's all coming?" Todd asked. "Be great to see everybody."

"Guys from my high school," said Lupo, wrapping his arm around Todd.

"So what's up?" Hope asked, pulling Leah aside. "You okay?"

"I'm fine." Leah managed a weak smile. "I'm totally psyched to see you."

Hope ladled punch into two plastic cups and set the cups on the counter. "Got a big surprise for you, sweetie." From her pocket, she produced a small pink pill with a butterfly stamp. She pressed the tablet into Leah's palm. "I got this especially for you."

"You're so cool. But I'm good," Leah said, pushing it back. "Thanks anyway."

"Go for it, girl. Seriously. You look like you could use it."

Thursday Night

The band arrived promptly at seven forty-five. By eight thirty, the house was rocking, the kitchen a wall of partygoers, laughing, talking, drinking, smoking weed. Three drunken girls, waving badminton rackets, challenged their boyfriends to a game of beer pong. Lupo's high school friends leaned against the cabinets, passing a crack pipe.

Leah wandered from the kitchen to the living room, where the band had rigged their stage, the raging electric guitars tempered by a hypnotic four-four backbeat. Tootsie Pops bulged inside the cheeks of the gyrating dancers, waving their glow sticks.

"Awesome," Leah shouted into Hope's ear. "Best party ever."

Hope nodded and grinned.

The Ecstasy had provided a welcome lift. The buzz wearing off, Leah pushed her way through the mob into the kitchen, and gulped four cups of punch in quick succession.

Giddy, she hunted for her boyfriend, found him snorting a line in the bathroom, and dragged him onto the dance floor, bubbles floating all around them as if they were under water.

At ten, on top of the world, she took a few hits from the crack pipe.

Shortly after eleven, a carload of out-of-towners showed up. Hope noticed the strange car in her driveway. After a brief conference, she and Lupo opted to send it away.

Fortunately, Leah beat Lupo to the door. Hope's bestie, she was practically a co-host, after all. "Hell-*lo*," she said, fanning herself, welcoming each new guest with a hug.

Wobbling on her tiptoes, she kissed the boys square on the lips. *All these hot guys. Ought to have an orgy*, she thought. Or maybe she said it. Either way, it was a brilliant idea. Tapping shoulders impatiently, she dragged the coffee table across the room.

The obliging partiers moved left and right, the crowd parting like the Red Sea.

"S'cuse me," she said, clapping to get the crowd's attention.

She climbed onto the table. Someone whistled. A boy handed her a Coke.

Leah waved the bottle. She felt like a queen. "Let's have some fun."

A crowd gathered around her, the sweat-drenched bodies intoxicating, sexy.

"I love you baby," she sang, shoulders pulsing, the band picking up on her song.

"Hey." Todd snagged her wrist, distracting her. "What the hell are you doing?"

Leah snatched her arm back. "Love, love, love," she sang, absorbed by the music. The band played to her, allowing her to take the lead, galvanizing the crowd.

Todd lunged for the table. Two of Lupo's high school thug-friends dove in after him. A team, they lifted him to his feet, twisting his arms behind his back. Out of the corner of her eye, Leah saw them shove her boyfriend out the front door, Todd fighting, his neck and back arched. She caught his eye, cringed, and launched back into her song.

The band raged, the bass pounding. Scanning the sea of faces, she located a pair of friendly eyes. She threw her head back, raking her hands through her hair, the music pulsing through her, filling her body. *Whoa, whoa, whoa, ba-by.* Hope and Lupo's friends poured into the room, the boys hooting, crowding the stage, the girls singing, dancing.

Leah had never felt so alive, so desperately empowered. *Hap-py birth-day, Mis-ter Pres-i-dent.* She unhooked her bra, tossed it to the frenzied crowd, and raised her arms over her head, her nipples taut and erect. The audience cheered, waving their hands.

"Go, go, go," the audience chanted. "Take it off. Take it all off."

Love, love, love. Her fingers slithered over her belly, teasing, reeling them in. "Go," they chanted. *They love me,* she thought—and pushed her panties over her hips.

The door crashed open, slamming the wall. And the music went dead.

"A gun," someone shouted. "Look out! He's got a gun!"

The sudden shift confused her. At first, Leah wasn't sure where she was. Then her boyfriend's ranting voice brought her to, and she realized, *oh God,* she was naked. Mortified, she crossed her arms and legs, covering her breasts and her crotch.

Her boyfriend waved the pistol. "Get away from her, fuckers," he shouted. His eyes flashed. He was out of his mind. "Now," he ordered. "All of you."

A girl sobbed and the crowd heaved, pushing backward, the room opening up.

"No!" Leah cried. "Don't shoot! Please!"

"Dude," Lupo pleaded. "Put it down, before someone gets hurt."

Todd swept up Leah's clothes, grabbed her, and hoisted her over his shoulder. Backing away, his gun pointed at the crowd, he carried her out of the house.

Thirty-Seven

Home Is Where the Heart Is

Friday, 3 p.m.

Leah squeezed her eyes shut, willing away the previous night. *This is a dream*, she told herself. *A movie. This can't be my life.*

"It's about time," her boyfriend chided. "Thought you'd never wake up."

Leah groaned, pulling the sheet over her face. Even her fingernails ached, and her mouth tasted like ass. *Again.* Leaving Hope's house last night, Todd had turned abruptly, and she'd slammed her leg against the doorjamb. She could barely bend her swollen knee.

"Let's go," he said, pulling the covers away her face. "Let's get outta here."

"Don't touch me," she said, pushing him away. "I feel like I'm gonna puke."

"No wonder." He snorted. "What'd you expect?"

"What time is it?"

"Three. Time to roll. I don't feel like driving the whole way in the dark."

"I need some aspirin."

"Sorry, babe. We don't keep that shit in the house."

"Seriously?" She sat, hugging the covers to her chest. "Could you get me some?"

He studied her face, as though trying to decide if she was sick enough to justify the effort. Finally, he said, "Sure, I guess. But you're coming. I ain't going alone."

"No. Huh-uh. No way."

"Why? What's the problem? I talked to Lupo this morning. Everything's cool."

"That's not what I meant," she said quietly, averting her eyes. "I'm embarrassed."

"Forget about it. They were all wasted. They probably don't even remember."

Please. She'd stripped. Naked. Like a whore. Of course they remembered.

"Whatever, babe. It's your call. I told you. I ain't leaving here without you."

It was a depressing afternoon, cold and overcast, yesterday's snow a filthy gray slush. Leah stared at the window, part of her frozen from mortification, the rest terrified, waiting for a siren, picturing a high-speed car chase, followed by fifteen years in prison.

"What're you so freaking uptight about?" He looked weird behind the wheel of his mother's Taurus, a kid playing at being a grownup. "Car's new. Nobody knows it."

What was *wrong* with him? This was serious. What if someone at the party, one of the out-of-towners, the strangers with no skin in the game, had heard about the robbery and recognized them? They'd hardly kept a low profile. "What if they reported us?"

"Get real. All the shit that went down last night? Crack? H? Who's gonna call? You really think anybody wants the cops asking questions, putting the finger on them?"

"Guess not," she said begrudgingly, and they rode the rest of the way in silence.

Todd turned into the busy shopping center lot and parked the Taurus between two SUVs. "I'm not going in," Leah announced. "I'll wait here."

He cut the engine, and climbed out, slamming his door.

CVS sat at the far end of the *L*-shaped strip, next to the Natural Grocer. Harried mothers wheeled carriages in and out of the market. Toddlers, in the seat of the cart, clutched bagels or boxes of raisins or pieces of dried fruit, while older kids in oversized parkas and bright rubber boots stomped gleefully through the puddles.

To kill time, Leah conjured phrases to match the number-letter combinations on the license plates of the other cars in the lot. A blue Escort backed into the spot in front of the truck, spewing oily fumes. 93RJMA. Ninety-three royal jackasses moving to Alaska. *Ha!* The driver looked like a jackass, with her long horse-shaped nose.

Someone tapped on the window.

Leah slid lower in her seat, tightening the drawstring on her hooded sweatshirt.

Another tap, and then three more. *Tap, tap, tap,* like a drumbeat. Relentless.

Leah slid her eyes sideways. *Shit.* Of all people to run in to today. *Cissy Hanson.*

Cissy bent, leaning forward, peering in the window. Typical fashion plate Cissy: suede jacket, bold geometric scarf, red doeskin gloves. "Hey, girl. Leah? Open up."

"Hey." Leah pressed the button, lowering the window a few inches. "What's up?"

"Where've you been hiding?" Cissy flashed a fake smile. "We've missed you."

"Sure," Leah said, rolling her eyes. "Whatever." Cissy had no doubt heard all about last night's fiasco, her humiliating striptease. *The whole town probably knows,* she thought glumly, imagining a chorus of derisive laughter. She should have stayed in New Hampshire. She'd have been better off taking her chances with that perverted motel manager than coming back here, making a total fool of herself. "What do you want?"

Cissy leaned in closer, glancing surreptitiously around the lot. "I heard you quit school," she whispered. "You're coming back, aren't you? I mean, it's not *true,* is it?"

So that was it. Leah's stomach heaved. She was looking for road kill. Leah eyed the glove compartment. She wondered what Cissy would do if she whipped out the gun.

"I've been so *worried,*" Cissy cooed. "I hate hearing bad things about you."

Leah's throat ached. "Yeah, right," she said, glaring. "Fuck off."

"Really?" Cissy snickered. "That's the best you can do?"

"Fuck you, Cissy," Leah spat, fighting back tears. "Go fuck yourself."

"I feel bad for you." Cissy shook her head. "You really are pathetic. By the way, sweetheart," she purred, as she backed away. "Nice act. Too bad they didn't have a pole."

Friday, 5 p.m.

Justine sat with her father in a booth at Mac's, a local hangout near her school, pushing food around her plate. The diner stank of day-old grease and packed-in people. The entrance was mobbed, a bunch of nerds milling around the door, waiting for seats. The boisterous Friday night regulars were gathered around the bar, the hopeful flirting unabashedly, the defeated drowning their workday sorrows in pitchers of American beer.

The door pitched open, admitting a rush of cold air accompanied by four college-age prepsters in pea coats and knitted skull caps, rubbing their hands together, chattering.

Justine picked her burger apart, setting the bun aside, stabbed the beef with her fork and shook it onto her bread plate. She was thinking seriously of becoming a vegan. After switching to an all-lettuce diet, a girl in her English class had dropped twenty-five pounds. If Justine lost twenty-five pounds, she'd look like a model, a cool heroin waif.

She had no clue why her father had dragged her out tonight. She wanted to yack, thinking about traipsing around the gym, poring over the ridiculous science fair projects. She pulled the spongy insides from her bun, tore off a tiny piece, and put it in her mouth.

A plate of greasy onion rings sat at the center of the table. "Think I'll ask for a doggie bag," her father said. "Bring these with us for Mom. She loves onion rings."

"Yeah," Justine said absently, twirling her mother's button bracelet. "Good idea."

"Hopefully she'll get to eat them before they get cold."

Please. Justine rolled her eyes. Who was her father lying for? Justine? Or himself? Her mother had no intention of showing up tonight. Since her father returned from Maine, her mother had left the house once: to go to the doctor to weasel another prescription. Her mother sat by the window all day, waiting for the phone to ring. It was pitiful. Justine wanted to shake her. *I'm hurting, too,* she wanted to say. *What about me?*

"You look pretty tonight, Jus. That sweater looks nice on you."

"Thanks." Justine smirked. The baby blue sweater belonged to Leah. Her father went ape-shit the first time he'd seen it on her sister. *He said I look like a slut,* Leah cried. He'd ordered her to return it. After that, she'd worn it only when he wasn't around. Justine fingered the plunging V neckline. She'd stuffed socks in her bra to give herself cleavage.

Her father, catching the waitress's eye, ordered a second Bud Light. When the server left, he asked Justine if she was excited. "You never did show me your project."

Justine mashed her burger with the back of her fork. Beef was disgusting.

"Jus? Honey? I asked you a question."

"Sure," she said, looking up at him through hooded eyes. "I'm psyched."

"Want to tell me about it?" he pressed, squirting ketchup onto his plate. "Saw the box in your room. Looked pretty complex." He dragged an onion ring through the puddle and stuffed the bloody ring in his mouth. Justine winced. "You did a video, too, right?"

Gagging, she grabbed her purse. "Bathroom," she croaked, and slid off the bench.

Justine opened the door to the stall and pushed her mother's bracelet up her arm. Kneeling, staring into the bowl, she thrust her finger down her throat, anticipating the welcome release, the exhilarating emptiness in her belly. She heaved, pushing deeper. Her stomach clenched and she felt the explosion, the tingling acid searing her throat.

Friday, 7:30 p.m.

Todd lounged, bleary-eyed, on his bed, his legs stretched out, with a nearly empty quart of Jack Daniels between his thighs. A Machine Head disc blared from the stereo.

On the way back from CVS, they'd stopped at Papa Gino's for garden salads and a large mushroom and pepperoni pizza. They'd eaten dinner with his mother, and she'd convinced him to spend the night. It was safer to drive in daylight, she'd pointed out. And so here they were, in his dank basement bedroom, squandering another hopeless night.

Her boyfriend took a long pull from the Daniels, sucking it down like water.

Leah studied her face in the hand mirror. She looked like a vagrant, with blotchy skin, hollow bloodshot eyes. With the pads of her fingers, she patted her bloated cheek. If she continued this lifestyle, she'd be dead in a few years. Or locked away in a loony bin.

She tightened the drawstring on her pajama bottoms and flopped on the bed. "I'm such a *loser*," she whined. "What's wrong with me?"

"You ain't a loser. Fuck that Hanson bitch. And quit obsessing. It's a turnoff."

Like he was some prize catch. *Whatever.* She wanted no part of so-called her boyfriend tonight. She was sick of his antics, his recklessness, his headlong march into the abyss. She didn't want to hear his voice. She didn't want to look at his face or see the chip on his shoulder. He could go to Hell, for all she cared. He was headed there anyway.

She missed her family. Her mother and father. Her sister.

If only she had a pair of ruby slippers. She could go home.

Your family loves you, Officer Johnson had told her that night at the hospital. *They'll always be there for you.* He'd been wrong, dead wrong. They were already gone.

She used to wonder how people went on after a loved one passed away. She'd been too young to understand death when her grandmother died. She wondered how it felt to stare into the face of such darkness, to lose someone you desperately loved. Grief tore a hole in your heart. A tear rolled down her cheek. It hurt so badly your teeth ached.

"Hey, babe." He flashed a shitty grin and patted the bed. "Got a surprise for you." Reaching, he snatched her wrist and dragged her open hand over his bulging crotch.

"Let *go.*" He made her skin crawl. She jerked her hand back.

He kicked out of his pants. "What do you think, babe?" He turned on his side.

"You're disgusting," she spat.

"Oh, yeah?" He swung right, grabbing her. She screamed and he pushed her onto the bed, holding her down. She cried, struggling, twisting away from him. "Shut up and hold still." Clamping her face, he kissed her, his mouth open, his hot breath reeking of alcohol, and lifted her shirt. "Now who's disgusting?" Groping her, he kissed her again.

"Stop," she begged, when he came up for air. "Please. You're hurting me."

"What's the matter?" He pinned her arms over her head, and pushed up her bra.

Shame consumed her. She twisted, pleading, arching her back.

"What's the matter? Wanted to show the world last night." He yanked her pajama bottoms. "Now it's my turn, you little bitch," he sneered, and ripped off her panties.

Mercifully, he stopped short.

"Thought you loved me." He rolled off. "You make me sick."

Sobbing, she tugged the blanket, humiliated, covering herself.

He threw her clothes at her. "Now you know what it feels like."

Friday, 8 p.m.

Justine tagged along with her father as he circled the noisy gymnasium, ogling the exhibits. At each table, he stopped, asked a question, offered a compliment. *Socially conscious, I see. How original, recycled garbage!* Her father's gusto embarrassed her. When she and Leah were little, unless the girls were involved, he'd refused to attend school functions. On the few occasions when their mother prodded him into going to a concert or fundraising event, he'd parked by the wall, and stood with arms crossed over his chest, looking bored and grim. It was bizarre to see him trying so hard.

"Impressive," he said, loud enough to be heard in China. The cloud chamber was bogus. The pockmarked dork who'd created it hung on her father's every insincere word.

"Project sucks," Justine said under her breath. "Who made it for you? Daddy?"

"Got to tell you, Jus. You've got some talented kids at your school."

"Mmm," she said, trailing her father down the center aisle.

At Justine's table, her father stepped back, stroking his chin. He scanned the room, making a poor attempt at discretion, his gaze lingering on the door.

"Phenomenal," he proclaimed, and patted Justine on the head. "Hell of a lot better than third place," he whispered. "The judges must be blind. I'd at least give it second."

Justine rolled her eyes. "Can we go now?"

"Let's give her a few more minutes." He insisted on circling yet again, in case they'd overlooked a project on their first, second, or third time around. "She'll be here."

By eight, everyone except for Justine and her father had begun packing. Kids toted cardboard boxes while their parents, conversing across the tables, disassembled the projects. At eight, when the gym had all but emptied out, her father finally agreed to go.

"Sorry, hon. Mom probably lost track of the time. What do you think? What do you want to do with this box?"

Whatever. "Throw it out."

They'd stowed their coats under the table. Crouching, she reached behind the cotton panel for her father's overcoat. Justine was zipping her parka when she spotted her mother by the gym door. Justine could hardly believe her eyes. Her mother looked beautiful. She'd even worn makeup.

Her mom peered around the room, grinning broadly. Justine waved, directing her to their table. Her mom shifted right. There was someone behind her. Justine's heart surged. The girl's face was hidden. Justine recognized the coat, her sister's distinctive athlete's gait. *She's home.* Justine pinched herself to prove this was real. *She came, after all.*

Her father was busy pulling her project apart.

"Dad," Justine said, "look who's here"—and took off.

The janitors had waxed the floor to a shine. Her feet slipped, her cartoon legs propelling her forward. Her mom turned, smiling, her lips moving. Justine's heart ripped through her chest. She was dying to know what her mother said. What Leah said to her.

"Lee," Justine called, from about ten feet away. *"Leah—"*

"Jus?" Her mother gave her a quizzical look. From behind her mom stepped a girl Justine had never seen before. The girl went by without acknowledging Justine. "Hi, sweetie," Justine's mom said.

"Mom." Justine's eyes pooled. "I thought that was Leah."

Friday, 8:15 p.m.

Jerry parked the cruiser at the bottom of the hill on Old Orchard Road. Hard to believe this was his final night on the streets. Martin Healy had accepted a position at his alma mater, as chief of the Rutgers University Police Department. The Board of Selectman had voted unanimously to promote Jerry to Chief. The promotion meant greater responsibility, more headaches—budgets, meetings, accountability to the Board. On the flip side, it paid more and, theoretically, offered better hours, meaning less time away from home, a chance to spend more quality time with the boys—six months old already, amazing!—and get reacquainted with his wife. He looked forward to that.

It was a cold night. He opened his window, enjoying the cool air on his face.

His computer blinked, Millie sending info on a tag.

Millie was good people, hardworking, intuitive, smart. He was damn lucky to have her. Meghan, Hollingshead, O'Rourke—he was fortunate. He had a good staff. The town had also granted a new hire. He'd sent his request to the Academy and they'd sent a stack of resumes, which Millie had already sorted, ordered, and ranked for his perusal.

He still thought regularly about the Tylers. Leah had been gone for six weeks, a long time. He'd kept track—the officers all had; they talked about her sometimes. They felt responsible. It was their job to keep the citizens and community safe. Losing her—it felt like a loss—realistically or not, like a breach of duty. He checked in with the family now and then to see how they were holding up, offer moral support. Not much else he could do. His buddy, Ray, had turned up nothing in California. They were fairly certain Corbett had held up the deli in Maine. The old man died of a heart attack, and they'd thought the case dead. Last week, out of the blue, a witness had come forward, a tourist from New York, picked him out of a photo array. When they arrested Corbett—when, not if—she'd agreed to come in, look at a lineup. Until then, the investigation was stalled.

According to the witness the Tyler girl was not on the scene. When he delivered the news, told her parents she was off the hook, they'd just nodded and said, "Thanks." He understood. What good was a dismissal if their daughter wasn't around?

Friday, 8:30 p.m.

The jeep plowed down Main Street. The moon was full, the night sky clear and bright. The temperature had plunged since the afternoon, the road a sheet of black ice.

Leah leaned against the door, her heart hammering.

They'd talked. Angry, he'd agreed to drive her home. He'd changed his mind, but she'd stood her ground. She couldn't be with him anymore. It was time to grow up, settle down, go back to school. Maybe her parents would send her to a private school, where nobody knew her and she could start fresh. With her athletic ability—if she committed and she would—she should be able to land a scholarship for next year. In the meantime, she'd find a job, her days of being a burden behind her.

When Todd went to the bathroom, she'd called home. It was only fair to give her family a warning. She could hardly show up on the doorstep after six weeks, put them in shock, and expect them to greet her with open arms. This way they could prepare. She'd reached voice service. "It's me," she said, disappointed. "Leah," she added, in case they failed to recognize her voice. "I miss you guys. I miss you so much. I'm coming home."

Todd gripped the wheel, his shoulders ticking. "We're supposed to get married."

He careened onto Old Orchard Road, moonlight illuminating the slick icy street. The truck skidded around the corner and shot over a hill, accelerating, airborne.

Leah braced herself. "Please," she begged. "Slow down. You're scaring me."

"What about our band? What about us?"

"We'll have our band," she lied. "Don't do this, Todd."

A cruiser nosed out of a clearing at the foot of the hill.

"Look—" She tugged his sleeve. *A cop.* "They'll arrest us." Never mind the coke in the glove compartment. Never mind the gun. "You don't want to go to jail, do you?"

"I don't give a shit. We had *plans*," he bellowed. "We're supposed to be a team."

A deer bounded over the stone wall, and stopped dead, caught in the headlights.

"A deer," Leah shrieked. "Look out!"

He slammed on the brakes, sending the jeep into a tailspin.

Oh, my God. Leah's hands flew to her face. *The wall.*

A blue light pulsed, the cruiser's siren screaming. The impact rang in her ears, the gruesome sound of metal grinding her ribs. A light flashed. Todd howled, his voice braying.

Leah gasped, struggling for air. She was cold. Spittle dribbled out of the side of her mouth.

Her door squeaked open. "Sweetheart?" She reached for the policeman, her arms heavy. He brushed her forehead. "That's it, baby. I've got you." Sliding his arms under her back and legs, he lifted her gently out of her seat.

"Mommy?" she gurgled, the words ringing in her ears. "Want my mommy."

"She's on the way, sweetheart. She'll be here soon." He laid her on the pavement, cold, cold, the deep dark sky overhead.

Starry, starry night.

In the distance, a siren, its scream drawing closer. Lights. A jumble of voices. Shuffling, a struggle. "Corbett," a female cop said. "We finally got him."

Am I gonna die?

"Found coke, Jer," another cop said. "A gun," added the woman. "He's screwed."

Officer Johnson covered Leah with a blanket.

Am I dying?

That's it, Jus. Listen. One, two, three, four. Let the music lead you. She holds Justine's hand, and she and her sister dance around her room. *BOOM, boom, boom. One, two, three, four.*

They're in the yard, making snow angels, a crystal blue sky overhead. Their mother calls from the front door, offering hot chocolate. With her foot, her mom pushes a shovel into the dirt. She's digging a grave for Hammy. Leah cries, trying to shake the hamster back to life.

"Not your fault, baby," she says. "All creatures die. That's part of God's plan."

She felt the policeman's lips. Tasted his breath.

A car door slammed.

She moaned. Pain shot through her hips.

"Come on, baby." Officer Johnson pushed on her chest. "Stay with me."

Leah dances into the sun, the light on her face. "Ring around the Rosie." She's holding hands with Justine. Her dad, her mom. In a circle, twirling. "Pocket full of posies," her mother sings, her voice pure and sweet as a hand bell. "One. Two. Three." They bend their knees, all four of them together, and leap, holding onto each other. "We all. Fall—"

"Breathe, baby. Stay with me. Breathe."

She felt a warm hand on her forehead. "Leah,"—her father's voice.

Her head floated. "Hi," she said. "Hi." Her sister was crying. "Jus—don't cry. I'm right here."

The weight again on her chest.

"Come on, baby." *Breathe.*

Her mother squeezed Leah's hand. "Leah, sweetie. I'm here."

Mommy?

"Mommy," Leah whispered, "Daddy, Jus—" *I love you guys.* A board slid under her back. *Mommy?* And then they lifted her up— *Mommy, I love you*—and carried her away.

Epilogue

Confirmation

It's unseasonable weather for late-March, the falling snow a swirl of spiraling crystals. The weather steadily worsens as Justine, in the vestibule at the back of the church, waits for the Confirmation Mass to begin. A door opens, an icy wind rushing in. A family enters, huddled together against the eddying wind, the father stamping his feet.

Through the open door, Justine watches the whirling snow blanketing the sidewalks, the trees, snowflakes blowing onto the sign in front of the church. All around her, her classmates whisper behind cupped palms about the parties, the fancy receptions their parents are hosting after the Mass. Justine's parents and grandparents sit one pew behind the pews reserved for the Confirmation candidates. Yesterday, her grandparents flew up from Philadelphia. After the Mass, they'll go to an Italian restaurant in Westford, for "an intimate celebration," her mother called it, and then her grandparents fly home.

Since her accident, Leah refuses to leave the house. She spends all day in her room, reading or listening to music—soulful, introspective songs by the Cowboy Junkies or Lucinda Williams or Sarah McLachlan. Once a week, she takes a cab to the home of the tutor the town of Cortland provides. Justine's sister is lucky to be alive. The pelvic fracture, her doctors had said, would have killed most people. Her strength from playing soccer all those years probably saved her. When the air bag deployed, she'd broken her nose. After the reconstructive surgery, scheduled for early next week, she'll look normal again. Now, Leah says, she looks like a monster, her nose buckled, the bridge flat.

The Cardinal wears a white chasuble trimmed in gold, a precious Mitre on his head. In his right hand, he carries a staff. He assumes his place at the head of the line. The pastor slides into the line behind the Cardinal. Behind the pastor the lecture, and behind the lector, Justine.

Justine adjusts the wreath in her hair. Her white Confirmation robe falls to mid-calf. Under the robe, she wears Leah's plaid skirt and her sister's blue silk blouse.

The organist strikes the first note. A hush falls over the church. The congregation stands as the Cardinal steps into the nave.

The church is packed. Parents at the centers of the pews crane their necks, angling for a better view of their children. A camera clicks and a lone soprano leads the choir in song. The cantor raises her hands and the congregation joins in.

Justine enters the church proper. To her left, someone snaps a picture. She stares straight ahead. Sprays of white lilies in gilded vases line the steps leading to the sacristy, and lilies decorate the marble candle-bench below the crucifix on the altar. Near the podium burns a thick white candle etched in gold—a symbol of life, a symbol of light.

At the foot of the altar, Justine bows her head, takes a sharp left.

The candidates behind Justine process in pairs to the end of the aisle, where the lines split, one turning left, the other right. The candidates file into their designated rows.

When the song ends, the candidates settled in place, the Cardinal, spreading his arms majestically, recites the opening prayer. "The Lord be with you."

"And also with you," the congregation responds.

Justine is scheduled to speak immediately after the Gospel. Her mind wanders. She stares at the pale purple paint on her nails, pushes her cuticles back, picks at a hangnail on her pinky. She feels like a hypocrite. Someone else should give this speech, someone whose family is normal. Someone whose mind is clear. Who isn't a mess.

This morning, when she went downstairs for breakfast, her mom was in the kitchen, setting the table, the griddle warming, pancake batter set out on the counter. Her father was in his office above the garage, checking his telephone and e-mail messages.

Two weeks ago, her father found a new job with a local construction company specializing in municipal buildings. Though he makes less money, he enjoys the work. He likes his boss, the other employees. Best of all, he said happily, "No more traveling, Jus." From now on, he'd work out of his home office. "I can spend time with you."

Her mom returned to work part-time, and she's applying to law school. A colleague arranged a meeting with the dean at Suffolk

University. If she's admitted—she's studying hard for the LSAT—the dean pledged to support her request for a grant.

Last week, her parents put their house on the market. Justine thought she would be sad to leave the house where she and her sister grew up. Her parents explained the financial burden, and she'd understood the reward. Even Leah seems vaguely pleased.

At nine, her dad came down from his office. "Sweetie?" He exchanged a look with her mom. "We have a little surprise for you," he said, and led Justine to the garage.

As a Confirmation gift, Justine's parents bought her a puppy, a Golden Retriever. Justine squatted and the puppy hopped up, licking her face.

She feels a tap on her shoulder, blinks, and sees Miss Green smiling down at her. "Good luck," whispers Miss Green. "You'll be terrific."

No, Justine thinks. *I won't.*

Holding onto the rail in front of her pew, she drags herself up. Her body tingles, her knees weak. She thinks she might faint. She steadies herself, glides across the front of the pew to the sacristy, up the two steps. On the altar, she bows her head, bending a knee.

She makes the sign of the cross, turns left, and approaches the lectern.

There must be a thousand people in the audience. Justine scans the crowd, picks out the faces she recognizes. She smiles when she spots Holly with her mother in a pew near the back. Officer Johnson and his wife each with a baby. Hope. Hope's mother, Mindy. Bobby Sullivan and his wife, Mary Ann. Coach Thomas. The principal of Justine's school. Cissy Hanson is here. The girls from the soccer team. All these people have come here for someone, a sister, a cousin, a niece or nephew. A neighbor.

She lays her folded paper on the lectern.

Her classmates fidget. Justine's grandmother beams. Justine's mother touches an earring. Her hair is swept back in a French twist, spiral curls framing her beautiful face.

Her father signals a silent message. *What's going on? Why haven't you started?*

Justine swallows, blessing herself. "My dear friends," she begins. "The Holy Spirit—" She planned to say, "in receiving." *In receiving the Holy Spirit.*

Her father nods, encouraging her to continue. Two thousand eyes focus on her. She breathes deeply, looks out at the audience, and down at her paper, her cheat sheet. She'd practiced, intending to recite the speech by heart. The words have slipped away.

She flattens the paper, the microphone amplifying the crackling noise.

"My dear," she stammers. Justine wrote this speech for her sister. What will happen if she simply steps down? Says, "Thank you," and returns to her pew?

The smell of incense drifts across the sacristy.

The director winks. "Doing fine," she mouths.

Am not, Justine wants to say. *I'm not fine at all.*

Her mother's eyes partially close, and her lips move. She's saying a prayer. Justine's throat catches. She swallows again. "Dear Friends, in receiving the Holy Sp—"

The wind howls, rattling the stained glass windows depicting the agony of Christ, and the church falls silent. Beyond the stained glass windows, the snow roils, whipping in circles.

Somebody coughs. The audience waits patiently.

Justine stares until the words on her paper dissolve.

All her life, until this winter, Justine believed that God would take care of her. If she prayed long enough, hard enough, if she believed, truly believed, if she gave herself over fully and honestly to her faith, God would answer her prayers. She prayed fervently. She had faith. In her time of greatest need, He left her to figure out things on her own.

A baby cries. His mother lays him over her shoulder.

Justine takes in the altar, hard and sturdy and real, constructed of wood, material, physical—like her—born of this earth. She takes in the eyelet altar cover, the golden chalice she once believed, literally believed, held the blood of the Lord. *Whose blood is it*, she wonders, *inside that cup?* Leah's? Her own? The blood of the parishioners?

The blood of them all.

In the balcony, the lone violinist in front of the choir tucks her instrument under her arm. The choir shuffles, and the violinist turns toward the wing. She smiles, nodding, and steps aside. Justine's breath catches as Leah takes the violinist's place at the rail.

Leah raises a palm, her face lit by a radiant smile. Justine raises her hand. Even with her scarred face, her sister is gorgeous.

And she's come here for me.

The congregation follows Justine's gaze to the balcony. For a crazy second, she expects applause. The Cardinal smiles beatifically.

"In receiving the Holy Spirit," Justine says, her voice wavering, "we become full-fledged members of God's family."

A young man in the row behind Justine's parents nods in agreement. Justine's mother reaches for her father's hand. Her grandparents look over at them and smile.

"We're a family," Justine continues, "parents and children. Brothers and sisters."

A family. The beautiful and the ugly. The perfect and the broken.

Her pulse echoes inside her temples, blood pulsing through her neck, her arms, the tips of her fingers. At home, Justine's brand new puppy waits in her crate. *I'll call her Daisy,* Justine thinks, for the crown of flowers Leah wore the day she was confirmed.

This is who we are, Justine sees. A community of sinners struggling to make our way in an imperfect world—torn by sorrow, united by faith. A family. United by need.

"Family," she says. "For God, for one another…"

As she speaks, her voice grows stronger, the words flowing into the microphone, out through the speakers. She imagines a nameless sound, rich and full and real, drifting outward in waves, touching her parents, her grandparents, her friends, the people here in this church, rippling, spreading across town, to all the people and places under the sun, reaching past pain and affliction, beyond the confines of this crazy, wonderful, battered old world, the sound, like the beat of her heart, circling back. *Touching her sister.*

Sisters, Justine thinks. And rising to the balls of her feet, she goes on.

Author's Notes

Real People, Real Places, Real Things

I am grateful to Bob Sullivan, owner-operator of Sullivan Farms Ice Cream in Tyngsboro, MA, and Dorothy Klein, owner and designer of Ruby Slippers Designs, in Newton, MA, for allowing me to include them in this book.

Bob Sullivan

I met Bob in 1990, when our eldest daughter, Jen, began working at an ice cream shop owned by his older brother. A kind, generous, good-natured manager, Bob inspires the devotion of his employees, many of whom work for him through college and even into their late twenties.

For more than 10 years, Bob has sponsored, organized and directed the annual John Carson Fourth of July 2 Mile Road Race. This memorial event for John Carson, a talented Chelmsford High distance runner hit by a train during a practice run, began as a fun race for local runners. Today, this highly competitive event draws 2000 athletes from across the US and 60,000 spectators.

Bob and his wife, Mary Ann, opened Sullivan Farms Homemade Ice Cream, on the bank of the Merrimack River, in 1997. Customers immediately flocked to the store. With thirty employees and eight serving windows, Sullivan Farms makes and serves over 100 flavors of ice cream—my favorite, Almond Joy—as well as sherbet, Italian ice and many varieties of yogurt. For info about the John Carson 2 Mile Road Race or directions to Sullivan Farms Homemade Ice Cream, please visit their website: http://www.sullivanfarmsicecream.com.

Acknowledgments

To family, friends, colleagues and students—for blessing my life with your kindness and grace, my heartfelt thanks.

Over the last year, my family and friends have spread the news about *In Leah's Wake*; book bloggers, the fairy godmothers and godfathers of the literary world, have recommended it; and countless colleagues have encouraged me, held my hand and worked tirelessly to spread the word. Last summer, Book Bundlz selected *In Leah's Wake* as their 2011 Book Pick; the Indie Book Collective made ILW Bestseller For a Day; and the lovely Naomi Blackburn, founder of the Sisterhood of the Traveling Book, introduced me to her Goodreads book club. Thanks to their efforts, their kindness, encouragement and dedication, this quiet literary novel has sold close to 100,000 copies. In expressing my gratitude, the words "thank you" fall woefully short.

Special thanks to my dear friend Emlyn Chand, brilliant writer and founder of Novel Publicity, for her friendship and guidance; my gifted campaign director and lovely friend, Donna Brown, for inspiring me, supporting me, and leading my marketing efforts; the talented Kira McFadden, for dropping everything to edit; Sara-Jayne Slack, a gracious woman, the innovative founder of Inspired Quill Press, for her thoughtful editorial direction.

Deepest thanks to Reverend James A. Woods, S.J., for believing in me and giving me hope; my mentor, teacher, and cherished friend, Jessica Treadway, a stunning writer, for guiding and encouraging me; my sister Audrey LeBourdais, CRNA, as gorgeous as she is smart, for medical expertise; my wonderful parents, Jerry and Audrey Giuliano, for their abiding love and for teaching me to persist. And my beautiful family, Dave and Chris, treasured sons by marriage, my beloved daughters, Jen, Lib, Natalie and KK, our little princes, Sam, Matthew and Griffin, and our princess, Alexandra, for their encouragement and love—and for giving my life wonder and light.

Above all, my husband, Dave, the love of my life—for all and for everything.

Interview with Terri Giuliano Long

A Few Minutes with the Author

Q: Tell us what you hope readers take away from reading your book.

It's tempting to believe that only bad kids from bad families get in trouble. This attitude allows us to distance ourselves – this could never happen to *us*. Too often, when families have problems, we judge and ostracize them, only adding to the difficulties they're already facing. The truth is, when problems arise, the fallout affects the entire community. The epigraph from *The Grand Inquisitor* says it best: "everyone is really responsible to all men for all men and for everything."

Although the Tyler family is far from perfect, they love one another. Had the community rallied around and supported them, perhaps Leah would not have gotten as lost. Like adults, most teens just want to feel accepted and loved – not for what they accomplish or contribute, but for who they are. I'd be thrilled if my novel inspired readers to suspend judgment, to look less harshly at troubled teens and their families. I think we owe it to our teens, to our communities, and to ourselves to work harder to support and encourage *all* kids, not just those who conform. As Hillary Clinton famously said, *it takes a village to raise a child*. For the sake of our children, we must all do our part to be supportive members of the village.

Q: Your book is the story of a contemporary American family caught in the throes of adolescent rebellion. Do you feel that they represent the typical American family of today? If so, how so?

In the sense that the Tylers want what's best for their children, yes, I think they do represent most families. Will and Zoe are invested in providing for and doing well by their children, which means they work harder than perhaps they should. Work takes them away from their children; one day, they wake up and realize that, while they were working, pushing themselves to get ahead and succeed, their eldest child has gone off in a dangerous new direction.

As a culture, we put tremendous pressure on children to succeed, but we define success very narrowly, in terms of money and achievement. Leah recognizes the hypocrisy in the rat race. She's lived her own version in soccer. She's pushed herself hard; by most measures, she's succeeded. Yet success does not make her happy – any more than achievements at work make Zoe or Will happy. Leah sees this and wants to simplify her life. That's a positive impulse; unfortunately, partly because it's nonconforming, it takes her in a negative direction.

I think these questions and impulses arise in many children. The more creative and independent their nature, the more likely they seem to be to follow their impulses. They push boundaries, as Leah does. Happily they don't all follow down the dangerous path she chooses.

Q: Why do you feel Leah got so out of control?

It was a combination of factors –first, rebellion against outside pressure to conform and achieve. As long as she's willing to live up to the expectations of others, she's accepted and even celebrated. As soon as she tries to take control of her own life, questions the rules, spreads her wings, she meets resistance.

Rather than listen to Leah, accept that she's growing up and her choices may differ from theirs and guide her, Zoe and Will pull the reins tighter. This is a classic problem with teens. The minute we tell them *no*, they can't do something, they focus their energy in that very direction. The more Zoe and Will try to control Leah's behavior, the more she pulls away. Escalating attempts to control her result in her getting more and more out of control. That's a difficult cycle to break.

Q: Do you think Todd was to blame for Leah's actions?

Todd is an easy target to blame, but he's more of a conduit. He makes Leah feel comfortable and safe and encourages her blossoming independence. By the time she realizes that he's also controlling her – albeit in a different way – it's too late. By committing to him, she pushes her family away. If only she realized how deeply they love her and how desperately they want her back, she might have avoided the dire consequences she suffers. That's the central irony in the book – perhaps the irony in many relationships between parents and teens.

Q: Can you pick a part of the book that makes us want to scream at Leah?

As a parent, I want to scream at Leah pretty much throughout the book. Although I do feel that she's a decent person with a kind heart, she's also a brat. She can be self-centered, belligerent, and rude. Her saving grace is that she does have moments of clarity when she realizes this. In other words, she has a conscience. When she hurts people or lets others down – her parents, her sister, her coach, even the girls on her soccer team – she feels guilty. She understands that she's behaved badly and she pays an emotional price for her negative actions.

Q: Can you pick a part of the book that makes us cheer for Leah?

While I don't condone Leah's behavior, her heart is often in the right place. Hope's mother is crass, a bit rough around the edges, yet unlike her peers – unlike her own mother – Leah sees beyond this.

Hope's mother is far too lenient, thus contributing to Hope's delinquency she's kind to Leah. Leah sees and appreciates this. Leah doesn't want to be judged and she doesn't judge others. I love this about her. In "Sisters Redux," when she shares a cigarette with Justine then reassures Justine afterward and teaches her to dance – in all those tender moments when her true personality shines, I want to stand up and cheer.

Q: Who are your favorite characters in the story?

My characters are all imperfect - they behave badly and they're sometimes, for some readers perhaps often, irritating - but I love them all, for their strengths as well as their weaknesses and vulnerabilities. Justine is sweet and caring and kind, so she's easy to love, but I also love Leah. Leah drives the parent in me crazy, but her heart is in the right place. The same applies to Zoe and Will - they often make terrible choices; despite their failures, they act out of love.

Jerry Johnson, the police officer, is the only non-family member with a voice in the novel. Though flawed like all the characters, he takes his responsibility for others to heart. I've always admired Gail Mullen Beaudoin, a police officer in Chelmsford, MA. Gail brings strength, dignity and grace to a very difficult job. I see police officers as the connecting force in communities. Every day they put their lives on the line. To me, they're our real life heroes. As the connecting force in this novel and for this family, Jerry is my favorite.

Q: Your book is set in the imaginary town of Cortland, Massachusetts. Can you tell us why you chose this city in particular?

Geographically, the town of Cortland is modeled after the town of Harvard, MA. In the fall, we used to go there to pick apples. Harvard is stunningly beautiful – with the rolling hills, the stone walls, the orchards. Sometimes, Dave and I would drive there and just ride around. This family is in tremendous pain; they're struggling. That these fierce struggles might take place in this bucolic setting felt surprising, and that tension felt important to the book.

Q: Does setting play a major part in the development of your story?

Judging from the stories I hear, the social and political climate in the imaginary town of Cortland is similar to that in many middle- and upper-middle class towns. I've talked with many parents who've expressed frustrations similar to Zoe and Will's. Culturally – not always or only by their parents - children feel pressure to live up to impossible expectations. When children step out of line, the parents and families often feel judged.

Community plays an important role in setting expectations and shaping and maintaining connections. The expectations, the constant demand to perform, can be overwhelming, especially in small towns where everyone knows everyone else, by sight if not by name. You can't hide. If you or a family member is in trouble, everyone knows it. That claustrophobia, the feeling of condemnation, informs the inner lives of these characters and influences their behavior.

Q: What are your favorite aspects of writing?

I'm passionate about writing. I enjoy every aspect of the process, from the initial burst of inspiration through the painstaking, sometimes frustrating, months or years of revision. Most exciting - that *aha* moment, when the work suddenly comes together, you understand what you're writing about, and the relationships among the various scenes and chapters suddenly make sense.

Q: What is the greatest piece of advice that you have heard?

Be grateful and appreciate others. At the end of the day, the people in our life are all we have. No one ever dies wishing she'd worked longer hours or made more money or sold more books. It's tough, because our culture values things over people and rewards monetary success. It's important to remember that, in fact, we've got it backward. People – our friends, our family, our community – are our most valuable and precious assets. It's far easier to recognize this and appreciate others if we're grateful for what we have and all we've been given.

Discussion Topics

1. "In Leah's Wake" is told from the perspective of five characters—Zoe, Will, Leah, Justine, and Jerry. With whom did you identify the most? Which character did you have the most difficulty understanding? How do the multiple viewpoints weave together to form a cohesive story?

2. Leah often changes her mind. One moment she misses her family, the next she hates them. She alternately wants to marry Todd and to break up with him. Why is Leah so fickle? Is this common of teenagers, or something unique to (or excessive in) Leah? Did you ever find yourself wanting to yell at her through the pages—to warn her that she was making the wrong decision?

3. If Leah had remained on the soccer team could the events of the story have been prevented? What about if she had remained friends with Cissy? Are there any other what-ifs that stand out to you?

4. How does Leah's cutting her hair serve as a turning-point for her character? Which other changes to Leah's appearance, thought process, and behavior redirect the story?

5. The first time Leah runs away Zoe insists upon giving her space. Was this the right decision? Would you have reacted the same way had it been your child?

6. In the end, Justine presents some worrying behavior. What causes her to unravel? Is it her desire for Leah to think she is cool? The impact of her sister's abandonment? Having to act as the caregiver while both of her parents struggled with their own issues? Will Justine revert back to her old self, or is she destined to follow in Leah's footsteps?

7. Zoe and Will have very different ideas of what it means to be a good parent. Zoe wants to keep the peace, she wants to be liked. Will desires to keep his children safe, and to do this, he often

responds in anger. Which parenting style did you identify with most? Would they have been more effective had they presented a united front? How does Leah drive a wedge between her parents?

8. Will's job situation becomes uncertain during the course of the novel. How does this difficulty play into the plot? How does it affect his character? Would he have been more level-headed in dealing with Leah and Todd had he not been under this added stress?

9. In the beginning of the novel, Zoe is a strong and capable woman. She leads self-improvement seminars and works as a therapist. As the story progresses, she slowly unravels finally developing an addiction to Oxycotin. What drove her to this point? Do you believe she will be able to recover the life she lived before Leah's rebellion?

10. What role does Jerry play in the story? How does he help bring the family back together? Does he truly love Zoe, or is he just overwhelmed by being a new father? Does Zoe love him back? Is she truthful with Will about not having an affair?

11. Todd, Hope, and Lupo undeniably are negative influences on Leah, but at times the author discusses each of these characters with compassion and understanding. Were these three really "bad" people, or did they just come from bad circumstances? Did you find yourself going back and forth between distaste and affinity for these characters?

12. Discuss the significance of the bracelet Zoe buys for Leah, Stormy. Does the birthstone ring she presents to Leah at Christmas hold an added significance; what is it? Are there any other important symbols in the story? What about the rope swing? Justine's science project? The strangled hamster? Zoe's flashbacks of a young Leah?

13. Music plays a huge role in the story. From Zoe and Will's affinity for older tunes (such as those by The Beatles, Tom Petty, and Van Morrison) to Leah's obsession with Ani diFranco, and Justine's attempts to understand rap. How did these musical allusions add to the plot and help us to better understand the characters?

14. Thematically, what struck you most about this novel? Did it lead you to contemplate any deeper questions about family, responsibility, and life?

15. How much control should parents exert over a child's life? Do Zoe and Will push Leah too hard? Is it necessary for parents to push their children in order for them to succeed? How do Zoe and Will's actions protect and in what ways do they fail their children? Does their intervention help or does it backfire? How might Zoe and Will have better handled Leah's rebellion? How do micro-managed children fare later in life?

16. What might cause a seemingly "perfect" child to rebel? Is Leah's anxiety caused by her parents' expectations or is it genetic, part of her personality? Is there such a thing as a perfect child? If so, how would you define the perfect child?

17. Do zero-tolerance policies work? Why or why not? Are they necessary? Should schools ban adolescents from participating in activities, such as sports, that could keep them out of trouble? Did Coach Thomas respond properly to Leah's outburst? Should Will and Zoe have exercised greater tolerance? Or were they too lax?

18. How do parents prevent children from falling under the influence of the wrong people? How might Zoe and Will have prevented Leah's relationship with Todd from getting serious? Should they have banned Todd from their home? Why or why not?

19. Are a child's personality and conduct influenced primarily by nature? Nurture? Both? How are Justine and Leah's personalities a result of their parents' influence? Might parts of Justine and Leah's personalities be inherent? If so, which?

20. Hillary Clinton said it takes a community to raise a child. What role does a community play in the lives of its children? Is the community responsible for the actions of an ostracized child? Why or why not? How do gossip and judgment affect adolescents? Are the effects always negative?

Watch for Terri's New
Psychological Thriller

Nowhere to Run

After the brutal unsolved murder of her six-year-old daughter, award-winning writer Abby Minot put her laptop away. A year later, emerging from a deep depression, she accepts her first assignment—a human-interest story on the wealthy Chase clan, the immediate family of Matthias Chase, a popular Republican congressman from northern New Hampshire.

Congressman Chase has built his political platform on unsubstantiated claims that his ancestors were abolitionists. During a major renovation, a subterranean chamber is discovered under the barn, and the Chase family estate is declared an official stop on the Underground Railroad. Within weeks, Chase launches a campaign for the presidency.

After accepting the assignment, Abby travels with her two surviving children to the Chase estate in the White Mountains. In her initial research, she glimpses darkness under the shiny veneer. Digging deeper, she uncovers a shocking web of lies and betrayal, dating back to the nineteenth century. Abby soon finds herself trapped—between an editor obsessed with uncovering the truth and the town and family who will stop at nothing to ensure that it stays hidden.

Read the first chapter on Terri's website: www.tglong.com

18351258R00176

Made in the USA
Lexington, KY
30 October 2012